B. G.

3-17

SO-BSV-803

FLIRTATION WALK

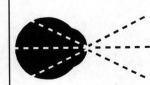

This Large Print Book carries the
Seal of Approval of N.A.V.H.

FLIRTATION WALK

SIRI MITCHELL

THORNDIKE PRESS
A part of Gale, Cengage Learning

GALE
CENGAGE Learning·

Farmington Hills, Mich • San Francisco • New York • Waterville, Maine
Meriden, Conn • Mason, Ohio • Chicago

GALE
CENGAGE Learning

LIBRARY OF CONGRESS CATALOGING-IN-PUBLICATION DATA

Names: Mitchell, Siri L., 1969– author.
Title: Flirtation walk / by Siri Mitchell.
Description: Waterville, Maine : Thorndike Press, 2017. | Series: Thorndike Press large print Christian historical fiction
Identifiers: LCCN 2016045091| ISBN 9781410497178 (hardcover) | ISBN 1410497178 (hardcover)
Subjects: LCSH: Military cadets—Fiction. | West Point (N.Y.)—Fiction. | Swindlers and swindling—Fiction. | Large type books. | GSAFD: Love stories. | Christian fiction.
Classification: LCC PS3613.I866 F58 2017 | DDC 813/.6—dc23
LC record available at https://lccn.loc.gov/2016045091

Published in 2017 by arrangement with Bethany House Publishers, a division of Baker Publishing Group

Printed in Mexico
1 2 3 4 5 6 7 21 20 19 18 17

For Tony.
Thanks for giving me the time and space to write and for putting up with all the craziness. You've always been my hero.

And for K.
Dreams take a lot of hard work, but you've always been so good at doing things that are hard to do. Can't wait to see your dreams come true.

This story takes place at a U.S. Military Academy that looked quite unlike the West Point of recent memory. Academic courses were taught in a single building (the Academy); the old mess hall and old barracks were quite new back then. There was no Camp Buckner for summer training, and Callum Hall wasn't yet in existence. Highland Falls was known as Buttermilk Falls. The corps of cadets numbered about 250 in 1855, and it was organized into one battalion composed of four companies; there was no brigade. The cadets ranking lowest in the order of merit were called Immortals.

Though the setting might feel strange, it's my hope that those who are acquainted with the military academy might come to find it surprisingly familiar.

MAKE US TO CHOOSE THE HARDER RIGHT
INSTEAD OF THE EASIER WRONG, AND
NEVER TO BE CONTENT WITH A HALF TRUTH
WHEN THE WHOLE CAN BE WON.

— FROM THE *WEST POINT CADET PRAYER*

1

LUCINDA

August 1855

The churning of the steamboat was relentless as it chugged down the Hudson River. Columns of steam and smoke trailed from twin chimneys, defiling an otherwise cloudless sky. Wrapped around the iron railing, my gloved fingers buzzed with the vibrations of the engine. Though the wheel was covered, I could imagine its paddles slicing into the river to scoop up water only to fling it all off at the top and plunge down into the current to do it again.

It put me in mind of my father.

Everything did, ever since I had received the notice of his death. Though my green-and-salmon-colored tartan dress didn't show it, I was still mourning my loss. Still uncertain what I should do.

Madame Mercier, my finishing school headmistress back in St. Louis, had drawn me into her office to give me the letter. I

11

didn't have to retrieve it from my reticule to remember what it said.

I regret to inform Miss Lucinda Pennyworth that her father, Mr. Ezra Pennyworth, has died. He succumbed to the ravages of his long illness on July 4th. His affairs have been taken over by me.

It had been signed by a Mr. Christopher Barnett. But I'd never heard of the man. And my father hadn't been suffering from the ravages of a long illness. He'd never been ill that I could recall.

Granted, I hadn't seen him since he'd left me at the finishing school early in March, but that wasn't unusual. He always came to retrieve me when he had need of me for one of his schemes. But now, nothing was going according to plan, and that in itself was quite dire. My father had always had a plan. *"If you keep one step ahead of everyone else, they'll never be able to trip you up, my dear. No need to panic. If you can't go out the front door, then you'll just have to go out the back."*

I'd grown up going out the back door with him, sneaking out of frontier towns or slipping away on the steamboats that plied the Mississippi River. Of course, just as often, we'd lodge ourselves at the finest of hotels as a much-deserved reward for our troubles. We'd had dreams, my father and I. Dreams of establishing ourselves in one of Europe's finest cities . . . just as soon as he came into his fortune.

The sunlight no longer glanced so glaringly off the water, so I adjusted the tilt of my bonnet, allowing my face to emerge from the long late-afternoon shadows. The gusting wind seized the chance to steal beneath my hat and ruffle the ringlets I'd carefully arranged atop my ears. Closing my eyes, I fixed my mind on my imagined paddlewheel. Just like the river's waters, there had been no end to the people willing to invest their money in one of my father's schemes. Out west, he had plunged into a town, sold deeds to plots of land that didn't exist, and then shoved off to do it somewhere else all over again.

"Most people are waiting for someone to give them hope. If you can do that, then they're more than happy to give you their money in exchange."

That's what father had always called it: an exchange. Perhaps in taking their money we got the more useful part of the bargain, but my father insisted they got what they were after as well. He gave them hope in return. Hope for wealth, hope for prominence.

Hope for success.

But I couldn't rely upon my father's provision anymore. And I couldn't do what he had done. I was a woman, after all. Who would entrust their money to me for the purposes of investment? In fact, we had begun discussing how best to make me someone's wife. Someone quite important. Someone worth the effort. But I couldn't vault myself into society now. Not without help.

Cigar smoke drifted back from the front of the boat, where a group of men had gathered. They were military men, dressed in blue uniforms.

I stole another glance at them. My, but they were fine to behold.

And I stopped myself from doing so immediately!

If I was to present myself as a respectable girl from a proper family, I would have to act like one, and a lady never solicited the interest of a gentleman.

Turning my gaze from them, I tugged my bonnet back over my eyes. My father had always had as little to do with the military as possible. I put a hand to my temple, beneath the spread of my bonnet, where my head was beginning to pound.

I was doing the right thing, wasn't I?

There had been nothing left me but to strike out on my own — no matter that a lady wasn't to travel by herself. *"Do what's expected until you have to do what's necessary."* That's what my father had always said. The danger of being attached to his memory could not be discounted. It was precisely why he had moved about so often and why I had been stashed at boarding schools in more places than I could remember.

Since I could no longer be my father's daughter, I'd decided to become my mother's. I put a hand to her locket, which hung beneath my bodice. Before the day was out, I would have to throw myself upon the good graces of her family. But they owed me something. At the very least, if they were not as welcoming as I hoped, any hospitality they extended would give me a bit more time to come up with a better idea.

As the men in uniform disembarked, a deckhand approached. "You for Buttermilk Falls, miss?"

"I am."

He pointed downstream. "Next stop. At Cozzen's Landing."

Five minutes later, the boat pulled in to a landing that lay at the base of an enormous cliff. Atop the cliff, overlooking the river, sat á large establishment, but the area appeared to be wilderness. That was disappointing. I'd imagined a setting much like Paducah. Or even Natchez. But I smiled my thanks to the deckhand and let myself and my trunk be handed off the steamer.

At the foot of the rugged road that climbed a rapidly rising hill, an old man was loading a pyramid of crates onto a cart. I asked him the way to Buttermilk Falls.

"Why? You going there?"

I nodded.

He pushed back his cap with the heel of his hand and scratched at his grizzled side-whiskers. "Then you might as well ride with me. Road's a bit rough. You'd probably get there faster if you walked, but you'd risk getting that dress of yours dirty." He loaded my trunk into his wagon, took a sprightly hop up onto the seat, and leaned down to offer his hand. I put mine in his, and he hoisted me up.

As I settled my satchel beside me, he pointed the horse up the hill.

"There were quite a few men in uniform on the boat, but they all got off at the last stop. Where were they going?"

"Up to the Point." The road wound between a tall boulder that towered over us and a tree-topped cliff that looked capable

16

of subsuming us. " 'Bout a mile back there."
He nodded behind us.

"The Point is a . . . What is it exactly?"

He gave me a long look. "It's West Point.
The military academy."

Military academy? "And Buttermilk Falls
is quite close?"

"We're just about there. Couple minutes
more."

If my father could see me now! Soldiers
were even worse than sheriffs and their
deputies in his opinion. I'd fled the West
and its territories only to find myself a short
walk from the nation's military academy.

The old man chuckled. "Don't you worry
none. They don't get let out much."

I hadn't realized my thoughts were so
obvious.

"Which don't mean you're entirely safe.
They have hops over in the mess hall every
Saturday in the summer — dance until the
wee hours sometimes. And they give concerts now and then. Don't mean you have
to go though. Have to say, they look all
bright and shiny, but the soldiers' life isn't
meant for ladies like you."

Ladies like me from a well-established
family of good reputation. *Seeming is just
as good as being.* "Do you know, are there
any Curtises still left in town?"

17

"Curtises? Well, sure. There's the Curtis girl — only she isn't a Curtis anymore. She married a Hammond, the fellow that teaches over at the Point."

"He teaches there? Is he a soldier?"

"No." He scratched at an ear. "Yes. It's hard to say. So many of those fellers started off in uniform. He might be a soldier, and then again, he might not."

"And Mr. Curtis?"

He sighed. "Died of a broken heart about . . ." His words trailed off as he consulted with the sky about something. "Must be ten years ago this winter. One of his girls ran off a while back. He was never the same after."

One of the cart's wheels dipped into a hole, and I grabbed for my satchel to keep it from tumbling onto the road.

"You here to look up the Curtises, then?"

What was I to say? News was likely to spread quickly, so I might as well use that to my advantage. "I am. You might say we're family." They might not like me, they might not want me, but if I made it known they were my relations, fear of public opinion might keep them from casting me out.

He grinned. "Good. That's real good. Mrs. Hammond sure could use the help." He halted the horses in the middle of the

18

road. "We're here."

"Here?" Here was just a few houses scattered over a rise in the land divided by a road that seemed to go nowhere. "Here . . . where?"

"Buttermilk Falls."

This was Buttermilk Falls? "But . . . isn't there supposed to be a waterfall?" And an actual town? My mother had been the Belle of Buttermilk Falls. *"Annabel Curtis, Belle of Buttermilk Falls."* That's what my father had always said. And though he'd said it with a wink and a smile, although he'd always mentioned it as a place it was better to be coming from than going to, it had sounded as if it meant something. As if she could just as easily have been the Belle of Boston or Burlington. As if she'd lived in a place that had Society. Where there had been more than just her competing for the title.

I'd always wondered where it was.

When the postal clerk in St. Louis told me it was in New York State, I couldn't have been more surprised.

The only times my father had ever mentioned it was when things hadn't worked out the way he'd hoped. "I suppose we could just go back to Buttermilk Falls . . ." he would start. "But I was thinking that

19

maybe . . ." A smile would overcome the words and then he'd chuckle while he told me of his latest scheme. Buttermilk Falls had been the symbol of all that was respectable, dull, and dreary, of all that was wrong in the world.

Which was why I'd decided to come.

And now I was here.

As I looked around for signs of civilization, I couldn't say that I disagreed with my father's assessment. My mother might have been from here, but for the first time I wondered where my father was from. Where had he once called home? I had never thought to ask. The future was where our expectations lay, where our hopes and dreams had always been fixed. We'd spent so much time longing for the day when Lady Luck would smile upon us that we'd rarely ever spoken of the past.

The old man gestured off behind us. "The falls're down over there, along with the grist mill. It's a nice walk if you want to take it, even when it hasn't rained and there's not much of a waterfall." He turned and nodded toward a dignified white clapboard house with black shutters. Chimneys jutted from both ends and a porch ran the length of its front, while a picket fence marked off its shallow yard. "That's Richard Hammond's place." He clambered down from his seat and then walked over to my side of the cart and helped me out.

I eyed the house as he shouldered my trunk.

I had that feeling in my stomach again. That disconcerting, weighted feeling that always preceded my entrance into a new place. But this time it was heavier. This time, if the plan didn't work, I had nowhere else to go.

Squaring my shoulders, I set out across the street, skirting holes, as I approached the house. My past was gone. It had died along with my father. My future was entirely up to me.

Smiling, as much to cheer myself as to make a good impression, I opened the gate, went up the front steps, and rapped on the sturdy wooden door.

By that time, the old man had deposited my trunk on the porch and gone on about his business. There were few people on the street. In truth, it wasn't much of a street, in the same way that Buttermilk Falls wasn't much of a town. I'd seen bigger settlements out in the territories. I shifted my satchel to my other hand.

Footsteps scuffed across the floor inside. I heard the latch lifting. As the door cracked

21

open, the scent of supper, of a roast, of onions and carrots, and freshly baked bread, drifted out. The woman who was silhouetted in the door's opening turned back toward the interior of the house. "Just a —" She broke off in a sigh and turned to face me as she opened the door wider.

"Mrs. Hammond? Aunt Catherine?"

I had the impression of auburn hair gently pulled back into a bun and hazel eyes set into a face quite surprisingly like my own before her eyes went wide. The color drained from her cheeks, and she lifted a trembling hand to her bosom. "Oh, my stars!"

2
SETH

Blinking, I tried to force myself to listen to what Professor Hammond was saying. I found myself doing that lately, trying to gain purchase in a conversation I hadn't even remembered joining. I'd enjoyed dozens of Sunday suppers at the Hammonds' over the years since I'd been attending the military academy. But this time, though I was present in body, my mind was elsewhere, my heart still grieving for the mother I had lost. She'd died ten weeks before, in Nebraska, leaving behind fifty acres of land, four cows, a dozen pigs, and numerous chickens, as well as my eighteen-year-old sister, Elizabeth.

But the military academy wouldn't give me leave to go home.

The commandant had been very apologetic, sympathetic even. But it hadn't mattered what I'd said, what argument I'd used. In the end, he'd clapped a hand to my shoulder as he escorted me from his office. *"If I let you go, I'll have to let everyone go. And soon the academy would be emptied due to weddings and birthdays and family balls. A soldier has to do what a soldier has to do. Needs of the army. You understand."*

The problem was, I didn't. For the first time since I'd received my appointment to the academy, I didn't understand.

For the hundredth time I reminded myself that I wouldn't have made it home for the funeral anyway. News of my mother's death had taken six weeks to reach me, and it would have taken three more for me to travel home.

But I was the eldest, the only son. Why couldn't I have been allowed to see to the sale of the farm? What would have been wrong with seeing my sister safely settled with family in Kentucky?

My fingers had curled into fists behind my back again. Taking a deep breath, glancing around the professor's sitting room, I spread my hands wide, forcing them to relax. And then I tried my best to follow the conversation between my classmate, Campbell Conklin, and my favorite professor.

But as my thoughts had been wandering, the conversation had stopped. Campbell was looking at me, one brow lifted. Had he asked me something?

Mrs. Hammond had gone to answer the door — I did remember that — and now the professor's attention was caught by whatever was taking place in his front hall. He blinked as he returned his gaze to me. "I'm sorry, Mr. Westcott. You were saying . . . ?"

Had I said something?

Campbell answered in my stead. "I believe he was making a point about the decidedly deplorable state of this year's appointees."

I couldn't have been. I didn't think they were deplorable. I simply thought they had arrived untrained and a summer's worth of drills had provided the cure, just like they did every year. But Campbell always took every opportunity to expound on others' deficiencies in order to promote his own merits. This time, though, the professor wasn't listening. His eyes narrowed as he took a step toward the hall. "Excuse me for a moment, gentlemen."

I might have offered my assistance, but the sharp words he was soon exchanging with his wife obliged both Campbell and me to pretend to a polite ignorance of the situation. Putting away all thoughts of my mother, I turned my attention to his oldest daughter, Phoebe. Walking the several paces to the tufted, hump-backed sofa where she sat, I cleared my throat. "I hope you're able to attend one of our concerts this summer, Miss Hammond."

She, too, had been listening to the goings-on in the hallway, but she took no pains to hide her interest. Seeming to stare right through me to the hall, her blue eyes hardly moved as she replied. "Perhaps I shall. We hear your concerts sometimes in Buttermilk Falls . . . if the wind is blowing in the right direction."

The Hammond son was attempting to play jackstraws while the youngest sister was begging to join him in the game.

Just as the boy had cast the sticks onto the floor, Professor Hammond returned, his wife leaning heavily upon his arm. There was a trace of tears upon her cheeks that any gentleman would know it was best to ignore. And there was a set to the professor's jaw that boded ill for the person who had caused it. As Mrs. Hammond allowed herself to be helped into a chair, I saw exactly who that person was.

Professor Hammond was scowling as he gestured to the young woman behind him. "Mr. Westcott, Mr. Conklin? My niece."

Of an age with the eldest Miss Hammond and my sister, she was as pretty as a china

26

doll. Prettier even with her hair bunched into curls and her golden-green eyes.

Campbell and I bowed at the same moment, as if obeying a martinet's command, while the younger Hammond children left off playing to look on with great interest.

Though the smile she offered in return seemed genuine, she clung to her satchel with both hands, the way a cadet clings to a letter from home.

"Have you traveled far, Miss Hammond?" Campbell's inquiry was politely subdued, but his interest was plain.

"Far enough." Professor Hammond nearly barked the words. Had I been in his classroom I might have feared for my grade.

Campbell retreated a step or two.

"Father?" Phoebe rose from the couch, reaching a hand toward him.

He crossed to her quickly, tucked her hand under his arm, and led her to her cousin, introducing them.

Mrs. Hammond hadn't taken her eyes from her niece since she'd reentered the room, but the sound of her third daughter sliding dishes across the dining room table seemed to spur her to action. She took the satchel from her niece, setting it in the hall, and then she excused herself and headed for the dining room.

27

While the Miss Hammonds conversed in low tones, Campbell and I pretended not to notice the professor glowering at them. Since it would have been rude to carry on a conversation without him, and since it was plain that he was in no mood to speak, we resorted to tricks learned during three years' worth of parades.

I raised a brow.

Campbell responded by pointing to the collar of his gray coat. I adjusted the black stock that sat beneath the collar of my own coat.

He nodded and raised a brow at me.

I put a hand to the red silk sash that was tied about my waist and extended a finger down toward the fringed ends that spilled past the thigh of my white cotton trousers.

He raked his fingers through the ends of his sash, untangling them.

Professor Hammond was still glowering, so I turned my attention to the room. Number of dainties and dust catchers on the mantel? Seven. Number of chairs? Three. In tufted green velvet. Gently worn. Sofa? One. Also in velvet. Pictures on the wall? Two. Indistinct, vague drawings of rural landscapes. Mirrors? One. With a carved, round frame, reflecting the simple, homey appeal of the room. Ways of ingress?

Two — through the hall and the dining room. Of egress, counting the windows when necessary? Five. I smiled at Campbell.

He smiled at me.

It was a great relief when we were called to the dining room.

As we approached the table, I gave Milly, the middle daughter, a wink.

She wrinkled her nose at me in return. Milly always put me in mind of my sister. Though younger by several years, she had that same restless, spirited nature.

Generally, when we were given passes to come to supper, Mr. Hammond escorted his eldest daughter to the table and I escorted Mrs. Hammond. I would have expected Mr. Hammond to have escorted his niece that evening as an honored guest. Apparently she did too, for when he took up his daughter's arm instead, the niece's step faltered.

I caught Campbell's eye, nodded toward Mrs. Hammond, and offered my arm to the niece. "Miss Hammond?"

Her smile, though swift, was tremulous. "There are too many Miss Hammonds here for clarity's sake. Please think of me as Lucinda."

I knew I would never think of her as

anything but plucky. She'd understood her uncle's insult the same way I had, but she'd simply lifted her chin and smiled all the wider. It took gumption to respond to rebuff like that. I wasn't privy to their family relations, but rude was rude no matter the circumstance. "I'm the only Mr. Westcott, but you could think of me as Seth."

"Thank you." As she whispered the words, her hand tightened on my arm.

She ought to have been seated to the right of the professor, but it wasn't my place to quibble over niceties. I drew out the seat between Campbell and myself, hoping my classmate would have the good sense to help me smooth things over.

I needn't have worried. Campbell always had an eye for pretty girls, and he employed every tactic possible to ingratiate himself with the military academy's faculty. Before the bread had made it halfway around the table, he'd already made it known to Lucinda that he was a cadet lieutenant and the adjutant of our company.

To the professor's credit, he pointed out that I was not only the captain of that company but also first captain of the entire Military Academy Corps of Cadets.

Lucinda looked from one of us to the other. "Your titles sound impressive, but I confess that I've no idea what they mean."

The professor seemed to take her ignorance as a joke, but it soon became apparent she was serious. "It means you're in the presence of two of the best men the military academy has to offer."

She didn't show any signs of contracting "cadet fever," of fluttering or simpering the way other girls visiting the Point were wont to do. She simply nodded. But though she carried on with the buttering of a piece of bread, her hand trembled.

Her uncle continued speaking. "When they graduate in June, they can look forward to the most prestigious of assignments. Perhaps even to the Corps of Engineers." He scowled.

I wasn't quite certain whether that was meant to be a warning. Apparently, Campbell wasn't either. "I had thought, sir . . . That is, I hoped —"

"Nothing is ever guaranteed. Even the most distinguished of cadets can prove himself a disappointment." He seemed very intent on communicating a point.

Campbell and I exchanged a glance. It was a worrisome thought. After all this time and all the work I'd put into academics, I couldn't afford to fall short of that goal. And neither could he. His father had attended West Point. His grandfather, a senator, had urged the establishment of West Point.

Silence ruled the table for several long minutes as we ate, but then the professor addressed his son and Campbell began to monopolize Lucinda's attentions. It was time to fulfill my obligations as both a gentleman and a guest. I conversed for some time with Mrs. Hammond and then with Milly, who sat opposite me.

When Campbell paused to put in a perfunctory word with Phoebe, Lucinda turned toward me. "Forgive my asking, but is something wrong with Miss Hammond?"

I followed her troubled gaze across the table to the eldest daughter. The professor was cutting her meat for her.

"In my experience, there's nothing wrong with the youngest Miss Hammond that turning five won't cure."

She smiled just as I'd hoped she'd do.

I nodded toward Phoebe. "The eldest Miss Hammond, however, is blind, and no one's yet found a way to cure that."

She gasped. "I didn't know."

"There's no reason you should have."

Her cheeks colored as she glanced across the table at her cousin.

Hoping to ease her embarrassment, I

inquired as to where she lived.

"At the moment? I'm not quite certain. I was living in St. Louis, but my father recently died and I wished to spend some time with family."

It was unaccountable how grief could overwhelm a man so suddenly. I had to force myself to take in a breath before responding. "I'm sorry. Does your uncle know that your father just died?"

She looked me in the eye. "I told him, yes."

And still he'd treated her so coldly? It was troubling to think that a man I looked up to could be so indifferent to his own niece. "My mother died recently. In June."

Something shifted in her eyes when I said those words. For a moment they shimmered with tears, but then she blinked them clear. It made me wonder if Elizabeth was still staring into the same gaping chasm of loss that Lucinda was. That I was.

"My mother died when I was a young child." Her eyes widened. "I suppose my father's death makes me an orphan now. But I'm . . . I'm fine. It's fine."

Young child? She didn't look so old just now. And her smile didn't seem to convince her of those words any more than it convinced me. Anyone could see that she wasn't fine, but I didn't know her well enough to do anything, and proper decorum meant I shouldn't say anything. At least not here, at the supper table. But I could most definitely sympathize. "My father's gone as well. A while ago. Several years now. I have a sister, but . . ."

"But you're alone now too." Tears were flooding her eyes again. "It wouldn't be so terrible if it didn't feel as if everything were up to you now. As if . . . Do *you* still feel as if you have to make your father proud?"

"I've always tried to. I think I did. I have. Most of the time. That's what my mother always says. 'You made your father proud. You made him so proud.' " I found that I could smile after all. But now, my mother was dead. I felt my smile fade. "I still want to make him proud."

She put a hand to my arm and then looked up at me with a startled glance, as if the gesture had surprised her as much as it had surprised me. "Now *you* have to make all the decisions. And you don't know quite what to do. Or what you *should* do. Or what he would even want you to do."

"That's it. That's it exactly."

"I was . . . angry. I still am. I'm angry that he died without telling me." She shook her head. "I know that sounds foolish. No one

34

knows when they're about to die. But I feel as if . . . it ruined all my plans. Is that terrible to say?"

"No. I think it's very honest of you."

"I wish . . . I just wish I'd known. I wish that the last time I said good-bye to him I'd known."

I couldn't speak for the lump that was in my throat, so I nodded and returned my attention to my plate. Around us, conversations continued. Voices rose and fell. The Hammond boy was scoffing at something. The youngest girl was being admonished for not eating her peas. They were all talking, all eating as if nothing was wrong. But finally, in talking to Lucinda, I felt as if one day things might somehow turn out right.

Campbell chortled as we hoofed it down the road back to the Point. "That was a bit of luck!"

We had to hurry if we were going to make it back in time for the parade at sunset. He was a good five paces in front of me, so I hadn't heard him clearly. "What was?"

He turned his head to look at me, though he didn't break his stride. "Professor Hammond having a niece. Anyone gets in good with her ought to benefit from the relationship."

"What do you mean by that?" I was accustomed to Campbell's schemes, having been his tentmate that summer, but this seemed a bit mercenary. Even for him.

"I mean what I said. If you want Professor Hammond to favor you, maybe the best thing you could do is find favor with the niece."

"The niece has a name."

He winked as he raked a shock of dark hair back from his eyes. "Sure she does. And it sounds a lot like the *Corps of Engineers* to me. You heard Old Hammond. Nothing is ever guaranteed."

"I don't think he was speaking about us." But if he wasn't, then what was the explanation for his tirade? There was something . . . something odd about his words. They'd left me as uneasy as a plebe standing midnight guard duty. I shook my head. I was just being fanciful. And fancy had no place at the U.S. Military Academy.

3
LUCINDA

Once supper was done and the cadets had departed, I breathed a sigh of relief as I took stock of the situation. By coming on a Sunday and so late in the afternoon, I'd been hoping my aunt would have the decency not to turn me away. From the encouraging smiles she was giving me, I thought I could depend upon her favor. I hadn't, however, counted on my uncle. In his case, fair-haired did not mean mild mannered. It didn't seem to matter to him that my father had so recently died. My aunt had had to plead with him to let me even enter the house. And then I had to endure his snubs as well as dine between two men who were, for all intents and purposes, military officers.

And preeminent ones at that!

I'd been so fixed on my plight, I hadn't even tried to flirt with them. Perhaps I'd miscalculated there. The man on my right,

Mr. Conklin, had the confident bearing and intense gaze of a man who would make his mark on destiny. From the sweep of his dark hair to the set of his strong jaw, he looked like money. The one on my left, Seth Westcott, while not so forceful in personality, was equally as acquainted with power, if I didn't miss my guess. But he wore it as casually as his fair, wavy hair — as a man in possession of himself.

Seth.

I'd told him my given name. He might consider me forward, but I had hoped I could trust him not to use it injudiciously. After our conversation at the table, I was quite certain that I could. More than anything, at that moment, I'd wanted someone to know me. Even now I didn't regret that decision; I didn't think my instincts were wrong.

My aunt ushered us all into the sitting room, taking the eldest daughter, Phoebe, on her arm and then pairing us together on the couch. The boy, Bobby, returned to his game of jackstraws as Milly gathered a sulky, rosy-cheeked Ella into her arms.

"Don't want to go bed!"

Milly winked at me. "Better stop pouting, or someone's going to come along and pluck that lip of yours right off your face."

The little girl's eyes went wide as she

covered her mouth with a hand.

While the girls were headed for the stairs, my uncle grabbed a pipe from the desk and stalked outdoors with it.

As the front door slammed, threatening the vases and other pretty pieces on the mantel, my aunt's brow rose. "Please don't worry yourself. He's just a bit . . . a bit . . . surprised by your presence. You must tell me everything about your mother. How is she? *Where* is she?"

"My mother?" Hadn't she heard? "She's . . . well she's . . . She's dead."

My aunt's brow folded as she gasped. "She's . . . ?"

"I assumed you knew. She died when I was three years old."

"She's dead." All the joy had fled from her face. "Why wasn't I told?"

"I . . . I thought my father . . . That is, I assumed that he had written . . ."

"If he did, my father — *our* father — never told me."

"She had cholera."

"Poor Annabel." Her hand found the cameo that nested at her collar.

I hadn't ever thought of things from the other side. From their side. Never realized they might have mourned my mother's leaving. But that just ought to make it easier to convince them to give me what I wanted. "Maybe . . . maybe my father thought you didn't care to hear from us. He told me he and my mother left Buttermilk Falls in rather a hurry."

My aunt glanced over toward Phoebe. Sending me an apologetic look, she rose and took her daughter by the hand. "Why don't you and Bobby join your sisters upstairs? You can ready yourselves for bed while I speak to your cousin."

Bobby pulled a face, but he gathered up his jackstraws, stuffing them into a pocket. "I don't see why I have to go up so early." His dark eyes were sullen. "I'm nearly eleven." The words came out as a boast.

I swallowed my smile. "At finishing school they always said a gentleman is as a gentleman does. As I recall, a gentleman *always* obeys his mother."

Though his scowl was nearly identical to his father's, his actions were gentle as took his sister's hand in his and led her toward the hall.

My aunt watched them walk away and then turned back to me, disapproval etching lines around her mouth. "They did leave in quite a hurry, your father and my sister. She climbed out her window one night and never . . . She never came back."

"Considering the way they left, perhaps my father didn't think you'd wish to know about her death." Frankly, I would have thought the same thing.

She pressed a hand to her heart. "Why would I not want to know? She was my sister. I cried over her for days. And she broke my father's heart, the way she left."

The poor woman seemed genuinely affected. "I didn't know my father hadn't told you."

She left her chair to sit beside me on the sofa. "My dear girl, it's not your fault."

I risked meeting her eyes. "It was my mother's dying wish that I return to her family." *Probably.* If I had been her, it would have been. I gave the smallest of shrugs. "When my father died, I was freed to follow her wishes."

"Poor child. And you've come alone?"

"There is no one else. Although I was not without companions on the train. Two very kind women agreed to accompany me." There must not be one whiff of impropriety regarding my actions.

"I'm just so glad you've finally come home."

Home. That was exactly what I'd been hoping she'd say. But why did I feel so duplicitous? "I don't want to be a bother. I

41

just wanted the chance to meet my mother's family."

"Of course you did. You must stay with us." She gave me a swift embrace and then dropped her arms, clasping my hands between hers. "Just look at you. So pretty. Such a lady."

"My father sent me to finishing school."

"Finishing school!"

"In St. Louis." And Chicago and Natchez and several other places in between.

"I never went to finishing school. I've never even left Buttermilk Falls."

"You've spent your whole life here?" I couldn't imagine such a thing.

She smiled. "It's not been as bad as all that. I was born here, as was your mother. I like it here. But my point is that you've had advantages that I have not. Perhaps you could share that knowledge with the children."

"The children?" In truth, I hadn't had much to do with children. They were too young to have much utility. Now and then they had proved to be useful distractions, but as a rule, I didn't have much need of them. I smiled anyway. Most of the time, people took a smile as a sign of agreement.

"I'm just so glad you've come back to us!"

If my aunt was overjoyed to see me, it was quite evident my uncle did not share the sentiment. Mr. Hammond was inscrutable. He might take me in out of a sense of duty, or he might just as happily show me the door. One thing was clear — he did not approve of my father. As he came back into the sitting room that evening, I cast my gaze down toward my hands.

He came to a stop in front of me. "At least your father's dead. Thank God for small mercies."

My aunt gasped.

I couldn't keep my chin from snapping up. "It happened quite suddenly. It was a very great shock."

My uncle spared me no sympathy. "How old are you, then?"

"I've nineteen years."

He glanced away from me in apparent distaste. "At least we know now why Annabel ran away with the lout."

My aunt's cheeks were flaming. "Richard!"

I'd never felt quite so humiliated as I did just then.

"I've no shame to spare for the

shameless."

My aunt had joined him, cajoling. "None of it was Lucinda's fault."

He appeared to consider that as he returned his pipe to the desk, looking at me from beneath his beetled brow. "What have you been doing that you've just now decided to find us?"

I forced myself to meet his gaze straight on. "We lived in the territories and —"

"Which one?" He was quite as terrifying as the headmistress in Chicago.

"Iowa. And Wisconsin, when I was younger. But I've come to you from Madame Mercier's Finishing School in St. Louis. That's where I was when I received word of my father's death."

"Finishing school. So he did well for himself, then?"

"He did." *Some of the time.*

"And your mother?"

"She died when I was three years old. Of cholera."

He said nothing in reply, but my aunt pulled a handkerchief from her sleeve and dabbed at her eyes.

My aunt's tears provided the perfect opportunity for me to press my case. "I don't know anything about my mother. I was hoping that I could spend some time, if you would have me, learning about her. And about all of you."

"We are not a boardinghouse. And I won't be taken advantage of."

The tears I blinked back were entirely real. "I hadn't hoped to take advantage of you. I had hoped to make your acquaintance."

"Why did you make no effort to correspond with us or contact us before now?"

"Because I was under the impression that my mother had been disowned by her family when she left with my father."

"At least he told you the truth about that."

Sometimes when things were going poorly, my father would simply give in. "I don't mean to trouble you." I looked toward my aunt. "I am happy to have had the chance to meet you, and I will always look upon this day we spent together fondly." I rose. "If you'll excuse me, I think it best if I went on my way."

My uncle eyed me. "What will you do?"

"What will I do?" I was hoping I wouldn't have to do anything. At this point, usually the other party would give in out of a sense of shame and do what my father and I had originally intended. Clearly, this man was no ordinary citizen. "I've been to finishing school. I am not without contacts and accomplishments." I smiled as if he were the

45

most gallant of men instead of a boorish toad, and I walked toward my satchel.

"Richard!" My aunt's tone was pleading.

I bent to pick up my things and continued toward the door, as if I weren't listening to them.

"She hasn't anything in this world. If she can't depend upon her family, then who can she depend upon?"

"I only wanted to make sure this wasn't some scheme of her father's." I heard the tap of footsteps across the room's bare floorboards. "Lucinda!"

I looked over my shoulder to see him coming through the room toward me.

"Lucinda, wait. Please." He ran a hand through his hair before extending his arm to clasp me about the shoulder, turning me from the door. "I'm sorry. I don't mean to be rude, but in the case of your father, I've learned one can't be too careful. Please. Come back. Sit with us. Give us a chance to decide what would be best for you. And for us."

4

SETH

Campbell slunk off to find the commandant, Major Walker, while I strolled the streets of the encampment. In the summer, immediately after graduation, the corps of cadets moved from the barracks out onto the flat, treeless Plain. Shaped like a coal scuttle, its base was to the south, along the road that fronted the barracks, academy building, and the chapel. It fanned out toward the river to the east and toward the row of faculty housing to the west. The West Point Hotel marked its farthest, tree-fringed reaches, and the tumbled, star-shaped ruins of Fort Clinton kept an eternal watch at its extreme northeastern point. West of its center the sunken, spherical bowl of Execution Hollow marked the site's revolutionary past.

Here, at the oldest post in the United States Army, we were forever being forced to comply with the army's wishes. Even the river itself had been required to bend at

West Point's command, causing boats to slow, passengers to gaze in wonderment, and railroad men to despair of ever conquering its nearly vertical cliffs. But that high ground and the vast, open space of the Plain comprised the chief parade ground of the military reservation. There we performed artillery and infantry drills, packed shells, mounted guns, constructed earthworks, trained the incoming appointees, and slept in musty canvas tents as practice for what it would be like in the real army.

As first captain, my visible presence was expected in the encampment, but that summer, I'd walked those tent-lined "streets" mostly for personal reasons. I did it to keep moving, to keep myself from thinking too much about my mother. My sister. The farm. But the more I tried not to think about them, the more I thought about them.

It was always a relief when I came upon groups of cadets and I was obliged to turn my thoughts outward. That evening, some of the plebes were suspiciously teary-eyed as they leaped to their feet to throw me a salute. And some of the yearlings were suspiciously bright-eyed as they went about gathering items like brooms and sheets that I knew from experience would be used that night for hazing the new appointees. But I didn't inquire; some things weren't worth knowing. And it wasn't possible to punish someone for something they hadn't yet done.

Out beyond the tents, in the middle of the parade ground, where the dust eddied over the remnants of the day's maneuvers, lanterns were being lit and fiddles were being tuned.

There'd be a stag dance tonight.

The tuning of a fiddle used to be a friendly sound. Now it just made me lonely.

Beyond the Plain, among the trees, lightning bugs twinkled and up along the river's bend, the West Point Hotel glowed in the twilight. The sounds of silverware on china dishes and trilling laughter drifted out through its windows. On its porches I could still see the light-colored smudges of wide skirts and lace-edged sleeves. And I could imagine I heard the rustle of silks. About the time the fellows started with their dancing, the girls at the hotel would wander in a gaggle across the Plain to watch the cadets cut up.

This was all the home I had now.

These cadets, my only family.

There was still Elizabeth, of course, but she'd already begun making a new life for herself, with Mother's family, in Kentucky.

I'd never been to Kentucky. She hadn't either. Could be I'd have time to visit after graduation, before I started off for my first assignment, but Professor Hammond was dropping hints about the possibility of my touring the military academy at Sandhurst in England directly after graduation. Or studying at École Polytechnique in France. In that case I might not have the chance to see her for another couple years.

If the army really was considering sending me to France, then I'd best try to get some help with my French from Dandy Delagarde. Though I was at the top of our class in all the subjects that mattered, Dandy had everyone beat when it came to French, and he was the best marksman in the corps of cadets as well.

As I approached his tent, I slowed to take a look inside.

Glancing up from a book he was reading, he nodded. "General." Dandy was the only cadet I knew who had more trouble being at ease than he did snapping to attention. Even this late in the day, his coat was buttoned up to his chin and his white cotton trousers were spotless, whereas mine needed a good coating of pipe clay to cover the day's stains. His shoes shone like mirrors reflecting back the candle's light, and that black, curly hair of his was slicked back in precise rows. There wasn't a finer-looking gentleman among us, and he lent an exotic air to the academy with his New Orleans accent. "May I help you?"

Dandy was numbered among the proud few we called Immortals. While Campbell and I battled each other for the top grades in our class, the Immortals lounged about at the very bottom, applying themselves to their studies only when it was truly necessary. It didn't mean they were bad sorts or any less willing to pull their share of the duty when they had to. They were just very . . . spirited. In ways the academy didn't condone.

I put a foot to the wooden floorboards and nodded out beyond the encampment. "They're getting up a dance on the parade ground." A fiddle screeched in the distance.

"So I hear."

"Just thought . . ." Just *hoped* was more like it. Dandy had never, in the three years I'd known him, ever joined in cadet diversions willingly. "Just thought you'd want to know."

"I think I'll pass tonight." His eyes flicked back down to the book he'd been reading.

I started to move on, but Otter Ames, Dandy's tentmate, hailed me. Another Immortal, he wasn't the smartest cadet at the Point, but he was as good-natured as a calliope. Every time his failure at exams seemed certain, a beatific smile would cross his face like the first rays of a sunrise and inspiration would rescue him. It defied explanation how many times he managed to hang on by just a single point. His features were open, his eyes bright, and his grin was so wide a fellow could see it in the dark. He was also from the South, but no one would have accused him of being a wealthy planter's son.

Never one to miss a stag dance, he didn't care if he danced the part of the girl, just so long as there was dancing to be had. "General! Hey there." He slipped by me into the tent. "Got a letter from Mother today."

That was no surprise. Otter's mother wrote him every day. And on Sundays, she wrote him twice.

"You oughter come back later. I'll read it to you when you got the time."

I tried to smile. "I'll do that." I nodded and withdrew through the tent's flap to continue on my way.

After settling a scuffle between two yearlings, I made my way to the tent of my barracks mate, Deacon Hollingsworth. While we couldn't share a tent during Encampment, due to my rank, I looked forward to our return to the barracks when we could room together again.

The candle flickered as I lifted the tent flap and ducked inside.

Deke was our class reprobate, the last of our class Immortals, but everyone loved him for it. He might not often choose to do the right thing, but he consistently did the wrong thing with such style and good humor that a fellow could never quite fault him for his failings. Except Campbell Conklin. He could fault anyone for myriad failings both real and imagined.

Other fellows might have been polishing their shoes on account of the girls who would be looking on at the dance that evening, but Deacon was lounging in a camp chair, sketching pad in hand. He was slowly filling it with portraits of girls to represent what he called "the delectable Greek goddesses of old." As I set my plumed cap on his tentmate's folded bedding and then loosened my red silk sash, he shot a glance at me. "You aren't planning to dance?"

"Maybe. Eventually." If I showed up too early, it might put a damper on the fun for the younger cadets. And if they needed anything after the long weeks in Encampment, it was the opportunity to forget that a long academic year still awaited.

"How's the good professor?"

I shrugged as I sat down in the other chair. "He has a niece come to visit."

He stopped drawing. "She pretty?"

"As a china doll. And she's got character too."

His smile was mocking. "Character! Is that what you been looking for all these years? Shoot, and here the rest of us have been willing to settle for pretty. You ask for too much, Seth. You always have. But that's why you'll be a general when the rest of us get stuck at captain."

The fellows were always saying things like that. I tried to ignore them. Flopping back into the chair, I put an arm up across my eyes. More than being tired, lately I was bone-deep weary.

"Only ten more months. You can make it."

"I know I can. I will." But June graduation still seemed so infernally far away.

I heard Deke's pencil scratch across his sketching book. "Won't be that difficult. Any of us who were going to be found deficient already have been. All a fellow has to do is stay the course."

"Stay the course and not be stupid." I gave

him what I hoped was a warning glance.

"Caught a cadet today crying like a girl over being homesick. Know why? He's from Philadelphia, and he says it's too danged noisy here. Can't sleep for the fish jumping in the river and that owl hooting from Fort Putnam and the cows lowing all over the place. Wanted to know didn't we have carts and wagons round here? Wasn't there any-one to come around and make deliveries and call their wares of a morning?"

I joined Deke in a smile. His family owned land out in Ohio somewhere. He was as used to being outdoors as I was.

One of the plebes stopped by and nearly propelled himself into the tent with a hardy salute. Deke winked at me before he addressed him. "You there!"

"Yes, sir!"

"What are you doing, fouling this tent with your miserable presence?"

The poor boy didn't quite know what to say.

"Dismissed." Deke tossed off a salute. "Get out of here."

The plebe started to turn on his heel but then stopped so quickly, he nearly fell right over.

"Didn't I tell you to leave?"

"Yes, sir. Only . . . sir?"

Deke grunted.

"I came to deliver a letter, sir. To the captain."

"And you didn't deliver it? Are you telling me you're derelict in the performance of your duty?"

The boy's face was wreathed with indecision. Deciding to show him pity, I pointed toward the foot of Deke's mattress. "Just leave it there."

"Yes, sir." He fairly flung it at us before wheeling and running off.

Deke took it up. "Seems like plebes were better when they were us."

"You already nostalgic for old time's sake?"

"It's just that I've noticed a lamentable lack of temerity in youth these days." He tossed the envelope to me.

I took it up and recognized my sister Elizabeth's script. "It's from home." Not home. Not anymore. This one must be from Kentucky. As I opened it, loss and longing pulled at my gut. I tilted it toward the candle's wavering light.

June 29th, 1855

Dear Seth,
I ought to have written you long before

now, but I just couldn't come by the words to do it. With Mama's death and arranging the sale of the farm, there just wasn't time. I know I said I was going to Kentucky, but as I was getting the sale recorded in town, I met a man named Mr. Pennyworth. Though he was on his way to a town called Greenfield, he was kind enough to escort me to the boardinghouse where I was staying and sit with me through dinner. He got to talking about Greenfield, and it sounded like the loveliest place. He said the Oregon Trail goes right through it, that it's a natural place to stop and catch a breath before heading over the mountains.

I was afraid, Seth. You heard all those stories Mama used to tell about Granny and her sisters. I didn't want to go to Kentucky, and when he said there was a hotel going up in Greenfield, it sounded like the perfect opportunity for me. For us. I figured I'd invest the money from the farm in the hotel, and in a few years' time, with all the people coming west, we'd have more than we'd started with.

He seemed quite surprised that I was interested and tried to talk me out of my idea, but I insisted on giving him our money to buy the hotel. I wish I could have told you about it, but how could I? He was headed out of town just then, so I didn't have much time to make a decision.

He went on ahead of me by a week, and after I had said my good-byes and visited Mama's grave one last time, I followed. I got as far as Fort Laramie, and I was talking to one of the officers there when he told me I'd been swindled. This man, Pennyworth, goes by different names, but he's taken folks for their money from Texas to Kansas. Everyone here seems to know about him. Wish I had too.

Seth, there is no Greenfield. There never was. I've enclosed the deed he gave me, but it's worthless.

Please don't be mad at me.

I'm so very sorry.

You're not to worry about me. I'm still at Fort Laramie and probably safer than I was out on the farm. With all the soldiers here, there's a heap of laundry to be done. I've been hired on by the woman who takes in their washing. She pays me in room and board.

I figure to stay the winter here. Come

spring, once I figure out what to do, I'll write again.

I remain, as always,
your loving sister

5

LUCINDA

My aunt took me upstairs and opened the door to a room that was plain in the extreme. "You'll sleep in here, with Phoebe." A bed draped in a fringed coverlet woven with stars and roses had been pushed against the far wall, and a chest of drawers sat beneath a window. My trunk had been placed beside it. Next to the door was a row of pegs upon which a bodice, several skirts, and a nightdress were hanging. There was little else in the room of which to take note.

My aunt pressed a kiss to my cheek and excused herself.

Phoebe was sitting on the bed unbuttoning her bodice. As I stood watching, she pulled her arms from her sleeves and then unfastened her skirt and pushed it to the floor. Pulling her feet from the skirt, she stepped out over it and stood.

I stepped back, pressing my back against the wall to give her space. I didn't know what to say or where to look. It seemed rude to watch her, since she didn't know I was doing so, but the room was so small; there was nowhere else to look.

She walked past me, hand extended, in the general direction of the pegs. When her hand touched the wall, she patted it until she found them. Taking up a nightdress, she replaced it with the skirt and bodice she'd just removed. After pulling it on over her head she looked straight at me.

How did she know where I was? It was uncanny.

"Didn't you wish to change?"

"I . . . um . . . yes. Thank you."

As she burrowed into the bed, I placed my satchel atop her chest of drawers and proceeded to undress. As I rolled my stockings down my legs and drew them off, I had to place my feet on the bare floor. Had they never heard of carpets? For a family my father had declared to be wealthy, there was a surprising lack of . . . just about everything in this house. Even the finishing school in Natchez, which was known for its parsimony, had placed carpets on the floors of our bedrooms. "I wonder that there's no rug." Wondered, in fact, that there weren't any in the house at all.

"I used to have one. But I tripped on it

and hit my head." Her fingers probed her temple. "After that, my parents took up all the carpets in the house." Her hand disappeared as she drew the bedclothes up toward her ears.

I lifted a corner of the blankets and climbed into the bed beside her.

They had taken me in, which was exactly what I had planned. But I would not be able to discount my uncle. If I stayed — and how could I leave at this point — I would have to mind my step.

I'd never been made to feel ashamed of myself before, and I didn't mind admitting I didn't like the feeling. I'd never been ashamed of my father either. I'd been proud of the way he knew how to talk to people and convince them to do the things he wanted them to. It hadn't mattered that he'd dragged me from town to town or that we'd often had to leave everything behind.

The best plan, the most expedient means to a secure future, would be to allow my aunt and uncle to embrace me as one of their family. As of this night, I would leave my past as my father's daughter behind. Here, I would marry, just as we had always planned, but I would marry for respectability, not wealth.

Respectability!

I nearly laughed into the night.

It wasn't the worst of things. I knew how to be good. I knew the appropriate things to say, the right things to do. And I was not unattractive. I would just look on it as a new sort of scheme. One might even say I was more prepared for this one than for any I'd ever undertaken. I had every expectation of success.

Phoebe woke before the sun had even dawned. She said nothing, but her stirring about woke me as well. I should think that if I ever had the misfortune of being blinded, I might find some way to benefit from never knowing where the sun was in the sky.

I lay abed for some time, unwilling to admit my day had begun, but there was no use in trying to return to sleep. The scent of breakfast had begun to infuse the room, and now that I was awake I could hear a clatter of cooking in the kitchen. Despite the bother and the early hour, if there was assistance I could offer to the household, I ought to do it. I needed to erase any doubt regarding my intentions from my uncle's mind.

Slipping from the bed, I grimaced as my feet hit those bare floorboards.

Phoebe was directing her sightless gaze toward the ceiling.

"Can I . . . can I get you anything, Phoebe?"

"No. Thank you."

I wished I hadn't been so rash in jumping out of bed so quickly. "Do you want to dress? Shall I get a skirt and bodice for you?"

"Not yet. I stay out of the way until Papa leaves for the Point and Bobby heads to the rectory for his studies. School doesn't start until next month, but Papa still makes him undertake a course of study with the rector. If I stay up here, no one has to bother about me."

I didn't want to be a bother either. "Perhaps I should stay here as well."

"You can help. Milly always minds Ella, but you could help in the kitchen. You *should* help. It's just that I . . . I can't."

Leaving Phoebe behind, I went downstairs to find the family at breakfast. My uncle nodded a greeting as I moved to take a seat.

My aunt came in just then, bearing a platter of biscuits. They'd been baked to a golden brown, and steam curled from their tops. "Lucinda! How perfect of you to appear. Here." She handed me the platter. "You can give them these and then come and help me in the kitchen."

Bobby reached up and stuck his fork into one and used it to pull several from the platter.

At least his father waited until I set the platter down to take his.

I flipped one onto Milly's plate and one onto Ella's and then carried the empty platter back into the kitchen, dodging the wiry, gray-haired maid who was arranging slices of what must be yesterday's roast on a plate.

"Just put it . . ." My aunt glanced wildly about. "Just set it over there, atop the cupboard by Susan. Then maybe you could take over here, with the eggs."

They were piled in a bowl. "What did you want me to do with them?"

"Just scramble them. Nothing fancy."

I picked one up. *Scramble?* I knew what scrambled eggs were, of course. I'd eaten them many times. But I didn't know how they got from the egg to the plate. "I don't know how to do that. I'm sorry."

My aunt turned toward me with a puzzled twist to her brow.

Susan was regarding me with something close to fascination. She took a swipe at her nose with the back of her hand.

"Then what did they teach you at that finishing school?"

"French. Drawing. Dance."

At mention of the last, she sent me a quick smile as she took the plate of meat from Susan's hand and poured some gravy over it. "That, at least, will come in handy. There's a grand ball at the military academy this Friday. But . . . they didn't teach you how to cook? Or . . . or . . ." The disappointment that had shadowed her face was overcome by hope. "They taught you how to do laundry, didn't they?"

Susan's eyes widened with expectation.

"Not exactly. The hope was that I would marry . . ." And that I would do it well. Well above my station, in any case. And then I would have servants to command. I did know how to do that. "I can keep accounts. And manage servants."

Susan wheezed a sigh.

"Well . . ." My aunt handed the plate back to Susan and nodded toward the dining room. Then she took my place in front of the bowl. Removing all the eggs, she cracked them one-by-one, releasing their contents back into the bowl. Her lips quirked into a smile. "I'm afraid the only servant we have here is Susan. And now there's you as well."

"Me?"

She laughed outright as she collected the eggshells and handed them to me.

"Where should I . . . ?"

"Put them right there." She pointed to a second bowl. "We'll use them to scrub the skillet when we're done cooking." She whipped the eggs together with a fork. "I don't expect you to do everything. But perhaps, if you could provide some companionship to Phoebe . . . ? You're close in age. She's eighteen."

I suspected it would be vastly preferable to laundry. And it had the added benefit of my cousin's not being able to see. I could do whatever I wanted when I was with her. "Of course. I would be happy to."

Taking the eggs to the oven, she poured them into the skillet that sat atop it. They sizzled as they hit the metal and soon they lost their translucence. After pronouncing them done and scraping them onto the platter that had formerly held the biscuits, she had me take them into the dining room, where they were quickly consumed.

My uncle left for the military academy and Bobby left for the parsonage. Soon after the front door closed behind them, Phoebe joined a restive Milly and a squirmy Ella at the table.

As Milly dragged Ella into the kitchen to clean her honey-smeared mouth, my aunt came in carrying a plate of bread. Hand at

67

her hip, she surveyed the crumb-strewn table and emptied platters.

Heaving a sigh, she pulled out the chair next to Phoebe's. "I don't guess I should complain about hearty appetites . . . but the fact of the matter is that I have one too." She picked up a knife and began sawing at the bread. "Lucinda? Can you bring us some plates?" When I began to glance about, she nodded toward the sideboard with her chin. "In the cabinet, beneath."

Milly and Ella rejoined us as my aunt was soaking up the last bit of gravy from the platter with Phoebe's bread. My aunt drained the remains of the tea into cups for us, but I demurred. Surely it was tepid; I preferred to drink mine hot.

While I swept the floor, Milly and Ella were sent out back to shake the tablecloth. Once the dining room was put to rights, we all repaired upstairs. But when I moved to enter Phoebe's room, my aunt stopped me with a hand to my shoulder. "Your uncle and I have decided you should stay with us as long as you'd like. So we ought to make space for you, should we not?" After considering both my trunk and my satchel, she went to Phoebe's chest, where she opened one of the drawers and began to push the contents to one side.

I opened my satchel and began to empty it. My brush and mirror. A fall and some ribbons. The gold crest that had been my mother's. A wreath and the silvered letters USMA adorned it. I'd always wondered what they stood for.

As I lay it atop the chest, my aunt snatched it up. "Where did you get this? Who gave it to you?"

I hoped she planned to return it. "My father did. He said it was my mother's."

My aunt set it back down on the dresser top and traced its letters with a finger. "United States Military Academy. You have probably never heard of it, but there's a tradition among cadets on furlough. They're allowed to travel the summer after their second year, and as they go they flirt. My, how they flirt!"

Her eyes went soft, as if gazing on days long past. "As they do, they give away the buttons from their coats. There are ten of them, you understand, so they can't mean anything special. But that plate of yours belonged to a cadet's hat, and there's only one of those."

"My mother was given one?" I'd never considered how she'd come to have it.

"Your mother was given several. Every year, it seemed. But this was the only one she kept. She seemed prouder of having that one than she was any of the others."

I'd never heard any stories about my mother. There'd been no one to tell them to me. "Who gave it to her?"

"Why . . . your father did!"

6
SETH

On Monday, on the way back from artillery drill, I stepped around one of the tents and ran into one of my classmates.

A pack of cards, trussed with string, tumbled from his coat. He sent a salute in deference to my rank and then bent, sending a quick glance around. Grabbing up the cards, he stuffed them back up his sleeve. "Please don't report me! I've already got twenty demerits and the semester hasn't even started. I'm going to be walking tours all year if I don't want to get dismissed."

Though playing cards was expressly forbidden, I wasn't going to report him. Campbell would have, and he would have also reported him for chewing what was probably tobacco, but I wouldn't. Can't report something you don't actually see. "You're a smart fellow. Why is it that you're always courting trouble?"

When he answered, it was with a glint in

his eye. "I'm not courting trouble. Not on purpose. But with Campbell Conklin around, doesn't seem a man can much avoid it." He nodded and continued on down the street.

It bothered me that a fellow like him, and Deacon and Dandy for that matter, didn't even seem to try to keep the rules. On the whole, unlike me, it seemed they'd been much more successful at furlough than they were in life at the academy.

I went back to my tent and set about sweeping the wooden platform. Campbell Conklin and I had tracked memories of the morning's field work in on our boots.

Deacon came along and scoffed at my efforts from the comforts of my mattress, where he set about working on another of his sketches. "You can't think that floor is going to stay clean until the next inspection."

"I can hope."

"You ever stop to think how much time we spend being looked at and our things being gone over? Way I figure it, we spend at least an hour a day in roll calls and forming up to march somewhere. And that doesn't count drills and parades, which I calculate at two hours. Every blessed day, that's three hours we're not doing anything but trying to look pretty and showing up where we're supposed to."

"I don't know that I'd count drills as parts of the —"

"I would! And I haven't even mentioned inspections. Do you know how many people get to look at my things every day? Start with police call in the morning. That's the subdivision inspector, and he comes back later at lights-out. The tactical officer looks everything over twice a day too. And then he comes back later at night! And then there's the officer of the day who looks in twice, in case anything I own has the temerity to move of its own volition during the two minutes nobody's watching it. And those sentinels get to look in on everything three times. That's —"

"That's four people."

"That's right. And do you know how many separate inspections?"

"Ten."

"Ten!" He spat out into the street.

"You aren't just now figuring all that out are you?"

"No. Just feeling envious of all those second classmen out on furlough."

"Don't. They'll take twice as long to get used to it all over again once they return. We did. Remember?"

He harrumphed. "Maybe I'll go sweep my own floor after I finish this sketch." He tilted his head as he looked at it. "Or maybe I won't."

"Last chance to impress the academic board, Deke. You going to try harder this year? If you tried even half the time, I wager you could make it up a few files. Maybe even get an assignment to the infantry."

He snorted. After pausing to contemplate his sketch again, he resumed drawing.

"You honestly don't care to do as well as you can?" It was a conversation we'd had a hundred times, but I'd never come to understand his answer.

"Well . . ." He spent several moments shading in something before he continued. "There's doing as well as you *can* and there's doing as well as you'd *like*. If doing as well as I can means spending my nights worrying about whether folks like you are going to get three more points than me on the January exam and whether that would kick me down from fourth in the class to sixth, then thanks but no. I'd rather spend some of those hours down at Benny Havens worrying about whether the quartermaster sergeant is on the prowl for me. They can order me to get my hair cut once a month. They can order me to march to the mess hall for meals, but they can't order me to turn myself into Campbell Conklin."

"Not everyone's like him."

"No." My contradiction didn't seem to bother him much. "There's people like you too. There's cadets who could have a lot more fun if they cared a little less about academics. The way I see it, it's not that I don't study enough, it's that cadets like you study too much. If you look at me and you look at you, you'll realize that I get lots more done than you."

"You hardly do anything at all."

He pointed his pencil in my direction. "You, sir, are mistaken. Here you are, getting everything in order, reporting *where* you're supposed to be *when* you're supposed to be, and I've already been down to the hotel —"

"You're not supposed to —"

"Down to the wharf —"

"When!"

"And over to the riding hall *and* done everything else I'm supposed to do. If you're talking about efficiency, I've got you beat."

"And you've probably got your uniform spread around your tent and your books in disarray."

He shrugged the criticism away as he pulled his flask from his pocket.

"Any demerits this week?"

"Two. I ran into Campbell Conklin. But we're not talking about me. We're talking about you. Can you really say you've had any fun since you got here?" He took a drink from his flask.

"That's not the reason I came."

"Doesn't mean there's no fun to be had as you go along. With that chiseled jaw of yours, that fair hair, and those blue eyes, you too could start wooing the belles of the Hudson Valley." He sat up and leaned forward as if to scrutinize my looks. "Why, bless my heart, Mr. Westcott! As our legendary drawing teacher would say, 'You're a regular Adonis.' Shame is, no one will ever know it if you keep your nose to the grindstone."

I turned round, took up the stiff-brimmed forage cap he'd dumped on the mattress and threw it at him.

He dodged, laughing.

It was always about girls with him. Thing was, all we had to look forward to after graduation was life as a lowly lieutenant. And the path to promotion was both long and treacherous. I couldn't help but agree with the privates who swore that if the army wanted you to have a wife, they'd issue you one.

Deke was peering at me through narrowed eyes. "Speaking of fun, usually you'd have chased me out of here by now. What's wrong?" Deacon was as gossipy as an old woman, and I knew he wouldn't leave me alone until I gave him something to jaw about.

"It's the news I got from my sister in that letter."

He screwed the top back on his flask and sat up. "What about?"

I shrugged, hoping he'd let me leave it at that.

"You might as well just tell me and get it over with."

"You ever hear of anybody selling deeds to property that doesn't exist?"

"My pa usually drums those folks right of town. They come around now and then. But most of the time they're selling liniments or snake oil."

"My sister met one selling the rights to property in a town out west of Laramie. I told you she was headed to Kentucky?"

He nodded.

"Well, she bought some hotel from him instead . . . only there wasn't one. Wasn't even any town."

"That's tough."

"Tougher that I'm here and she's stuck at

77

Laramie doing laundry all winter."

"Wouldn't want any sister of mine out there. All those privates . . ."

"Exactly."

He cocked his head as he sat there watching me. "You going to do something about it?"

"I already wrote and told her to stay right where she was, that I'd come get her once I graduate. What else can I do? They wouldn't even give me leave to go home and see my mother buried and the farm sold! I've some money in my account with the treasurer. I'd send it to her and tell her to come here, but you know they won't let me have any of it until after graduation."

"Well . . . there's things you *should* do, but there's a whole lot of other things you *can* do. You want to leave right now to go get her, why don't you get yourself dismissed? I'll lend you my flask, and you could let old Campbell Conklin see you take a drink from it. Or you could take a deck of cards down to supper tonight and deal yourself a hand. Hate to see you go, but if that's what you want to do, I'll help you any way I can."

I'd already thought of that, but it would be pointless. "What's being dismissed going to do for me? Or Elizabeth? I'm all she has now. At least if I graduate, I'll have lieutenant's pay. . . . That would be something."

"Guess you can hope she survives the winter without getting talked into marrying one of those privates."

That's exactly what I feared would happen.

"And then you can use your furlough to go get her. Take her with you to your new assignment."

"I might not get a furlough. Professor Hammond's talking like I'm going to be sent straight to Europe."

"No furlough! Furlough's the only reason I'm still here."

"Even if I don't get the chance to see her, I could still send her some money. Trust that she'll get herself to Kentucky. . . ."

Deke didn't look as if he thought any better of that idea than I did. "But what about that fellow?"

"What fellow?"

"The swindler."

That was the other part of the problem. Elizabeth's rightful inheritance, as well as my own, would still be gone. Stolen. "I was thinking I could hire one of those detectives to track him down. Elizabeth said they've heard of him out there at Laramie."

"They've probably heard of him at more

forts than just Laramie. There's really only those two trails heading west. I know settlers are scattered every which way across the frontier, but with the cavalry, it's different. All those trips for resupplying and with reassignments . . . soldiers see each other so often it's like they're neighbors. Too bad they won't give you furlough. If you could have the summer out west, put the word out that you were looking for him, you could probably run him to ground."

He gave me an appraising glance. "Why don't you get assigned to the cavalry and do that detecting yourself? Could be it will take longer than a summer, but you'd find him eventually."

"That's an idea. . . ." I hadn't thought about the cavalry before.

His lips twisted in a sardonic smile. "Not all of us are bound for the engineers."

"It's not like I could just tell Colonel Lee I want to be assigned to the cavalry . . . do you think?"

He lifted a brow, though he seemed to be more interested in assessing his handiwork than in continuing the conversation. "You mean old Robert E. I don't know. You could ask him."

7
LUCINDA

I was staring wide eyed at my aunt, I knew that I was, but I couldn't help myself. "My father was a *cadet*?"

"He was."

"At the *military* academy? *This* military academy?" Wouldn't he have told me about something like that?

"At West Point."

"But . . . are you sure?"

"Quite."

"I just . . . he never told me."

"And why would he have? He left before he graduated. That doesn't make him look very good."

"He . . . he really was a cadet?"

She took up my hand and squeezed it. "He truly was a cadet. And a good one. A very clever one. He might have been at the top of his class if he'd applied himself."

"What happened?"

She shrugged, a delicate lift of a shoulder.

Then she sat down on the bed by Phoebe, who must have entered the room in my moments of shock. "He had a way about him. He was quite charming. Very handsome. He drew people like a flower draws bees. But after a while, I came to realize that he wasn't laughing with us; he was always laughing at us. As if he considered himself smarter than everyone else."

"He did." He had. And generally speaking, he was.

"I always imagined that it must have been difficult for him at the academy, obeying everyone else's orders when he felt as if he should be the one giving them."

"I can't picture him as a cadet. I thought . . . I mean . . ." He'd always avoided soldiers. Had he been afraid of them? I discarded the thought almost as soon as it had formed. He hadn't been afraid of them. He must have been afraid of being *recognized* by them. That explained quite a bit, although it didn't resolve the contrast between his way of life and his time at the academy. "I just can't . . . I can't imagine it. My father, here. One of them."

She looked to Phoebe and then back to me. "You can only be as good as you are. They come here as boys and they leave as men. But at what other place in the world are men issued their undergarments and taught to march as if they'd never learned how to walk? So they learn how to comply with the letter of the law rather than its spirit. Sometimes a person has to in order to survive."

"And I suppose some don't comply at all."

"The military academy is not for everyone." The way in which she said it left little doubt that she had identified my father as *everyone.* "But there's no point in dwelling on his record at West Point."

"He had a record?" I suppose that shouldn't have surprised me. He had a record out west too.

"He has . . . *had* the distinction of amassing the most demerits in the least amount of time."

I almost smiled, knowing how proud he would have been of that. "Does it still hold?"

"It does." Something flashed in her eyes.

"So you met him? You knew him?"

"Oh yes. And so did your uncle. They were barracks mates."

I felt my mouth drop open once again.

"Your father pulled him into several of his schemes. It was only thanks to the superintendent's mercy that your uncle was saved from dismissal. You can see, then, why the subject of John Barns is so distasteful to him."

"John Barns?" Who was John Barns? And how did he figure into any of this?

Her brow puckered. "John Barns. Your father."

John Barns was a name I'd never heard. It sounded like one of those men my father always made fun of. One of those stolid, serious men of good character and very little imagination. Ezra Pennyworth — or Pennwith or Penfield or Pennman, depending upon the situation — couldn't be a John Barns, could he?

"I'm sorry, my dear. It must pain you to hear me speak of such things. He was your father after all. I'll try to remember that. Only please don't think the worst of us if it seems as if we cannot speak of him charitably."

It didn't pain me to hear her words, it just . . . it . . . unnerved me. Unanchored me. Set me drifting. To think that the man I had spent my life looking up to was just a . . . a . . . a *John Barns*! If I didn't know these basic facts about him, if I'd never known his real name, then what else didn't I know? What else hadn't he told me?

Down the hall, Ella began to protest something quite vigorously. Milly's reply was rather testy, and soon the little girl began to wail. My aunt left us to see to them.

Was this what it felt like to fall prey to one of my father's schemes? To place all of one's hope and one's trust in his words and then to find out that they meant nothing? That *he* was nothing?

"Lucinda?" Phoebe's voice was gentle and kind, but I wanted to bark at her. Punish her for being so noble, so good.

My father had told me so many things through the years, given me countless pieces of advice. I'd secreted them away in my soul, every one of them, as if they were treasures. I'd been hoarding them as one would jewels, but . . . "I've so been wrong." It was as if I'd been living my life inside a kaleidoscope not realizing that what was real was on the *outside,* not the inside, of the tube. Rotating did nothing to rearrange what was true and real. It only jumbled up the images and distorted the truth. "I didn't know . . ."

I felt Phoebe's hand patting tentatively up my arm, then increasing in firmness as she grabbed hold of my shoulders and pulled me to her breast.

"I don't know anything anymore. I just don't —" I choked on my own sobs, on the tears streaming down my cheeks.

"Hush. You'll be fine. I'll help you."

I couldn't keep myself from smiling. And then I was laughing through my tears. "*You'll* help me?"

"I'll help you. I will." She was quite serious.

A blind girl would help *me*? Lucinda Pennyworth . . . rather Lucinda Barns? My soul wavered between hysteria and despair. But I knew, as surely as I'd ever known anything, that Phoebe would. She *would* help me. And that was worst of all. I was so unfit for normal life that the only person I could count on was a girl even more unsuited to it than I. She would help me not because I deserved it — heaven knew I didn't — but because she was a kind and decent soul.

Which only served to underscore that I was not.

I never had been, even at my best.

Would I ever be?

8
SETH

I *could* have asked the superintendent, Colonel Lee, about an assignment to the cavalry, but upon reflection I decided I didn't want to. For wouldn't he want to know why his top cadet wanted to go for the cavalry? And who could think honorably of a man whose family had been taken in by a swindler? Whose sister was, at this moment, taking in laundry for her room and board? This might be a military academy, but it was still a school for gentlemen, and Colonel Lee was the most distinguished gentleman of us all.

I decided to speak to Professor Hammond instead. In spite of my concern about the way he had treated his niece, he still had great influence over assignments, so I went over to the academy during recreation to find him. He looked up from his desk at my knock with what I took to be a smile. His lips hadn't moved, but there was an easing of the lines above his brow.

"Mr. Westcott. How may I help you?"

"I uh . . . well . . . I was thinking about Dirichlet's unit theorem, and I just wanted to make certain I understood the principles."

"I wish more cadets would take the time to make sure they understood mathematical principles. Why don't you try a problem and we'll see how far you get." Professor Hammond gestured toward the board. I took up a piece of chalk and sponge and then went to the board and stood at attention.

After he gave me the problem, I wheeled around, wrote it on the board, and went to work on it. It wasn't so difficult that I didn't understand it, although I took my time in solving it. In truth, I was hesitating for I hadn't yet decided what I should say to him. By the time I had finished, spun around, and recited the answer, I still didn't know.

"Well done."

I turned around once more and sponged the chalk off the board.

"You didn't have any trouble with that your yearling year. At least not that I noted."

I hadn't.

"What was it you thought to be confusing?"

That was the question, wasn't it? "I

guess . . . I should say . . . I figured it out, sir."

"I shouldn't worry, Mr. Westcott. With the talent you've shown, and your grasp of theories, I should imagine you'll stay at the top of your class this year. It's men like you, men with your grasp of mathematics and engineering, who are needed abroad. Men of understanding who can study at foreign academies, make true friends of our allies, and then bring all that knowledge and those experiences back home."

"I hope so. That is, I know our assignments after graduation depend upon our performance as cadets."

"You've scarcely stumbled since you've been here."

"But . . . what if I do?"

"For a cadet of your obvious talents, at this late date, a few missteps could be forgiven. Although you should keep in mind that an assignment to the Corps of Engineers is never guaranteed."

"Yes, sir. But I've heard some of the fellows, some of those who might go as ordnance or artillerymen, say they'd give it all up to go cavalry."

He frowned as he leaned forward, hands clasped in front of him. "I understand what it is to hear the call of the untamed wilderness, and I'd like to see a bison for myself one day, but what would happen to the army if soldiers were allowed to decide their own assignments? There are no options for a soldier, Mr. Westcott. You must know that by now. There are only orders. The best and brightest must go where we've the most need for them — to the engineers. If they're not acceptable to the engineers, they must go to ordnance. If ordnance won't take them, the artillery will."

"But not the cavalry?"

He gave me a stern look. "The cavalry, sir, must make do with what's left."

There was no need to inquire as to what he thought of those cadets like Deacon and Dandy who had settled, quite comfortably, to the bottom of the class.

"The road to success is found through hard work and study, Mr. Westcott. Keep on the straight path, and your future will be secured." Incredibly, then he winked. "You can trust me on that."

Which is exactly what I'd been afraid of.

Deacon caught me as I came out of the academy.

He was strolling up the tree-lined road, looking for all the world as if he were free to do whatever he wished. And it looked as

90

if . . . Was he wearing my officer's sash? He hailed me as I jogged down the steps, throwing a salute in deference to the chevrons on my coat.

I returned it.

"What were you doing in there?" He lifted his chin toward the building. "Are you that anxious for classes to start?"

"Just asking Hammond a question."

"Isn't he the one who usually *asks* the questions?"

"Don't you have somewhere else to be? And why are you wearing my sash?"

"Well, blast my buttons, I surely do." He flashed a smile. "Just borrowing it. I'm supposed to see the tactical officer about something."

"Supposed to? Then why aren't you?"

"I've more important things to do."

"Like what?"

"I'd say most anything is more important than reporting to the tactical officer, wouldn't you?" He lifted a hand when I would have protested. "But don't you worry, I've a yearling pledged to cover for me."

"If you would put as much time into doing your work as you do getting out of it, neither Campbell Conklin nor I would hold a candle to you, Deke."

"Right. And don't you forget it. Now about getting you into the cavalry —"

"There's no hope for it. That's what I was doing in there. Asking Hammond if there was any way a fellow could choose a lesser assignment. No offense."

"None taken." He stretched up his chin and wrestled his top button into its buttonhole. Then he adjusted the white-web crossbelt over his chest and turned the red sash around his waist so that the knot rode his left hip, riffling through the fringe that fell from the ends in order to straighten it. "But that's the trouble with you fellows at the top. You're always asking questions about everything, ruining all the surprises."

"Where are you headed again?" He hadn't really said, had he?

"Heard there's a new family visiting up at the hotel with a pair of pretty girls. I decided it was my responsibility to tell them about the grand ball on Friday. Got to make folks feel welcome."

I might have known there was a girl or two involved. "Then you might want to do something with that thatch of straw you call hair."

He lifted his dress cap with its black pompon and tried to smooth his hair down with his hand. "Can't help what I was born with. I just have to make up for it with my stunning good looks." He gave a glance off behind us and then tilted his hat just enough to put it off-regulation. "Meet me in Otter and Dandy's tent after exercises tonight. I think I've figured out the solution to your problem."

I didn't know whether I ought to go. On the one hand he was right: asking questions of Professor Hammond hadn't done anything but confirmed answers I already knew. On the other hand, being caught where I wasn't supposed to be was punishable by demerits, and what sort of example would I be to the new plebes and the yearlings if I were caught disobeying the rules?

Campbell decided it for me. I heard him out in the street skinning one of the plebes for some infraction. He was such a grind that it pained me to imagine anyone might think the same of me. So that evening, I snuck down the street and slipped into Otter and Dandy's tent, letting the flap fall into place behind me.

It looked exactly the same as my tent, with its pair of mattresses and wooden floorboards, only here, the scent of flowers perfumed the air. Otter must have gotten another letter from his mother; she was known to scent her stationery. While I was trying to figure out how to politely push open the flap for ventilation, Deacon swore and reached over to do it himself. "Don't see why she has to use a whole gol-darned bottle of skunk water all the time. What is it you call those flowers again?"

Otter seemed to take no offense. "Jasmine." He said it with a smile. Unlike Deacon and Dandy, he owed his place at the bottom of the class wholly to merit. He truly deserved to be there. He was loyal to a fault, and he sat a horse better than anyone else in the corps of cadets, but he wasn't very smart.

Deke gave the flap a shake, trying to get the stink out. "Well, we're not a bunch of girls. And besides. We got work to do." Releasing the flap, he took a stance in front of it, clasping his hands behind his back. He nodded at me. "I took it upon myself to apprise everyone of the situation."

There was a murmur of "tough luck" and "too bad."

As I nodded in acknowledgment, a flush crept up my cheeks. Had it really been necessary for him to tell Otter and Dandy that my sister was destitute because some swindler had stolen all of our money?

He continued speaking. "I know what

you're thinking. I know you're wondering why I went and told the other Immortals about your . . . well . . . you know. But they had to understand the lay of the land if we're hoping to get their help."

We were hoping for their help? I enjoyed the fellows, and there was no one I'd rather room with than Deacon Hollingsworth, but why had *he* suddenly become a *we* with *me*?

"On account of the way you got Otter through math and that time you covered for Dandy when he was late for parade —"

I shrugged. "I only figured —"

"And the way you volunteered to carry water that week during plebe year when you knew I was sick —"

"It was the decent thing to do —"

"We've decided we're in. We're going to help you. Besides, we're the only solution to the whole problem."

"*You* are?" My gaze fell on Otter and Dandy, who were, even now, playing cards. And if I wasn't mistaken, they were drinking too.

"That's right. *We* are."

"I fail to see how —"

"You want to be assigned to cavalry, don't you?"

"I do." Didn't I? Wasn't that the only way to rescue Elizabeth and find that Pennyworth fellow?

"And you aren't going to get there by studying your head off, are you?"

"No." Professor Hammond had made that quite clear.

"So what you're asking for is help."

"I don't think I actually meant to —"

"I've given it quite a lot of thought, and I've decided that what you need to do is fail this next semester."

"*Fail?* That's not quite the solution I was after."

That's when Otter lived up to his nickname. "I just don't see how . . ." He paused to blink. "What I mean to say is, you worked hard to get to the top of the class these past few years, so if you want to get to the bottom, hadn't you oughter start failing right quick? Once the semester starts?"

"I don't have any intention of failing."

Deacon held up a hand as if he were conducting a lecture. "Listen. We're not here to corrupt you. We don't want to do that. Do we, men?"

They chorused a denial.

"We simply want to help you. If *we* needed help with ethics or rhetoric or —"

"Geology," Dandy suggested.

"Or civil engineering. Then we'd come to you — wouldn't we, fellows?"

They nodded.

"So it just makes sense that if you wanted help with failing, then you'd come to us."

"I don't quite understand — how it is that you decided I needed to fail?"

"How else are you going to get into the cavalry? Do you think you can just walk into Colonel Lee's office and ask him for a favor? And how would you put that exactly?" He struck a pose. "Colonel Lee, sir, no matter my class standing, no matter that I've achieved the highest grade in engineering since the foundation of the military academy, I was wondering, would you mind terribly if I threw away all this education and the goodwill of the academy board and joined up with the cavalry?"

"Of course I wouldn't do that. I just think —"

He came forward to take me by the arm. "That's just it. You've been thinking way too much these past three years. What you need to do now is let us do the thinking for you. And we have! We've got a plan. So here's the way we'll do it. If you'll just stop studying —"

"Stop studying? I can't *stop studying.* You don't just stop studying. Not at the best engineering school — the only engineering school — in the nation."

"I do. Don't both of you?" Deacon looked at the other two.

They nodded over their cards.

He looked at me again. "So it seems you *can* stop studying. Leastwise until December. And then there's a bit of hard work needed to catch up for January exams, you understand. You *do* have to start studying at some point, but at least you're not wasting all that time every dad-blamed day over your books. That's the first thing we're going to teach you."

"I don't . . . I don't quite understand how you *teach* someone not to study."

Otter interjected. "Mother always says you might as well stop to smell the roses, because someday soon enough, you're going to be pushing up daisies. Maybe we oughter say that we're going to teach you how to have some fun." He nodded. "That's what we're going to do."

Dandy glanced up at me over his cards. "And how to earn demerits."

I shook my head. "I've only gotten a couple demerits since I've been here. I really don't think demerits are necessary, do you?"

Otter skewered me with a look of pure disappointment. "Then you *don't* want to find that cheating, thieving swindler? Because we were all planning on helping you

98

do it once we're gone from here and assigned to forts out in the territories somewheres."

"Of course I do."

Dandy laid his cards down and gave me his legendary dark-eyed glower. The one that had caused many a cadet much bigger and older than he to back up a step or two and reconsider what he was about to do. "Then you *don't* want to avenge your sister's honor?"

Good grief. It sounded as if he was challenging *my* honor. "No! I mean yes, I —"

Deacon came over and planted himself right in front of me, glaring. "Then you *don't* want to have to be assigned to the cavalry because there's just no other place to put you?"

"Yes. I mean . . . I do."

He grinned. "That's fine, then. It's settled. So what you got to do now, once school starts on Monday, is stop studying and just leave the rest to us." He took up a hand of cards that was sitting on the table and settled down to join the others.

Apparently I'd been dismissed.

9
LUCINDA

On Tuesday evening after the supper dishes were put away and the young ones put to bed, Milly brought a cup of tea from the kitchen for Phoebe, spooning some sugar into it. She sat down beside her sister at the table and started telling of a recent encounter with one of the townswomen. I hadn't realized she was such a mimic, but it was all in good fun and she soon made her older sister laugh so hard Phoebe was crooking a finger to her eyes to wipe away tears. I didn't have the chance to listen to the end of the story, for my aunt drew me into the sitting room to talk with my uncle. It was really rather fearsome the way he looked at a person.

"Your aunt and I wish to speak to you of your future. I think it prudent that you use my family's name. Some in town still remember your mother, and it would be best for everyone, I think, to leave the past behind us."

I agreed. Wholeheartedly.

"If you call yourself our niece, of course it will still be true. But the Hammond name will protect you from your father's misdeeds and give you a chance at a respectable future."

The scrutiny of his piercing gaze made me want to squirm, but I forced my lips into a smile. "That's very generous."

"None of what happened in the past was your fault. I can't bring myself to think you should be punished for it. And it would be a shame not to take advantage of the opportunity the military academy offers. Your aunt and I think that would be the best place for you to find a man of merit to marry. I suggest you consider this a chance to begin again, to forge a new life for yourself."

That fit exactly with my own plans. "If you think it best."

My aunt joined the conversation. "Of course the life of a military wife is not always easy, but you're familiar with the West. You're probably more suited to the life than many of the girls who flock here in the summer. Your uncle has agreed to be your escort to the cadet dances and —"

"Hops, they call them."

"— and to introduce you to those cadets he deems acceptable."

"If I see any signs of history beginning to repeat itself, of you taking up with a cadet who displays the worst traits of your father, I will be obliged to ask you to leave."

I swallowed. Hard. "I won't. I promise you that I won't." My days of deceit were behind me.

"Promises are easily made. I'm more interested in seeing them kept."

"I will." I had to. In this new world of mine, there was no room for a girl with a tarnished past. At least they thought me innocent of my father's schemes. And how would they ever learn I'd been an active participant? My secret was safe. No one would ever know I wasn't as spotless an as angel.

The first dance I would attend, a grand ball to celebrate the end of something called Encampment, was to take place Friday evening, on the last day of August. But I had the rest of the week to get through first. Helping Milly mind Ella, assisting my aunt and Susan with the cooking, and reading to Phoebe left hardly any time for me to think about cadets, let alone to ready myself for the dance. Had I had the time, I might have salved my hands with glycerin jelly and rinsed my hair in alcohol and castor oil. As it was, Friday morning found me trying to coax Ella into eating her breakfast and chasing Milly down from the apple trees out behind the house.

She dropped to the ground with a thud. "God wouldn't have made the branches so low if He hadn't meant them for climbing."

Now Ella was trying to climb it as well, hugging the trunk with her arms and kicking a leg up toward the branch.

I caught her up about the waist as I admonished Milly. "If God made trees for climbing, then He was intending them for boys." I picked a twig from her hair. "Girls were made for better things."

She pulled a face as she ran to the back door. As always, Ella trailed along behind.

I spent the afternoon telling stories about my life in boarding schools to Phoebe and Milly as I helped my aunt and Susan cook. Most of the stories were inventions, but they would never know.

By suppertime, my sleeves were powdered with flour and my forehead was slick with perspiration. I was halfway through talking to Phoebe about the classes I'd taken at Madame Mercier's finishing school in St. Louis when my aunt pronounced her stew done. She set about serving supper before I even had the chance to remove the apron she'd lent me. And I still had pie crust underneath my fingernails. I'd found that the lard did wonders for my hands, but I feared baking pies and minding the gravy had made me smell like a tavern.

After supper, Susan tended to the dishes while I went upstairs to change. I didn't have many choices. My delicate blossom-sprinkled barège or my printed organdy. I settled on the barège with its lace trim. Its pale pink color suited me, and the bodice was cut to flatter, presenting me as respectably demure and understatedly wealthy. A pair of shining rock crystal earrings only added to the effect.

Pulling my gloves on over ragged fingernails, I hoped there wasn't too much dough still stuck beneath them. And I could only hope that I didn't smell like gravy or the evening's stew. But if I did, what was there to do about it? In frustration, I put a hand to my hair. There was no hope of curling it. I ought to have started earlier in the day for that. I pulled out the pins, smoothed it to dip over my ears and then plaited it into a braid and wound it into a bun at the back of my neck. Securing it with a comb, I turned toward Phoebe, who was sitting on the bed. "Do you think —" I was going to ask her about my hair; I'd forgotten again that she couldn't see.

"Do I think what?"

"Do you think . . ." What could I say that wouldn't underscore how different her life was from mine? And when had I come to care so much about her feelings? But she was so . . . sincere and kind and generous and selfless. She evidenced all the worst qualities of an upstanding citizen! Of course, it was those same qualities that made them so easy to deceive. There were a dozen ways I could have turned her solicitation to my favor, to make her do what I wanted. But since coming to Buttermilk Falls, I seemed to have lost my will to do so — at least in her case. I sighed, turning to pull a hand mirror from a drawer. "Do you think autumn will be long in coming?"

She frowned. "I shouldn't think so. Just wait. In a month's time, you'll find yourself shivering of a night." She began to unbutton her bodice. Her evening was ending while mine was just beginning.

I pushed aside the pang of pity that wrenched at my heart and left. My uncle was waiting for me at the bottom of the stairs. My aunt stood beside him, twisting a handkerchief in her hands. "Remember, you don't have to dance if you don't wish to."

I adored dancing, but I didn't say so. I simply nodded.

"And don't let any of the cadets take you away from the ballroom. For any reason."

"I won't."

"And don't —"

My uncle leaned down and kissed my aunt on the cheek. "We'll be fine."

"I just don't know if —"

"We'll be fine. One of the benefits of keeping a conduct-roll in addition to a merit-roll is that the cadets have to mind themselves outside the classroom as well as inside." He pulled on his gloves and helped me on with my lace-trimmed mantle.

I only had the carriage bonnet I'd come with. It wasn't the proper accompaniment for a ball gown, but it was the best I could do. As I settled it at the back of my head, my aunt presented me with a headdress of flowers fixed atop a fan of lace. As I took it from her, she removed my bonnet and set it on the hallstand. The headdress was outmoded but still quite pretty, the sort of touch one commonly calls charming. If I had been in danger when I came down the stairs, of being overlooked, her gift had cured me of that fate. Having settled it upon my head, my aunt stood back to take a look at me. She dabbed at an eye with her handkerchief. "It was your mother's. Her favorite. One hates to discard such pretty things. . . ."

My uncle saved me from a reply by opening the door and ushering me through it. But still, I put a hand to the flowers. I might have thought them a good omen, but the more I discovered about the past, the less I was certain of anything.

As we walked along, my uncle sent a glance toward me. "Your aunt is right. You shouldn't leave the room under any circumstances. And you don't have to dance if you don't wish to. At this ball, for instance, I believe over four hundred invitations were sent. But as the school year commences, there will be many cadets at the hops and not so many girls, so if you can find it in your heart, it would be kind if you could dance as many dances as you can."

The memory of the sun lingered in the clear night sky, though the moon was already climbing to take its place. After we passed through the academy's gate, as we walked up the long road, I could see the silhouette of the academy's buildings.

My uncle gestured to the left, beyond them. "We were to have been given one of the faculty houses here on the reservation, but it was in such disrepair that we had to take the house in Buttermilk Falls instead. I think they must have forgotten we're there."

I had never seen any of the military academy's buildings, by day or by night, but the light that spilled from the windows of one of them left little doubt as to where the dance was being held. Several dozen conveyances and their accompanying horses were waiting in front.

My uncle ushered me through them and into the building and then escorted me into a vast columned hall. It was decorated in a military fashion, with an abundance of flags. Swords and knives gleamed beneath blazing chandeliers, but it was the men who were the most decorative. Cadets wore their white trousers and gray coats, red sashes circling their waists. Older men sported blue frock coats with shining brass buttons.

Buttermilk Falls was such a small, sleepy hamlet that I could not account for all of the women at the ball. Perhaps they'd come up by boat from the city. They were wearing the very latest in fashions. I wished, and not for the first time, that I'd been able to fit all of my gowns into my trunk.

I must have paused in my step, for my uncle took my arm in his and pulled me forward. He introduced me to all of the instructors and professors and soldiers who were assigned to the military academy. I smiled and conversed and tried my best to comport myself in a manner befitting my finishing school training.

Mercy, but a uniform did wonders for a man!

I met captains and sergeants and colonels, but I could not keep them straight, and in truth did not know, aside from my uncle's deference, to whom I ought to give the most attention. And all the while, I could feel the eyes of cadets upon me.

There was a clutch of younger girls who formed a giggling knot toward the back of the room. They were ringed, at a respectable distance, by cadets who were sending long looks in their direction, gesturing toward them with sharp nods. Some older cadets were standing near the punch table, no less aware of the girls in the room, but much less obvious in their attentions. I took a step back, away from the obstruction of my uncle's shoulder, ostensibly to shift my feet, but I looked for those cadets I'd met at supper upon my arrival.

Mr. Conklin saw me and bowed from the waist.

I nodded.

And — oh! — there was Seth Westcott. I

blushed as his gaze fixed on me.

When the music struck up a lively gallopade, Mr. Conklin crossed the floor and joined me. He nodded at my uncle and extended a gloved hand to me. "May I have the pleasure of this dance?"

I took his hand and he placed his other at my waist and swept me across the floor. He was quite proficient at the steps. As he whirled me first one way and then the other, my dress swirled about my ankles and I knew all the flounces of my skirt were being put to good use. Had Madame Mercier seen me, she would have thought my future secured.

Mr. Conklin returned me to my uncle and had just stepped away when a second cadet presented himself.

My uncle frowned, and I could see that he didn't want to introduce me, but the cadet had a twinkle in his eyes to which I couldn't help but respond. I nodded at him, and my uncle was forced to make the introductions. "Mr. Hollinsgworth, my niece, Miss Hammond."

Mr. Hollingsworth crooked his arm for me, and I tucked my hand around it. "Might as well call me Deacon. Or Deke," he said as he escorted me to the dance floor. "Everyone does."

"Do you have aspirations for the pulpit?"

He laughed, flashing straight white teeth. "You'd have no reason to know this, but that's what some folks might call a contradiction in terms." The dance was a polka, which suited him. He was all high spirits and restless energy, and the music gave him occasion to put it to good use. As the dance came to an end, he had me laughing, even though I was gasping for breath.

He winked. "I feel that I should tell you this liaison of ours is doomed to end in heartbreak."

"Is it?"

"Has to."

I was captivated by the mischief in his eyes, and I could not keep myself from smiling once again. "Now why is that? Do you think me so heartless? So cruel?"

He gave me a knowing look. "Oh, I think you could be. You could be the girl every man in this room dreams of. But, sadly, my sentiments are not so easily won this evening. I am simply an emissary for a heart much truer, much more noble than mine."

"That's very generous of you. But what if I'm not interested in a noble heart?"

He cocked a brow. "What other kind would you be interested in?"

I forced the smile from my face though

my eyes were probably still dancing. "A respectable one." *Noble* was fine for some heroines, but in novels, *noble* quite often happened to be paired with the adjective *poor*. Or *humble*.

He laughed once more. "Then I'm twice rebuffed. That wouldn't be me either. But if respectability is your goal, you shouldn't look any farther than my friend Seth Westcott." He lifted his chin toward the opposite wall. "I think he'd like to dance with you."

The cadet in question, however, was glaring at his friend.

"Then perhaps he should do me the favor of asking for one."

"He's a fine fellow . . ." Deacon leaned close, "but I need to warn you — he's not much of a dancer."

"I'd think I would be the better judge of that."

"Don't think any less of him for it, will you?"

"I wouldn't be much of a lady if I did, would I?"

10
SETH

I'd given Deacon as much time with Lucinda as I was willing to. I could have kicked myself for pointing her out to him. If he spent any more time at her side, she'd be falling in love with him just the same as all the other girls between here and Ohio. It didn't seem fair that a fellow who could win hearts so easily always seemed to want more of them. Not that I wanted her heart, of course. I was just . . . trying to be friendly.

I straightened my shoulder belt and checked my sash, and then I stepped out across the dance floor, glaring at several of the yearlings and second classmen who had started for her as well. They mumbled their apologies and moved out of my way.

She bent in a slight curtsy. "Mr. Westcott. How wonderful to renew our acquaintance."

I bowed and gave Deacon a sidelong glance.

He looked at me speculatively. "I'll wager

he never told you he's our first captain."

"He did not. Although my uncle did, but I still have no idea what a first captain does. And I'm afraid I have to confess myself quite ignorant of uniforms and ranks."

Deke rapped me on the chest. "It's easy. All you got to do is count the chevrons." He took up my arm and pointed to those I was wearing at the top of my sleeve. "The more you've got, the better the man. Take me for instance." He dropped my arm and offered up his own, twisting it so we could see his sleeve. "I've got no chevrons at all, I'm just a private — a high private since I'll be graduating this year, but a private none-theless. So you can assume that I'm one of the poorest, sorriest excuses for a cadet that you'll ever meet. Old Seth here, though, he's got . . . Well, how many have you got?"

"Four."

"You see? So you can just about count on the fact that he's one of the sharpest, smart-est, most brilliant cadets you'd ever wish to know."

She was laughing. "You're too late, Mr. Hollingsworth. I've already discovered that for myself."

The band started in on another polka and Deke looked at me pointedly. She curtsied as if I'd asked her to dance, and before I knew it we actually were.

I repositioned my hand at the small of her back. "I apologize for Deacon — for his lack of manners."

"But all those things he said are true, aren't they?"

"Well . . . I wouldn't say that."

"I would. I would say them all and then add a few more. You were very kind to me at dinner on Sunday. Thank you."

I'd only done what any gentleman would do. Was kindness so foreign to her that my words had seemed exceptional? "I can't imagine anyone ever being unkind to you."

She flashed a smile. "Then perhaps I've discovered your only fault. I'll have to let Mr. Hollingsworth know that you're lacking in imagination."

I guided her forward into a chassé, and we completed one of those turning hops that made the polka one of the most favored dances at the academy. "I'd like to apologize for your uncle's behavior too."

"He's not your responsibility. I'm the one who's related to him."

"But he's my favorite professor, and I have to tell you that the man you saw that night is not the man I know."

She glanced over my shoulder, and as we turned I saw she'd been looking at him.

"Perhaps he was only trying to protect his family."

"From you?" That didn't make any kind of sense.

"I'm a stranger to him. To all of them. I'd never met them before."

"But you're family."

"Imagine I had showed up on your doorstep, unannounced. You might have felt the same way."

I was certain that I wouldn't have — I would have thanked God for my great fortune — but I had sense enough to know saying so would only have embarrassed a lady like her. "Will you be staying in Buttermilk Falls?"

"I will."

I hadn't known I'd been holding my breath until she answered. "Your father would have been relieved to know you're with them. My sister was left alone after my mother died. She was supposed to have traveled to stay with family as well."

"Supposed to have? You mean she didn't?"

Maybe I'd said too much. But if anyone could understand, it would be Lucinda. "She's at Fort Laramie. I just found out. I thought she'd already made it to Kentucky."

Concern clouded Lucinda's eyes. "I'm so sorry, Seth."

116

"I wish . . . I just wish I could do something." I *was* doing something, or planning to in any case. I just wished I could do something more immediate. "Or at least be there with her."

"Is there not some way? I don't mean to pry, but could you not bring her here? There must be a boardinghouse where she could stay."

"I've my pay, from being here for the past three years, but the treasurer keeps it for us. I can't have any of it until after graduation."

"Then I'm doubly sorry. To have the means without being able to do anything for her . . ."

That china-doll mouth of hers had gone pensive. And suddenly, right then, what I wanted more than anything was to see her smile. "She's surrounded by soldiers, she's probably safer at Laramie than she ever has been." At least her person was. I hoped her virtue would be too.

Lucinda smiled.

How could she be so impossibly pretty? And why had I been willing to tell her so quickly what I'd wanted to hide from my friends?

We executed another chassé. It was one thing to dance at the academy dance master's command, but another thing entirely to dance with her. If I could just fall into those green eyes, I'd happily drown. Maybe that was the problem. Maybe if I stopped looking into her eyes as I danced, I'd be able to remember the steps.

She came toward me at the same moment I stepped toward her and collided with my chest. I pulled her close to keep her from reeling away. "I'm so sorry."

"It's fine." She smiled up as she leaned into me, her earrings shimmering in the candlelight.

I couldn't help smiling in return. There was an advantage to not being the best of dancers. And I can't say that I didn't enjoy it, feeling her small, warm hand against my chest, holding her close. Her perfume was a kind I wished Otter's mother would use. It smelled like . . . gravy and cinnamon.

When the song ended, I kept hold of her hand. "I hope we have the occasion to dance again at the next hop."

"I would be honored to dance with you anytime, Mr. Westcott."

I had to let her dance with some of the others. It wasn't polite to keep a girl to yourself. So I watched with Dandy as the better part of the corps of cadets swept her across the dance floor that night.

Otter and Deke walked over, saluting us with cups of punch. "If I was looking for a girl, I think I'd try for her." Otter nodded in Lucinda's direction.

Deke answered. "Too late. Seth already met her. And now he's gone completely soft in the head."

"That's good, then. Real good."

I eyed Otter. "What would Mother say about a girl like her?"

His brow folded in irritation. "That's Mrs. Ames to you. But . . . I suppose . . . she'd probably say some girls smell like roses and some girls *are* roses. But you oughter pay attention. Roses come with thorns."

Deke grunted.

I ignored him. "But . . . do you think she'd mean that in a good way or in a bad way?"

"What do you mean good or bad? Thorns just is. You oughter figure out where they are before you grab hold of one — that's all." He sighed. "You can take it from me."

Deke and I exchanged a glance. Otter had never talked about any girl in particular that I could remember. Deke nudged him with an elbow. "You have some fun down home during furlough, Otter?"

He put up a hand to ruffle the hair at the back of his neck. "Oh . . . I should say so."

Deke slapped him on the back. "Good for

119

you! Any girl in particular?"

"I should hope so!"

Deke blinked at the vehemence in Otter's words. "Just asking." He turned his attention to me. "You going to go ask Professor Hammond about seeing Miss Hammond during recreation on Saturday?"

"I don't know." I wanted to.

"You don't *know*? You're his favorite student!"

And he was my favorite professor. But would that favor extend beyond the classroom? "These things take time. Let me just . . . I have to think about it." A good campaign took planning. No soldier ever wished for less time when it came to doing something important. Mostly, I had to figure out how to approach Professor Hammond. I would have had plenty to say to him if the subject were geometry or calculus, but I didn't know how to get from mathematics to the topic of his niece.

"No one ever won any wars by sitting back and *thinking* about anything. Wars are won by *doing*. And if you don't do something soon, you might just end up having to surrender to Campbell Conklin."

As I followed Deke's gaze, I saw Conklin talk himself into a second dance with Lucinda.

"Maybe I'll just go give Professor Hammond my regrets . . . er, my regards."

Deke was trying hard not to laugh. "You got a handkerchief?"

"Sure. Why?"

"Going gets rough, you just hold that up like this" — he waved his hand in the air — "and I'll send the cavalry to your rescue." He doubled over in laughter, and Otter joined him.

11
LUCINDA

Mr. Conklin asked me to dance a second time. Though I would have preferred a second dance with Seth Westcott, he hadn't asked me for one. So I accepted Mr. Conklin's arm, and he escorted me out to the dance floor. There was nothing wrong with him, he was really quite impressive. And quite impressed with himself. But he just . . . wasn't Seth. That didn't mean, however, that he couldn't still be useful.

"It's so kind of you to ask me for a second dance, Mr. Conklin. There are so many women here, you would never have to dance with the same one twice."

"Some might like variety, but why take a chance when you like what you've found?"

"Ah. So you're a proponent of a bird in the hand?"

"Being worth two in the bush? Do you not believe in romance, Miss Hammond?"

"I do. But I'm more inclined to admire

expediency."

He laughed. "My grandfather would like you very much. He's a senator down in Washington, and he admires the very same thing."

His grandfather was a senator? That was a whole different higher level of society than that for which I'd been aiming. Just the possibility of marrying into such a family made my feet stutter in their steps. But that was silly. I wasn't the kind of person that I had been. Mr. Conklin didn't know anything about my father and he never would. "And what do *you* admire, Mr. Conklin?"

"A graceful dancer." He turned us in a circle. "And an engaging smile."

"You're easily pleased."

He laughed at me. "And you're easily baited."

I couldn't exactly say the man was charming. He was too much in possession of himself. Those who deployed charm as a weapon usually cared what others thought of them. But he did radiate power and privilege.

After the dance, he escorted me back to my uncle, who was speaking with Seth.

My uncle paused in his conversation, nodding to us.

Mr. Conklin bowed and took his leave.

My uncle addressed himself to me. "We were just speaking of a theorem of geometry. Mr. Westcott has done exceedingly well in his studies. I suppose it's no secret that I have high hopes for him."

As did I.

But as I stood listening, as the dance swirled on without us, my heart sank. Despite how attentive Seth had been during our dance, he didn't seem to have any interest in me now. For a while, I tried to follow their conversation, but I didn't understand the mathematical principles of which they spoke, and really, it was all quite dull. I glanced about the room, hoping that one of the other cadets would ask me to dance — at least that would have been diverting — but not even Mr. Hollingsworth would let me catch his eye.

I finally decided to take matters into my own hands. Laying a hand on my uncle's arm, I smiled at Seth. "I can't think that there are very many dances left before the refreshments we've been promised at midnight."

Seth shook his head. "Probably not."

I lifted a brow, hoping he would take it as an invitation . . . but he kept conversing with my uncle. When they paused once more in their conversation, I spoke again. "I so enjoyed our dance this evening, Mr. West-cott."

He bowed. "I did as well." But he didn't take that opening either!

I'd never had to work so hard for a gentleman's attention before. I was about to give up entirely when I noticed a sheen of sweat above Seth's upper lip and saw the way his gaze kept drifting in my direction before he pulled it back to focus on my uncle. At the next opportunity I inserted myself into the conversation once more. "This is such a lovely landscape, and the river is so beautiful. I wonder, Mr. Westcott, is there any vantage point from which the whole of the valley can be seen?"

"There's Fort Putnam."

I sighed, putting my heart into it. "I don't suppose it's safe for a girl to go up there by herself . . . ?"

He blinked. "It's on the military reservation. I don't think anyone would bother you up there."

"But I've the worst sense of direction. I've been known to get lost in my own house."

"It's not so difficult to find. You can see it when you're standing on the Plain." He sent my uncle a glance. "You can see it from just about anywhere. It's the perfect defensive position, towering above the military academy . . ."

"Maybe you could point it out to me sometime."

"I would . . . That is, if it were possible, maybe . . ." His words had been directed at my uncle rather than me, which was rather curious.

Taking a chance, I decided to try one last time. "I wonder, Uncle, could Mr. Westcott show me Fort Putnam sometime? Would it be permissible for him to accompany me?"

He blinked his brows wide. "Well . . . Oh! Yes. Yes, of course. Mr. Westcott, I would be grateful if you could show my niece the sights here at West Point. Next Saturday, perhaps?"

The ball ended around four o'clock that next morning. The moon was slipping behind the hills as we walked home, and a mist was rising off the river. Owls hooted somewhere out in the forest that swept up and over the valley's steep hills. Despite the calendar, the early morning air was cool, and I made good use of my mantle.

My uncle pulled a pipe from his coat pocket, paused to light it, and then smoked as we walked along.

I felt quite satisfied with the ball. The impression I'd formed of Seth was confirmed. He was a genuinely nice man. Honest and noble, he could be depended upon to come to the rescue of a woman in trouble. I had used that trait in men like him more than once during my time with my father.

Here, in my new situation, I found that very comforting.

I felt badly for his sister, all alone out on the frontier. Chances were, he'd find her married when he went to retrieve her next summer. It didn't do to be a woman alone. Of course, I'd spent half my life alone, waiting for my father to come take me from my boarding schools or finishing schools. But I knew a dozen different ways to make it look as if I belonged to someone. Without my particular skills of deception, it was difficult to imagine his sister could fend for herself.

My impression of Mr. Conklin was also confirmed. Had I been searching for a husband out west, I would have decided upon him without a second thought. But there was something to be said for a man like Seth, who took time to do for others before he did for himself.

Once home, my uncle bid me good-night, urging me to sleep as long as I could. As I climbed the stairs, he took his pipe into the sitting room. Its spicy scent followed me. Though I tried to be quiet, I woke Phoebe when I slipped into bed.

She rolled over to face me. "Tell me all about it. I want to know everything."

"It was nice. A very many cadets and so many guests. There might have been five hundred people. And the refreshments were quite delicious."

"I mean *everything.* Please, Lucinda. I'll never go to a ball, and I want to hear what it was like. You're the only way I'll ever know."

It didn't seem like a good idea. Wouldn't it only make her feel worse about the way things were? "Phoebe —"

"Please. I won't feel badly or left out or anything but glad that you told me. I promise."

"Well then . . ." I turned on my side to face her. "It was delightful, although the music was very regimented. The band was quite accomplished — I'm not saying that they weren't — but it was very precise. Even the dances made me think of marches."

She laughed.

"You should have seen all the cadets, dressed in their uniforms — gray and white — they stood along the edge of the room, straight as pins. There were ever so many people. I've never been to a bigger ball. And it felt as if everyone was staring at me as I walked in."

"Of course they were. You're beautiful. Why shouldn't they stare?"

She didn't know the first thing about how I looked, but the ferocity of her loyalty warmed me. "I danced nearly every song."

"With whom? Tell me about each one. And which was best."

"I can hardly remember all of them, there were so many! My first partner, you already know."

"I do?"

"It was Mr. Conklin."

"Oh! I do know him."

"He whirled me across the dance floor, steering us right through the other couples, not caring who had to alter their path, and we never missed a step. But my next partner, Mr. Deacon Hollingsworth, was the most amusing. I was laughing so hard at the end of our dance that I could hardly catch a breath."

"But there was someone better than either of them, wasn't there? I can tell by your voice."

"You know him too. He's Mr. Westcott."

"Mr. Westcott! Is he handsome? I've always wondered."

"In a quiet, confident sort of way. He looks like a soldier. A very competent one."

"More competent than Mr. Conklin?"

"Mr. Conklin has the look of a politician. And his grandfather is one." I rolled onto my back. "But I can imagine if I were in the middle of a battle and Mr. Westcott rode up on his horse, I would know that everything would turn out right."

"And the one who made you laugh? What was his name again?"

"Deacon. Mr. Hollingsworth. I've met dozens like him on the —" I stopped myself before I could say too much.

"On the . . . ?"

On the riverboats. In the gambling saloons. "I meant out west. On the frontier. When I traveled with my father."

"Do you mean to say he's . . . Is he a rough character?"

"No. He's quite safe. But very flirtatious."

"Maybe you shouldn't —"

"Don't worry. I won't pay him any mind." I let my thoughts wander back through the night's events. "Mr. Conklin will do very well for himself. He has that way about him. He made me hope my skirts were straight and my hair in place and that I was performing the steps of the dance correctly."

"I would think that would be tiring, trying to make sure you were perfect all the time."

In the dark, I smiled to myself. Looking

perfect was what I had been trained to do. How happily coincidental I'd come to a place where that was considered a virtue.

"But you said you danced with more boys than those, didn't you?"

"Boys? My goodness. They aren't boys — if they ever were. They're most definitely men! And what nature didn't see fit to supply them in looks or stature, the uniform more than makes up for."

"Lucinda!" I could feel the bed shaking with her laughter.

"It's true. You would have thought the same." My laughter died. "I wish you could have seen it."

"Don't feel badly for me. You're the one who had to do all the dancing. I should tell you that I heard Mama and Papa talking to you. About finding someone to marry. I'm so glad I'll never have to. Deciding on a man would be the hardest part."

Not for me. I'd already decided. At least . . . I think I had. The hardest part would probably be helping Seth Westcott work up the courage to ask for my hand!

12
SETH

How had she done it?

I asked myself that question in the mirror as I washed my face back at the encampment. I'd been talking to Professor Hammond, trying to figure out a way to ask him if I could see Lucinda next Saturday, and then all of the sudden he was asking me. To ask her. Or . . . he didn't ask me at all, really. He just told me to show her the Point next Saturday. We'd been talking about geometry . . . and then I was agreeing to take her up to Fort Putnam. In military tactical terms, we'd call that a masking maneuver.

It was a West Point tradition to break camp the day after the grand ball. We emptied our tents of cots and belongings and tramped a path to the barracks as we carried it all inside. Once in the barracks, the echo of footsteps and the creak of doors summoned visions of the academic year to come. Of courses and study hours, recitations and examinations. As the new second classmen who'd spent their summer on furlough began to report to the barracks, their tales of home only added to our misery.

But it wouldn't do for the first captain to be so melancholy on this day.

I ordered the corps of cadets back to our tent city. As the drums beat a cadence, at my command, lines were untied, and then tent poles were withdrawn to allow the canvas to collapse. The tents were folded and the wooden floors swept. Trusting the other company captains to divvy the plebes and yearlings up by pairs, I placed my own men at the back corners of my company's tents. The first classmen already knew what to do. They took up brooms and clubs. When everyone stood at the ready, I gave the signal. As the wooden floors were lifted and tilted from their back corners, dozens of rats scurried out and into the waiting ambush of the upperclassmen.

They must have flattened a good hundred of them before I halted their efforts.

After tidying up the Plain and carrying the floors into storage, the corps fell in for the march back to the barracks. Soon after, we found ourselves marching to chapel.

After our return from chapel, I decided to

see if Otter had received any letters from his mother. Some of the fellows gathered round whenever somebody received a letter from a sweetheart, but Deacon, Dandy, and I preferred his mother's missives to the sighs and promises of lovers. Though heavily scented, the pages were always filled with news about Otter's young brothers, the state of the homestead, the wanderings of the neighbor's cow, the preacher's sermons, the price of flour, and other homely details that made a man feel as if he'd been allowed a glimpse of life beyond the academy's gates.

A life that wasn't calibrated according to bugle calls and orders to "fall in." A life that wasn't based on how many equations you could recite or the condition of your uniform. A life I increasingly worried I might never have again.

I'd put countless hours into doing the right thing. Studying. Obeying orders. Conforming to the shining ideal of what every cadet should be. And now it looked as if none of it had mattered. If Deacon was right, I had to find the quickest way to shed all of those high marks and all of the goodwill I'd earned.

Was everything I'd done here a waste of time and effort? Was coming to West Point a mistake?

The only people who could help me, the only people who seemed to care about my mother's death and Elizabeth's plight, were the Immortals. But they were the repudiation of everything I would have said I believed. If they were my only hope, then what use were all those principles and fine morals the academy taught? If the gentlemen I had looked up to for so long wouldn't allow a man to care for his own family, why was I trying so hard to become one of them?

Otter's mother always had something to say about everything, and I was hoping he might share some of her advice. As I ducked into their room, I nodded at Dandy. Otter grinned at me as if I were the person he'd been waiting all day to see. "Mr. Westcott! General! To what do we owe this great honor?"

"I was just . . . uh . . . wondering . . . Heard you got another letter."

His smile seemed to grow even wider. "Got a letter from Mother just today." He reached out and pulled an envelope from beneath his pillow. Even as I was overcome by the scent of flowers, Dandy was using his book to push the odor toward the open window.

Otter extended it to me. "You want to read it?"

I deferred. "You can."

He pulled the pages from the envelope and opened them with a snap of his wrist. Dandy and I sat on his bed. As we settled in to listen, Deacon appeared in the doorway. "Heard there was a letter." He flopped onto Otter's bed and propped his head in his hand.

Otter looked up from the pages and nodded a greeting. Then he turned his attention once more to the letter. "It's dated July 15."

"My dear one, I suppose I ought to start with first things and tell you that the youngsters been missing you something terrible, asking after you, wanting to know when you'll be coming back. Course I tell them what I always do about you having to be up there at that academy and how you make us all proud, but I know you'll understand that's little consolation when Junior's kite got broke and we haven't been able to fix it yet."

Deke interrupted. "Is that the same kite that broke last year before furlough?"

Otter nodded. "I fixed it when I was there."

"You should tell her to make sure that

frame is made of soft wood. Spruce, maybe."

I added my own opinion. "Or yellow pine. Won't break so easy, then."

Otter was chewing at his cheek. "Hadn't thought of that. Wished I had when I was there. I'll let her know." He took up a pen and bent to the table to flatten the letter out. Then he scribbled a note in the margin. He continued reading. " 'Mr. Chisholm's cow got into my petunias again. I'm at my wits' end trying to think of a way to keep that beast out of —' "

I interrupted him. "Did she try a hedge? Do you know?" That had always worked for my mother.

Otter beamed in admiration. "Fancy you knowing a thing like that!"

He bent to write again, and after he was done, he continued. " '. . . been trying to think of a way to keep that beast out of my pretties.' "

He looked up from the letter. "I put in two more of those flower beds while I was back home last summer. Mother loves her petunias."

He cleared his throat. "Where was I? 'That shep dog you got me isn't any use at all, except to chew on my shoes and keep the garden dug up. But they say the thought is what counts and that's most important.' "

"Had a dog once . . ." Dandy was staring off toward who knew what. We waited for him to say something else, but he didn't.

Otter kept reading. " 'Apples are ripe for the picking. We'll have more this year than I'll know what to do with. I suspect some of those Faircloth boys are sneaking around, taking some off the trees for their moonshine.' "

Deke stopped him. "Didn't she say back spring before last that one of those Faircloths was jailed for . . . What was it again?"

Otter looked up. "For thieving. Only the judge is a Faircloth, on account of being married to the sister of the cousin of *that* Faircloth's mother, and he got let out. Had a talk with him when I went home, wore my uniform even. I thought we'd settled everything, but I guess . . ." He sighed. In the sound was the echo of all the men at the Point who ought to be allowed to do as men do instead of being cooped up here like a flock of chickens.

He returned to the letter. " 'I been making sauce and jams. Wish I could figure out how to send you some pies.' "

I wished she could too.

" 'You always did say apple was your favorite. Don't forget to tell me what I ought to do about that sale of land. With love in my heart.' "

With love in my heart. That's how she always ended her letters.

Otter folded the paper back up and pushed it down into the envelope. "That's all she said."

"What land is she talking about selling?" Deke had pushed himself up to sitting.

"The Holifields asked about buying a parcel that sits next to theirs. They made an offer when I was home."

I had a bad feeling about the offer. "The Holifields? Aren't those the ones you said weren't to be trusted? What kind of offer did they make?"

"Wasn't a bad offer . . . Not exactly . . ."

Dandy snorted. "But it wasn't good either? Is that what you're saying?"

"They've been real helpful since I've been here at the Point."

Dandy was scowling now. "Don't mistake a helping hand for them helping themselves to your land."

"Well . . . it's a tricky kind of business. See, Mother's related on account of —"

Deke called out from the bed. "Is everyone related down there where you're from?"

"I'm not related."

We looked at each other in puzzlement. "But if *she's* related . . ."

"Oh. Well. I guess that follows. My daddy, he wasn't from there, but with Mother related by marriage . . . That's the way it works, doesn't it?"

I don't think any of us were quite sure the way it worked down where Otter was from. I suppose that's why we tried to help him and his mother any way we could. We weren't much use to anyone, secluded as we were at the Point, but it made us feel as if we were making a difference if we could pass on suggestions for fixing a kite or keeping the cows out of her petunias. For a few short minutes every day, Otter's mother made us feel as if we were normal men doing things that men normally do.

13

LUCINDA

Some things never changed. No matter if I were in St. Louis or Buttermilk Falls, Sunday was for church. It provided as good an excuse as any for seeing and being seen. I'd been with my aunt for a week, but until I attended church I was still new to town. Father had always supplied me with the very latest in gowns, knowing that when I wore them out into society, it would perpetuate the deception that I was from one of the nation's finest families. But when I left St. Louis, in order to keep from paying the finishing school's bills, I'd had to tell the headmistress I'd be returning and I'd left most of my wardrobe there. Buttermilk Falls was a small town, though, and what I had would do. For now. If I showed myself to be a devoted niece and cousin, I had every expectation that my aunt and uncle would supply what was missing. Perhaps not in the style I was accustomed to, but they wouldn't let me shame their family.

As I waited in the yard for everyone to appear, I shook out my skirt and made certain my costume was spotless. As spotless as I could make it. Susan didn't come on Sundays, so I'd had to work harder in the kitchen than I had expected to. There was a small smear of biscuit batter on the inside of one sleeve, but if I held my arms just so, it would never be seen.

My aunt asked me to keep an eye on Bobby and Ella while she replaited Milly's unruly hair.

"The children? But I don't know if —"

She'd already disappeared back inside the house.

"Catch me, Bobby!" Ella dashed around behind me as Bobby wandered farther into the yard, kicking at the path that led to the gate. "Bobby?" Ella grasped my skirts as she leaned out to take a peek. "Bobby!" The stamp of her small foot sent up a cloud of dust, which promptly clung to the hem of the same salmon-and-green tartan dress I'd worn on the steamboat.

As I tried to shake it out, I encountered a sticky splotch of . . . something.

Ella ran over to Bobby and pushed at him. "Catch me."

He reached out and grabbed hold of her

arm. "Caught you."

"That's not fair!" Her words ended in a wail as she struck out at him.

Mindful of the rapidly deteriorating state of my dress, I didn't even attempt to separate them. I clapped my hands instead. "No fighting. If you stop right now, I'll buy you candy."

No sooner had I bribed them than my aunt appeared and took them both in hand to stop the squabble. She asked me to escort Phoebe instead. Milly tripped along beside us as we walked up the street. Though both sisters had the same fair hair and blue eyes, Milly's high-spirited chatter was a contrast to Phoebe's soft, gentle nature.

Wearing a simple bodice and skirt in a blue stripe, which matched her shining cornflower-blue eyes, Phoebe was serenely beautiful. Even her glass buttons seemed to wink with good-natured benevolence. Had she had her sight, I might have taken her for a rival. But as it was, how could I do anything but pity her?

The church wasn't far — just a short walk down the road toward the military academy. It looked as charming as a painting. Dressed in stone with a tower at one corner, it sat diagonal to the road, as if trying to entice passersby. I helped Phoebe negotiate its arched red door and walked with her to the pew. After the others filed in, I placed her hand along the back of the bench. She found the seat with the back of her knee and then sat and slid down to join the others.

As we waited for the service to begin, greetings were called between the pews and the sound of laughter floated about us. This church was different than the others I had attended. Those had been filled with people proud and formal. Their greetings had been cold, their smiles mocking. But the people in Buttermilk Falls, while much more modest in means, all seemed to know and like each other.

As the rector took his place at the front, conversations ceased. There were prayers and songs and readings, all of which I had known to expect. But the God the rector spoke of was not the one I'd come to know through my father and at my finishing schools. That God was by turns vindictive and cold.

My father had taught me that God was always waiting to catch you out in your schemes. Although we'd always attended church when my father was playing the role of upstanding citizen, when left to our own choices, we'd stayed as far away from God as we could.

My finishing schools had taught me that God was much more concerned with social status than He was with sin or redemption. That God was best appeased by attending church regularly and doing good works that would serve to propel you and your husband upward in society's circles.

But here it seemed, if what the rector said was really true, that God cared. That He saw. That He . . . loved. God and love had been quite far apart in my experience. So far apart that one might have even called them opposites.

I thought about the sermon as we walked back to the house, as I ate dinner, and as I helped my aunt and Milly with the dishes. Afterward, when we all repaired to the sitting room, I was asked to read to Phoebe. I took up the book my aunt offered and settled us on the sofa while Milly and Bobby played at marbles. Ella crooned one of her dolls to sleep as my aunt and uncle conversed in a pair of matching chairs by the fireplace.

When a stray marble rolled my way, I left off reading for a moment and bent to send it rolling back in Bobby's direction.

He thanked me with a grin.

145

Phoebe was staring toward the hearth, a smile softening her lips. "I must admit that I like Sundays best of all."

The book had tumbled from my lap while I'd tended to the marble, so I opened it once more and flipped through the pages to find my place.

"Sitting in the pew at church, I don't feel so out of place. All anyone is there for is to listen, and I can do that as well as anyone. And after, everyone is home and in each other's way, so there's no reason to keep myself apart." There was a wistful note to the words. "On Sundays, I can be a part of it all."

"I don't know that anyone believes you ever to be in their way."

Her gaze shifted toward me. "It's only because I try so often to keep myself from being in it." The smile had left her face. Her voice had gone low.

How lonely her life must be. Always sitting off to the side, always listening, but rarely ever joining in. I'd often done the same, but I'd been scouring the crowds to identify the most gullible, the most vulnerable, and the man whose eyes strayed just a bit too far from his wife. But after, I'd plunge into the thick of a crowd in order to do my father's bidding. To place a timely comment that would plant the seeds of suggestion in an innocent's mind. To send a come-hither look in the direction of a would-be philanderer.

If we couldn't swindle a man honestly, then sometimes we'd had to do it dishonestly, accepting his money as a way of ensuring that embarrassing tales never reached the ears of his wife. I was no scarlet woman, of course, but it was surprising how often a whispered word could convince a man to meet me in a darkened corner. I had to say that I'd often felt apart from others in my work with my father, but had I ever truly felt lonely?

Concern swept Phoebe's face. "I hope you don't find Sundays too lonely."

How had she read my thoughts? "Me?" Why on earth would she worry about *me*?

"With your father gone. And you at a new church. It must bring back painful memories."

Of a cramped backside, perhaps. "I'm fine."

"Did you find the preaching to your liking?"

It was better than I was used to. "The rector spent so much time talking about how much God loves us . . ."

Her smile unfurled once more. "He always

says that. Every Sunday. But you sound rather astonished. Had you never heard that before?"

"No."

"Now *I* am astonished! What had you heard about Him?"

"Nothing good. I've been under the impression that He's continually watching us to catch us doing the wrong thing. Like some crotchety old bachelor who resents it when others have fun."

"That sounds . . . Forgive me for saying it, but I wonder if the person who told you that actually knows Him?"

It had been my father who had given me that impression. I had always accepted his words as truth, but now, I was beginning to wonder about the veracity of some of the things he had taught me. "I don't think that person likes — liked — God very much. Perhaps that's why."

"I'm sorry to bring back old memories."

"Enough about God." I opened the book once more and began reading a description of the story's springtime setting.

"Spring!" Phoebe clasped her hands to her chest. "That's my favorite time of year. The air smells so delicious, and the hills are reborn in that pale, delicate green. As long as there's spring, I don't think I could ever truly despair of anything."

I waited to see if she would say anything else, but she didn't, so I took up where I had left off. I finished the chapter and had started the next when the meaning of her words struck me. "You mean . . . you mean you haven't always been blind?"

She blinked. "I could see as well as anyone up until I was six."

Courtesy would have dictated that I not ask questions about such a personal matter, but no one else was listening, and I couldn't keep myself from asking. Besides, I'm not ashamed to admit that I had already considered how pretending to be blind might be used to my advantage at some point. "What happened?"

"I wanted to see the soldiers. That's what I called the cadets back then. Papa teaches at the military academy, you know, and I was always begging him to take me with him. I didn't understand that he had to work, I just thought . . . Well . . . it matters little what I thought. Of course, he always refused to take me, and normally, though disappointed, I took it as a firm decision. But Milly was still sleeping and Mama was busy with Bobby that day. He'd just been born, you see, and somehow, Papa's refusal seemed so unreasonable. So *I* decided."

As she'd been talking, dread had begun to press against my throat. I motioned for her to stop, forgetting that she couldn't see me. She opened her mouth to continue, so I put a hand to her arm.

She paused.

"It was rude of me to ask you about your condition. Let me just . . ." I fumbled with the book. "I'll just keep reading." I did not wish to know, anymore, what had happened to her.

"I don't mind. It's true that I don't speak of it often, but it's only because everyone already knows. It's odd, isn't it, how we make decisions every day. Big ones and small ones, without even thinking twice. But some decisions . . . this one I knew that I was making. I need you to understand, to know that *I* know, because otherwise . . ."

I'd given myself over to a fit of fidgeting, and at that point, the book slipped over my knee and fell to the floor with a resounding thud. "I'm sorry." I retrieved it and opened it to where I'd stopped. "Shall I commence reading again?"

"We have to take life as it comes to us, cousin."

Not me. Not my father and I. We'd taken the life we'd wanted. We always had. We took the good and worked our way around

150

the bad. I could get out of most any scrape. But I didn't know how to get around what had happened to Phoebe. I'd changed my mind about pretending to be blind. I couldn't imagine I'd seen anything useful about it at all.

"So I decided. I decided that I wasn't going to obey and I was going to go with him to work anyway. I waited until he was well along the road, and then I slipped out of the house and followed him."

I forced my hands to untangle themselves.

"I was wearing a green dress. I still remember it as a favorite. There was a bit of a mist along the river and its banks, but anyone could tell it would soon burn off. As I followed Papa, I became less interested in where he was going and much more concerned about the goings-on around me." Her smile broke out. "There were butterflies by the dozens, with their bright orange wings. Surely you've seen some. They come by the thousands in autumn. By then I'd forgotten all about following Papa. I'd veered off across the Plain, toward the river."

Had she fallen from those steep cliffs? Is that what she was trying to say?

"I knew the cadets undertook artillery drills, we heard them from Buttermilk Falls, but I didn't know they used the Plain for them. And they weren't expecting a little girl to be there chasing butterflies. In any case, they couldn't see me because of the mist."

I felt my heart stutter.

"It seemed as if the whole world was . . . it was crumbling. The air replaced with dirt. I couldn't see anything; the butterflies had disappeared. I couldn't hear anything; the birds had gone silent. There was just . . . nothing. And then . . . It sounds foolish to say, but I felt as if I was flying, and after that I really don't remember much more."

I couldn't breathe for wanting to weep so badly.

"I had the most awful headache for weeks. They were hopeful my eyes would work once it went away, but they never have."

"I'm so . . . I'm so, so sorry." I brought my hand to my mouth.

"I knew what I was doing. I didn't know it would end the way it did, but I made a choice. You understand that, don't you?"

"So unfair."

"But how would you have wanted it to end? For me to wander back home again with no one the wiser? If nothing at all had happened, if there hadn't been any consequence for my disobedience, would that not have been unfair as well?"

"You were just a child." Tears were streaming down my cheeks.

She smiled, extending a hand toward me. I took it up. "Perhaps I was. But I was also a child who knew better."

14
Seth

The first day of the semester was like falling into a dream I'd dreamt before. I knew where all the bad parts were, but I couldn't figure out how to wake myself up. I had to suffer through it all over again.

So I sat in civil engineering with Campbell Conklin and the other men in the top section. I stood and recited when called upon; and I went to the board to work problems when required; and it all went on as if it would never end.

The worst part was, I knew that it wouldn't. Not for another ten months.

I wasn't supposed to be trying so hard, but I couldn't just stop studying. It wasn't in my nature. I liked geology and even political science. Drawing wasn't my strongest subject, but I did enjoy rhetoric. And if I didn't learn all these things while I was here, then when would I ever have the chance to do it later? To be presented with

154

opportunity and then fail to make use of it was worse than laziness in my opinion. It was a betrayal of all the army asked of us.

So while I didn't quit studying, I tried not to be so quick in my board work. And I certainly didn't volunteer any answers in class. But on Friday, when class rankings were posted, my name was still at the top.

Deacon fell into step with me as we left the mess hall for recreation. "Are you finally going to stop studying now?"

"I didn't study quite so hard as —"

"For such a smart cadet, you're awful stupid. Weren't you the best in mathematics?"

"I was." I had been.

"Then I have a subtraction problem for you. Given that Cadet Westcott is at the top of his class, what do you have to take away in order for him to slide all the way down to the bottom?"

"I . . . uh . . ."

"Stumped you, huh?" He gave me a knowing glance. "Thought I might. The answer is . . . you've got to take away his grades *and* tarnish his comportment. Those are the two variables in the problem. So if the grades aren't going down fast enough, looks like the conduct has got to go into a steeper slope of decline."

"There isn't really a *slope* of decline. There's a negative slope —"

He was shaking his head as if truly disgusted with me. "That's what you get for all that studying. A bunch of claptrap and no good sense. Consider this a warning. You can't say I didn't tell you. If you're not going to do your part on the studying, then we're going to have to increase our efforts in comportment. Understood?"

He had already hailed one of the other fellows and was walking off toward the artillery depot, but for some reason, I felt like saluting.

That afternoon, after our last class, the fellows hailed me as I left the academy.

"Where you headed?" They fell into step along with me.

I'd intended to go to the library. "Just . . . uh . . . just wanted to do some reading."

" 'Bout what?" Otter smiled genially.

"Just . . . things."

Deke gave me a sharp glance. "Wouldn't be about geology, would it?"

"No!" I'd actually hoped to find some more information about the political science we were studying.

"That's good. Because you're not supposed to be studying. Remember?"

I remembered.

Dandy hadn't quit glowering since they'd caught up with me. "I'd hate for us to be working so hard to help you when you're going behind our backs to sabotage our efforts."

"I'm not sabo—"

"Because that might as well be a slap in the face."

I stopped walking. "Listen, fellows, I've thought it over and I don't know that this is the best plan. It doesn't feel right to aim to fail. It's not honest. I just don't think I'm cut out for any of this."

"We don't think you are either." Dandy reached over and knocked my cap askew.

I set it right. "What'd you do that for?"

"To try to knock some sense into you."

As I'd been fixing my cap, Otter was kicking dust up onto my shoes.

"Stop that!"

He glanced up at me with an apologetic sort of grin. "Mother always says you got to get dirty if you're going to play with the boys."

"She does?" Otter's mother said a lot of things, but she'd never seemed quite that mercenary before.

Deacon reached out with a penknife and cut off the top button of my gray coat. "It pains me to do this, but sometimes, sacrifices have to be made."

I shrugged them both off and pushed Otter away. "Just — just *stop!*"

"All we're trying to do is help you look the part."

"What part? Part of what?"

Deke took me by the elbow and turned me around, marching me away from the library. "The part of a cadet who doesn't care much about pointless things."

"If I go around with my coat undone and my shoes dirtied up, I'm going to get reported."

"Exactly."

"In front of everyone at formation."

"Yes. It's going to be perfect. We're going to find a way for you to beat the record for amassing the most demerits in the least amount of time. You need to get a hundred before the semester is over."

"There's a record for that?"

Deacon scoffed. " 'Course there is. John Barns. No one's beat it for nineteen years. But you're going to. That way everyone will know you've embarked on a new endeavor this year." He looked round, both in front and behind us, and then he pulled something from his sleeve and handed it to me.

It was a cigar. I dropped it.

"That was a perfectly good — !" He stooped and scooped it up. Holding it up in front of his nose, he blew some dust from it and then whipped out a handkerchief and wiped it clean. "You'd better hope it's still smokeable." He handed it to me again.

"But I don't smoke."

He grinned. "You do now."

We spent the afternoon's short recreation period on the terrace of Battery Knox, above the river, as they coached me on the finer points of loafing about doing nothing in particular. Otter was held up as an example in dishevelment.

"See there?" Deacon gestured toward him as he stood there before us.

I surveyed him from my position on the ground. "I don't quite . . . How do you do that, Otter?"

"Do what?" He pulled his chin in, grimacing, as he glanced down toward his chest.

There was nothing actually wrong with his uniform. He was wearing all the pieces. His coat was completely buttoned. His shoes were tied. His cap was firmly fixed to the top of his head, but he looked nothing like Dandy. His barracks mate was near to gleaming.

"What's wrong with me?"

I appealed to Deke. "How am I supposed to duplicate that?"

Deacon and Dandy sat beside me, scrutinizing Otter through narrowed eyes. It was Deacon who finely forfeited. "You're right." He stood and clapped Otter on the shoulder. "You've worked nonchalance into an art form. I don't know anyone who can do it better than you."

Otter beamed at the compliment.

"However, expecting the same of old Seth here might be asking for too much." He squinted as he looked at me. "For the moment, we'll just help you along."

"Help me . . . ?" I would have asked what that meant, but I decided I didn't want to know.

"Dandy." Deke nodded at him. "You're next."

Dandy drew himself to attention as he stood before us, chin tipped, chest out, hand hovering where the haft of a sword might have hung.

"See there?" Deacon strode back and forth in front of him like a drill sergeant. "You have to let the rest of the military academy know you take this seriously."

"But . . . that's just the point. You don't want me to take any of this seriously anymore. That's what you all are trying to do, isn't it? Inspire me to . . . what exactly?"

"What I'm saying is, you have to take the idea of not being serious, seriously. It's not as easy as it looks. Take Dandy here." Deke came to a halt beside him. "What you need to think about is, How do I look like that? How do I achieve that same look of scorn, disregard, and utter contempt?"

"I have no earthly idea."

Deke tapped him on the chest with his forehand. "Why don't you tell him how you do it, Dandy?"

Dandy looked down at Deacon's hand with distaste and took a step away from him.

"There. Just like that! What is it you think of, Dandy, when you stand there looking that way?"

Dandy's face closed up. "Nothing."

"See there? That is . . . why, that is . . . That's *art*!"

Deacon wasn't far wrong. And since he'd mention it, I *did* wonder what Dandy was thinking. What was it that made him look as if he wanted to keep the world at bay?

"So you just stand up here." He hauled me up by the hand. "And you give it a try." He took my place, regarding me with a raised brow of encouragement.

I probably couldn't have felt more like a fool if I'd tried. But I stood there, chin up,

161

chest pushed out, glaring as if I were mad at the world.

Dandy's glance flicked up and then away from me in apparent disgust.

Otter was shaking his head. "Not working. You just . . . Hate to tell you, but Mother would say that you look constipated. And then she'd dose you with castor oil." He shuddered.

I let my chest deflate and flopped to the ground beside them.

Deke nodded with something close to approval. "There. That. What you just did. That's the way."

"What's the way?"

"The way you threw yourself on the ground — like you were so sure you couldn't do it, why should you even try." He grinned as he pulled the cigar out and sniffed at it. "I knew this would work." He gave me a careful, studied look. "But we still got to figure out what to do about your uniform."

15
LUCINDA

My aunt had introduced me at church as her niece, freshly graduated from finishing school. The former was true — the latter, most definitely not. In this new beginning to my life, I had determined to tell no lies that were not strictly necessary, but I couldn't see how being honest about that would gain me anything. Especially as I had already filled Milly's and Phoebe's ears with stories about my accomplishments. I hadn't expected, however, that they would share those stories with others.

Or that those others would talk my aunt into allowing me to establish a sort of finishing school for the daughters of Buttermilk Falls. By the middle of my second week in town I found myself agreeing to welcome a half dozen of Milly's contemporaries into the sitting room three afternoons a week for a course of study dedicated to turning them into accomplished ladies.

Surprisingly, however, the tasks I enjoyed the most were those I had first been given — acting as companion to Phoebe and aiding my aunt in the kitchen. It wasn't the cooking or the scrubbing of pots I looked forward to so much as the opportunity to find out more about my mother.

After Susan had gone home on Friday evening, my aunt put me to work scouring a pot while she assembled a pie for the next morning's breakfast. It gave me the chance to ask a question that had been plaguing me. "My father had intimated that your father, my grandfather . . ." There was no way to put it politely. "He said my mother was disowned when they left, that she was denied an inheritance."

"An inheritance!" My aunt laughed. "That would have tickled your mother's fancy, to be thought of as an heiress!" She laughed some more, wiping tears from her eyes as I stood there in utter consternation. "I'm sorry, my dear. It was just so unexpected. My family was never well-to-do. We had enough, we had each other, but . . ." She smiled again. "We were never wealthy. Perhaps you've mistaken your father's family for ours."

"He always said he was denied my mother's inheritance."

Her brows drew close. "He was denied his *own* inheritance. What he considered to be his inheritance in any case. Perhaps you misunderstood him."

"He always said —"

"In my remembrance, a person could never trust anything he said. He said whatever was needed to make himself look better, and he said it with such confidence it was difficult not to believe him. He could convince anyone of anything. But the truth is that his *own* family was quite wealthy."

I didn't know anything about my grandparents. I'd asked . . . I was sure I had. He'd somehow always managed to change the topic. I'd seen him do it a thousand times to other people. It was the first time I'd realized he'd done it to me as well.

"It was rather sad, really. His mother remarried after his father died and had another family. Your father never saw eye to eye with his stepfather, and when his mother died . . . that would be your grandmother . . ."

She was talking about people I ought to know, but didn't. I'd never even known they existed. It was all very unsettling.

"When your grandmother died, all of her money, all of the wealth from the first marriage went to the second husband and the children she'd had with him."

"That doesn't seem fair."

"Your father didn't think so either. He'd been counting on an inheritance, and when it didn't come to him . . . well . . . it changed him. He'd tried to be the son his stepfather wanted. He tried, for a while, to be the cadet the army said they needed. But if you're following the rules simply to get a reward . . . ?" She shrugged. "Sometimes you can do everything right, obey all the rules, and still end up with nothing. I think he finally decided it wasn't worth it."

I wanted to know more. "What was my mother like?"

She paused in rolling out the pie crust as she seemed to consider. "Very much like you." She started rolling again.

"How?" I already knew she hadn't looked anything like me.

My aunt paused in her work again, mouth working, brows knotted. Finally she put her plate down altogether. "In almost every way. You could be her twin but for your years."

Her twin? "But I look nothing like her!"

"You're her very image. Her hazel eyes. Her auburn hair. The way you speak. The way you hold yourself. Perhaps you're not so flirtatious as she was . . ."

"But I don't look anything like her."

"Who told you that?"

"My mother had blond hair. She was very fair, and she —"

"She was not."

"She was blond." I stopped scouring and dried my hands on my skirts, heedless of staining it. Then I pulled my locket from the depths of my bodice, opening it with shaking hands. "She had blond hair." I tilted the necklace so my aunt could see it. "Blond." It was important that she understand.

She dried her own hands and came beside me, cupping her hands around my own, cradling the locket with me. "This isn't your mother's hair."

Taking my hands from hers, I snapped the locket shut. "My father said I looked nothing like her."

She waited until I settled the locket back beneath my blouse, and then she took my hands in hers. "Your father was known to . . ." She glanced down at our hands, squeezing them, and looked back up into my eyes. "Your father didn't always tell the truth."

"Why would he lie about that? Why would he lie about my mother?"

"I don't know. Why did he lie about anything?"

I turned back to my pot. "But I don't look anything like her!"

My aunt turned away and I heard her rummaging through the cupboard. Then she came back to me, metal platter in hand. "This was from our mother, passed on by her mother, and her own mother before that." She held it up in front of us. It reflected back our faces. "The Curtis women have always been known for their hazel eyes. And their auburn hair. Like mine, and hers, and yours." She set the tray down.

"Phoebe's blond."

My aunt smiled, her eyes washed in tears. She put a hand to a tendril that had escaped my bun and pushed it back behind my ears. "Phoebe takes after the Hammonds."

My chin began to tremble, and then my mouth collapsed and I couldn't hold back my own tears anymore. "I can't be like my mother because I don't know who she is. Don't you see?"

"Oh, my dear." She enfolded me in her arms.

I clung to her sobbing, hot tears coursing down my cheeks. "Why would he lie to me? Why would he lie to me about that?"

She spent long moments rubbing my back and stroking my hair as if I were a child.

"Shall I tell you about your mother?"

I nodded, not trusting myself to speak.

"I hear her in your laugh. I see her in your smile. She had a very winning way about her. It was no wonder she caught your father's eye. She caught everyone's eye. She always did, even as a child. She was such a pretty thing. Everyone thought she was flighty, but she wasn't. Sometimes I think maybe I was the only one who knew that."

I took a long snuffling sniff and moved from her embrace to wipe at my eyes.

"I was timid. I still am, if truth be told. But she protected me. She took care of me in much the same way you take care of Phoebe." She tipped my chin up, making me meet her eyes. "That's how I know that I can trust you." She smiled.

As I smiled back, I vowed to make myself worthy of that trust.

16
SETH

They wouldn't let up about my uniform. On Saturday morning, right before we reported for drill, Dandy and Otter crowded into the room just as Deke held his hand out toward me. "Let me have it."

"Have what?"

"Your coat."

"I don't think so. We're going to be late if we don't leave now."

"I keep telling you, you got to quit caring so much about things like that. Next lesson, we'll talk about how to be unashamedly tardy. So hand it over."

"Why?"

"Don't worry. I'm not going to do anything bad to it."

I didn't trust him, but I didn't have any reason not to do it, so I undid the buttons, took it off, and handed it to him.

He dropped it on the floor and started stomping all over it. Though we'd swept the floor for inspection that morning, it had already become dirtied with the muck we'd tracked in from breakfast.

"What in tarnation are you — !" I lunged at him, but Dandy was quick. He got between me and Deacon and stood there until I stepped away. Then he put a finger to my chest and made me back up one step more. When he moved away, I could have sworn it was with the sound of a sword being sheathed.

Otter was looking sadly on. "I told you about boys getting dirty and all . . ."

"There." Deacon gave it one last stomp. "Now you can have it back."

I reached down and grabbed it up. "This doesn't even look respectably worn. It just looks like I rolled around in the dirt." I searched for something to beat it on but couldn't find anything. My chair would have to do. As I clapped it against chair's back, a great cloud of dust arose. Half of it stuck to my trousers.

"Hope you don't mind, we'll just step away for a minute."

"Oh, sure. Go on. After you've been lecturing me on how to look worn and moth-eaten."

"Hey! Look at that, Dandy. He might just turn into you after all."

I gave them both a glare filled with pure poison.

Deacon winked.

I went after him, but Dandy grabbed me by the collar and hauled me off. For loafing about so much, he was a quite a bit stronger than he looked. "No need to be fractious about it. It's us doing you the favor, remember?"

I gave the coat one last shake and then pulled it back on. Starting off for the stairs, I buttoned it as I went. In twenty paces, I had stepped out well ahead of the rest of them. I was out the door before they even appeared . . . which wasn't necessarily a good thing, for when I encountered Campbell Conklin, I was all alone.

He tilted his head as his cool-eyed gaze traveled from the top of my cap to the tips of my shoes. "You lose your way, Mr. West-cott? The home for widows and orphans is back down the river a mile or two." He smirked.

It was awfully hard to feel righteously indignant when I knew I looked the truant. And then I thought of Dandy and remembered my position as cadet captain. I felt my chin lift. Though I didn't say anything, his smile disappeared.

"I feel I have to report you for appearance

unbecoming a cadet at the U.S. Military Academy."

What would Deacon say to that? I shrugged. "Do what you have to do." I moved to pass him as if I didn't care that my coat had just been trampled and there was dust clinging to my trousers.

"And for defacing government property."

Touching the brim of my cap, I sauntered on past.

I paid for it, though, as Campbell Conklin announced my name later at parade in a voice that echoed through the ranks. "Conklin; Westcott, first captain; appearance unbecoming, defacement of government property."

Deacon and Otter took turns slapping me on the back afterward. "That's the way to do it. See how easy that was?"

It didn't make me feel any better. What sort of example had I been to all of those plebes and yearlings who'd borne witness to my shame? "Maybe I can get out of it with a written explanation —"

Deke was shaking his head. "For appearance unbecoming? Isn't worth it. Besides, you need all the demerits you can get!"

Otter grinned at me. "Cheer up. Just think what that fellow . . . Penworth?"

"Pennyworth."

173

"Just imagine his face when you walk up to him and tell him who you are and would he rather pay you back now or talk to a judge. It'll all be worth it. You'll see."

I hoped so. It had better be. If I'd been allowed leave to take my sister to Kentucky, she never would have met Pennyworth, and he'd never have taken our money. "Maybe I should just go home."

Deke looked at me askance. "Home? You mean leave?"

"Have you ever been in Nebraska Territory in the winter?"

"I've been in Ohio in the winter."

"Then you'll know what it's going to be like at Laramie."

"You can't go now. Leaving now would be desertion. Federal offense. They catch you, they'd put you into prison. You'd be locked up and Pennyworth would still be free. Unless you want to get yourself dismissed. I said I'd help you. Offer still stands."

"No." Getting dismissed didn't make any sense either. "Guess I'm just stuck."

"As a pig. But come on now, Little Sally Walker, and wipe those weeping eyes." He mimicked children who sang the song, turning to the west and then to the east. "You want a handkerchief? I think I got one somewhere."

"I don't think you're taking this seriously."

"I *am* taking it seriously. But the only thing to do now is concentrate on what can be done. Listen to me good. You already got through the hard parts. You made it through the first three years. Through geometry. And calculus. You even did the best at optics. Everyone who's not going to make it gets found deficient by now. You know that. So you got to put your heart into failing or no one's going to believe you're in earnest. And it's going to take some really, truly bad things for you to make it far enough down the list. You understand?"

"Are you trying to warn me about something?"

"Me? No. 'Course I'm not. Why would I do that?"

"That's what it sounded like."

"I don't know why it would sound like something it doesn't sound like."

"Is there something I should know, Deke?"

"Well . . . come to think of it, you should probably know that I'm not the sainted choirboy people believe me to be." He winked as men flowed around us on their way back to the barracks.

I took a step closer. "I'm a grown man. I ought to be able to do something about this. I ought to be able to take care of my sister.

She's my responsibility now."

"Which is why you're going about this in such a responsible way. Just a few more months and the army will pay you for all the trouble they're putting you through. Isn't that better than running away and offering her nothing at all? The only reasonable choice left you is to do exactly what you're doing."

"But what if Pennyworth disappears before I can find him?"

"Man like that? With the whole western half of the nation to swindle? He won't stop while he's ahead. And people being like they are — no offense — he's always going to be ahead."

"What if I can't catch up to him? What if he just gets away with it?"

"The way I see it, the more time you let him wander around, the easier he'll be to find. His trail will be so obvious, you'll be able to just waltz right up to him. Won't be any trouble to find him at all."

"You really think so?"

He nodded. "I really think so."

There's no way Deacon could be certain, but it made me feel better.

17
LUCINDA

I woke on Saturday morning with a smile. Today I was going to see Seth . . . but I still had a morning to get through first. I kept Ella out of trouble while Milly and Phoebe sorted through several bushels of apples in the kitchen, checking for overripe ones as my uncle quizzed Bobby on his Latin. I dumped out the pouch of clay marbles, letting Ella line them up by color, as Bobby kept glancing over in envy. Feeling sorry for the lad, I sent him a wink. He blushed and then made a good show of pretending disinterest.

After his lesson, Bobby took Ella in hand . . . or perhaps I should say she took him in hand, as I went to help my aunt with cooking. She must have noticed my impatience, for she soon sent me upstairs with the charge to "Ready yourself for that cadet of yours."

Phoebe turned an amused face toward

me. "Would that be Mr. Westcott?"

My aunt turned to me. "It would be a grievous sin if you made that poor cadet wait. They've only a few hours of their own each week. It's very flattering that he's chosen to spend his with you."

Phoebe offered her bucket up to her mother and held out a hand toward me. "I'll help you with your hair."

"My . . . hair?"

My aunt was smiling, though Phoebe could have no way of knowing it. "She's very good with a brush."

I took my cousin by the hand and helped her to stand, then looped her arm through mine and walked her to the stairs. Once there, she put a hand to the railing and went up quite on her own. By the time I reached our room, she was waiting for me, hairbrush in hand.

As I entered, she bid me sit.

I pulled the pins from my hair and let it spill down over my shoulders. I placed her hand atop my head and she patted down its sides and gathered my hair into her hand. Smoothing it down my back, she began to pull the brush through it. She really did have a lovely hand. At her last pull, she gathered up my hair, twisted it into a hank, and then released it to spin down my back.

"You've such nice hair."

I picked up her braid and tickled her cheek with it. "As do you."

She grabbed hold of it. "For all the good it does me. I might as well be twelve years old with it plaited like this."

"I'll put it up for you tomorrow if you'd like."

"There's no need. I've only myself to please with it." She said it not with pity but with quiet resignation.

I would have embraced her, but it might have frightened her rather than comforted her. And besides, I was in danger of being late as it was.

After braiding my own hair and fastening it into a bun, I settled my bonnet atop it and picked up my reticule.

Phoebe was reaching for my shoulders, so I let her find them. From there, her hands patted up my neck and glided over my bonnet. "Beautiful. You look beautiful."

Not nearly as beautiful as I had looked at finishing school with a full wardrobe of gowns at my disposal, but her saying so made me feel as if I were.

I took her hands in my own and squeezed them before releasing them. "If I don't leave now, I'll keep Mr. Westcott waiting."

■ ■ ■ ■

My uncle walked to the academy with me. He wasn't the kind of man to engage in idle chatter, so I was surprised when he began to speak. "We're quite gratified, the way you've taken to Phoebe. Thank you. She's needed the companionship of a girl her age."

"I feel as if I should thank her for taking to me." I wasn't being untruthful.

"It's very . . . It's good of you."

We walked on in silence, picking our way around holes in the road. A cooling north wind had blown in during the night, sweeping away August's haze and sharpening the outlines of the distant hills. It was the kind of day that whet the appetite for autumn's vivid, sparkling days.

"I must confess that when your aunt said you'd come, I expected that you had brought trouble with you. But I've been quite pleased with the help you've given to my household."

I nodded. Mostly because I couldn't trust myself to speak. His words had stirred up a strange compulsion to confess my sins. But that was pointless. My past was behind me. From my present I had nothing to fear. What would confession do but place a question mark where I had apparently already established a firm period?

We approached the military reservation in amiable silence. He stopped at the gate and spoke to the guard for a moment, and then we passed through and walked on to the academy area, toward a building he told me was the barracks. Some cadets were marching back and forth in front of it, muskets in hand. He pointed toward them. "It's generally supposed that a cadet would meet you there."

"Why are all of those men marching?"

"They're marching tours as punishment. Just ignore them."

I might have done a better job of it if they hadn't looked so dour and if they weren't carrying weapons.

My uncle cleared his throat. "I hope you enjoy yourself. The view of the valley from Fort Putnam is unparalleled, although I do wish to remind you of all of the misfortune a cadet has caused us in the past."

I didn't dare to meet his eyes.

"But I have great trust in Mr. Westcott. He's one of the best of his class."

Seth came down the steps of the barracks just then. He bowed to my uncle and then to me.

I nodded.

My uncle sent him a stern glance through his spectacles. "I'll be at the academy and will expect to have Miss Hammond returned to me by drill."

Seth crooked his arm for me, and I took it up. "Yes, sir." He glanced down at me. Though his face was shadowed by the brim of his hat, I could see the quirk in his lips quite plainly. We took a few steps before he resumed speaking. "You had asked me to show you Fort Putnam, Miss Hammond —"

"Lucinda." There was no need to move backward in our acquaintance. Not when I was quite happy with what I'd seen in him.

He tightened his arm. "Lucinda. But there's a path along the river that's very pleasant this time of year."

I'd moved relationships forward with deceit in the past. This time, with this man, I decided to try the truth. "I only asked you to show me Fort Putnam because I wanted to make sure I could see you again. I hope I wasn't being too forward." *Blast!* I oughtn't have said it that way. I was relying too much on old tricks, trying to force the answers I wanted. No gentleman, no man, would have replied in the affirmative. Any fool would have known that wouldn't be polite.

"No! Not at all."

Seth Westcott was no fool.

He continued. "In fact, I was trying to do the same. Though perhaps not as successfully as you. . . . What I was most hoping for that night was an opportunity to see you again as well."

The way his gaze slanted down toward me brought a blush to my cheeks. "Then please lead on. I'm happy to see whatever you'd like to show me."

We walked out across a large flat area Seth called the Plain. He took me over to a sunken area he called Execution Hollow and pointed out the West Point Hotel, where visitors were sitting on the covered, columned porch. Then we walked to Fort Clinton, where stonework walls supported mounds of grass-covered earth. Lending a hand, he helped me up to the top, where we looked in the direction of what I presumed was the river.

"I thought there'd be a better view from here."

"There is. In the winter."

I laughed.

"That path I mentioned starts out there." He nodded out ahead of us into the trees. "It follows the river and the view is better."

"Then why don't we take it and see where it leads?"

The climb up Fort Clinton had been difficult, but Seth's river path was downright treacherous. With a bit of sliding and quite a bit of handholding, however, I made it down the smooth rock-faced slope to the trail below.

As we walked along, we encountered several other couples coming from the opposite direction. Seth stepped off the path to let them pass. Cliffs fell away from the path's edge at some points, and as we walked, we wound up and over inclines and through a rock-studded landscape. At one point we strolled beneath a cliff with a ledge that protruded out over the trail. But the view through the trees was idyllic, and the river, dazzling under a cloudless sky.

"You've told me of Execution Hollow and old Fort Clinton. Surely a path this lovely must have a name."

He colored. "It does."

"And what is it?"

"It's called Flirtation Walk."

"Why, that's perfect!"

He gave me a sharp glance. "It-it is?"

"The river flirts with the sun and the path flirts with the cliff and the view flirts with the trees. If the purpose of flirtation is to pique the interest, then this path succeeds."

"And so do you." He put a hand to mine and unwound it from his arm, turning to face me. Then he took up my other hand with his. "Miss Hammond, Lucinda?" His hands tightened on mine. "I would very much like to —"

"Captain? Captain Westcott?" At that moment a cadet ran up, saluted, and said something about a fight. Seth asked the cadet to escort me back to my uncle, bowed, and took his leave . . . leaving me to wonder what it was that he would very much like to have done.

18
SETH

I walked away from Lucinda, trying my best not to curse. Heaven only knew how much I wanted to strangle whichever cadets were squandering their recreation time fighting! But maybe it was all for the best.

If I'd stayed, I would have kissed her. And then what would I have done?

A career in the military wasn't easy at the best of times. Even with the engineers, I'd be subject to picking up and moving whenever my assignments changed. Lucinda might be from St. Louis, but I'd bet she'd never seen the foul side of a stable. Or a chicken coop or anything else, for that matter. She deserved better than I could ever give her . . . even when I hadn't been trying for the cavalry.

The person I ought to be cursing was Pennyworth!

I jogged across the Plain and over to the cadet area where I heard some fellows hooting and hollering. The fight was over, but there was still blame to be handed out.

And Campbell Conklin was already there to do it.

By rights, as my adjutant, the honor was his. But fights were tricky. Cadets could be dismissed for fighting. And sentinels or those pulling guard duty had been dismissed for letting one continue unimpeded. In the close quarters of the Point, sometimes feelings ran hot. But I wasn't of the mind that a man ought to be dismissed for that. For bodily harm, maybe. But for goading someone to throw a punch? Sometimes both men came out of a fight better friends than they went into one.

Two second classmen stood off to the side, chests heaving. One had a blackened eye and split lip. The other was flexing his fist.

"Sir!" The one with the swollen eye saluted me. "It wasn't my fault. He threw the first punch."

"So I see."

Campbell interrupted. "I recommend dismissal for both men."

Of course he did. I addressed the other cadet. "Is there a reason you chose to pick a fight with him?"

"Didn't choose it. Didn't have any choice

once he maligned my honor. Sir."

Heaven save us from men with a delicate sense of honor. I wished they'd put as much effort into doing their duty. I told Campbell to escort them to the commandant. He was generally a fair man with an eye for character as well as for justice.

I dispersed the rest of the cadets and then followed on their heels toward the barracks.

Word of the fight had spread, for we met a wave of cadets coming toward us on the way back. "Fight's over. Get ready for drill."

There was an audible sigh of disappointment as they all turned around and we trudged back to the barracks together.

Deke fell into step with me in the stairwell.

I nodded. "Didn't see you there. Were you watching the fight?"

"Me? Naw. Got better things to do."

I didn't ask what those better things had been because I didn't want to know. Sometimes ignorance provided its own protection.

"How was Miss Hammond?"

I didn't answer until we were in our room. Some information didn't have to be shared with the whole corps of cadets. "I don't think I'll be seeing her anymore."

"She doesn't have that character you were so interested in?"

"She does."

"Did she lose her looks overnight?"

"She didn't. But what's the point, Deke? If I can do this right, I'm headed for the cavalry. A girl like her shouldn't be subjected to that." I unstrapped my sword and hung it over my rifle. "You ever get the feeling that life isn't fair?"

"I was born knowing that. Look at this." He gestured to his mop of hair. "And look at you."

"What about me?"

"If God were fair, He would have given me, the consummate ladies' man, your hair."

I felt a corner of my mouth lift in the start of a smile. "Or to go with your hair He could have given you my —"

"Your cool determination and practical indifference to the female of our species?"

I grunted. "Or Otter a bit more smarts to go with his good intentions."

"Or Dandy . . ." He *hmphed.* "Can't say what I'd have done with Dandy. But I'd sure as anything have taken away most of Campbell Conklin's smarts." He turned the page of his sketchbook, scribbled furiously for a long minute, and then showed it to me with a flourish. It was Campbell Conklin, looking decidedly stupid. "Then his looks might have matched his personality."

I laughed. I couldn't help it.

"But I suppose fair is all relative. He'll end up with some girl he can lead around by the nose. I'll end up with someone willing to put up with my wild ways. And Dandy will end up with some girl who can overlook that fearsome glare of his. And you'll end up with — ?"

"No one at all. That's what I was saying. How could I ask anyone to share the sort of life I'll have?"

He frowned. "Well . . . that's the funny thing, don't you think? Professor Hammond knows all about this kind of life, doesn't he?"

I supposed, on reflection, that he did.

"If he was so dead set against it, if he thought it was so terrible, don't you think he'd persuade his niece to look elsewhere for a beau?"

Maybe.

"And I'd give Miss Hammond more credit."

"You would? For what?"

"For seeing what the rest of us do. So don't give her up. Not just yet."

"Thanks, Deke."

"*Pshaw.* Weren't nothing you wouldn't have figured out for yourself. Eventually.

Once you stopped making cow's eyes at the girl."

"I wasn't —"

"But can I ask you for a favor?"

I nodded.

"I still haven't found a Venus for my book. Do you mind if I use your Miss Hammond?"

"As Venus?! Get your own inspiration, Deke. She's mine."

"That's fine. I see how it is." He picked up his sketchbook and went back to work, but I could tell, behind that drawing, that he was laughing at me.

19
LUCINDA

Along with teaching at my finishing school, my days had fallen into a rhythm of helping Phoebe, helping my aunt, and helping Milly with the children. My aunt and Phoebe were pleasant company. Bobby and Ella, however, could be quite trying whenever they found themselves together. I'd solved their unwillingness to be reasonable, however, with an old trick I'd learned from my father: I promised them whatever it took to get the behavior I wanted. Whatever it took had turned out to be candy. I'm sure I must have promised them nearly a jarful by the beginning of that third week. They never seemed to tire, however, of the thought of gumdrops and lollipops. But when Ella and I tussled over her getting dressed one morning, she demanded immediate payment for compliance.

"I'll get you some candy when I go to the store next. I promise." I hadn't been there

192

yet and hadn't planned on going anytime soon, but she didn't need to know that.

"Now!"

"I can't very well go to the store right now, can I? And leave you here undressed? I hardly think your mother would approve."

"I want candy!" Her little fists were clenched into tiny balls, and that plump little chin of hers was unwavering.

"I *will* get you candy, I just can't do it right now. But when I do go, what shall I get you? A peppermint stick?"

"A Gibraltar."

"Fine. I'll get you a Gibraltar."

"Lemon."

I turned her round and tied the back of her pinafore.

"Now!"

"I'm quite certain getting dressed includes shoes."

She picked them up and tried to shove them onto her feet.

"And stockings."

Eventually the child was dressed, hands and face washed, and I'd only had to promise her two more pieces of candy.

I picked up the brush, which she must have taken for a device of torture, for she burst into tears. "There now. What's to become of those candies if you cry at the slightest provocation?"

"More."

"More what?"

"Candy."

I promised her what I had to, and in the end, she appeared downstairs with her pinafore neatly tied and her hair drawn back from her face and bound with a ribbon.

My aunt greeted her with a smile.

Her eyes turned stormy and she seized my hand. "I want candy."

My aunt's brow rose. "I'm sure we'd all like candy, but we've none here, and even if we did have some, I wouldn't give it to a sulky girl like you."

Her mouth dropped open, her eyes screwed shut, and she let out an ear-splitting wail. "Lucinda said she'd give me candy! I want my candy!"

I felt my cheeks flame. "I don't know that I said that exactly . . ."

My aunt kneeled to draw Ella into her arms. "Hush now."

"I want my candy! She promised! She said if I got dressed —"

"She promised you candy for getting dressed?"

Snuffling, Ella nodded.

My aunt eyed me over the top of Ella's head. "But you ought to have done that because you were supposed to, not because you were offered candy."

"But she said! And she promised me candy last time too."

"Last time?"

"When you told me to stop pestering Bobby."

Would the child not stop talking?

"Do you get candy for everything you're supposed to do?"

"No."

A look very much like relief crossed my aunt's face.

"Sometimes we get other things."

"Things like . . . ?"

"She promised me ribbons."

That was true. I had.

"Or a story when I'm supposed to be sleeping."

After kissing the girl on the cheek, my aunt rose. "I want you to do all those things not because of candy or some other promise of reward, but because you know that those are the right things to do. Sometimes there isn't anyone to see the choices we make. I want to know that in those cases, you can be counted on to do what's right."

"I'm not getting candy?"

"You're not getting candy. Or anything

else. Now. Off you go to help Milly out back."

As the little girl tramped down the hall, my aunt looked pointedly at me. "Sit with me for a moment."

I took a seat on the sofa while my aunt sat in a chair.

"I'm a bit concerned."

"By what?"

"The children adore you, there's no doubt about that, but I see you appealing to their baser nature."

"They've been perfectly behaved, haven't they?" Or nearly so.

"Yes . . . but you've been manipulating them to achieve that behavior, haven't you?"

"I wouldn't call it manipulating."

Her brow rose. "What would you call it?"

"Persuading. People will do almost anything if you can convince them it's in their own best interest."

"That sounds very much like your father speaking."

Was it such a very bad thing to believe? "It's true, isn't it?"

"It is, but . . . you could convince someone to do almost anything that way."

I had. I could convince someone to do just about anything for me.

"Both right and wrong."

"I've only ever asked them to do things you've wanted them to do."

"But at some point, they'll have to do those things not because it's in their best interest but because it's in your best interest. Or mine. Or their father's. If you teach them to act selfishly, they always will. If you reward them with gain at another's expense, they will think that's the only way to ever obtain anything."

Wasn't it?

"Life is about caring for others, not taking things from them."

My life wasn't. It never had been. "But . . . they've been doing all the things you've been asking them to do."

"They have been, yes, but I didn't want them done like that."

"I don't understand. If I'm not to make them mind that way . . . what other way is there?"

"They're to mind because it's the right thing to do. They're to help you because they've been asked to. They're to put others' needs first because they ought to care for others as well as themselves."

"I . . . I wasn't . . . That is . . . no one ever taught me any of those things."

She came off her chair to sit beside me on the sofa and to lay a hand on my cheek.

197

"That's no surprise, considering who raised you. And I don't want you to consider that I think any less of you because of what you were taught. I just don't want you to pass those things on to my children."

"But . . . I still don't understand. They've done all the right things."

"But it's all been for the wrong reasons."

"The result was the same, wasn't it?"

"Maybe for you, but not for the children. They were serving for a reward, not out of kindness or compassion."

"Does it matter?"

Her jaw dropped.

Clearly I'd said the wrong thing.

"What did that man do to you? How is it that you could grow up in this day and age and never know anything about selflessness or responsibility? Did he use you in those schemes of his?"

"He didn't —"

She cocked a brow.

"Perhaps I helped. Some."

She was looking at me with such compassion, with such pity, that I felt quite naked. As if she could see right inside me.

"Dear child, he wronged you. And quite grievously."

"He always said . . . he said when we took things from others that they deserved it.

That if they were smarter, they wouldn't let us. It was as if we were teaching them a lesson. He said that if they could be talked out of their money that they didn't deserve to have it."

"Sweet child, none of us deserve anything." She searched my eyes. "But he didn't tell you that, did he?"

He hadn't.

"Everything we get, we get from God. And not because we've earned it, but because He loves us. And those things He withholds, He withholds out of love as well."

"But we never took anything from anyone who couldn't afford it. And really, we didn't take those things for nothing. He said we were giving them what they were looking for."

"And what was that?"

"In exchange for their money, we were giving them hope."

"Hope? Perhaps. For a moment. But wouldn't you say that in the end, it was a false hope?"

It was. It had been. There was no getting around that. "He said . . . he said you didn't approve of him."

"We didn't. The question is, do you?"

■ ■ ■ ■

Did I?

What my father had done always seemed quite reasonable to me. And he had provided for both of us, hadn't he? Of course . . . we did have to run away from a town once in a while. And we did tend to avoid lawmen. But they just hadn't understood things the way we had.

It seemed so odd that my aunt saw things differently. But the way she explained it also seemed quite reasonable. Only it made me ashamed of all the things I'd said and done. All those people I'd convinced to do things that were for my benefit instead of for their own.

Was I truly that selfish?

Perhaps I was, but was there any harm in it? I was alone in the world. If I didn't take care of myself, who would? For the moment, I relied upon my aunt and uncle. If they insisted upon selflessness and morality and kind generosity, then I would do so . . . but would that not be considered selfish as well? Since I would be doing those things in order to earn my room and board?

I couldn't quite see that all this talk about selflessness led anywhere but to self serving.

If my father and I had been more honest about our motives, was that truly all bad?

20
SETH

Deke tried to push me out of the room on Tuesday morning. "Come on, come on, come on. Don't you hear that drum?"

"There's a scuff on my shoes. I just have to —" I grabbed up a rag and prepared to spit on the toe of my shoe.

But Deacon stepped down on my shoe with his heel and twisted his foot.

I bit back an ungentlemanly response. "Would you mind telling me why you did that?"

"Because it will be good for a demerit. At least one."

Maybe. And now it would take me a good hour to layer the shoe black on thick enough to cover up the mark his heel had made. But I couldn't do anything about it right then. I risked being late.

That's about how the rest of the day went: expecting the best but getting the worst. It's true that I needed to use these first weeks of the semester to set an expectation for my failure, but old habits died hard. In fencing exercises, the only course Dandy and I shared, I didn't dare meet the instructor's eye for fear Dandy would accuse me of trying too hard. But that didn't stop me from being called to demonstrate. Keeping in mind Deke's warning, I tried my best not to be too quick or too good. In fact, I was hoping to delay my demonstration long enough to be saved by the bugle's call to dinner.

I'd never been good at feigning anything, though.

The professor finally called a halt to my fumblings and ordered me to stop. "I see you practiced quite hard for this, Mr. Westcott." Sarcasm was a weapon he yielded with great facility.

"Yes, sir?"

Dandy kicked out at my ankle. "Ouch!"

"What's that, Mr. Westcott?"

"I, uh. I . . . yawned."

"You *yawned*?"

"Yes, sir."

He glanced about as if unsure whether I was making a joke. "In the future, could you do so a bit more quietly?"

It didn't take long for word of the incident

to make its way through the mess hall at dinner that afternoon. Deacon was thoroughly disgusted. "Could you yawn a bit more quietly? A bit more *quietly*!" He tormented the plebes for a few minutes and then turned his attention back to my failings. "If that had been me, I'd have been reported."

He smashed his rice into his boiled potatoes and attached a lump of it to some stringy roast beef. "You, sir, are going to have to work on your answers! *And* you're going to have to study quite a bit less than you did last year if our plan is going to work."

"I already told you — I can't not study. I won't. Least not in rhetoric or civil engineering. I will not just sit in class and twiddle my thumbs. I want to learn something while I'm here. Anyone who doesn't is just wasting the opportunity."

"But what good is rhetoric going to do when you're out in the middle of . . . of *Kansas* dodging arrows?"

"Learning is never wasted. And how do you know you'll never have a use for it? How can you know what lies ahead? How can any of us?"

"What lies ahead of us is what the army says lies ahead of us. And that, sir, is that."

"I'm *not* not studying. And if you want me to help all of you out in subjects like tactics and civil engineering, then I have to."

Deke bolted down the rest of his meal. "Fine. Study all you want. Just don't use any of it in your recitations or examinations. How's that for a compromise?"

I had no intention of changing my habits, so I studied that night the way I'd studied the past three years at the academy. Cadets were expected to come to class ready to recite, prepared to discuss the assigned materials. I figured the trick of it would be not to remember, in the morning, all the studying I'd done the night before. Not that I would forget. I just wouldn't be able to . . . I let my head drop into my hands. Who was I kidding?

I was a failure at failing.

Dandy and Otter appeared promptly at nine thirty when our half hour of recreation began. They took cigars from Deke's floorboard hiding place and lit them once the door was shut. I crossed to the window and wrestled it open. "It smells like a saloon in here."

Deacon took in a hearty whiff of the air. "Smells like heaven to me." He sat down in my chair and put his feet up on my table.

I took my pillow from the bed, lifted his feet, and stuck it beneath them. I'd spent a whole lot of time polishing that table, and I wasn't willing to have it all go to waste.

With a long look at me, he kicked the pillow away, took his cigar, and ground the butt into the tabletop.

"What did you go and do that for?"

"It's an experiment."

"Experiment!"

"If I did that, I'd probably get three demerits for it."

Dandy was already disagreeing. "You'd get two."

A rather long discussion ensued, but ultimately, they agreed that Deacon could have expected either two or three demerits for defacing government property.

I protested. "There's nothing experimental about that. An experiment requires answering a question you don't know the answer to."

"Exactly." He took the cigar from his lips and blew smoke rings at the ceiling. "You're the experiment. You've never been given a demerit during room inspection. Are you going to be given three, same as I would be, or are they going to give you less? That's the question. And we're going to do this experiment in order to find the answer."

The answer was two. I received two demerits for the offense of defacing government property even though I happened to own that particular table. My account with the treasurer had been docked in payment for it.

Deacon and the fellows kept tutoring me on what it took to be an Immortal. On Thursday night before lights-out, Deacon took my coat from its peg. He shook it out and then pulled it on and carefully buttoned it up.

"What are you doing?"

"You are going to owe me so many favors by the time we graduate . . ." He poured some water from the pitcher into the bowl and cupped his hands in it. Lifting them out, he clapped them against the body of the coat. Then he did it again, releasing a dribble of water onto each sleeve. After that, he rubbed the water in.

"You are going to stink to high heaven of wet wool."

He crawled into bed and pulled his blanket up to his chin. "I know it. See what a good friend I am? I've got to start thinking on how you can repay me." He crossed his arms behind his head.

"Why are you wearing my coat to bed?"

"I noticed that none of that dust I stomped into it last week is still there. What'd you do to get it all out?"

"I beat it on the windowsill. And I brushed at it." It had taken the better part of an hour.

"Well, all that hard work is going to be for no use because I'm going to sleep in it. And in the morning, because of this water? All the wrinkles will be nice and set. See if they aren't." He closed his eyes.

"You can't sleep in my coat."

"Well I'm not going to sleep in mine!"

"Don't do that, Deke."

"Why. You want to?"

"No. I just —"

"Then go to sleep."

21
LUCINDA

I woke the next Monday morning with the worst of knots in my stomach. Today I would, once again, be holding a class for my finishing school students. On the whole, they were very nice girls. Except for Milly. And it's not just that she wasn't nice. She was also devious.

The weather was fine that afternoon, so I brought chairs out into the orchard behind the house and placed them beneath an apple tree.

When class commenced, Milly sprawled in her chair, tossed her braid behind her shoulder, and began plucking at the ragged edges of her fingernails. "I don't know why Mama thinks I need a finishing school."

Several of the girls twittered.

I wished I had a ruler and a desk to rap it on. "Every lady ought to go to a finishing school. I went."

She eyed me with a skeptical tilt to her

brow. "Are you finished, then?" There was laughter in her eyes and a challenge in her words.

"Am I . . . ?" People out west were generally quite impressed when I told them about school.

She grinned. "That's what I've always wondered. When you finish finishing school what exactly have you finished?"

"Well, I suppose . . . I've finished . . . learning how to be a lady." Or I would have, if I had ever graduated from one.

"So what, exactly, do you need to know to be a lady?"

"I studied singing —"

"I already know how to sing. And don't you, girls?" Two of them nodded.

"And French."

"But why? Why would I need to know French if I never plan to go to France?"

"The cadets all learn French." Phoebe broke into the conversation.

Class was not going well, and it hadn't been since I'd first started teaching. Milly had always been so busy watching Ella that I hadn't realized just how recalcitrant she was. I needed to gain the upper hand in the conversation. "I also learned how to play the piano. And I have a very fine hand at embroidery, if I do say so myself."

Milly snorted. "None of that sounds very useful. Did they teach you how to make pies? Or darn a sock? I'm not so good at those."

"Well . . . no."

"Please don't let Mama know you're not going to teach me anything useful!"

Another of the girls chortled.

"At least if I'm attending your lessons I don't have to mind Ella."

"I can teach you how to walk."

"I already know how to walk."

"I'm sure you don't know how to do it properly. I can also teach you how to talk."

"I already —"

"*Politely.* Without contradicting everything a person says."

"So what are you going to teach us today?" Milly arched a brow as if she knew I was an imposter.

"There's . . . comportment."

"What's that?"

"The way one holds oneself. You shouldn't ever, for instance, lounge about."

"Why ever not?"

"It's not appropriate. It's slatternly. And louche."

"Louche! Is that French?"

"It might as well be." I spoke the words between my clenched teeth.

211

"If I can't do this." She slid off her chair and sprawled on the grass, arms out-stretched, eyes closed. "Then what should I do?" She cracked one eye open.

I grabbed her hand and hauled her up. "You must give attention to your posture."

"*My* posture? What about Phoebe's?"

Phoebe placed her hands in her lap and straightened her spine.

"Phoebe is doing quite well. It's you who worries me." I pushed her into the chair. "Now then, you're not to rest against the back of the chair." I cast an eye over the rest of the class as they adjusted their positions. "Keep yourself at the very edge of the seat."

"If we're not supposed to use the back of the chair, why do we have them? Why don't we just use stools?"

"I don't make the rules, I'm simply telling you what they are. If you want to be a lady, then —"

"Fine." She repositioned herself on the chair. "What's next?"

"You've slouched again."

"Have I?" She straightened her shoulders, lifting her chin. Glancing toward Phoebe, she nodded her head. "You'd better pay attention to her. She's slouching now too."

Phoebe straightened as well. "I don't see

why you have to be so mean about it. I'm
blind!"

"And I'm only fourteen. And I'm ornery."
Milly reached over and poked her in the
ribs.

Phoebe was so startled she fell off her
chair onto the grass.

The other girls were looking on, mouths
slack with shock.

Such behavior was unconscionable!
"What's wrong with you? She's blind! Of all
the — !"

But Phoebe was laughing.

"Being blind gets her out of all the hard
work. It always has. Maybe you could teach
me to be blind too."

"Milly!"

"Good grief! You act as if she hasn't any
sense of humor."

Phoebe was wiping tears from her eyes. "I
haven't laughed so hard in ages." She put a
hand up to feel for her chair.

I guided her up and helped her sit.

Milly was grinning. "See?"

I shot her a dagger of a look. "All I see is
that you're incorrigible."

"And so is Phoebe."

"Phoebe doesn't have anything to do with
this. She's —"

"She's just as bad as I am. Admit it! I

don't think it's fair that you give her special treatment just because she can't see. She can hear, can't she? And speak too."

"She's —"

"You're talking as if she's not even here. Phoebe can speak for herself. Can't you, Phoebe?"

"I can. Thank you." She said it quite primly, although her lips were still twitching.

I glared at Milly. "I don't think finishing school is the right place for you."

"Probably not. Maybe I should ask Mama to find me a starting school instead." She and the rest of the girls broke out into great guffaws of laughter and collapsed against each other.

"I can see none of you really wish to learn anything."

Milly stopped laughing and took in a deep breath. "We're not making fun. Honest! It's just that I can't see what use all this is. It's not like some gentleman will ever want to court me. And I don't think anyone is going to offer for any of us anytime soon and —"

"Milly!"

"So why can't people just let us be the way we are?"

Phoebe interjected timidly. "At least Milly isn't afraid to say what's true."

So they were in this together now? "She doesn't have to say it quite so plainly!"

"I've had people tiptoe about me all my life."

"But I'm meant to help make ladies out of you. Out of all of you. And if your mothers don't see any change in you, then . . ." Then one of the main reasons for my aunt allowing me to stay in Buttermilk Falls was gone.

Milly sighed. "I'm not completely stupid. Just tell me what to do, I'll learn it, and then we can go back to having fun. I don't want to waste this whole hour on a lesson."

"I went to school for several years to learn all these things, and you think you can learn it in ten minutes?"

"Maybe not *all* of if it. But I'm supposed to have three lessons a week, aren't I? And I've already told you I know how to sing and I don't need to know French. So what can be so difficult?"

"Being a lady is not a set of skills you can just learn and then put behind you. It's a way of life. It's a way of treating people." All of which I had managed to learn and then use to extort other people — which was the antithesis of everything a lady was supposed to be.

I sighed. What I needed was some motivation. Something to offer them to make these classes worth their while. "What if . . ." *What if what?* What would give them reason to take what I was teaching seriously? Perhaps . . . an opportunity to use the information! "What if I organized a dinner party at the end of three weeks' time, so that you could put your new skills to good use?"

That gained the interest of several of the girls. From Milly, however, it only provoked another challenge. "With who?"

"With *whom* would be the proper way to ask that question."

"Well?"

"With all of you."

"We see each other all the time."

That was a good point. "What if . . . I also invited some guests?"

"Whom?"

"That would be who."

Milly scowled. "*What other people* would be invited?"

"How about . . . if . . . I invited some cadets?"

22
SETH

"Careful there. You're going to rub the shine right off that."

I looked up at Deacon from the musket I was polishing on Wednesday morning for inspection. "Why should it matter? It'll just get me more demerits. Isn't that a good thing?" It had been tougher than I thought it would be to not be the smartest one in my classes. It was three weeks into the semester, and I'd already been sent back at least one section in all of them. I might be one step closer to retrieving my sister, but I was that much further away now from ever being assigned to the engineers. Not that I blamed my sister — all the blame fell to Mr. Pennyworth, in my opinion — but it was a blow all the same and made even worse because the blow was to my pride.

That wasn't something I was pleased to admit.

No man likes to admit to finding vice in

himself. The people who knew me best knew I wasn't really an Immortal. What rankled was that I cared so much about the opinion of those who didn't really know me at all. Why should I constantly have to fight the almost overwhelming urge to explain to them that my sudden lack of effort was for an entirely noble cause?

"It's not that we don't care about your plight, because we do. Each one of us. But personal destruction is not what we're here for. You've got to remember the goal."

"Which is?" I worked the rotten-stone powder into the brass with my buff stick to give it a good polish.

"Which is to get assigned to the cavalry. Can't do that if you get lost in your own melancholy. That won't do any of us any good. You've got to fail at this with a *cheerful* spirit. You've got to put your heart into it. That's all I'm saying."

"And what good is it that I'm doing for you, Deacon? What good is it that I'm doing for anyone?" And why did my musket have to get so blasted dirty all the time?

"When we first decided to help you, we agreed that it would be mostly helping ourselves. Purely selfish, you see?"

"No . . . I don't." I picked at some rust with my fingernail to try to scrape it off.

"Who else gets to pick who they report to? Me and the fellows figure that even out in the territories, you'll be promoted so fast, it'll make a hummingbird look slow. To tell you the truth, we've always thought you were a decent sort, so if we have to report to anyone, it might as well be you."

I put my buff stick down. "That's actually . . . quite kind. I'm touched."

Deke scoffed. "Don't be. Like I said — purely selfish on our part." He belied his protests with a wink.

But I *was* touched. Moved in fact. It was one thing to be respected, but another thing entirely to be genuinely liked. And not for being best in mathematics or first in natural philosophy. I stepped out into the hall before I let the compliment go to my head. Or my eyes. I took a swipe at them with my sleeve. What was wrong with me these days?

That evening, I received a letter.

Deke quirked a brow. "Anything interesting?"

"Hmm?" It was from Lucinda. Her handwriting looked just the way she did: composed, elegant. Maybe Deacon was right. Maybe I shouldn't be so hasty in deciding not to see her again. Her uncle wouldn't have introduced us, wouldn't have let me

219

spend a Saturday with her, if he didn't think me worthy of her time. Although he assumed I'd be heading to the engineers. This plan of mine kept getting in the way of everything! "What's that?"

"Anything interesting?"

"It's from Lucinda. She wants to know, can I come to a dinner party at the Professor's on the sixth of October."

"Better you than me."

"And she wants me to bring my friends." I consulted the letter. " *'That nice Mr. Hollingsworth,'* she says."

He grunted. "Nice? I suppose I ought to get to work, then, on not being so conventionally dull."

"And she'd like me to invite several others if they wouldn't mind the favor of indulging her students."

"What students are those?"

"She's holding some sort of finishing school in the Falls."

"She's got character, looks, *and* accomplishments? Don't move too slow or someone's liable to flank you."

"Will you go?"

"To dinner?"

"It's better than staying on the reservation."

"And the food's got to be better than at

the mess hall. I'll make Dandy and Otter come too."

By Friday I was less prepared for my recitations than I ever had been before. What's more, it showed. I'd probably be moved down another section in my classes. And then I'd have to start all over again, forcing my instructors to dislike me, all but insisting they not give me the benefit of doubt.

Deke clapped me on the back as we left the academy building for the mess hall. Dandy joined us, and we caught up with Otter on the way in to dinner.

He grinned at me. "I heard some bad reports about you, General. Congratulations. That's the way to do it!"

"Listen, fellows. This not studying is not going to work."

Deacon didn't seem overly concerned. "No need to panic. I never said not to study."

"You most certainly did!" We sat down together at one of the long tables.

"Perhaps I did. But what I meant was, don't *only* study. If all you do is study, you don't have time to do other things."

"Which is exactly why I used to be at the top of my class! I didn't have time for foolishness."

"And you also didn't have time to get any demerits." He sent me a long glance. "There comes a time in any campaign when the days grow long and the injustices begin to chafe and a soldier starts to wonder if the war will ever be won."

I couldn't stop my eyes from rolling. "God save us from poetical men."

Dandy raised his fork in our direction. "Hear, hear."

"But" — Deacon had increased the volume of his voice and the gravity of his look — "may I remind you gentlemen that the war is won by *battles,* and not the battle by the war."

I had tired of his bluster. "That doesn't mean anything!"

"What I'm trying to say is, *buck up*!" He gave me a shove that nearly knocked me off my chair. "We didn't take you on so you can sit around like some gloomy Gus and complain about how you're failing. By failing, you're succeeding. By losing, you're winning. Don't you see? This is all part of the plan. You can't give up now."

"I'm just . . . I'm used to being looked up to." Somehow, I was shamed by those words.

"And that's the beauty of all of this. We're used to being looked down on. Now you're looking up to us and we're looking down on you. Change is good, don't you think?"

23

LUCINDA

I made the girls work hard at their lessons for three full weeks with the promise of a dinner party at the end. Seth graciously agreed to attend and to bring along three of his friends. I'd spent half my waking hours in the kitchen that first week of October, helping to prepare cakes and pies, the meats and other dishes, and now it was too late to do anything else. The girls had gathered, the men had arrived. For better or worse, my dinner party was under way.

Mr. Hollingsworth was regaling Milly with some sort of tale. Mr. Ames was listening in polite anguish to one of the girls who was trying to say something in French. Mr. Delagarde was . . . Where was he? I glanced about. There he was, sitting on the sofa talking to Phoebe. But he was pale as a . . . Was he ill?

Seth appeared at my elbow and saw me watching them. "I introduced him to Miss

Hammond. She can't see him, and I figured he'd scare all the other girls away."

I touched his arm. "Thank you. For this. For bringing them."

He smiled down into my eyes . . . and then reached out to cover my hand with his. When I looked up at him his gaze held a question.

"Lucinda!" At the sound of my aunt's voice, I quickly withdrew my hand and turned to see her nodding toward the clock. "It's time."

Phoebe was gesturing wildly in my general direction.

I walked over to her and took up her hand.

"Where did Mr. Delagarde go?"

I looked about for Dandy, but I didn't see him. "I don't know. He was just here, wasn't he?"

She sighed. "He probably left."

"Left? He can't have gone. I'm sure he'll be back in a moment."

"I don't think so. He's like me. He doesn't belong here."

I almost laughed, but I didn't want to hurt her feelings. "If you could see him, you'd know he's the one who belongs here the most. They call him Dandy. He's the perfect gentleman."

"Dandy?"

"It's what they call him."

"That can't be right. You must mean the other friend. Mr. Hollingsworth."

I was about to explain that his name was Deacon, but then thought the better of it. I didn't have time for Phoebe's musings. Later, in bed, I'd help her sort all the men out. But right now, I had to give my attention to my charges. "Mr. Hollingsworth is definitely not a dandy."

"Describe him to me. Describe Mr. Delagarde."

"Well he's . . . tall. Dark. Very handsome, but in a most intimidating sort of way. Everything about him is perfect. His posture. His uniform. His hair. Not one thing out of place."

"Don't you see? He's not a dandy. He's just afraid."

"Mr. Delagarde? Afraid? I'm sure he's not afraid of anything! There's something . . . something dangerous about him. A disdain that wafts from him. He makes other people afraid. Of *him.*"

She was shaking her head quite decidedly. "You couldn't think that if you would just hear him."

"I do." I had. The few times he'd spoken to me. "I've spoken with him several times."

"But you didn't *hear* him."

Sometimes Phoebe was just so maddening! I leaned down to take her hand in mine. "I'm sure he'll be just fine." As I glanced toward the center of the room I saw Milly whispering with one of the other girls. "Forgive me, but I have to go."

When I got to Milly, she tugged at my arm and leaned over to whisper into my ear.

I shook my head at her request.

But Milly stamped her foot and then stepped into the middle of the room. Folding her hands in front of her, she began to address us all. "Ladies and gentlemen. Thank you for coming to our dinner today. In the interest of furthering our finishing, don't you think it would be best if Miss Hammond tells us all what we ought to do as we go about doing it? That way we might keep from making mistakes in the first place."

I looped an arm through hers as a means to secure her person and in hopes of stopping her from saying anything else. "I'm quite satisfied with my instruction. I think you girls know everything there is to know about dining with guests."

Milly extracted herself from my arm. "I think if you depend on my remembering anything, you're liable to be mortified."

That was a threat if I'd ever heard one,

but before I could reply, my aunt gestured toward the dining room. The rest of us followed her lead.

She touched me on the elbow as she passed. "I don't think there would be any harm in it. I daresay we could all do with a reminder."

There was triumph in Milly's grin, and she quickly went to her friends, pointing toward the table as they conferred.

I decided to accept defeat gracefully. "The host is always first to the dining table, and he takes with him the lady who has the most status, which —" I might as well have been lecturing myself. None of the girls were in sight. "Girls?"

Seth and his friends stepped aside to let them pass.

"Girls!" I gestured Milly to my side and then took Phoebe by the hand and drew her close. "As I was saying, the host enters first and escorts the lady with the most status. It might be the oldest or it might be the one who has the higher position in society. For today, we'll have it be the elder Miss Hammond."

My uncle came and took up Phoebe's hand.

"Now then, the host always sits at the foot of the table, and —"

Milly interrupted. "How do you know which end that is?"

"The foot is at the bottom, opposite the head."

"They both look the same."

"I've always thought that myself." Otter might have thought he was whispering, but his voice carried, and one of my students began to giggle.

"But the foot is —" Taking in a deep breath, I smiled. "The foot is wherever your father sits. And generally he sits there." I gestured to his accustomed seat. "Uncle?"

He went to stand behind his chair.

"This being a more informal sort of meal, the lady he escorts, being first among the ladies, will have her choice of seats." I gestured to the chair next to her uncle. "The seat to the host's right, however, is always considered the seat of greatest honor. Now then, the hostess will come in last and the most senior gentleman will escort her."

Seth offered his arm to my aunt.

"And where do you think they will sit?" I asked the question of Milly, who didn't take long in answering.

"I should think she'd sit at the head of the table and he right beside her . . . if they could figure out where that is!"

If there weren't so many guests with us, I

might have wrung her neck. "The rest of us would then pair up and walk into the dining room in the middle of the procession. We would take our seats based upon where the host's partner has chosen to sit. If Miss Hammond prefers not to take the seat of honor at his right, then the next ranking lady may do so. That would be —"

"That would be you. Or my mother." Milly smiled as if she deserved a prize.

"So it would." I paired up the cadets and Bobby with the girls. My poor cousin was a bit too young yet to appreciate this opportunity. Perhaps I ought to have charged him with caring for Ella instead of leaving her in the kitchen with Susan. No use in dwelling on it now. "Generally speaking, married couples are not to sit together." I sent a look in Bobby and Milly's direction. He was furtively tugging at one of the ribbons that bound her braid. I moved to stand between them. "And probably not siblings either. And it's best if ladies alternate with the gentlemen. You see? It's all very simple."

By the time everyone stood behind a chair, due to the uneven numbers, Phoebe and Milly stood next to each other. Seth and I were next to each other as well.

"Gentlemen, please assist the lady to your

left in sitting. And now you may seat your-selves."

As they sat, all eyes were on me.

"You must not think, gentlemen, that this is the end of your duties. We will depend on you for conversation throughout the meal. You may speak with those beside you as well as those directly across the table from you. Please do your best to avoid unpleasant top-ics."

Milly piped up. "How do I know what's unpleasant?"

"That's a very good question. Even adults sometimes find it confounding. Politics, religion, and money are best avoided."

"So I could talk about baseball if I wanted to?"

"If a gentleman asks you about baseball, you may feel free to respond."

"Is Phoebe supposed to be the gentleman or am I?"

"At the moment, I have every expectation that you will both be ladies."

Milly's face fell. "Blast!"

Bobby laughed outright while the other girls giggled.

I felt quite in danger of exploding with frustration. Beneath the table, my hands were balled into fists. As I sat there trying to maintain my composure, Seth reached over and covered one of my hands with his own.

I glanced up at him, but he was looking down the table toward where my uncle sat. I turned my hand over and he grasped it, giving it a squeeze. "Please keep in mind that uncouth words are not appropriate at anytime, anywhere."

"That's why I was hoping to be a gentle-man."

Before I could respond, Seth came to my rescue. "Gentlemen don't use such words, Miss Hammond. And neither do soldiers."

Milly leaned back against the chair with a huff, but a glance from me made her scoot forward and sit up straight.

"Now then, let's enjoy our meal."

Seth withdrew his hand, but he leaned a bit closer, as if to adjust his silverware. "Stop worrying. You're doing just fine."

24
SETH

Lucinda's dinner party was a success. Her girls might have been new to etiquette, but they did everything they were supposed to and, probably more importantly, nothing that they shouldn't have. The fellows had enjoyed the food.

"Think you might be able to get us another invitation, General?" Otter was practically pleading as we walked back to the Point. "I haven't had a pie like that since furlough last summer."

"I wouldn't mind the chance to have ham again before graduation." Deke might shovel down his food at the mess hall, but that didn't mean he enjoyed it. None of us did.

"I'll see what I can do."

Even Dandy smiled at that.

But the good cheer didn't last long once Deke turned the topic to me. "I was thinking . . . this campaign to help Seth fail is going to be tougher than we expected."

Otter squinted in my direction. "How much tougher?"

"Looks like it's going to require the ultimate sacrifice."

Dandy's brow bent in annoyance. "The *ultimate* sacrifice? What's that?"

"I've come to the decision that we've got to take the long view on this." He slid a look in my direction. "In case you didn't realize, it takes quite a bit of work to become an Immortal."

I agreed. Much more effort than I'd ever thought.

"I know you've all been helping when you can. And I've seen some brilliant use of strategy, but we've come to the point where the last full measure of our devotion is going to be required. Who's with me?"

Otter didn't hesitate. "I'm in."

Dandy looked rather disgruntled at being required to sacrifice anything, but he declared himself committed as well. "So what's the plan?"

"We're going to have to start studying."

Shouts echoed and birds lifted from the trees as the fellows protested vociferously. Otter even got quite heated in his opposition. "I mean, I like you and all, General, but some things you just can't ask a man to do."

Deacon was trying to regain control of the conversation. "This is the last resort. I wouldn't ask it of you either if it weren't truly necessary. Here's the problem. No one's been willing to give out enough demerits. They're not taking any of this seriously. So if we can't get Seth to the bottom honestly, we're going to have to try and meet him halfway."

Dandy had been drinking from his flask, but now he screwed the top back on and hid it away in his coat. "Explain."

"If Seth can't get to the bottom on his own, then the bottom's got to rise enough to meet him. Understand?"

Otter seemed to be trying to take it all in. "So . . . what you're saying is we got to get better grades?"

"Exactly."

"Then you oughter told us that to begin with. I wouldn't have agreed to it."

Dandy sent me a dark look. "Me neither. No offense, General."

"None taken."

Deacon raised a hand as if to preempt any more dissent. "It's not going to be that hard, because I figure we've got our own personal tutor."

Otter looked around as if he was trying to identify that someone. "Really? Who's that?"

235

Deke grinned. "Seth."

They were still Immortals, so mostly the tutoring sessions took place as they were getting ready for inspection, or running down the halls to make it to parade on time. By the middle of the next week, I finally had to protest. "If you mean to learn, you need to put some time into it. And some concentrated effort."

Deacon lifted his head from the book I'd planted in front of his nose. "I agree."

"You do?"

"I do. So I've arranged for a session with all of us."

I wasn't a naturally suspicious person, but this seemed to be going entirely too well. "When?"

"Tonight. After call to quarters."

"*After* call to quarters? Where?"

"In Otter and Dandy's room. But make sure you're wearing your overcoat."

My overcoat?

I was there, as ordered, wearing my overcoat. But I couldn't make any sense of Deke's instructions. We had just had our rooms inspected, and lights were expected to be extinguished. It was too late to go anywhere. "Where is it we're going again?"

"*We're* going again. Apparently *you're* going for the first time."

There weren't too many places at the academy I'd never been. "Just tell me where."

"Benny Havens."

"No!"

Otter grabbed one of my arms and Dandy grabbed the other. Deacon followed along behind, talking all the while. "If you're going to make us study, then we're going to make you do it in a place amenable to our proclivities."

"You could get dismissed for being caught at Benny's. It's strictly off limits."

He opened the door, placing a finger in front of his lips. When he spoke again, it was in a whisper. "The only thing strict about it is Benny. I'm hoping he'll take two of my candles in exchange for some whiskey." He patted his coat, where I'm sure those two candles were stashed. "Benny's been good to us. And he knows a thing or two about mathematics and the like, although I get the feeling civil engineering is a bit beyond the bounds of his expertise."

We kept silent, to avoid the sentinels and tactical officer, as we tiptoed through the hall, down the stairs, and out the door. Then we hoofed it out across the Plain and made it to the hotel before we broke stride.

I didn't have a good feeling about any of it. "What will we do if we run into some officers?"

"We're not going to. And do you know why? They'll expect us to try to sneak out the gate. But we're going to take the path along the river."

Once we'd gone beyond Flirtation Walk, the path along the river wasn't truly a path. Unless you happened to be a goat. Beneath the nearly full moon, I couldn't see any sign that anyone had ever walked along the cliffs there, but from the way Deacon and the fellows skirted the rocks and pointed out the most dangerous spots, it was clear they'd done it a time or two.

It pinched at the dignity of a man to have to run away under cover of darkness to do something other fellows his age could do in the daylight. A normal man could have walked the road to Buttermilk Falls any time he wanted to. He could have stayed all day even, and no one would have blinked if he bought himself a drink or two or three.

The fellows had to pull me back from falling into the river several times before we left the cliffs for the forest. Deacon held out an arm as we approached what looked like a road. "Let's just take a listen for a minute."

We all cocked an ear in the direction of the academy and listened for a long while before he declared it safe. Perhaps it was, but still, I cast a furtive glance over my shoulder before I joined the others.

After jogging down the road for several hundred yards, the fellows turned quite abruptly toward the river and then seemed to throw themselves off the face of a cliff.

"Deke?" I hissed his name as I approached the point where they'd disappeared.

"Down here!" His words came drifting up to me.

I could see a set of stairs built into the rock. They zigzagged down the face of the cliff.

As I descended, a chimney seemed to rise to greet me. From it curled a finger of smoke that smelled of food such as I hadn't had since my last meal at the Hammonds. "Smells like —" I took another great whiff of it — "ham and bread and steak." The chimney belonged to a ramshackle-looking house that had been built right up against the cliff.

Deacon hopped back up several steps to take my arm and tug me down the stairs. "Sooner we get there, the safer we'll be. Don't want to be taken by ambush when we've almost reached our goal."

After sliding down the last of the steps, I followed the rest of them, ducking into the cottage. Inside was dark with very little moonlight filtering in through the single window, but a great fire was snapping in the hearth, spreading its orange glow about the room, which hosted a full crowd among its tables. As I glanced about I recognized many of the faces. Nearly half the cadets in my class were eating and drinking at Benny's. To my shame, there were some second classmen among them too. But I soon realized no one seemed to care that I was there.

Deacon took hold of my elbow and dragged me toward the back of the room, where a woman was stacking plates behind a sort of counter. "Mrs. Havens? This here is Seth Westcott."

She smiled and leaned forward to pat my cheek. "You poor, dear boy." The look in her eye, the great sympathy in her voice, let me know she understood everything, every single day I'd spent at the Point.

I swallowed hard to keep an errant sob from leaping to my throat. Why hadn't I come here before?

Sitting at a table, a bowl of soup in front of me, and a warming fire behind me, I had to think this was a foretaste of heaven. Beside me, Deacon drew a sheaf of papers from one sleeve and a pencil from another. "Gather round, fellows."

Otter and Dandy both took another drink from their mugs and leaned in close.

Deacon cast a glance around the room before he continued in a low voice. "You don't have to be too obvious about it, but I think what we'd most like to work on is constitutional law."

"What?" In that place of sustenance and good cheer, talk of law and military tactics had very nearly become anathema. "Now? You want to talk about classwork *here*?"

"You going to help us or not?"

"I'll help you. Just . . . let me enjoy this while it's hot, will you?"

Deacon started on a cigar while Dandy worked his way through the tables toward the counter for another drink.

Once I'd finished, Otter stacked the mugs and dishes while I went to work explaining the concepts, writing them down. "Understand now?"

Deacon was nodding, but Dandy had long since lost interest, more intent on the conversation of a couple of cadets from Mississippi than he was on the lesson. Otter was staring at the piece of paper as if hop-

241

ing it might turn into something else. "No. That is . . . you'd think folks oughter just do what's right. Most folks want to — even those in Washington. But if the laws are this dad-blamed hard to understand, how are they going to do it?"

I sighed as I tried to think of a different way to explain things.

He eyed Deke. "I just don't know if this is going to work."

If truth be told, I didn't think it was going to work either. I was afraid I'd be stranded in the middle of the class, unwelcomed by the engineers, yet too far from the bottom to do myself any good. And what would become of me then?

25
LUCINDA

My aunt and my students' mothers were so pleased with the dinner party that they had begun touting me as a graduate of one of the West's finest finishing schools, an expert on society and good manners. A genius at French and a fine hand at embroidery. My father couldn't have done a better job campaigning for one of his schemes, and in spite of my protests, I soon had three more students for my thrice-weekly classes.

Perhaps I was earning money honestly, but a voice inside my head kept reminding me that I was a cheat and a fraud. If the town's good citizens knew who I really was, they would keep their children far from me, in hopes that they would never learn any of the lessons that I could best teach. If I was a genius at anything, it was lying through my teeth, getting out of paying boarding school fees, manipulating people to get my way, and profiting from the poor decisions of others.

It was true, perhaps, that I knew more about polite society than anyone else in Buttermilk Falls, but who was I to teach anyone how to behave? How to conform to society's expectations? I had defied, even gleefully broken, every convention of polite company. I was a sham. A sham who was succeeding brilliantly in making a new life for herself, but a sham nonetheless. Even when I was trying to be good, I was bad.

I cringed whenever I entered the doors of the church. I tried hard not to listen at night when my uncle read to the family from the Bible. The talk of love and mercy was so far from the life in which I'd been raised that it seemed fantastical. Irrelevant, even. It was no wonder my father found such ready takers in his schemes among church people. It was easy to believe in love and forgiveness when no one had ever harmed you. I had no doubt that, should my past become known, no one would offer to forgive my sins.

The problem with spending too much time thinking about God was that it led to other, even more troubling thoughts. By mid-October, I finally had no other choice than to believe that God himself was the ultimate fraud. The consummate hoaxer, promising kindness and grace and instead doling out death and punishment and pain.

Phoebe heard me sighing over those thoughts one afternoon as we waited for my students to come.

"What is it, cousin?"

I shook my head and waved off her inquiries, forgetting once again that she couldn't see me.

"You sound as if the cares of the world are weighing upon you."

That was one way to put it. Phoebe was my proof — the surefire evidence of my crusade against God. And as I looked at her, it made me quite angry. How could she be so . . . so . . . *accepting* about what had happened to her? "If God loves us, and if He truly does intend good things for us, as everyone here seems to think, did you ever wonder why He let you have that accident?"

"*Let* me?"

"He must have known of it, since He knows everything. At least that's what everyone says."

Lucinda seemed to pause to think, her sightless gaze drifting toward the right. "I suppose He must have, or He wouldn't be God, would He?"

I hated to snatch away a belief that seemed so foundational to her and everyone else in town, but wasn't I doing her a favor? "If He did, then why did He let it happen? I don't mean to speak ill of Him or to make you think less of Him, but it seems a cruel thing to do to a young girl."

"I don't know that He had much to do with it. I was the one who chose to disobey Papa. I was the one who snuck out of the house that morning. I've always been more inclined to thank Him for my life than to curse Him for my blindness."

I could have shaken her! But what had I expected? It was so difficult to make people see the truth once they bought into a scheme. That's how Father had been able to make all his money.

Phoebe cocked her head. "You don't like my answer?"

"I don't understand your answer."

"God isn't some amulet or charm to be used to avoid life and its consequences."

"But if He loved us the way people around here insist —"

"Since He loves us — and I believe that He does — He promises to be with us. I suppose I might have railed on about how things might have been so much better all these years if I had my sight, but I find myself thinking so often of how they might have been much worse. I've been blessed, don't you see?" She smiled. Then she laughed. "I supposed that's just it, isn't it? I *don't* see. And you don't see how much there is to see."

How could she be so flippant, so dismissive of her tragedy? "You don't mind, then? Is that what you're saying?"

"I mind as much as anyone. I mind *more* than anyone. I hear you all go on about your lives around me and I can never really take part. I'll never be married. Or have children. Or . . . choose my own gowns or bake anyone a pie. But I've never thought that makes me any less loved by God."

"My father would have said you were unlucky."

"Luck?" She frowned, brows drawing together. "I don't think luck had anything to do with it. I would much rather believe in love, wouldn't you?"

Would I? As I sat there next to her, gazing at all the things she would never see, I pondered her words. Would I rather believe in love rather than luck? Neither luck nor love were within my control. They were both things that simply happened. So either I believed that luck was somehow dispensed regardless of person or merit or that love was dispensed in the same way.

If I believed in luck, I would think every

man had to watch out for himself. If I believed in love, if I could imagine that there was a God who loved us no matter what we had or had not done, that would mean love came to us regardless of whether or not we recognized it. Wouldn't it be nice if God was watching out for me? And for Phoebe and my aunt and my uncle, all at the same time? That if something happened for my benefit, it didn't mean it was taken away from theirs?

I slipped my hand into Phoebe's and rested my head on her shoulder. "I still don't understand. I don't know that I ever will. But I think . . . I'm almost certain . . . that I want to believe in love as well."

She smiled.

She might not have done so, however, if she had seen the tears coursing down my cheeks. I did want to believe in love. But how could I, when I'd been so bad?

26
SETH

On the last Thursday in October, Deacon tromped into our room and tossed his hat onto his bed. "The commandant's called for a parade with swords, instead of arms, this evening."

I nodded. I'd heard.

"So you'll give him what he's asked for."

"I was planning on it."

"You'll do anything in order to catch that crook who cheated your sister, won't you?"

"Just about."

"Will you or won't you?"

"Of course I will."

"Good. Just so we're understood. I've got to go down the hall and talk to the others about this first, but we'll figure out the details and tell you all about it later."

I wasn't sure I liked being treated as their project, but a good officer knows when to trust the talents of his staff.

■ ■ ■ ■

"So you understand, then?" Deacon was standing by the wall that evening, just before dress parade, elbow propped on the bookshelf, looking me over.

"I understand all right." I was starting to understand that the fellows weren't quite so talented as I'd thought.

Otter frowned at me. "Hadn't you oughter just button up that first button, right there . . ." He was pointing to the top button on his coat.

My fingers were itching to do that very thing, but I knew that if I didn't approach the matter philosophically, I wouldn't be able to go through with it at all. "I hardly think it matters."

He tilted his head as he looked at me. "I suppose not."

The tattoo of drums and the call of bugles drifted in through the open window.

Deacon walked over and stuck his head out. "Would you look at that!"

I looked out to where Deacon had nodded. There, at the edge of the Plain, a crowd of onlookers had gathered. In the summer, excursion boats came up the river from New York City and dropped the tourists off at

Cozzen's Landing. They toured the academy grounds, watching us drill and ride at the stables as if we were steers up for auction. The biggest draw was always the sunset parade. At night, afterward, the boats anchored just off the landing to listen to the army band. There were always a few tourists about, no matter the time of year, but I wouldn't have expected such a large crowd at the end of October. The fine weather must have drawn them up the river. "Maybe I ought to go back and put my —"

Deke put a hand to my shoulder. "Can't back out now. All this will just make it better."

"Better for whom?"

"Worse. I mean worse. It'll be better for you because it will be worse. You haven't fallen as many files as we'd hoped, so you need to make a grand gesture. That's what we all decided earlier. You know all this. If you can humiliate the commandant, especially in front of a crowd, you're bound to get a really good number of demerits." He glanced off toward the Plain again as he straightened the hem of his coat. "You ready?"

I nodded.

Leaving the barracks at a run, I fell into formation along with the rest, at the front of my company. To the sound of their snickers, I marched us out, away from the barracks and onto the Plain.

I thought I heard a gasp and maybe a shriek.

I couldn't help but glance in that direction. My cheeks, which had been flush with embarrassment, now went hot with shame.

None of the cadets said anything, no change registered in the tempo of our marching, but I felt the entire company wince just the same.

"Company halt."

We halted.

"Mr. Westcott!" The commandant barked my name.

I stepped out of formation and marched to him.

"Explain yourself!"

I tried to act as nonchalant as Deacon or as insolent as Dandy, but a sweat broke out behind my ears as I considered how to respond. It was hard to maintain a sense of dignity in my underclothes as the long tails of my unbuttoned undershirt were flapping in the breeze and the ties of my drawers had come undone around my ankles. "We were told to report to the parade with swords, sir."

"To which parade, a cadet is generally

intelligent enough to add a coat, trousers, and proper shoes!"

I glanced toward the stockings that covered my feet.

"Do you think this is funny, sir?"

Somewhere behind me in the lines, someone snickered.

"No, sir. Just trying to follow orders, sir."

"Then report to the superintendent's office directly so you can explain yourself to him."

Before I spun on my heel to do just that, I couldn't help but steal one last glance at the crowd. I wished I hadn't. Because standing front and center were Professor Hammond and Lucinda.

27
LUCINDA

I blinked, unwilling to believe my eyes. Standing before us, in his drawers and nightshirt, was Seth Westcott. Seth! The man I'd come to respect. The man I relied upon. The man I was . . . was I coming to love him?

His cheeks were flushed, his shoulders hunched, his gaze downcast. Why had he done such a thing?

I wasn't the only one to gasp at his antics. My uncle *tsk*ed. And the woman standing beside us even shrieked.

It was a long walk back to Buttermilk Falls, and I had to ask my uncle twice if he might slow his pace. "I'm sorry, my dear. It's just that I had such high hopes for Mr. Westcott. And he behaved with such . . . crassness. Frankly, he reminded me of your father at his very worst. I'm afraid I was much mistaken regarding his worth. It's very . . . extremely . . . disappointing to have been so wrong about him."

If my uncle had been wrong about him, I had too. But I couldn't figure out why, couldn't figure out how, I'd misjudged him.

"I'm afraid I have to forbid you to have anything more to do with him."

"I wouldn't *want* anything more to do with him." Listen to me. I sounded positively respectable! But mostly I was angry. I'd welcomed Seth's protection that first night in town. Relished it even! I'd gone hiking with him. I'd looked forward to seeing him every Sunday at supper. And now it looked as if he was nothing more than a rogue.

"I'm glad to hear it." He peered at me, lips pursed. "Mr. Westcott was going to take you to Fort Putnam this Saturday, wasn't he?"

I nodded.

"I'll invite Mr. Conklin to take you instead."

After Milly, Phoebe, and Ella had gone upstairs that evening, my uncle sat at his desk, cheek propped against a fist as he glared at the fireplace.

My aunt sent Bobby upstairs and walked over to my uncle, pushing a lock of hair back from his face.

He looked up at her as if startled from his thoughts, and then he straightened, taking her hand in his own.

"What is it?"

"One of my cadets. You know him. Mr. Westcott. He's joined us often for supper. But this semester, he just seems . . ." He looked up into her face and shook his head. "It's almost as if he's bent on his own destruction. I can't explain his actions any other way."

"You've known cadets like that before."

"I know cadets like that now. But they're different. They've been that way since their first day at the Point. And they're clever about it. If they gave the same attention to their studies, they'd be among the best in their class. But this one . . ."

My aunt bent to kiss his forehead.

"This cadet . . . I had great hopes for him. I just don't understand. Of all the men in his class, I would have put my money on Seth Westcott. Sometimes, you just know. The good ones just have something . . . something *more.* I can't understand why he's trying so hard to be less."

I had expected that Phoebe would already be in bed when I went upstairs, but she wasn't. She was sitting on the bed. As I

256

walked in, her face turned toward the door. "What happened at the parade?"

Should I tell her? Probably not. "It was very nice. Very . . . military."

She came as close to a pout as I'd ever seen her come. "I know *something* happened. Mama and Papa only ever whisper when they're saying something they don't want me to hear, but I can hear better than they think I can. Something happened to Mr. Westcott, didn't it?"

"Not . . . not exactly."

She tried to give me a look of disapprobation. She gave it to the chest of drawers instead. "Cousin! Tell me."

"He, um . . . Nothing happened *to* him."

She raised a brow.

"It's just that he did something. Or rather, he didn't do something."

Now she was frowning.

"He didn't get dressed for the parade."

"He came out in the wrong uniform?"

"He . . . came out in no uniform at all."

She gasped. "Mr. *Westcott* did that?"

I nodded before I remembered she couldn't see me. "He did."

"But why?"

"I don't know. Neither does your father. It really . . . Your father was very . . ." He was hurt by it. He seemed to take it quite personally. "He was more than disappointed. He seemed offended."

"As am I."

"You? You didn't even see it."

"But I know him. He's come for Sunday supper so many times. And I would never have expected something like that of him."

"Perhaps . . . maybe it was just a prank."

"A prank?" Her brows peaked as she discounted the idea. "He has a sense of humor, but he's not crass. That sounds like someone else entirely."

"I wouldn't have thought it of him either. Not if I hadn't seen it myself."

"He wasn't . . . he wasn't laughing, was he?"

"No. He looked humiliated. He looked . . . as if he would rather have been anywhere but on the field."

She nodded, as if confirming something to herself. "Mr. Westcott has always taken great pains to put us all at ease. Me especially. He always speaks to me whenever he comes. About real things. As if he's interested in my opinions. So I can't think him capable of doing something that would embarrass anyone."

"But he did."

"I wonder why." She puzzled over the thought as she undressed and climbed into bed. I did the same and then extinguished the lamp. "What on earth would make him want to be bad, cousin?"

"I've no idea."

"Well . . . when would *you* wish to do the wrong thing?"

Me? I wished to do the wrong thing almost all the time. What's more, I usually did it! Maybe the better question would be, When would I try to be good? That answer wasn't difficult to come by. I'd try to be good when it was in my own best interest, when I could use it to my advantage. But what possible interest could Seth Westcott have in turning bad?

28
SETH

The superintendent, Colonel Lee, was not pleased. He didn't even put me at ease. So I stood there, in front of his desk, holding a salute. There had to be an easier way to fail, didn't there? One that didn't require humiliating myself in front of the entire corps of cadets, my professors, *and* Lucinda?

"I've had my eye on you for quite some time now."

"Yes, sir."

"I'd always considered you to be one of the finest young men at the academy."

"Yes, sir."

He gave me a long look, which communicated quite clearly his distinct displeasure with my behavior. "At ease."

I shifted my left foot outward and fixed my hands at the small of my back.

"Sometimes things happen, Mr. Westcott. Things that can be quite overwhelming and disheartening. But if the academy teaches cadets anything, it teaches how to over-come."

"Yes, sir."

"Would you like to tell me what happened to change my top cadet into a ne'er-do-well?"

"No, sir."

"I'm asking as a concerned citizen, as an admirer of sorts, not as your superinten-dent."

I wished I could tell him. I truly did. But it was too late. He hadn't helped when it would have made a difference, when I'd requested leave to see to my mother's death and my sister's safety. If I wanted help, I was going to have to find it myself.

"You may speak frankly."

"Frankly, sir, I wish I could, but I can't." Nobody liked a complainer. I'd rather he discounted me as an Immortal than think me a malcontent.

The compassion that had relaxed his features and warmed his eyes evaporated. "So this is just a cadet prank?"

"Yes, sir." I had to steel myself in order to look him in the eyes as I said it.

"It was in remarkably poor taste. Some-thing no gentleman would ever think of do-ing. You understand I have no choice but to punish you."

"Yes, sir."

"I'm giving you three demerits for reporting for parade in the wrong uniform. And five demerits for behavior unbecoming a member of the corps of cadets."

Eight demerits? Deacon wouldn't believe it when I told him. Maybe the plan was going to work after all.

There was a knock on the door, and an orderly entered.

The colonel nodded at me. "You're dismissed."

On my way out of the building, Campbell Conklin came up the stairs toward me. His lips were crimped in a smirk.

I wished I could have knocked it off his face. "On your way to reporting another plebe?"

"None of your business." He passed me by without another glance.

"What's it for this time? Boots not polished to your satisfaction? Books not in the right order?"

He stopped and turned around to face me. "Irregularities have to be nipped in the bud before those plebes become first classmen who walk around in their underclothes."

What could I say in reply?

"I'll never understand why a smart man

262

like you would fraternize with those Immortals."

"Maybe because they're kind and decent. And they'd never stab a man in the back just to see if their knife is sharp enough."

He smiled. "Maybe not. But reporting to parade in your drawers won't get you in good with Professor Hammond's niece either." He squinted off toward the river. "I'm betting a man could see clear to Peekskill from Fort Putnam on Saturday. Too bad you won't be with her."

I stalked back to the barracks and drew Professor Mahan's text on tactics from the shelf before I remembered I wasn't supposed to be studying. Closing the book, I shoved it back onto the shelf. I went to take up the broom but reminded myself another demerit or two for not cleaning our quarters wouldn't hurt my cause. I ended up stranded in the middle of the floor, trying to figure out what to do with myself.

No wonder the Immortals got themselves into so much trouble. Not studying freed up a whole lot of time.

I glanced over at Deacon, who was sketching in that book of his. "What are you thinking about with that smile on your face? You look like the tomcat who found a bottle of cream."

"Mandy."

"What?"

"Amanda de Carondelet."

"Who's she?"

He simply smiled.

I took the sketchbook from him and flipped through the pages. It bothered me that so many of the girls in his sketches had bared shoulders that faded into the white of the page. It was all respectably done, and I wouldn't want to accuse Deacon of anything tawdry, but . . . "Don't any of those belles of yours own a gown with sleeves?"

He barked a laugh as he took it back from me. "Wouldn't you like to know?" He lifted a brow. "Thing is, I always think it a shame to have to bother with clothes when the essence of a woman is in her face."

I reached over and closed up his sketchbook for him. "Don't let Campbell Conklin catch you with that. He's on a tear."

"He wouldn't know a girl to look at one. He'd be more likely to criticize me for the way I hold my pencil than for drawing pictures of girls."

On consideration, I couldn't say I disagreed.

"What about your girl?" He smiled.

"I don't have a girl."

"Miss Hammond, I believe her name is."

"She's Conklin's Miss Hammond now."

He sat up with a frown. "When did that happen?"

"About the same time I appeared for parade nearly naked this evening. Don't you remember that? I do. Because Professor Hammond showed up. And his niece too."

"Well, now. Don't people in hell want ice in their water! Sometimes in war there are casualties."

"I didn't mean for them —"

"And if your sterling reputation has to suffer for the year, I'm sure it will all be worth it to see that swindler thrown in jail. I hope you don't make a habit of being so morose. I'll not often be willing to give speeches on spirit and resolve. Makes me feel as if I should care about such things."

I barely refrained from saluting.

He picked himself up off the bed. "I'm going down the hall to Otter and Dandy's. When you're done feeling sorry for yourself, you can come join us." He tucked his sketchbook back behind his headboard, and with a flash of his grin, he was gone.

29
LUCINDA

When my uncle came back from the academy on Friday evening, he handed me two messages. The first was from Seth Westcott, regretting that he was unable to escort me to Fort Putnam on Saturday as we had planned. The message was brief, the tone terse, the effect much more of a blow than I would have expected.

My aunt was watching me. "Are you all right?"

I forced myself to smile. "I'm fine. Thank you."

It was the first message I'd ever received from Seth, and it would probably be my last. I swallowed down the lump in my throat.

My uncle picked up his pipe and asked Bobby to recount the day's schoolwork as I opened the second message.

It was from Mr. Conklin. He wondered if I might be available to join him for a walk on Saturday. My uncle had thought him a worthy substitute, but his invitation just made me feel worse about everything.

When my aunt asked me for help in the kitchen, I placed the letters on my uncle's desk, intending to take them upstairs after supper. My aunt handed me a plate of bread and called out for Milly to see to the butter. Out in the dining room, I set the plate on the table without much thought. I was halfway back to the kitchen when I realized what I'd done.

Leaving the bread in front of Bobby's place would ensure that no one else had the chance to eat any. Retracing my steps, I slid it farther down the table, toward my aunt's seat.

Seth wouldn't be coming for dinner anymore.

My heart ached at the thought.

Mr. Conklin had been present at our Sunday suppers just as often as Seth had. Though Mr. Conklin could ably direct a conversation, though he was undeniably handsome and polite to a fault, Seth's quiet presence, his self-effacing smile, his genuine kindness were what I looked forward to most on Sunday afternoon. I would not have missed Mr. Conklin were he ever to be absent. But just the thought of Seth's not

being there made me feel lonely. Abandoned.

Milly and I set the table as my aunt and
Susan readied the food for serving.

"Aren't the forks to go on the left side?"

I blinked. "What's that?"

Milly was holding up a fork. "You told us
they're to go on the left."

"That's right. Forks on the left. Knives
and spoons on the right."

She looked pointedly at my side of the
table where I'd placed all the forks on the
right.

What was wrong with me? I hastily
changed all the silverware around.

I supposed . . . Mr. Conklin was pleasant
company, but he always spoke of his position, his grades, and his illustrious family.
But maybe pride was actually a virtue. The
academy seemed to think so. They'd made
him a cadet officer. Perhaps what seemed
like arrogance was simply competence.

As I waited for the family to assemble
around the table, I tried my best to warm
to the thought of Mr. Conklin. But in spite
of everything I had seen at the parade, in
spite of Mr. Conklin offering himself as the
perfect replacement, I couldn't force myself
to be pleased with the substitution.

It used to be that my personal opinions

268

about a man didn't matter, just so long as he could be useful. My father used to say, *"If the first plan doesn't work, then just start right in on the next one. No need to sulk, if the result is the same in the end."* I had been assiduously trained by him to ignore my heart when it conflicted with what really mattered. Since I'd come to Buttermilk Falls, I was having trouble remembering all the lessons he'd taught me.

I took the last serving dish from Susan and found a place for it on the table.

Whether I convinced Seth to marry me or Mr. Conklin to marry me, the result would be the same in the end, wouldn't it? I'd be married. So why couldn't I simply adapt to changing circumstances the way I'd always done?

Why?

Because it made me angry.

I helped Ella into her seat and placed her napkin in her lap.

I was angry Seth wasn't the man I thought he was. Angry that he had left us all with Mr. Conklin, who didn't have half of Seth's worth. And that made me wonder if I'd been wrong, once more, about everything. Maybe in this world where selflessness was a virtue and people truly cared for each other, my intuition had misled me.

I slipped into my chair and pulled my own napkin down to my lap.

Maybe my instincts had been calibrated to the wrong standard. Maybe they didn't work here. Perhaps the man whose interest I ought to have been pursuing all along was Mr. Conklin. If I could take the gleam in his eye as a sign, he was willing to court me. I ought to have been pleased; his family's connections could do nothing but assure my future.

It galled me to no end that I was wasting this much time, evidencing this much heartache, over a man who couldn't bother to dress himself!

I bowed my head along with the others while my uncle prayed over the meal.

A man like Mr. Conklin who cared for nothing but his own interests was entirely predictable and easily managed. I'd been brought up by such a man; I'd done the bidding of such a man. If I could give him what he wanted, then I would get what I wanted as well. Taking care of him would be the same as taking care of me.

Love didn't have to come into it.

It was simply a matter of expediency.

I'd been hoping, eventually, for a proposal from Seth, but I recognized now that those hopes were unrealistic. Wealth was what I'd been raised to pursue. When I met Seth, I was sidetracked by thoughts of love, so maybe this was all for the best.

I helped myself to potatoes when they came to me and then passed the bowl along.

Love was heartache.

Happiness was wealth and power and a tour of Europe.

All I had to do was remember my goal and stick with my plan.

I helped myself to meat and turnips and bread.

I could learn to overlook Mr. Conklin's pomposity and tendency to promote himself at every opportunity . . . couldn't I?

I could. I would force myself to.

But my feelings made me wonder if I would always be drawn to scoundrels and rogues. Was it in my blood, passed down to me by my mother? Maybe I was doomed to repeat her tragic past. Why else would my heart prefer Seth Westcott to Campbell Conklin?

I brought my napkin to my lips, crooking a finger to hide a treacherous tear.

Why should I be so overwrought about a wayward cadet? I would just have to keep trusting my uncle to guide me. He'd been respectable for his whole life, so his instincts were entirely trustworthy . . . unlike my own.

But was not one forearmed when forewarned?

As long as I recognized a tendency in myself toward ruination, then could I not compensate for it? If only I could marry myself to Mr. Conklin immediately! Then I could keep my faithless heart from wandering. Feelings didn't really matter, did they? And in my case, weren't they liable to lead me astray?

"And how was your day, Lucinda?" My uncle was smiling at me from the end of the table.

"My day?" I blinked. Smiled. "My day was fine. Just fine."

30
SETH

Friday evening, as I walked down the hall with my bucket, intending to get some water, Campbell Conklin hailed me.

There was nothing to do but stop to talk to him.

"This is providential!" His lip curled into what passed for a smile. "I have the great pleasure to inform you that you've been demoted."

"What?"

"You've been demoted."

He really had said what I'd thought he had. "Demoted? To what?"

"To nothing. Cadet officers are appointed by merit, if you'll remember. And you, sir, have none. Not anymore. I think we'd all agree on that, the way you've been earning demerits by the handful . . . and with that crude display of yourself at parade." He held out his hand toward me.

"What do you want me to do? Shake it?"

His smile widened into a grin. "I need your coats. All of them."

"All my . . . ?"

"They've got captain's chevrons on them and you're nothing but a regular first class-man now, a private."

Maybe I should have expected it, but I couldn't have been more astonished if the academy had been attacked. "But . . . who's going to be first captain?"

"Me."

By Saturday morning, I needed some time to myself. Some space to remember who I was and what I was doing. I meant to climb up to Fort Putnam, but I'd heard Campbell Conklin tell it around that he was walking out with Lucinda that afternoon. I'd seen the shock, the horror, the betrayal in her eyes at the parade. I didn't want to risk see-ing them again. So I took a walk in the direction of the hotel and, farther beyond it, to the river.

Some of the fellows preferred to go hunt-ing or hiking for their recreation, but I'd gotten into the habit of finding a perch somewhere to enjoy the scenery. When I was first captain everyone had always wanted something from me. Answers, assignments, approbation. I'd taken to savoring the few hours I had to myself and preferred to spend them alone.

Looking out over the river and its valley helped me put everything in perspective. The river swept along, reminding me that one day I too would leave these banks behind. In spite of autumn's chill, I unbuttoned my coat, took it off, and rolled it up. Then I lay down on the bluff, using my coat as a pillow. Looking up past the trees' bared branches, I stared up into a stark, blue sky that had been scoured raw by October's winds.

Though Deacon's plan appeared to be working, it sure made me feel like some kind of a fool. I rolled over onto an elbow, reached out to take hold of a rock, and threw it toward the river just to see how far it would go.

I'd never forget the look of disapproval in Professor Hammond's eyes or his stern warning for me to stay away from Lucinda. He knew I was better than that. What I couldn't decide is whether it would make me feel better or worse to let him know why I'd done it. Even if I did tell him, there was nothing he could do about the swindle. He'd probably advise me to just let the whole incident go. And then he'd pity me — the parentless son whose sister had been duped by some trickster.

Best not to tell him . . . or anyone else.

I heard the sounds of someone scuffing through the grasses. Probably a tourist. In that case, it wouldn't do any good to hide. I sat up, shook my coat out, and pulled it back on. I'd be darned if I buttoned it up, though. Glancing back toward the hotel, I saw a flash of blue bob in and out of view. Maybe a tip of my cap and a nod would be enough for the intruder to leave me to my solitude.

But the face that emerged wasn't a tourist's.

It was Lucinda Hammond's. Those golden-green eyes of hers widened, and the flush on her face deepened. "Oh! I'm sorry. I was just waiting for —" She cast a glance back over her shoulder as if tempted to turn around and go back to the hotel.

I stood, as any gentleman would have done in the presence of a lady.

She looked up at me for just a moment, and then her gaze traveled out across the river to Constitution Island, skimming across its trees to rest on the shore beyond. Her breath caught as her eyes lost their suspicion and filled with wonder. "I never stopped being amazed by the beauty here. I should think I could see clear down to . . ."

"On a day like this? You can probably see five, ten miles." I stepped closer so I could share her view and pointed off behind us toward the mountain peaks. "Might even be able to see out toward the city from up there." I moved away from her, squatting to lean against a tree trunk. It's not as if I needed to impress her. Not anymore. No one who had observed me lately could fail to think that I was the poor excuse of a cadet that I was trying so hard to be. I took a drink from my canteen and held it up to her. "Want some?"

She gave me a wary look. "What is it?"

I almost laughed at her reticence. Had I really fallen so far? "Water."

"Oh. Then . . . please." She took a sip. And then a second one.

I offered her a handkerchief, and she used it to dab at her lips.

"Thank you." She returned the canteen and the handkerchief, all prim and proper about it.

"How's Campbell?"

She blinked. "Fine. I was to meet him at the hotel. I should probably . . ." She nodded back in the direction she'd come. "I should probably go back."

"I suppose he's taking you down to Flirtation Walk."

She raised a brow. "I suppose it's no business of yours where I'm going with him."

"Just . . . be careful. He's not what he seems."

"Unlike you, he seems to be able to dress himself of a morning."

I felt my face flush and shoved that handkerchief back into my coat.

"I'm sorry. That wasn't kind. But . . . I thought you were different than that, Seth Westcott. I thought you were more."

She couldn't have hurt me worse if she'd tried.

"And Campbell Conklin is a perfect example of an officer and a gentleman. . . ."

Was she hoping I'd disagree? She sure looked like it. Sure sounded like it. But there was no point in caring anymore. I took another swig from my canteen and then jammed the top back onto it. "He might be one of those, but I promise you he isn't both."

Her face closed up, and she looked alone, in the same way she had in the Hammonds' dining room that first night I'd met her.

I stood. "I'm sorry. I wasn't being mannerly. You can go where you want, do what you want." What else could I say? What did I have to offer her? The fervent hope that I could sink my standing far enough that the army would have no choice but to assign me to the cavalry? What sort of life would that be for a lady like her? "Just . . . be careful. A lady like you deserves honor and respect."

A hand flew to her throat, and she clenched her fingers round the strings of her bonnet. "I just was hoping . . . you see . . . I'd wanted . . ." Her hand reached out toward me but I forced myself not to take it. "So that's it, then?"

I said nothing.

"Good-bye, Seth." Avoiding my gaze, she stepped away and headed back toward the hotel.

31
LUCINDA

My encounter with Seth Westcott had rattled me. Catching sight of Mr. Conklin, I blinked away tears as I determined to be everything I wasn't.

He was watching my approach, arms folded across his chest. "I had meant for you to wait for me."

I smiled. "I didn't really go anywhere. I thought the river must be just down there, on the other side of the bluff. I couldn't help taking a look."

"We'll see enough of the river where we're going." He crooked an arm, though he made no move to close the distance between us.

I did it for him. As I slipped my hand around his arm he flexed it, securing me to his side, drawing me close.

We strolled past the hotel and down toward the river, just to the right of where Seth Westcott was probably still sitting on the bank, watching the clouds scud by.

The path was as treacherous as I remembered, steep and slippery. There was quite a bit of handholding involved in order to ensure my safe passage along it. The trees that formed a tunnel for the path had now shed their leaves and were standing, branches bared, much like Seth Westcott. But why should I care about him? He was nothing but a buffoon. A clown.

To take my mind off Seth, I determined to engage Mr. Conklin in conversation. "Is this what they call Flirtation Walk?"

He smiled and covered my hand with his own. "What if it is? Is it such a terrible thing to want to flirt with you?"

I couldn't quite summon a blush, but I diverted my gaze. "I'm very flattered."

"*I'm* very flattered. It's not every day that I get to step out with a pretty girl like you." His hand tightened around mine.

It wouldn't do to have him think me quickly won. *"Too easily won, too easily parted."* I swayed away from him as a rock jutted up between us on the path. "You probably say that to all the girls."

"I won't say I haven't walked here before, but I've seen lots of girls, and I don't mind telling you that it's true. You're very pretty." He stopped with an abruptness that spun

281

me back toward him. Then he dropped his hands to my elbows, pulling me close. "Do you know what they say about that rock up ahead?"

I glanced over my shoulder down the trail to see that rocky outcrop with the ledge that jutted out over the path.

"I have no idea."

"If a cadet attempts to pass beneath it without first being kissed, legend says that it will crumble and fall on him."

Seth had never mentioned that. We'd walked right beneath and he hadn't said a thing.

"I swear to you, it's true."

"That would be a very great shame."

He made a show of looking at the rock and then looking back at me. "The greater shame would be to cut our walk short. The best views of the river await us on the other side."

I blinked wide, trying for levity, though my heart wasn't truly in it. But that had never bothered me before. Why did it feel so much like betrayal now? "You're willing to risk life and limb for my benefit? Are all cadets as brave as you?"

A corner of his mouth curved up into a smile. "I was hoping I wouldn't have to risk my life."

"Are you asking me to save you?" My father always said *"You have to make a man say what it is that he wants. Until then he's not committed — he's just hoping."*

His smile took its time as it spread across his lips. "I think you'll find it's worth the effort."

Mr. Conklin certainly knew what he wanted, and he didn't waste any time going after it. Madame Mercier would have said he was treating me with too much liberty. After a kiss like that, my father would have told me to encourage him even more. But I meant to have him respectably, with an engagement ring to seal the agreement, so dealing with Campbell Conklin required a defter hand than I was used to employing.

I took his hand in mine and drew away from him slowly, tugging him along the path with me. And then I gave a cry. Collapsing into him, I made a show of wincing.

"What is it?"

"I think . . . I might have turned my ankle. Perhaps — is there somewhere we could sit? For just a moment?" I'm sure it was already known that we had wandered down to Flirtation Walk, but if we had to cut short our walk, it could do nothing but preserve his interest.

He clasped me rather more tightly than

283

was necessary as he helped me along, but I can't say the sensation was unpleasant. He was strong. And efficient. Should I place myself in his hands, I daresay my life would be entirely taken care of. It was not an unpleasant thought.

"Would you like to go back?"

I glanced up at him and then let my gaze fall away. "No."

His chest puffed as if it had suddenly expanded two sizes.

I frowned. Just the tiniest bit. "But I don't think my ankle will allow me to proceed."

He crooked his arm for me. "I would offer to carry you, but your shoes might mark my trousers." He wasn't making an apology.

I didn't blame him. "I understand." I did. Truly. Maintaining appearances was the most important of things.

He looped an arm about my waist, and I leaned against him as we picked our way back down the path.

"I'll be graduating in June. After that, I hope I'll be assigned to the Corps of Engineers."

"And what do engineers do?"

"Everything worth doing. With my family's connections, I'm hoping they'll see me as a likely candidate for further study in Europe. Or as an attaché, perhaps."

I murmured, in French, that I hoped all would go well for him.

He blinked.

Perhaps I'd miscalculated. "Don't you speak the language? I thought you all studied French."

"We do. So we can learn about Napoleon's strategies. We mostly read it; we don't speak it." He was looking at me as if I'd done something untoward. "The only one who actually speaks it is Dandy Delagarde, but he's from New Orleans."

"That's practically the only phrase I know." It wasn't true, of course, but it wouldn't do to give him a reason to think less of me.

Phoebe was keen to know about my afternoon, pestering me from her perch on the sofa in the sitting room before I even had the chance to remove my bonnet. From the sound of the pots banging about, I guessed my aunt to be in the kitchen with Susan. Milly must have been upstairs with Ella, otherwise they both would have been underfoot. I placed my bonnet on the hallstand and settled myself beside Phoebe.

"Tell me everything. I've only ever heard Mr. Conklin when he comes here to supper, so I'm sure I must have a false impression of him. Tell me what he's like."

What was he like? "He's . . . what you'd imagine the finest cadet to be. A bit taller than most." Though not so tall as Seth Westcott. Not that it mattered in the least. "Quite trim. He holds himself with some gravity. He's very . . . dignified. Quite respectable."

"Is he affable? When he's not trying to impress Papa?"

"He is."

"Is he fair?"

"He's rather dark, in fact." Seth was the fair one.

"Brown-eyed?"

Was he? "I can't say that I recall."

"I should think that's the first thing I would notice about a person."

I should think so too. Deacon's eyes were brown. My aunt's eyes were hazel. Seth Westcott's were blue. "I'll tell you what color they are next time I see him. I suppose that will be for dinner tomorrow."

Her brow furrowed as she thought about my words. "Is he kind? I haven't been able to tell. He never talks much to me."

Kind? I wouldn't have used the word *kind* to describe him. "He's quite the gentleman. He looks like a cadet should. All straight lines and stiff motions."

She nodded, a smile softening her lips. "I remember. I remember how all those cadets look in their uniforms."

"He's quite smart. At the top of his class. Did I tell you that already?"

"*He's* told me. Every time he comes over. It's practically the only thing he ever says to me."

"I haven't spent that much time with him, you know — just a dance or two — and then this afternoon . . ."

"But what about Seth Westcott?"

"You know your father doesn't approve of him. If he keeps going as he is, your father says he might break my own father's record in amassing demerits. So you see why he can't be considered a suitable prospect."

"Why is that again?"

"Because he's just like my father! And I will not be like my mother. I'm not going to run away with some disreputable man."

She held her hand out toward me, and I put mine into it. She squeezed my hand. "I think you just have to make sure you're looking for the right things."

"Exactly. Which is why respectability has to triumph over" — over whatever else Seth had that Campbell didn't — "anything else." The important thing is that I was starting over, and this time I was going to do everything right. I was going to link my destiny to the right man . . . even if he didn't happen to make my heart flutter the way Seth did.

We passed the remainder of the afternoon in what my father might have called pleasant tedium. For supper we had what was left from dinner. When Phoebe decided to go to bed rather earlier than usual, I followed right behind her. I would have beat her into bed too, but for all the pins in my hair.

I had just found a comfortable position on my pillow and was drifting toward sleep when Phoebe rolled over and plucked at my sleeve.

"What is it like to kiss a man?"

I was glad she couldn't see the blush that stained my cheeks.

"You have . . . haven't you?"

I fisted the corner of my pillow in my hand. "I don't know why you'd think that."

"It's something about the way you speak of men." She rolled onto her back. "I don't think Mama kissed anyone . . . not before Papa. But you have, haven't you?"

How had she guessed? I said nothing. Perhaps if I didn't move, she'd think I'd fallen asleep.

"Haven't you? I'm not wrong, am I?"

I sighed and rolled to face her.

"Please. You must tell me. I'm not likely ever to be kissed, and who knows how long you'll be here —"

"I'm not planning to go any—"

"I've heard Mama and Papa talking. They plan that you'll marry. So if you don't tell me, nobody will."

Why did she have to be so kind? And innocent?

"Lucinda?"

I knew that if I didn't tell her, she'd just keep pestering me until I did. "Kissing is . . ." I faltered, thankful that those blue eyes of hers weren't really peering down into my soul. "Kissing is like anything else. The quality of the experience depends upon whom you do it with."

She was silent for quite some time before she moved. Then she patted the air next to my arm, searching for me.

I took her hand in mine.

She squeezed it. "I'm so sorry."

Speaking of kissing made me feel more like a fallen woman than I had when I'd pretended to be one. "Sorry for what?"

"I'm sorry you haven't ever kissed anyone worthwhile."

So was I. I leaned over and kissed her on the cheek. "There. I just did." She smiled, and I couldn't help but smile in return. "Now, then. You mustn't tell anyone."

"I'm flattered that you think I would. But really, cousin, who do I ever talk to but you?"

Her words pinched my heart, and I blinked hard to keep tears from my eyes, tried even harder to keep them from my voice. "Just goes to show how lucky I am, counting you among —" I meant to say *friends,* but I didn't really have any except for her. I never had.

"We're friends, aren't we?" She squeezed my hand.

"Of course we are."

"I'm so glad." She rolled back to face the wall then, and before long she was breathing the long, deep breaths of peaceful sleep.

Somehow Phoebe managed to pull the oddest confessions from me. I couldn't account for it. She didn't ever plead with me for anything; she didn't beg me to do her bidding. I could find no guile in her words, nor in her motives. But somehow she made me tell her things I'd never told anyone. Not even my father.

She saw more . . . I smiled at the thought. She *sensed* more than anyone I'd ever met. Why then, hadn't she discerned any hint of my past? Why had she not perceived the desperation with which I'd come to Buttermilk Falls?

I supposed it didn't matter. My hope was that she would never know. That she might always think of me as her dear cousin, her friend. But that was foolish. Who knew what demands tomorrow might make of me and when it would be more advantageous for me to go than to stay? It was dangerous to become more attached to her than I should.

"Ties were meant to be broken." That's what my father always said.

For the first time that I could remember, recalling his words didn't fill my heart with warmth. They just made me . . . sad.

32
SETH

My next week, the first in November, was hard fought, without even one victory at its end. If an instructor were to have looked solely at the results of my recitations, they might have thought me unsuited to life in general. Failing all my classes surely made me feel that way. But at least I hadn't partaken in much misconduct. On Saturday, I had the afternoon free once again. The fellows convinced me to go with them to Fort Putnam.

As we indulged in a forbidden game of cards, once again Lucinda managed to find me.

"Oh! I'm sorry. I was walking up here with Mr. Conklin. He had to go back for just a minute . . . There was a cadet . . ."

I couldn't help snorting as I rearranged my cards. "And the poor fellow was probably doing something wrong that Mr. Conklin felt obliged to report."

Lucinda didn't reply, but she didn't have to. The only thing Campbell Conklin liked more than courting a pretty girl was reporting on a fellow cadet. He'd gotten worse since he'd become first captain.

Deacon took the cigar from his mouth and waved it as if to excuse us all. "You'll have to forgive us, Miss Hammond. I know cards aren't a gentleman's pastime, but we've been gentlemen all week and we'd hoped for a bit of a respite."

Otter had folded his hand and tossed his cards into the middle of our circle. Dandy was trying to hide a flask in the sleeve of the coat he'd discarded.

She smiled in a way that made my heart turn over. Curse that Mr. Pennyworth. If it weren't for him I might have been able to declare my intentions. Feigning disinterest, I tried to ignore the sensation.

Sighing, she sent the cards what I might have thought was a look of longing. "I don't suppose any of you know of the game *vingt-et-un*?"

Otter cocked his head. "Can't say I've ever heard of it."

"My late father taught it to me."

Deacon gestured to a tumbled stone that was a good height for sitting upon. "Then why don't you show us how to play?"

She was wearing a dress that looked like milk froth topped with a dollop of cream, so I stripped off my coat and placed it atop the stone so she wouldn't ruin her skirts. Just because I was forbidden to continue courting her didn't mean I couldn't still be a gentleman.

Deke was already dealing cards. "How many?"

"Just one each. And then hand me the rest and I'll play dealer. The goal is to total your cards as close to twenty-one as you can without going over. Aces count as one."

"Sounds simple enough."

"What were you gentlemen playing for?"

Deacon chomped down on his cigar. If the playing of cards was forbidden, then gambling at cards was strictly outlawed. "What were we . . . ?"

Otter swallowed. "We . . . uh . . ."

Dandy's dark eyes were sparking with amusement.

"We're playing for the simple pleasure of it." I said it in a way that dared any of them to say anything different.

Otter sighed and then fessed up. "I oughter say that we *were* playing for sips from Dandy's last bottle of whiskey . . ."

She nodded. "You might as well all keep playing for sips, then."

Otter's grin was overcome by a frown. "But what about you?"

She smiled. "I'll just play for the pleasure of your company."

We played several hands, one of which she won. It was Dandy's turn to deal when Campbell Conklin came puffing over the top of the crumbling wall. "I'm sorry, Miss Hammond. I didn't mean to leave you alone for so long. Are you — ?"

In the heat of the game, I guess we'd forgotten all about him.

Lucinda's eyes went wide as she dropped her cards. Dandy's hand snaked out to cover the neck of the bottle that was stashed behind him. Deacon hadn't been quick enough to toss his cigar or his cards. But he didn't have anything to worry about because Conklin had fixed his ire on me. "Fancy seeing you here like this, Mr. Westcott. Out of uniform. Playing cards. Smoking."

"I wasn't smoking." I hated cigars.

"What do you think the commandant will say when I tell him the same cadet who showed up to parade in his drawers has also been caught out of uniform, playing cards? He might assume you were trying to get yourself dismissed. And you know what? I think he might just oblige you."

He might. If there had been any mark on

Conklin's record, any suggestion of him ever having bent the rules, then this would have been the time to mention them. But Campbell Conklin was one of the few who took great pleasure in doing everything exactly right . . . and even more pleasure in rubbing everyone else's face in it. There was nothing I could say, no room to even maneuver.

I stood, and in doing so I stepped a bit closer to him than was comfortable. I had a couple inches on him, and unless he took a step or two back, I knew he'd have to look up at me.

He fell back.

I held my hands up, palms out. "You caught me."

Beside me, Lucinda also came to her feet, stepping in front of me. She put a hand to Conklin's chest and turned, cozying up to him.

His hand dropped to her waist in a proprietary gesture. I knew I'd never have the right to dance with her, to touch her again, and I hated him for it.

She glanced up at him from beneath her bonnet. "I was the one who asked them to play."

"*You* did?"

"My father used to play a game called

vingt-et-un with me. You know he died this past summer, and I just . . ." She sighed a long, heartfelt sigh.

He let his hand drop from her waist, but he didn't step away from her side. "Cards aren't allowed at the Point. Just the fact that they have them is grounds for dismissal."

"I suppose I should probably take them with me then. I would hate for them to be a temptation to these gentlemen."

Deacon threw his cards atop the others and then hastily gathered them up and handed them to her. "Take good care of these, Miss Hammond. Some of the cadets round here are so starved for cards, you might find them prone to go missing."

Campbell's eyes looked as if they might pop right out of his head. "Those are *your* cards?"

She drew away from him as if surprised. "You ask that as if you're not convinced that I'm a lady!"

"I didn't mean —"

"Playing cards is all the rage in France." She turned her attention to us. "I didn't mean to get you gentlemen into trouble." She dropped the cards into her reticule and wound her arm around Campbell's. "They aren't in trouble, are they?"

Old Conklin couldn't seem to decide.

She bent and picked up my coat, offering it to me. "I can't thank you enough for saving my skirts from the dirt." She turned to Campbell, who was growing red in the face. "I know it's probably a grave offense for him to be seen without his coat, but with this dress being so wholly unsuited to a place like this . . ."

"It's not usually —"

"Isn't there some kind of medal to give cadets like these? When they've so kindly used their own free time to humor a girl like me while I was waiting for you?"

Deacon had stood, and now he was wringing his hands, though I could see laughter in his eyes. "We didn't figure it would be polite to insist that we couldn't play cards when she was so set on showing us what her Pa had taught her. And seeing as how he'd just died and all . . ."

"Yes, well . . ."

Lucinda took a few steps toward the edge of the drop-off. "I can't think how I got all the way up here on my own. It's quite far, isn't it? You were gone for such a long time, I suppose I'd better go back down or my uncle will wonder what's become of me." She turned to wave at us. "Farewell. Thank you for entertaining me. You'll have to show me your medals once you get them."

Campbell was spluttering as they started down the trail. We could hear them both as they left. "They give us all a bad name —"

"For what?" Lucinda's voice was all innocence.

"For . . . being out of uniform and —"

"They weren't out of uniform when I came upon them."

Maybe not. But we had been playing cards.

Dandy was already passing around the whiskey.

Deacon was effusive. "She was a brick. Saved our hides is what she did!"

Otter was grinning. "Mother sure would have smiled to see her. She always says a girl oughter have spunk if she has nothing else."

They were acting as if she'd won some kind of contest. "Hold on now, we still might get some demerits."

Dandy was eyeing me. "I don't think so. And she didn't waste any time jumping in front of you. She didn't have to do that. Especially not in front of old Conklin. If it was me, I think I'd find a way to thank her."

That was the thing of it. She hadn't had to do any of that, and yet she had. Why? "Don't sing her praises too quickly. She did take your cards, Deke."

"Dadgumit! She did, didn't she? So what are we going to do for the rest of the afternoon?"

I had an idea. "This is the perfect time for all of you to study."

Otter's face fell. "You just had to go and ruin Saturday afternoon, didn't you?"

Dandy jammed the top back on the whiskey with the flat of his palm. "We're all here, so you might as well tell us what we need to know."

"Which subject?"

The fellows looked at each other for a long moment. "Tactics."

I must have explained some of the principles in Jomini's *The Art of War* for over an hour, drawing diagrams in the dirt and answering the same question about offensive warfare over and over again. Finally there wasn't much more I could tell them. "Did you follow?"

Deacon nodded.

I looked over at Otter, who had just spit onto his shoe and then knelt to rub the toe of it to a shine. "Otter? How about you?"

"Well now . . . I was just thinking how in war, generally laws are disregarded . . . ? I mean, someone must be breaking the law if there's a war — right?"

"Right."

"I just don't understand why we got to study constitutional and international law if all we expect people to do is break them. I mean, hadn't we oughter —"

Deacon cut in. "Maybe . . . think about it this way: we study tactics for fighting and law for when the fighting's over."

"I think . . . maybe . . ." A sort of wonderment swept over his face, and he grinned. "It's just like when Mother —"

Deacon jabbed me in the ribs. "She knows something about everything, doesn't she."

On my other side, Otter was nodding. "She's really smart that way."

Heaven help us all. "Dandy? How about you?"

"I got it. And I appreciate all you said. So do me a favor and listen to what *I* said."

"About what?"

"About that Miss Hammond. You ought to find a way to thank her."

33
LUCINDA

The walk back down the hill had been pleasant if brisk. Mr. Conklin spent some time regaling me with stories of his illustrious ancestors, one of whom had been stationed, during the revolution, inside Fort Putnam's walls. At one point we paused to enjoy the views of the river. If he'd gotten rather close when he'd done so, I couldn't say it was disagreeable. The quickest way to help along a scheme like this was to flirt with a man. And after all this time, I could flirt without even half trying.

Mostly, he'd been a proper gentleman. He'd had to take my hand to assist me when the path became too steep, and in my opinion, he'd kept hold of it when he didn't really need to, so in that sense, things appeared to be progressing. But when I'd dropped my handkerchief, instead of keeping it as I offered, he had returned it with a bow, insisting that having it discovered in his possession would be in violation of the rules. I ought to have been glad, because I didn't have enough handkerchiefs to be quite so free with them, but somehow, the whole exchange had left me feeling peevish.

When I tried to coax him into forgetting his complaints about Seth and his friends, he began to lecture. "They try to make you feel sorry for them, but they deserve the demerits they get. They've earned them. If they're stupid enough to break the rules, they deserve to be caught — don't you think?"

He didn't have any idea who he was talking to. It was difficult to resist the impulse to laugh. "Perhaps they just don't care."

"How could they not care?" He took my words as an offense, though he lent me his hand to aid me down the path.

I had to start choosing my words more carefully when I was with him.

"I'm doing them a favor. If they don't learn how to obey rules now, how are they going to become good officers?"

How indeed? I picked my way around rocks and took care as I sidestepped down breaks in the path that had been made by cascading rivulets of rain.

"Could be, I'll end up commanding some of them one day. Why not whip them into

303

shape now and spare myself the trouble later?"

I nodded, glad to have firmly entrenched myself on his side of law and order.

"Although I wouldn't want them to reform too quickly. Some of them are quite smart. I can't be too careful. Especially in drawing. Professor Weir thinks I'm too mechanical, and I'll never be as good as Deacon Hollingsworth."

"Deacon's good at drawing?"

"He's brilliant."

"Truly? I didn't think he cared about his studies." I hadn't thought any of them did.

"He cares just enough not to be dismissed. Drawing is his one talent . . . along with the knack for hanging on by the skin of his teeth."

He did have the way of a rogue about him. I hid my smile, letting Mr. Conklin pass me by and then pausing to take a look at the valley. It truly was magnificent.

"If they were really ready to be officers, they would care about their uniforms and the damage that card playing might do to their reputations."

"Do you think we might stop for a moment? It's so beautiful up here."

He squinted up at me. "Better not. I'd hate to be late for supper."

Once back within the cadet area, many of the cadets saluted Mr. Conklin. Some also avoided him, if I was reading their actions correctly, ducking behind corners, or changing directions entirely.

He was feared, perhaps, but he did not appear to be liked.

But of what importance was people liking him when there was clearly respect? Being a man of merit didn't require the admiration of others. It required being worthy of honor. And if anyone was worthy of honor and accolades it was Campbell Conklin. With him, life would be mine for the making. The smart course of action was to link my life with someone who was going places. Someone who could take me along with him. Compassion wasn't required for that. There was plenty of compassion in my aunt's house, but that house was also located in humble Buttermilk Falls. My uncle might be a respectable man, but he was still just a professor.

My father had trained me for more than that. He'd trained me for a life of luxury and self-indulgence. *And his self-indulgence too,* a little voice inside my head declared.

Perhaps. But that didn't mean I couldn't appreciate merit where I found it. A man like Campbell needed to marry someone.

Why shouldn't that someone be me?

Mr. Conklin wasn't late. As a matter of fact, we reached the academy grounds about half an hour early. When I asked him to escort me to my uncle's office, he pointed out the building and excused himself by reason of having to consult with the commandant.

By that time, Seth Westcott and his friends had followed us down the hill. I made a point of ignoring him, but it quite quickly became apparent that we were both headed for the academy building.

With his long legs, he swiftly caught up with me and then matched his stride to mine. As I walked up the steps to the building, he dashed in front of me and held the door open.

"Thank you."

"Lucinda, I —"

"I'm not allowed to speak to you." Although I had, up there on that mountain. "Not in public in any case." And especially not when we were approaching my uncle's office.

"I just wanted to thank you. For what you did up there."

"I didn't do anything. Mr. Conklin just seemed to me to be a bit zealous in his pursuit of order and propriety. It didn't seem quite fair. That's all."

"I wish things could be different, Lucinda."

I wished they could be too. "Why can't they be?" I stepped closer so my voice wouldn't carry. "Why don't you care anymore, Seth?"

"Any*more*? Who says I ever cared at all?"

He wasn't very good at lying. I wanted to put my hand to his cheek and tell him everything was going to be all right. "My uncle."

"What does he know about anything?" The words would have sounded more defiant if they hadn't been mumbled.

"He told me you were one of the finest cadets he'd ever had the pleasure to teach." I took hold of his arm. "I want to believe that you're still the same man I met that evening in August. The man I've come to respect and admire. What happened to you?"

"Nothing you can help with."

"He's worried about you."

"That's very gratifying, but if he ever asks, you can tell him not to waste his time." He shrugged my hand off, wheeled around, and stalked back down the hall.

34
SETH

I was supposed to be not studying that night, but how could a man be expected to just sit by and do nothing when the girl of his dreams was being courted by a fellow like Campbell Conklin? And Deacon seemed glad to help me recount all the ways in which Campbell Conklin was a grind. "If she can't see Conklin for what he is, that's not my fault, is it?"

"No."

"And if she's too stubborn to admit that he's arrogant and pompous, that's not my fault either, is it?"

He sketched something with a swirl of his pencil. "No."

"And if she couldn't see what the rest of us did, up there at Fort Put, it's not up to me to explain it to her, is it?"

"No." He held his drawing at arm's length for a moment before taking it back to work on.

"Then why can't she just stay out of my way?"

"She's probably wondering why you can't seem to stay out of hers."

"Whose side are you on?"

"Yours. And hers." Putting a thumb to the page, he smudged his pencil lines.

"I thought you were my friend."

"I am your friend. I'm just saying that it's hard to take you seriously when you report to parade in your drawers."

"I'll have you remember that was your brilliant idea, not mine!"

"It was. It was brilliant. Best idea I've had in all the years I've been here!"

"You aren't helping."

"But I am helping. That's what we're all trying to do. We're trying to help you."

"Then tell me why it is I care too much about old Conklin and his girl."

"Because she ought to be *your* girl — that's why! Now, I like her as much as anybody —" He broke off when I glared at him. "Not as much as you, of course, but I think she's real nice. And smart. And if I'm not mistaken, she's going to open her eyes soon and see the same Campbell Conklin the rest of us do."

"None of the girls ever see the same Conklin the rest of us do. And haven't you ever wondered why that is?"

"Because some girls care more about dash than they do about substance."

"He's not that dashing."

"But he's got the scent of money on him. For some girls, that's better than cologne."

I grunted. "If that's why she wants him, then she's not worth my time. Or effort."

"I think you're in for a surprise. And soon."

I wasn't planning on holding my breath.

But I could have. The surprises came sooner than even Deacon had expected.

On Monday, I got put down two sections in International Law. And in Civil Engineering, I got put down one.

My former engineering instructor hadn't asked to have a word with me in private. He didn't plead with me to make more of an effort. He didn't even appeal to my honor or sense of integrity, didn't say anything about hoping to see me again soon. He simply bid me farewell and opened the door so that I could show myself to the next section down.

That's when it hit me: They truly thought I was a delinquent. My hands began to shake. A chill ran down my spine. It had happened. They believed me. I'd finally become the kind of cadet I'd been pretending so hard to be. I braced myself against the wall as I nodded at the cadet who was coming up from my new section to take my place in the old one.

I wouldn't be able to make it back from here. Not if the tide of opinion had truly turned against me. I hoped Deacon was right, that this really was the only choice. Otherwise, I'd ruined my grades, I'd given up Lucinda, and disappointed my professors for nothing.

After closing my eyes and sending up a prayer, I walked into my new section. I hadn't been with some of those fellows since the summer before my plebe year when we took entrance examinations together.

I shook hands all around before class started. The section marcher announced the results of the morning's roll call. The instructor glanced up from his desk and called five of us to the board. "Mr. Westcott. Welcome. I've been expecting you."

That night, as Deacon was drinking from his flask, I asked him something I'd never asked him before. "Let me have a drink of that, will you?"

His eyes blinked wide. "Why?"

"I got pushed down a section today in

engineering. And two in law."

"Congratulations."

"Thanks." I held out a hand for his flask.

He shook his head. "I don't think you should be drinking."

"On today, of all days, you don't want me to drink? You always ask me if I want to."

"Because I know you don't. I was just being friendly."

"I need a drink." I could practically taste it. I needed to taste it. I needed to turn myself into the shambling wreck of a man everyone else had decided I was.

"You don't need a drink. You just need to quit feeling sorry for yourself."

"You aren't feeling sorry for me. Someone has to."

"Otter got another letter from his mother. Why don't you head down there and see if he'll read it to you."

"I don't want to hear about his mother."

"I drew another girl in my book." He held it up so I could see. "Want to take a look at it? All I need now is Venus."

"I don't care about your girls."

"Well, that's a shame."

"All I ever cared about was school. And my grades and class standing. And now they're gone. I can't ever get them back. Everything's ruined."

"Well, that's a hill of beans if I've ever heard one. You might have ruined your grades, but you've always cared about justice and decency and everything that's good and right. Failing might have bruised your self-respect, but you've still got your honor, man!"

"I don't. I don't have anything."

"You do, or I'm not Deacon Hollingsworth. Nobody can give you honor — just like they can't take it from you. That's why we all hate Campbell Conklin. You've got to carry honor around inside of you. If you can't find it there, you're never going to find it anywhere else."

"Well, I don't have any left, and that's the truth."

"If you think that, if you're trying to find sympathy at the bottom of a bottle, then I can't help you anymore." He threw the flask at me.

I had to dodge so it wouldn't hit me.

"Drink all you want."

35
LUCINDA

Between teaching my students and helping my aunt, the second week of November was upon me before I knew it. During my childhood, my father would always take us to a city for the winter . . . or at least to a respectably-sized town. He presented us as a family, bereft of a wife and mother, that was hoping to settle in for some time. Insinuating himself into the leadership of the community, he became well-respected. Well enough that, come spring, we were always able to abscond with a small fortune donated by those very same citizens. When the air chilled and frost visited of a night, I usually got restless, ready to move on to the city.

But not this year.

This year, I was anticipating nothing but more of the same people, the same place, the same routine I'd had since I'd come. I'd even come to appreciate my chores. There was a joy I hadn't expected in the finishing of things.

Perhaps that's why I let myself be talked into preparing Milly for her first hop. She was a clever girl, and I'd come to understand that any deviation from those things I taught her was not from a lack of understanding but rather from a lack of motivation to employ them.

She and Phoebe were all whispers and laughter that second Saturday of the month. Phoebe brushed out her sister's hair while I concerned myself with the fall of her skirts. Though I attempted to persuade Milly's hair into ringlets, true to character, her locks refused to be coaxed, no matter what I tried. I finally just smoothed her hair over her ears and drew it into a bun, securing some ribbons at her crown. I stepped away, toward the back of the bedroom, tilting the hand mirror so she could see herself.

She clapped her hands in delight. "You should see me, Phoebe! How I wish you could. You'd never guess I've just turned fifteen. I look sixteen, at least."

In her golden yellow gown and pleated sleeves, with blue velvet ribbon at her waist and neck, she did indeed look lovely. The mischievous glint in her eyes was somehow softened by her long neck and slim, white arms. If she could just manage not to roll her shoulders, to stand up straight, she would look downright regal. In just a few years' time, those laughing eyes of hers could cause many a man to prostrate himself at her feet. Hopefully she'd get herself betrothed and then safely wed before she realized the true extent of her charms.

When we set off, my uncle handed us into the wagon and fixed a quilt about us. Milly began to chatter, but her father promptly hushed her. "There will be noise enough at the dance. No need to have to hear it before then."

She obeyed with good grace, though she fidgeted quite enough to make me take her hands in my own. "A lady never gives in to a fit of anxiety."

"Right now, I don't feel much like a lady. What I feel like is . . . quite a bit like Ella."

I smiled as I put an arm around her.

"Everyone's going to expect me to remember all those things you taught us, aren't they?"

"You'll do just fine."

"But what if I don't? What if I can't? What if I don't want to go anymore?"

My uncle answered. "It's too late to turn around now."

We arrived under a waxing moon. The

silvery rays softened the angles of the buildings and bathed the carriages and waiting horses in light. With the sound of the band and the windows glowing with candlelight, the scene was wholly enchanting. Milly's mouth dropped open as her father helped her down. Her eyes reflected the candlelight with wonder.

I grabbed up her hand and pulled her along. "Welcome to your first hop."

My uncle offered us both an arm, and we all walked up the stairs together. Just inside the door, we handed our mantles to a man in uniform. I pulled Milly aside to adjust her skirts and the ribbons in her hair. By that time, curiosity had overcome her trepidation, and she was all but climbing over me in order to see into the ballroom.

"I didn't realize there were so many cadets!"

"You'll have no lack of dancing partners. Just try to remember all that I've taught —"

"I will. I do. At least I think I do. . . ."

"If you're worried, I —"

"I'm not worried. Oh, look. There's Mr. Westcott!" She stepped out in front of me and waved as if she were trying to flag down a stagecoach.

I took hold of her arm and pulled it down.

"A lady does not wave down an acquaintance as if signaling a carriage."

"Then how does she do it?"

"She either begs an introduction from a mutual acquaintance —"

"I already know him."

"*Or* she waits until he looks in her direction, and then she may nod."

"Oh, look! He's looking!" Her arm shot out once more before I could stop it. I grabbed hold of her other one and turned her around. "Perhaps you don't know this, or maybe you don't remember, but Mr. Westcott is no longer an approved guest in your father's house."

"Why not?"

"Because he's not." I wish my uncle would have told her about the parade. At the moment he was engaged in conversation with one of his fellow instructors.

"But he's the best cadet at the Point!"

"Not any longer."

"Then who is?"

"Mr. Conklin."

She pulled a face. "Why?"

"Because he engaged in inappropriate behavior."

"Mr. *Westcott* did? Are you sure?"

I nodded.

Curiosity peaked her brow. "What did he do?"

There was no way I could demand her compliance without telling her why, so I leaned close and whispered into her ear.

"He did? I would have liked to have seen it!"

She was incorrigible. "The point being that you are not to recognize him."

"How can I not recognize him? It's not as if he's wearing a disguise."

I was going to throttle her. "You're to pretend that you don't know him."

"He's not pretending as if he doesn't know you."

I was well aware that he had not stopped looking in my direction since we'd entered the ballroom. "Be that as it may, I need you to do as I, and your father, request."

She scowled. "Fine. I'll try. But I'm warning you — I might forget."

I tried to be good, to take the advice I'd given Milly. I really did. But I couldn't keep myself from glancing across the room to where Seth stood with his friends. When our eyes met, I looked away. Feeling as if I ought to instead be searching for Mr. Conklin, I swept the room for his familiar form. There he was, at the far end of the room, standing alone, staring at his cup of punch with a sour look on his face.

I can't spend the rest of my life with him. I won't.

The thought had come uninvited, but that didn't make it any less true. I didn't like him. As a person or as a man. And here, on my own, there was no one to make me seek his attentions. My father didn't figure in to decisions like this anymore. My uncle was a kind man; my aunt had a generous heart. If I were to tell them I just didn't wish to marry anyone, then . . . that wouldn't exactly be true. I *did* wish to marry someone, I just didn't want that someone to be Mr. Conklin. But if I made my wishes plain, then I was almost certain they wouldn't push me into it.

For the first time since that awful parade, I felt as if I could breathe again.

I wasn't going to marry Mr. Conklin.

I wouldn't marry Mr. Conklin.

My eyes strayed back to the man I preferred. The man I admired. The one who was regarding me quite miserably.

What about Seth?

Maybe . . . maybe my instincts *were* right. Maybe Seth really was the truer, nobler man. And if he was, I needed to know why he'd done what he had. Not that I was a shining example of what any woman should be, but I'd put my past behind me. He could too, if that's what he wanted. But I needed to know why he was so set, all of a sudden, on becoming the worst example for a cadet that there could be.

It didn't make sense.

My uncle was still engaged in conversation. Milly was whispering over in the corner with some other girls from Buttermilk Falls. I decided to speak to Seth. Although I would be expressly violating my uncle's wishes, could I not be forgiven if Seth could give me an explanation for his behavior?

Sending one last glance in my uncle's direction, I crossed the floor toward Seth.

His eyes widened as he saw me coming. Handing his cup to Mr. Hollingsworth, he bent to say something to him and then came toward me. "Lucinda! If I had thought you would agree to a dance, I would have asked you for one. Do you —"

I took hold of his hand and pulled him toward the door. "There's no time!" Once I tugged him outside, down the steps, beyond the reach of the ballroom's light, I turned and put a hand to his arm.

His own hand dropped to cup my elbow, drawing me closer.

"My uncle has forbidden me to talk to you, but I want to ask you one last time. I know he would welcome you back to the house if you would just tell us why you're trying so hard to be someone you're not. Please. Tell me."

36
SETH

"Why, Seth?" Lucinda's voice was low. Insistent, pleading. It felt as if a weight had been lifted from my heart. She knew me. She believed in me. She understood I was not the man I'd been pretending to be. "Whatever it is, I'll understand. I promise you I will. And I won't think any less of you."

"It's rather complicated . . ."

I wanted to tell her, I really did. I just . . . I didn't quite know how.

She let go of my arm and my hand fell from her elbow.

I wanted to take her hand back, to hold on to it, but I didn't have any right to do that.

"I've never told anyone this before, but my father was not a good man." She glanced away. Swallowed. When she looked back up at me it was with resignation and guilt. "And I'm not . . . I'm not a very good person either, Seth." She'd tipped her chin down, as if in shame.

But whatever her father had done wasn't her responsibility. I put a finger to her chin and lifted it so I could look into her eyes. "He's dead now. He's gone. Whatever happened, it's not your fault, Lucinda."

Moonlight glinted off the tears that had pooled in her eyes. She glanced off toward the hall where the dance was taking place. "But Seth, that's what I want to tell you. I want you to know the truth. I want you to know that whatever it is that's making you this way, you can tell me. I'll understand because my father —"

Making her relive her father's mistakes wouldn't make me feel any better, so I stopped her from talking by taking her hands in mine and threading my fingers through hers.

She looked from our hands up toward me. "Seth . . . ?"

"This summer my mother died."

"I know she did. You told me." She took a step closer to me.

"That left my sister, Elizabeth, alone on our farm."

"I remember."

"I asked the commandant and the super-intendent for leave so that I could go out and settle things. So I could take Elizabeth to stay with relatives until I could come get her after graduation. But my request was denied."

"How could they! That's . . . that's inhuman!"

I tightened my grip on her hands so she wouldn't drop mine and move away. "This isn't a regular university; it's the army. As long as I'm in the army, it will always be like this." I was trying my best to tell her what army life was like. Trying to warn her away, if truth be told. "My sister had to sell the farm. Sell the livestock. She did it all herself."

Her eyes searched mine. "She must be very brave."

"She is. But while she was preparing to leave, her money — our money — was stolen."

"You mean . . . you mean all of it?"

"Everything. That's why she's stranded at Fort Laramie until I can go get her. And that's why I had to do it. You've heard your uncle. If I'm assigned to the engineers, I'll be shipped off to England as soon as I graduate. I wouldn't have the chance to go get her."

"Surely you could still send money to her.

Engage someone to take her from Fort Lara-mie."

"But I wouldn't be able to track down the man who did it. That's why I had to find a way to lower my grades and make it to the bottom of my class. If I can force the army to assign me to the cavalry, I'll be sent out west. Then I can find him and make him pay for what he did."

"But he must be long gone by now."

"Turns out his swindles are widely known. My sister was told Mr. Pennyworth has been in Texas and Kansas and everywhere in between."

She swayed.

I caught her by the elbows.

"Pennyworth?" The name came out in a whisper.

"That's the name of the man who took the money. He sold my sister some hotel in a made-up town."

"Your sister . . ."

"She's about the same age you are. Can you imagine someone taking advantage of a girl that way? Or taking advantage of you? That's why I've been doing all those things. If I want to make it to the bottom of the class, I have to do it quickly. It's the only way to rescue my sister and find Penny-worth. I *have* to head west. I *have* to be assigned to the cavalry."

Tears were coursing down her cheeks. She was shaking her head as if begging me to assure her none of what I'd just said was true. "But you can't throw your life away for that man. He's not worth it!"

"Wouldn't you do the same? If it were you?"

She kept right on talking as if she hadn't heard me. "What if you never find him? What if . . . what if he's dead! What if . . . what if he died and all your plans are useless? How can you do this, all of this, for him?"

I pulled her into my arms, trying to comfort her. Trying to calm her. "It's not for him. It's *because* of him. I have to do what I have to do. I have to try. Don't you understand? Wouldn't you do the same?"

"But if I had known. If I had just known. . . . My father . . ."

She was taking my words much too personally. "It's not your fault. Your father has nothing to do with this."

I felt her flinch.

"The man who swindled my sister has nothing to do with you."

327

37
LUCINDA

"Nothing to do with you."

My father had everything to do with this. And so did I.

I could picture Seth's sister. I'd seen dozens like her. It was easier to take advantage of a woman when she was bowed by grief. She was looking for hope. She was willing to believe in anything that seemed to offer her a better life or a way out. If I knew my father, he hadn't even had to work very hard to take her money. He'd offered her an opportunity with very little time to make a decision. Like all those other widows and orphans before her, she might as well have just thrown her money into his lap.

If I had been there with him, I would have helped him do it just the same as I had so many times in the past. I would have recognized that forlorn, frozen, worn look that those in the throes of grief always wore. I would have seen her red-rimmed eyes. I would have gotten her to tell me all about her sorrow . . . and then I would have given all that information to my father.

I would have betrayed her.

What a despicable creature I was. What a wretched, loathsome, hateful creature.

And Seth must never know.

I'd come to Buttermilk Falls, expecting my mother's family would receive me. And they had. But they'd given me so much more than I had been looking for. They'd given me themselves. Seth had done the same. And now I'd come to know how little I deserved any of them.

"It's not your fault."

Oh, how I wished that were true!

I stepped from Seth's embrace, not able to bear being comforted by a man whose life had been ruined by my father. If Seth had known to whom he spoke, he would never have been so generous with his love. Nor with his understanding.

I put a hand to his chest when he would have taken me back into his arms.

"I'm sorry. I didn't mean to take any liberties." He dropped his arms as he took a step away from me.

I wiped at my eyes with the back of my wrists. "I have to go. I have to go back now." If God were truly kind, I would never have to speak to Seth again. I'd never have to see the admiration in his eyes when he spoke to me. I would be able to forget how I'd felt in his arms.

"I know you do." He handed me a handkerchief. Just one more way in which he was a gentleman — always thinking of others, never for himself. That thought brought a new torrent of tears to my eyes. "Thank you, Lucinda. For believing in me. I know it's asking a lot of you. You can't know how much it means to me."

"I-I have to go. I have to go now."

Finding a dark corner along the edge of the building, I turned my face to the wall and wept.

My father had always insisted that he only took from people who could afford it. From those who had more than enough to spare or from those who were so stupid they didn't deserve to keep what they had. He told me the exchanges he made were generous, even philanthropic, because he was giving people hope. But Elizabeth and Seth hadn't received any hope. They'd been disheartened and demoralized. He'd taken their money and left them with nothing.

And now Seth had destroyed his career because of it.

I'd never imagined our victims to have lives. Never thought that our schemes would jeopardize their futures. I'd known they had names, of course, but I'd never known they could be Elizabeths. Or Seths. Never even considered they could be people I might come to love.

By the time I rejoined the crowd in the ballroom, I'd gained control of myself. It was a terrible coincidence that my father had taken advantage of Seth's sister, but I had to remind myself that the past was in the past. I was still safe. No one would ever be able to connect my father with Mr. Pennyworth. I would say nothing to my uncle of the reasons for Seth's poor behavior and failing grades. Seth would simply think him unreasonably strict and would attribute my reluctance to speak with him to my wanting to obey my uncle's wishes.

It would all be for the best.

In time, he would forget about me.

But still, my heart pinched as Milly danced by on the arm of Seth's friend Deacon. And it very nearly cracked as I thought about the plight of Seth's sister and his vow to find my father. Maybe I could find an obituary. There must be one. Somewhere. And if I mailed it to Seth anonymously, maybe he would stop his search. Maybe he would stop trying to fail his classes. Maybe it would make up for what my father had done.

"Lucinda!" Milly bounced up to me, a young cadet on her arm. "I remembered them."

I blinked. "Remembered what?"

"The dances. I remembered every one!"

"Good. That's very good."

"Why aren't you dancing?"

"I . . . My head. I'm not feeling well."

She dropped the cadet's arm. "Do you want me to get Papa?"

"No! No. I'm fine. I'm sure it will go away soon."

I excused myself from Milly just as quickly as I could. Walking about the outskirts of the room, I told myself that it didn't matter. None of it mattered. What my father had done was terrible, but no one had forced Seth into ruining his grades or trying to slide to the bottom of his class. It wasn't my fault that my father had died and that Seth would never be able to confront him. I could be sympathetic — and why wouldn't I be — without needing to take responsibility for any of it.

I was living a new life now, and I had determined to do everything differently. The past had no hold on my present or my future. Seth had said it best. None of this was my fault.

And suddenly Mr. Conklin was presenting himself to me. "Would you care to dance?"

No. I didn't care to. Not with him. I didn't deserve the society of Seth or his friends. The company of men like Mr. Conklin was all that was left me. My past had left me with very few options and no chance at happiness. Not if I were to keep my secrets safe. I smiled and I tried my best to put my heart into it. "Yes. Very much. Thank you."

38
SETH

I waited a good long time to let Lucinda get back inside before I followed. I didn't want anyone to start any rumors about us. Not before she was able to speak to her uncle about me. I hoped she could make him understand.

Deacon saluted me as I walked back into the ballroom. "Did you talk to her?"

"I did." I nodded out toward the dance floor, where she was locked in Campbell Conklin's arms.

He followed my gaze, but then swept his eyes back to me. "Nothing wrong, then? She's all right?"

"Hmm? Fine."

"Fine is for fiddles."

"I told her."

"Told her what?"

"About my sister and the farm."

Deke's brow rose. "And?"

"And she understood. At least I think she

did. She started crying saying some swindler wasn't worth ruining my whole career for." I can't say I hadn't had that same thought before. I'd just chosen to ignore it until now.

"Going to ask her to dance?"

"Can't. Her uncle won't let her. I'm a bad influence." Just look at the way Campbell Conklin was holding her so tightly! "Why do girls always think he hung the moon?"

"Conklin? That's the way it is with weasels. They look so handsome and sleek."

"I'd like to sleek him up his —"

Deacon handed me his cup. "Have some of this."

I took it from him and tossed it back. To my great surprise it had quite a bite as it went down. I blinked, eyes watering. "That wasn't punch."

"It was a little punch . . . mixed with a lot of whiskey."

I coughed as he smiled benevolently. "Did I just drink a glassful?"

"Looks like it."

"You know I don't drink."

"But if you don't drink, you probably won't feel like reveling in your success."

"My success at what?

"At being the worst cadet in the class."

I pondered that for a while. I supposed I was, in fact, a success at failure. Quite a great success, really. "I'm doing a good job of it, aren't I?"

"That you are."

"A fellow might even say I was born to fail like this."

"He might."

"I'm probably the best at being the worst that there is."

He saluted me. "Amen."

"I'm so good at being bad that not even my favorite professor would suspect that I'm not." I watched for a while as the other cadets danced by, girls in their arms. Why did girls have to be so pretty? "So that means I am, right?"

"That means you're what?"

"It means I've become what I was pretending to be, haven't I?"

He smiled as he raised his own glass. Wait a second. He was raising *two* glasses. With the same hand.

I looked at my own glass. My hand wasn't big enough to hold two of them, so I wondered how Deke could do that with his. "You're not going to tell anyone about me, are you?"

"Now why would I do that?"

"I just . . . I don't want anyone to know. Because my sister's awful smart." I lifted my glass to look into the bottom of it. There wasn't anything left to drink. "She's really smart. And it wasn't fair that Mr. Pennilworth . . . Penneterth . . ."

"Pennyworth?"

"Him. It wasn't right. Because my father left me in charge. I was supposed to look after her. And I didn't do it."

"Not your fault."

"I should have looked after her. If anyone found out . . . can't be charged with the lives of good men, good soldiers, if I can't even look after my own sister. I used to think I was good. I used to think I was the best. But now I know."

"What do you know?"

"I know I'm not. That's what I know. I'm not the best. So it's a good thing I'm the worst."

It was funny the way Deke's mouth was hanging open like that. I laughed.

He frowned. "For being so tall, that liquor sure is hitting you awful fast." Deacon put a hand to my chest. "I wouldn't try to go anywhere right now if I were you."

"What do you mean?" And why was Deke's face suddenly upside down?

The next thing I knew, I was waking up. Had I been asleep? I must have been. I sat and banged my head against something.

Ouch! There was music playing somewhere. I wasn't in my room. But if I wasn't in my room, where was I?

I put a hand to my head and felt a rising bump.

Deacon had something to do with this. His face was the last thing I remembered before everything went black. I put my other hand out and touched . . . cloth? That was odd. Something hard above my head and cloth to the sides. I rolled to my knees.

Bad decision. My head felt as if it were going to wobble right off my shoulders.

"Psst!"

I squinted toward the sound. "Deacon?"

"You're awake."

"Wish I were asleep."

He crawled over and squatted beside me. "Feeling better?"

"Better than what?"

"Sorry. Guess I gave you too much whiskey."

Is that why my mouth felt funny? "Where are we?"

"Here?" He glanced at the board above our heads. "I'd say we're right beneath that platter of little cakes everyone keeps eating."

Footsteps scuffed against the wood floor. They stopped beside us, on the other side of the cloth.

"Has your uncle said anything about assignments?" That was Campbell Conklin.

"Assignments?" Lucinda's voice. "Assignments to what?"

"To our posts. After graduation. He's on the academic board. They're the ones who will make the decisions."

"He rarely mentions the academy at home."

"But surely he must speak of it sometimes. It's quite important."

"Why don't you ask him about it tomorrow when you come for dinner? I'm sure he can put your mind at ease."

"I'd hate to seem too pushy. I wouldn't want him to think poorly of me."

"I've never heard my uncle say anything bad about you. *Is* there anything bad about you?"

Sure there was! I could think of at least a dozen things.

Deke held a finger up, warning me not to say anything.

"Me? I should hope not! How could there be? I'm first in my class. My father graduated from the Point, you know. And his father, my grandfather, advocated for the establishment of the academy. I just want to make them proud. They have expectations, you understand. I'm sure your father had the same for you."

A glass hit the floor and shattered. Thankfully the tablecloth prevented its contents from soaking us, but glass shards skittered beneath the cloth toward us.

"I'm so sorry!" Lucinda's voice swooped toward us as the hem of her dress pooled on the floor.

Deacon and I looked at each other and froze.

"Don't trouble yourself." Campbell's voice was dismissive. "One of the stewards will clean it up."

The skirt moved away as her reply faded into the music.

I collapsed back to the floor. I really had ruined everything.

39
LUCINDA

Saturday's hop left me shaken. The more I tried not to think about my father swindling Seth's sister out of her money . . . the more I actually thought about it.

How I wished I could be the honest, upstanding citizen everyone assumed me to be!

I went about with my tongue clamped between my teeth, fearing that it wouldn't take much to make me admit to every swindle I had ever taken part in. I so desperately wanted not to feel guilty anymore. Not that I would ever be innocent. Not that telling my secrets wouldn't make me feel even worse. But in this town of cordiality and respectability, I just wanted to fit in. I was tired of being myself.

Feigning the need for air one mid-November afternoon, I grabbed my mantle, pulled on my bonnet and gloves, and took to the streets of Buttermilk Falls just before supper. The air was bracing and the wind was chill, but still there was a cluster of people coming up the hill from the river landing. I nodded at Mr. Dusenbury, smiled a greeting at Mrs. Parry, and then my gaze traveled beyond them to —

"Lucinda!" Walking up the street toward me was one of the most distinguished men I'd ever seen. Dark haired and green eyed, from the top of his flared hat to the tips of his highly polished shoes, he was the very picture of respectability. The gold-tipped cane he carried only added to the illusion.

I blinked. Hard. But when I opened my eyes, he was still there.

"Lucinda. My dear." My father approached me smiling, arms extended, as if proposing that I embrace him.

In times past, I would have, but things had changed. I was an orphan now. I was a Hammond. And I didn't want anything to do with him. His presence would ruin everything.

Galvanized by the danger, I stepped toward him, linking my arm with his, pulling him away from the others. "What are you doing here?" I queried him under my breath even as I smiled at the passing townspeople.

"What are *you* doing here?"

"I asked you first!" My words came out in a hiss.

He frowned, though his eyes still twinkled. "You don't look very happy to see me."

"You're supposed to be dead."

"Dead?"

"That's what the letter said."

"It said Mr. *Pennyworth* was dead."

I raised a brow.

"I had to improvise. I was in jail, you see, and —"

"Jail!"

"I thought you would be able to read between the lines. Mr. Christopher Barnett was taking over Mr. Pennyworth's affairs. I'd thought that was quite clear."

"You were in *jail*?"

He glanced about. "If you could speak a bit more quietly . . . ? They let me out several weeks after I wrote you that letter. For good behavior." He swept his hand into a flourish. "Behold . . . Mr. Christopher Barnett. I've left Pennyworth behind me for good."

"Is that supposed to make me happy?"

His smile dimmed. "Why wouldn't it? I had quite the time trying to determine where it was that you went. But then I thought about what I used to say. How when everything looked grim I would propose that we just go back to Buttermilk Falls . . . and here you are!" He sent another glance about. "We're back in business. So tell me, what's the lay of land?"

"The . . . the . . . ?" I couldn't breathe.

"Lucinda?" He gripped my arm as my steps faltered.

Mrs. Parry joined us, a worried tilt to her brow. "Miss Hammond?"

My father's brow peaked as he mouthed, *"Hammond?"*

"Are you quite all right?"

My father replied before I could. "There's nothing to worry about. I'm afraid I surprised her. Lucinda's my daughter, you see, and —"

The world swirled as I grabbed at him.

My father's grip tightened, nearly lifting me off my feet. "She's fine. That wind is terribly brisk, isn't it? Quite bracing." He squeezed me like a vise and pushed me forward, back onto my feet.

I tried to smile. "I'm fine, Mrs. Parry. Truly I am. Please tell your daughter I'll see her tomorrow afternoon for lessons."

Mrs. Parry regarded me with concern. "If you're sure? You look so peaked all of a sudden. . . ."

"It's just . . . It's the cold. I wasn't expecting it to be so cold."

As she walked off, my father examined me with a worried frown.

For the first time in my life, I didn't care what he might think of me or what he might say. I was worried about what my uncle would say. Or do. "You can't come home with me."

"Why not?"

"I'm staying with my aunt. And I have cousins and they have friends —"

"Your aunt? Your mother's sister?"

I nodded. "And my uncle."

"Who's your uncle?"

"Richard Hammond. Your old roommate. He's an instructor at the military academy now. And he doesn't approve of you."

"That didn't bother me when I was at the academy, and it certainly doesn't bother me now. Don't worry. I'll take care of it. Where is the house?" He was looking off up the street with an air of impatience. Never one to subject himself willingly to the elements, he was more at home in ornate steamboat saloons than the out-of-doors.

"I don't think this is something you can take care of."

"I've been in more difficult binds than this."

"I'm staying here. In Buttermilk Falls. I'm not coming with you this time." I couldn't.

Not after what he'd done to Seth and his sister. I wasn't going anywhere with him ever again.

He looked at me as if seeing me for the first time. "I didn't come to take you anywhere."

"What did you come to do, then?"

"I came to stay."

"Stay?" Did he say . . . Had he said *stay*? My whole body had suddenly gone numb.

"For a while, at least. Seems to me you've found the perfect place to operate. All these respectable people." He winked at me. "Just ready for the fleecing, wouldn't you say? On the way here, I came up with a scheme for the city, but it will work even better if I stay here while I'm doing it. Won't have to worry so much about being found out. I can just take the steamboat down the river when I need to." He nodded as he glanced about. "This is even better than I had planned."

"But they know you here. Everyone knows you. Even the cadets know about John Barns."

"I haven't been John Barns for quite a while now."

"They'll recognize you!"

"Here? Where cadets come and go every year? I have a beard now. Who would connect me with John Barns?"

"I wish you hadn't come east."

"And I wish you'd stayed out west." There seemed to be a sort of warning in his eyes. "Seems to me neither one of us got what we wanted. So let's make the best of it, shall we?"

"They won't want you."

"They might not want me, but I can guarantee you they'll have me." His smile had disappeared. "And it will all be thanks to you."

As we walked toward the house, I tried to think of all the reasons I could to get him to leave. "They're decent people. All of them here in town. Hardworking. Honest."

"That's the best kind. The easiest kind. What do I always tell you? The easiest people to dupe are respectable people. Once you help them admit to their secret hopes and dreams, they can hardly give you their money fast enough!" He was looking up and down the street as if taking the town's measure. He shook his head. "Hasn't changed much. At least it's close to the city."

"Do you really think the family is going to accept you? After you ran off with mother?"

"As I recall, she ran off with me." He chuckled. "They may not want to accept me, but they're going to have to."

I stopped walking, trying to gain some time. "There are quite a few of them in the house. They've four children. I have to room with the oldest."

"What's wrong? Are you worried?"

More than worried. I was deathly afraid. "I have a bad feeling about this."

"Then you should have left before now. Though I have to say I'm glad you didn't. I'd hate to have to chase after you again. It was hard enough tracking you here. Although I did come into a bit of a windfall on the railroads." He hefted the satchel he held in his hand. "I played a lot of three-card monte. Can you believe no one else is operating on the trains?"

That was exactly like him! But this time I wasn't impressed. I was horrified. "I'm not worried about me. I'm worried about you. I'm doing fine here." And I would continue to do so, if he would just leave.

"We're a team, you and I. We'll work it out."

I didn't want to be part of his team anymore.

"You don't look like you're happy to see me. What's happened?"

What's happened? I'd discovered the world wasn't at all like he'd taught me. What happened is that I'd discovered good, honest people — and I'd decided I wanted to be one of them. What happened is that I'd finally found my place. I wanted to stay in Buttermilk Falls with my aunt. With Phoebe and Bobby and Milly and Ella. With Campbell and Deacon and Dandy and Otter. And Seth. How would I ever be able to look him in the eyes again?

"I see what's happened!"

"You do?" He did? Relief suffused me with warmth. He understood. Maybe now I could convince him to leave.

"Of course I do! My little girl is growing up. You're running a swindle of your own, aren't you."

The relief that had just taken wing settled back into my stomach. "No — I'm not! I thought you'd died. I thought I was on my own. I came here to start a new life. I'm Lucinda Hammond now. No one knows about my past."

"So what's your plan?"

Plan? Hadn't he heard anything I'd said? Frustration and anxiety pushed tears toward my eyes. I shoved back my bonnet so I could see him clearly. "There is no plan. I have no plan. I'm trying to be respectable."

He looked at me, his gaze searching mine. His lips curved into a smile, settled back, and then curved again as he laughed. "You don't want to be *respectable*! Respectable people are . . . They're tedious. And boring."

"I *do* want to be respectable. I want to be an honest, upstanding citizen."

"But you can't be."

"Why not?"

"Because you aren't — that's why." He laughed again.

"I am. Did you know there's an order of merit at the military academy, and —"

"Oh, yes. I'd heard."

Of course he knew about it. "The top cadet in the graduating class has displayed a very flattering interest in me."

"So you're hoping . . . ?"

"I told you. I'm trying to be a normal person."

His brow twitched.

"I want to marry a normal person. The most normal, most respectable —"

"That's your plan?"

"It's not a plan."

"No. It is. And that's a good one. A very good plan. Much like what we were working toward when I so inconveniently died. So who is this cadet? What's his family like?"

I was the one who had brought up talk of marriage. I couldn't refuse to speak about it

now. "Campbell Conklin. His grandfather
—"

"His grandfather was a senator. And his
father was a graduate. You've set your cap
for quite a fine young fellow. He could come
in very handy."

"He's not going to come in handy. He's
not going to come into anything. I'm not
trying to take money from him. I plan to
marry him."

"Which is perfect. How can I help?"

"You can't."

"Why not? I can be anyone you want me
to. Your uncle? Your brother?"

"You can't help because I won't be able
to marry him if they find out who you are."

"So you *are* planning and scheming. You
are pretending."

"I'm not pretending. This is real. I want a
real life."

"A real life? *Pretending* to have a respectable background? And an honorable father,
I suppose?"

Tears pricked at my eyes. He didn't understand. He wasn't going to leave.

"I think this could be the best swindle
we've ever done, you and I. If you can manage it."

"I don't want to swindle anyone. I want
to marry Mr. Conklin and be . . . normal!

Why can't you understand?"

"Because you're not. And you never will be. Why can't *you* understand? So let me help, and I'll see how we can turn his interest in you to our benefit."

"I don't want your help. I don't want you."

His smile disappeared. "That's not exactly what I was hoping to hear, having traveled so far to find you. Having spent all these years training you. Knowing just how deeply involved you've been with my schemes. Why do you think I sent you to all those schools? Why do you think I've bought you the best of everything money can buy?"

"I know you only meant —"

"I need you; you need me. So if you do as I say, we'll both come out of our time here well."

I brought us to a halt in front of the house.

"Is this it?"

I nodded.

He offered me his arm.

There was nothing I could do but take it.

40
SETH

After a long morning of recitations in military engineering and ethics, I met up with the fellows at the mess hall. Halfway through dinner, Deacon nudged me with an elbow. "Dandy's making hash tonight. Early. Right after supper."

I raised a brow. Dandy didn't cook often, but when he did, he made a hash to admire.

"He traded at Benny Havens last night for some bacon. I'm bringing bread. You get some of those potatoes. Otter's good for the butter."

Just the thought of it made my mouth water. I hadn't eaten well since I'd stopped being invited to Professor Hammond's. Furtively, I pulled a handkerchief from my coat, spread it atop my lap, and dropped globs of potatoes onto it. Across the table from me, Otter was portioning off a good chunk of butter. After casting a glance up and down the table, it disappeared into his lap. Beside me, Deacon had reached out for what was left of the bread and overturned the platter into his own lap.

I tied my handkerchief into a knot as the fellows did the same. The trick of it would be to transfer our prizes to our hats and then clap them on before anyone noticed. We were drilling in cavalry tactics down at the riding-hall that afternoon, so we were expected to visit the barracks to change into our riding jackets.

It's just that we did so on the run.

Deacon opened up his hiding hole, and we dumped our handkerchief-wrapped food into it.

After changing into our riding jackets and reinforced trousers, we strapped on our spurs and buckled on our heavy cavalry sabers. Grabbing our buckskin gauntlets, Deke and I met the others out in the hall.

As we left the barracks we started to divvy up the hash-making tasks.

I glanced at Deacon. "You get a lookout?"

"I got one. A yearling. Offered him a serving in exchange for keeping an eye on the tactical officer."

"You have anyone watching for Campbell Conklin?"

"The adjutant's ready to report some mischief going on outside if need be. That should keep him away from the room."

I eyed Dandy. "Got your utensils?"

"Took a fork and a knife the other night. Sure would like a spoon, though."

"I'll get you one at supper."

"Much obliged."

As we'd been talking, one of the second classmen fell into step with us. "Heard you're making hash tonight. I got a wild onion I found down by the river."

Deke considered the offer. "An onion? I don't know. It's Dandy's hash." He leaned forward to speak around Otter. "Dandy? You want an onion?"

"Who's offering?"

Deacon nodded toward the cadet.

"How big is it?"

The cadet held up his thumb and forefinger in the shape of a C. " 'Bout that big."

"I'll take it."

The cadet flashed a grin. "Then I'll bring it."

As he left, another second classman came abreast to take his place. "Heard Mr. Delagarde's making hash. I think I can get you some eggs."

Dandy frowned. "Eggs? This time of year? From where?"

"I, uh . . . I got a girl . . . in the Falls." A flush was spreading across his face toward his ears.

"I can't do much with one or two, but I sure could use four."

He nodded. Saluted. "I'll see what I can do."

One of the plebes in our company was dragging his feet, sending looks in our direction. It was clear he wanted to talk to us, so I finally nodded him over.

"Mr. Westcott, sir. What if I could get me a rabbit?"

Deke answered on my behalf. "You? How?"

"I run a snare up in the hills above the academy."

The cadet, short and smooth-chinned as he was, looked about twelve years old. Deacon scoffed, but Dandy held up a hand. "Wait. You have a rabbit?"

"I might could have one. I got to check. But if I do, you can have it. If you want it."

"I'd want it."

He broke out into a grin before he remembered he was talking to upperclassmen. "Yes, sir. I'll bring it. If I got it."

There were two other men from our company who looked as if they wanted to have a word, but we had to consult first on how many servings we'd given away. "There's the four of us," Otter offered.

"And the two lookouts." Deke added.

I nodded. "That's six. And one for the onion and another for the rabbit and a third for the eggs. We're looking at nine."

Deacon winked. "Maybe eight, if there's no rabbit."

"I sure hope there is one." Otter sighed. "Mother makes the best rabbit stew I ever ate."

"I think that's all we can take, then?" I glanced round at the fellows.

They all nodded.

I gestured the other men over. "We got what we need. Sorry, men. Maybe next time."

Everyone who attended that evening brought a candle. That was the rule. And then we rigged some plates we'd borrowed from the mess hall atop them. There was, in fact, a rabbit in that plebe's snare. He skinned it before he brought it, leaving only its bushy, white tail. The man with the eggs brought us six. And the onion turned out to be a bit bigger than we had expected.

Dandy cooked in his shirtsleeves, taking his time over the onions, mixing them into the eggs. He directed Otter to make buttered toast with the bread and had Deacon fetch his flask so he could add a splash of whiskey to his concoction. By the time the rabbit was frying and the eggs and onions were cooking, my mouth was starting to water.

Otter was toasting the bread on the tip of his saber when the lookout cracked open the door and stuck his head in. "Better do something about that smell. Won't be able to help you much if you give yourselves away."

We placed the candles and the cooking apparatus nearer the window and stationed the plebe in front of it with one of Professor Mahan's books. He fanned the rising steam toward the window for all he was worth.

Once Dandy finally pronounced it done, we partook of it in friendly fashion. A man could down his food at the mess hall in three minutes flat. But Dandy's hash wasn't food. It was a meal. We all stayed for over an hour, eating and laughing and trying to forget the humiliations and the petty slights we'd suffered during the day.

Deke finally collapsed on the floor, hand on his belly. "I bet, out on the frontier next summer, we'll be able to scare us up some antelope. Maybe even a bison. Bet the eating'll be real good out there."

Otter and Dandy murmured consent while the second classmen and yearling listened on with envy.

Deke sighed. "You got to admit, don't you, isn't anything finer than partaking of a feast with the fellows."

Dandy raised his flask while Otter kept gnawing on his rabbit leg.

"No place I'd rather be, this minute, nothing I'd rather do than this. No, sir."

The rest of the men nodded their agreement, and I raised my fork, though I didn't really agree. I could think of something better. I could imagine someone I'd rather be with. Thing was, I didn't know if she would say the same for me.

It was a good thing I'd taken the time, earlier in the day, to clean my musket and put my books in order. And then sweep the floor. And fold my clothes. That evening's room inspection was especially thorough because Campbell Conklin was trailing the tactical officer. At least the scent of our hash was gone by then.

Conklin sauntered around our room, adjusting the sleeve of one of Deke's coats and running a gloved finger along the spines of our books. "Dust." He held up a finger so we could see the smudges. "Two demerits to the cadet charged with the keeping of the room this week."

That was me. I lifted a hand.

"Mr. Westcott. I expected better of you." The glee in his voice belied him, told me failure was exactly what he'd expected of me. There was no point in saying anything. The sooner he was finished with me, the sooner he'd leave.

"But I suppose a man like you can't be bothered with such things."

As the tactical offer went on to the next room with the orderly, Deke stepped forward, stopping Conklin from leaving. "You aren't making any friends here."

"I know I'm not liked, by you or anyone else." He tilted a book away from its place on the shelf and then shoved it back. "Does that surprise you? I've watched you and Seth and Dandy and Otter and wondered a time or two what it might be like to have the corps really admire me. Look up to me. Want to be me. But it looks like Westcott has taken things a bit too far, doesn't it?" He shifted his attention to me. "That's the trouble with you. You've taken your eye off what really matters. For which I suppose I ought to thank you. How does it feel to watch it all slip away?"

Behind my back, my fingers clenched into fists.

"Miss Hammond is very pretty, isn't she?

A delightful companion, though somewhat lacking in sophistication."

"If you so much as touch one —"

He put up a hand. "Don't worry. I'm not planning on doing anything to her."

"If your intentions are anything but respectable —"

"Sorry? Oh!" He smirked. "My intentions aren't respectable . . . or otherwise. I've no intentions at all. You see, the best thing about Miss Hammond is something you seemed to have forgotten rather quickly. She's the niece of Professor Hammond."

What was he trying to say?

"And Professor Hammond has quite a bit of influence with the Corps of Engineers. The cadets he recommends are just about guaranteed an assignment, by my calculations. Saturday afternoon, I'll take her down to Flirtation Walk. Saturday evening, I'll see her at the hop. I've even been invited to Sunday dinner. For the next few months, we're going to be practically inseparable."

"And then what?"

"Then what?" He lifted a shoulder in a shrug. "Then I'm afraid she's destined for a broken heart. You see, my father would never let me marry her. My mother would never deign to even speak to her. I'm practically engaged to be married. Didn't you

361

know that? I have one of the Phillips girls in Boston ready to run down the aisle with me after I graduate. The only thing I lacked was the assurance of a slot in the Engineers. That's what Lucinda's for. If I do it right, her uncle will vouch for me when the time comes. I have to tell you that it doesn't hurt that she's so pretty. I might as well have some fun while I can."

As I swung a fist at Conklin, Deacon caught my arm. "Don't do it. He's first captain. If you hit him, you're as good as dismissed."

"I've always been a step behind you, ever since I got here. But now . . . ? I feel like I *am* you. I've become you. I have the rank. I have the grades. I have the girl." Conklin sneered. "Why don't you hit me? You've been flirting with dismissal all term. Why don't you just get it over with?" He lifted his chin and turned his cheek toward me. "Take a swing."

I buried my fist beneath an arm as Deacon stood in front of me. "No. You're not worth it."

41
LUCINDA

As I entered the house, my father with me, Phoebe called out from the sitting room. "You've returned! We were so worried. You haven't caught a chill have you? The wind is all but howling."

I took my father's coat and hung it on the hallstand. Took his hat and gloves and set them on the bench. Then I did the same with my mantle and bonnet and gloves.

Motioning him to come with me, I went into the sitting room.

Phoebe was waiting for me, head turned toward the hall, an expectant smile on her face.

"Phoebe, I'd like you to meet . . ." How I wished I didn't have to say it.

My father stepped forward, nodding at her. "Lucinda's father. At your service." He extended his hand.

Phoebe, not seeing his gesture, turned her head in his general direction. "Lucinda's father? But . . . ?"

Gesturing for him to sit, I left him in Phoebe's care as I went to find my aunt.

She was tugging at a crock. "Lucinda! I'm so glad you've finally returned. Your uncle's late in coming home tonight. If I could just get some help with —"

"We have a visitor. He's in the sitting room."

"Now?"

I nodded, not willing, not wanting, to tell her it was my father.

"At this hour? It's nearly time for supper." She sighed, pushing a tendril of hair from her forehead with the back of her hand. "I suppose I'll have to greet him, then. Perhaps he'll want to stay and eat with us." After wiping her hands on her apron, she undid the pins that secured it to her bodice and unfastened it.

I tried to come up with the right words, I truly did, but I still hadn't settled on any by the time we reached the sitting room.

My aunt stopped when she caught sight of my father. "Oh!" The color drained from her face as she put out a hand and felt for a chair. Then she turned to me, betrayal and confusion rippling across her face.

Father stood as she sat with a thud.

Madame Mercier would have been proud.

We engaged, the four of us, in polite if banal conversation, as we completely avoided the obvious: My father had returned from the dead.

My aunt started as the front door opened. She pushed to her feet and swiftly walked into the front hall. There was a murmur of voices, both hers and my uncle's, and then a long silence.

"Here?" My uncle's voice was explosive.

My father winked at me.

In the past I might have responded with a wink of my own, but my stomach had clenched and my lungs didn't seem to be working.

Boots scraped against the floorboards to the accompanying staccato of my aunt's footsteps. My uncle soon appeared in the doorway, where he paused, hand at his hip, pushing back his long coat.

My father rose and moved toward him, hand extended. "Richard. Good to see you again."

"I'm afraid I cannot say the same." My uncle ignored the offer of a handshake and pushed past him to stand beside Phoebe's chair. He lobbed an accusatory glance at me. "Lucinda said you were dead."

"Happily, that isn't true."

"She assured me that it was."

My father extended his arms as if inviting us all to acknowledge that he was, indeed, among the living. "And I can assure you that she was quite mistaken."

My uncle faced me directly. "Were you mistaken? Or was this some scheme of yours?"

I stood, wringing my hands in violation of all my finishing school training. "I thought it was true. I was told that he'd died."

"And I told you I wouldn't countenance any deceit in my house."

"I haven't deceived you. I didn't! If I'd known he was alive, I wouldn't have come."

The eyes that were usually alight with intelligence and interest had gone cold and flat. "Well, he's here now. So you can both leave."

My aunt started toward me, her face stricken.

Phoebe gasped. "Leave? She can't leave!" She half rose toward her father, waving her arms, looking for him. "Papa, *please*!"

I couldn't bear it. I moved toward her and placed her hand on my uncle's arm. "I didn't know." I whispered the words, imploring him to believe me, but fearing any goodwill I earned over the past few months had abruptly expired.

Phoebe took up my cause. "She didn't

know, Papa. I know she didn't."

"Be that as it may, I cannot abide either of you under my roof."

My father stepped toward him. "Richard, this is all a misunderstanding. Can't we let bygones be bygones?"

"If you're asking whether I've forgiven you for what happened during our academy days, be assured that I have. That doesn't mean, however, that I can trust you. Or that I can allow my family to suffer from your misdeeds."

"That's too bad. I'd hoped for a friendly sort of greeting because I've decided to stay in Buttermilk Falls for a while. Seems a shame to turn around and leave when I've just gotten here. And winter isn't the best time of year to travel."

"I hope you'll understand when I ask that you not associate with us in any way." He swept an arm toward the front hall. There was no mistaking his intent.

But my father didn't move. "That's the thing about family that I've always admired — they take care of each other. You've accepted my daughter into your household as a niece. *Your* niece if I'm not mistaken. I don't see any reason why you can't accept me as your brother."

"Because I despise everything you stand for."

"You despise everything John Barns stood for. How embarrassing for you if he were to show up on your doorstep. I wouldn't blame you for not being able to accept *him* into your family. But I can assure you that your new brother, Christopher Hammond, is a different man entirely. You'll find him quite affable. Quite willing to fit into the community. To take advantage of all that Buttermilk Falls has to offer. I think if he found himself accepted . . . or at least not ostracized, he'd be happy to leave John Barns in the grave."

"Are you threatening me?"

"You?" Father laughed. "Of course not." His smile vanished. "I'm threatening your sense of propriety. And your precious career. Those very fragile, very important things that might just dry up and wither away at any hint of scandal."

"What is it that you want from me?"

"I just want to be allowed to live here, for a while, in peace, as I pursue some opportunities in the city. Is that too much to ask?"

"You can do anything you want as long as you and your daughter never darken my door again."

■ ■ ■ ■

I went upstairs and gathered my things as Father waited in the street for me. Phoebe came up the stairs, felt for the bed, and sat down upon it. "I wish you wouldn't go."

"Your father made it quite clear that I can't stay."

"I don't understand why —"

"If you knew my father, then you would."

"Then ask *my* father to let you stay. Just tell him you won't have anything to do with your father."

"It's not that easy."

"Why?"

"Because my father's threatened to do to me the same thing he threatened to do to your father."

"But what is that, exactly? Tell the truth? Why not do it yourself?"

"And let it be known that he —"

"Let it be known that you're nothing like him."

"But that's just it!" My voice caught on the tears that clogged my throat. "I'm exactly like him. And I don't know how to be anyone else."

"You're not. You're not like him."

"I most certainly —"

369

"You're not, Lucinda. I know you. But what will you do now? Where will you go?"

"I don't know." But that was a lie. I knew exactly what I'd do. I'd do anything my father said. I'd keep trying to interest Mr. Conklin. I'd probably accompany my father to New York City this winter in order to help him run a swindle or two. And in June I'd marry into the Conklin family and help my father gain access to greater power and influence. But Phoebe didn't need to know any of that. "When the weather is fit for travel we'll probably move on to somewhere else. That's what we've always done."

"But your home is here with us."

"*Your* home is here, and I've enjoyed sharing it, but it's not mine."

Her chin began to tremble.

"Don't cry. Please don't cry."

"I never had a friend before you. It won't be the same."

"It will be even better — you can have your bed to yourself again."

She laughed through her tears and reached both arms toward me.

I moved into her embrace.

She hugged me and then patted the sides of my head with both hands. "Hush, now. Dry your tears. Everything is going to be all right."

How had she known I was crying?

"It's going to be all right. I know it will."

42
SETH

That Saturday afternoon, as I was passing the hotel on my way to the river during recreation, I saw Lucinda standing on the porch. I lifted my hand in a wave, and her face went white.

Bounding up the steps, I reached out to grab her arm.

She intercepted my hand, cast a harried glance behind her, and pulled me toward the corner of the porch.

"I'm so glad to see you, Lucinda. I've been wanting to tell you . . . I've been giving a lot of thought to what you said at the hop."

"What did I say?"

I couldn't help smiling at the fear on her face. I covered her hand with my other one. "Nothing so bad as all that."

"I'm sorry. I just —"

"It was about not being able to find that Pennyworth fellow. The thing of it is, what if he *has* died? What if I *can't* find him?"

"That's something I was wanting to talk to you about as well."

"I've decided that you're right."

"*I'm* right?"

"You are. He's probably long gone. And maybe that's for the best. Why should I waste my time trying to track him down?"

Lucinda tugged her hand from mine. "I need to tell you something." She was glancing beyond my shoulder. "But not here." She moved around the corner, and I hurried to keep pace with her. As I looked back to the front porch I noticed a man who seemed to be following us. "I need to tell you that . . . Seth?"

I swung my gaze back to her. "Pardon me?"

"I want to tell you about my father."

"There's no point in bringing up bad memories. I was thinking, maybe it's best for both of us if we can just leave them in the past."

"Normally, I would agree with you. But my father isn't a good man."

"Wasn't."

"What?"

"He *wasn't* a good man. But he's dead now. You *can* leave the past behind."

"But that's what I need to tell you. I can't.

And neither can you."

"Why?"

"Because my father is Mr. Pennyworth."

"Your father . . . Mr. *Penny*worth?" That couldn't be what she'd just said. "There's no way your father could be as bad as Mr. Pennyworth."

"He is as bad, because he *is* Mr. Pennyworth."

"What are you saying?"

"Seth. Listen to me."

I just couldn't quite get her words to make any kind of sense.

"It was my father who swindled your sister. As soon as you told me his name was Pennyworth, I knew it was him."

"Your father? But then . . . That's why you said he was a bad man?" I was beginning to understand everything. "And that's why you said all that. About him being dead and everything. Why didn't you just tell me that night at the hop?"

"Because I didn't know what to say. I didn't want to think that he'd done that to you. I'm so sorry. I should have —"

Comprehension slammed me in the gut as everything shifted. But one thing remained unchanged. "It's still not your fault. What he did doesn't have anything to do with you. His past died with him."

"But —"

"You weren't there when it happened were you?"

"No, but —"

That man who had been trailing us was now quite close. I stepped in front of Lucinda to shield her from his gaze. "It doesn't change anything about what I feel for you."

"Seth, listen! That's not all. He's —"

I glanced behind me and saw the man smile in our direction. Did I know him? I glanced back down at her just as the man spoke. "Lucinda?"

He knew her name? "Do you know that man?"

"That's what I wanted to tell you. I . . ."

At that point, he had almost reached us. "There you are." He was nodding at Lucinda and he'd crooked his arm . . . for her?

She stepped past me and took it up.

He smiled at me with friendly interest as he glanced between the two of us. "Is this a friend of yours?"

Her gaze almost intersected with mine, but then it dropped toward the floorboards. "Yes." It came out in a whisper.

He patted the hand that curled around his arm. "Then aren't you going to introduce me?"

I didn't like the way he seemed so possessive of her. Something was wrong. And sometimes the best defensive move is to step forward instead of back. I put out my hand. "Seth Westcott."

He took it in his. "Mr. —"

Lucinda completed the introduction herself. "This is my father, Seth."

She couldn't have stunned me more if she had taken my saber and stabbed me with it. "Your father?"

"The name is Hammond."

"Hammond?"

"That's right." He looked at me as if he weren't a thieving, cheating, lowdown scoundrel.

"I was under the distinct impression that you were dead."

He laughed. "It was a simple misunderstanding. Fortunately, for my sake, I'm not."

"You haven't, by any chance, been in Nebraska Territory, have you?"

"Nebraska? I've never been there."

"How about Texas?"

"I can't say I've had the pleasure."

Liar! He'd changed his name. Now he was changing his story.

"This is what I was trying to tell you, Seth. My father's returned."

It took everything I had to shift my attention back to Lucinda. She *had* been trying to tell me about her father. About his return. "You must be very happy, Miss Hammond."

She shook her head. A small, hardly discernible motion.

Did she want me to do something? Was she in danger? "Would you care to keep our plans to meet tomorrow afternoon?" We had no plans to meet, but her father didn't know that.

"I think, in light of my father's coming, perhaps we should save our meeting for a different occasion. Maybe we could make a different plan?"

A *different* plan? We didn't even have a plan to begin with. Her uncle had forbidden her to speak to me. "Did you have a suggestion?"

"Not at the moment." She tried to smile. "But I'm sure you'll come up with something."

What was she trying to say? Why was she throwing it all back on me? "If you'll excuse me. I need to go." Before I did something I might greatly regret.

43

LUCINDA

Father and I watched Seth walk away. I hoped he understood what I'd been trying to tell him. We needed to meet. We needed to come up with a plan to get his money back.

My father was watching him through narrowed eyes. "I wonder why he asked about Nebraska?"

I smiled as if I hadn't a care in the world. "That's where he's from. He seems quite proud of the territory, doesn't he?"

"Sorriest excuse for country I ever saw."

"You *have* been there?"

"I sold some deeds out that way back at the beginning of summer. Did rather well at it too."

My father and I had spent the day at the West Point Hotel, trying to determine what sort of clientele they had. He was always ready to gamble on cards or dice or horses if he could find a willing party. Though tourists had come by the boatful in the summer, their numbers had decreased quite noticeably with the coming of winter. We'd eaten in the hotel's dining room, listening to conversations, lingering as long as we possibly could. After speaking with Seth, we walked back to Buttermilk Falls.

We could have taken rooms at the hotel, but my father was loath to spend money he didn't have to. We'd taken two rooms with a widow, Mrs. Holt, instead. Her boarding-house was up the road from my uncle's house, in the direction of the church. My father had smiled and winked and cajoled her into a discounted rate.

As I settled myself into a chair in the front parlor, he worked on lighting a cigar.

"I figured I'd go into the city this week. I got lucky on my way east. Took a pile off a man on the train to Cleveland and a small fortune from a man on the steamboat to Buffalo. We'll add to it this winter in the city, and in spring we'll be ready to travel again."

Travel again? Maybe he'd forgotten about Campbell Conklin.

"I figure if you play the Conklin cadet right, by Christmas he'll be ready to propose. If I take you away for a few months before graduation, it will make his heart

379

grow fonder. Isn't that what they say? With his family's connections and the territories growing, without too much trouble, I should be able to get myself appointed a federal judge or a territorial secretary even. When I head back west, this time it will be in style." He smiled. "Nice work you've done. Couldn't have managed better myself." He took a puff on his cigar. "Think I'll go outside for a smoke."

I'd come to Buttermilk Falls wanting nothing more than to make a respectable life for myself. But everything I'd done had only served to prepare the stage for my father. He was right. He couldn't have done it better himself.

There was no way out, nowhere I could go that he would not find me.

I had tried. I had come here intending to leave everything behind, to take up the name Lucinda Hammond, but even that had damned me. There was no escape. Not for me. But there could be for Seth. I could help him get his money back. It was the fair and decent thing to do. Only . . . I couldn't quite figure out how to do it. That's why I needed to talk to him.

If he was still willing to speak to me.

I sat on the bed that evening, arms

wrapped around my waist. It had been useless to wish for a different kind of life. This
is who I was. This is what I had been trained
to do. And trained so well that it was quite
apparent I couldn't do anything else. But it
was time, now, to ask some questions. It
was time to find out why.

When I heard my father come up the
stairs, I opened my door. "I'd like to know
about my mother."

He paused, hand on his doorknob. "What
is there to know?"

Everything. "She wasn't blond, was she?"

He dropped his hand and turned around.
"That's her locket you always wear around
your neck. I told you that."

He hadn't answered my question. "My
aunt told me I was the image of my mother.
So who was the woman with the blond
hair?"

He said nothing.

"That woman wasn't my mother."

"That woman might as well have been
your mother. She took care of you like a
mother."

"Did she have a name?"

"Cora."

Cora? It sounded familiar.

He sighed. Fiddled with his cane. Then he
looked up at me from beneath his brow.

The gestures were familiar. I'd used them before. He was trying to gain my sympathy.

I steeled myself.

"She took care of you while I traveled. When you were still too young to go to school."

"You *left* me with her?"

"She didn't mind. She looked after you as if you were her own."

"So you . . . you were married?" Had Cora been my stepmother?

"No."

"Did you love her?"

He smiled, amusement flickering in his eyes. "It wasn't like that, Lucinda."

"Then what was it like? Tell me."

He tilted his head, pursing his lips, as he seemed to consider. "She lived in Memphis. It was convenient. I couldn't very well take a child with me on the riverboats. How would I have been able to gamble? How would I have been able to do anything? I got her a place so I could stop in on my way up the river and on my way back down."

"You got her a place . . ." There was something . . . something not quite right in his words.

"It seemed best."

"For who?"

"For me. For you."

"So . . . you paid her. You paid her to take care of me?"

He looked at me patronizingly. As if what he wanted to do was laugh at me instead. "I paid her for other things too."

I heard myself gasp and clapped a hand to my mouth. "I was raised by a *whore*? Is that what you're saying? The woman I thought was my mother was your whore?"

He winced. "Don't pull out your morals and become righteous now. It's not becoming. I didn't raise you that way. You're too old for that, Lucinda."

"Is that . . . is that even my real name?"

He shrugged. "It's what I've always called you. It's what she called you."

She. Cora. His whore. I splayed my hands at my temples, trying to think. Trying to hold on to myself. "What did my mother call me?"

"I don't know. I wasn't there when you were born. I got there a year too late. I'd left your mother because she wasn't fit to travel. She wasn't good at breeding. She got fat. She got . . . She was very unpleasant. She didn't understand things the way I did. But eventually I realized she would have been useful in some of my schemes. So I came back into town to make amends, but she was already dead by then. The doctor and his wife were taking care of you. They called you Jane. Maybe that's what your mother called you."

My soul recoiled in horror for the baby I'd once been. "Why didn't you just leave me there with them?"

He shrugged. "They already knew that I was your father. That's my fault — I spoke too soon. What would they have thought if I just up and left you again?"

What would *they* have thought? I couldn't even . . . I couldn't even . . . couldn't . . . "And Cora? What happened to her?"

"She died."

"Of what?"

"Cholera."

"*She's* the one who died of cholera . . . ? I thought she was my mother."

"You called her your mother. She might as well have been your mother. You cried. You wouldn't stop crying. That's why I gave you that locket. I told you that way you'd always have her with you."

I wrapped my hand around it. "You mean, it wasn't hers?"

"The hair was hers. That part was true."

"But you always told me I looked nothing like my mother."

He opened his mouth to speak. Closed it. Opened it once more. "You didn't look anything like the woman you thought was your mother."

I was already shaking my head. "That wasn't necessary. None of those lies were necessary."

"They were to me." His voice had risen and his eyes were glinting. "Everyone in my class, everyone I was at the Point with, knew your mother. Annabel Curtis was the Belle of Buttermilk Falls. But now, all those men are out there, out west. In Texas and New Orleans and Memphis and Chicago. If they had seen you, they would have recognized you. They would have known who you were."

"Would that have been so terrible?"

"To all my schemes? Yes! They wouldn't have recognized me, but to see you? They would have known that —" He swallowed the words he was going to say. "Suffice to say that I wouldn't have been able to do the things I needed to. And my best defense, the best disguise, was for you not to know who you resembled."

I couldn't even begin to fathom all of the lies that I'd grown up with. "So you took me with you after Cora died?" Is that when it had all started for me?

"Had to. I couldn't convince anyone else to do what Cora had done. But you caught on quickly. You learned well. And I boarded you when I needed to. I have to say, you turned out quite well."

Quite well for a girl who'd been raised by a whore and serially abandoned at boarding schools and finishing establishments. My hands slid to my throat. I wasn't a lady after all. I never had been. I never would be.

"Come now. It doesn't do to get too emotional."

"I know that." I knew it doubly now. I'd become attached to one of the many people he'd swindled. I couldn't think of a greater irony. "Father? Please. I want this to be over."

"It will be. By the end of June you should be good and married, and Mr. Conklin will be starting his brilliant career. After that you won't have to take an active part in anything. Maybe steer some good opportunities my way a time or two, but —"

"I mean I want to be *finished*. I don't want to participate anymore."

"I'm sure you don't mean that. You're my best investment. All those schools I sent you to. All that polish you've acquired. I can talk a man out of his money, but you're the only one of us who can talk him out of his heart. That, right there? That's talent. A real gift."

"It's not a gift. It's a corruption of everything that's kind and decent."

"You're my good luck."

"Have you ever wondered . . . ? Maybe there's no such thing as luck. Maybe there's just love."

His brow lifted. "Love? You're sounding more and more like your mother every day. At first, she did whatever I asked. And it was easy to talk people out of money when she became so visibly pregnant. But she didn't like doing that, and she didn't like traveling, and she wanted me to just . . . just quit all of it and do something respectable. *'Don't you love me?'* she'd ask. Love is a trap. *'Won't you change for me?'* is what she really meant. I can only be who I am."

"But . . . what about God?"

"What about Him?"

"What if He's here?"

"Now?" He made a grand show of peering up and down the hall. Then he laughed. "Don't you think we'd see Him if He was here? God is just a delusion made up by people who need something to believe in. I believe in me. I believe in luck. And more and more, I'm beginning to believe in you."

I didn't want him to believe in me. I didn't believe in me. Not in the way he did. "What if God's not a delusion? Maybe God cares.

Maybe He sees. And maybe life is not about luck at all. Maybe God actually loves us."

"You don't really think that!"

"I might. I think . . . in fact, I do." I would much rather be like Phoebe than like my father. Even if it cost me everything.

44
SETH

"Lucinda's *father*? He's your Pennyworth?" Deke whistled as he glanced around at Otter and Dandy. I'd asked them to come down to our room after tattoo, at half past nine. "So what are you going to do?"

I'd been thinking on it all afternoon. "First of all, I'm going to try my best to get my grades back. Starting now. I know you all meant well, but I should have known better. I should have known a strength should never be looked at as a weakness, that you should never start playing by another man's rules. He'll always beat you at his own tactics."

Deacon was nodding. "That's . . . probably pretty true."

"And I'm going to find a way to get our money back while he's here."

Dandy looked up from his deck of cards. "How?"

"I don't know. Yet. But I'm going to make

389

a plan using my head this time. I just have to figure out what it is that I have to work with."

Otter blinked his eyes wide. "Outside of Professor Mahan's *Summary on the Cause of Permanent Fortifications and of the Attack and Defense of Permanent Works*? Not much."

"I've got you fellows."

Dandy's brow peaked. "Us?"

"Don't I?"

His nod was slow in coming, but when it did, I knew it meant something. "Well . . . sure."

Deke joined him. "Sure you do. We were going to help you once we got out west. Might as well help you now that Pennyworth's here. It's just . . ." Deke tugged at an earlobe. "I don't know that there's much we can do."

"We'll start as if we're planning a campaign. What's the enemy's weakness?"

Deke looked at me as if I were crazy. "How are we supposed to know that?"

"Got to be money, doesn't it? Since he's a swindler?"

Otter agreed. "Makes sense."

"So if we can think of a way to offer him a chance to make more of it, don't you think he'd take us up on it?"

I'd gotten Deke's full attention now. "I suppose. Depending."

"On what?"

"On what that chance is. And how are you going to make the offer to him?"

That's what I hadn't quite figured out yet. But I would. There had to be a way. "Well . . . what are our strengths?"

Otter answered that question. "We don't . . . We're just cadets. We don't have any money. We don't have any real weapons. And we aren't at liberty to do much at all off the military reservation."

Dandy scoffed. "Or even on it."

True. All those things were true.

Otter squinted, thinking hard. "Could you get him to go back out west? Once we're in the cavalry we'll have lots of strengths at our disposal. All those horses."

"And rifles," Dandy added.

"And soldiers at our disposal. And nothing to do but ride out on patrols, searching for news of Pennyworth, like I told you at the first." Deacon said the words wistfully. I didn't blame him. The plan would have been a good one if Pennyworth had stayed out west.

"He's here now, fellows. He came to me. I'm not going to retreat. So what are we good at?"

"*You're* good at most everything." There was no hint of envy in Otter's words. He made it sound as if he was just stating a fact.

"But Pennyworth has already seen me with Lucinda. He knows who I am. So forget about me. What about the rest of you?"

"Well . . . Mother says I'm good at young'uns, but there's not much use for that here."

"No . . . but you're good with horses."

He sat up straight as if I'd just reminded him. "I'm the best at horses."

Horses. It wasn't much, and it didn't count for hardly anything here, but Otter was right. He could sit a horse like nobody I'd ever seen. So that was something. Maybe.

I looked at Dandy. "You're good at . . ."

He raised a brow as if in challenge.

"You're good at . . . You're our best marksman, of course. . . ." But what else was he good at?

"He's good at striking fear into the heart of ordinary mortals."

Dandy turned around to glare at Deke and did just that. Or tried to. Might have worked if my barracks mate hadn't been shaking with laughter. Dandy stood up and looked at him with a combination of dignity and such disdain that I knew I had my answer. "He's good at being a gentleman. Put a fancy hat on him and hand him a cigar, and he'd be the best Southern gentleman in just about any room."

"And French."

"Pardon me?"

"I'm good at French."

"So noted." Horses, being a gentleman, and French. It wasn't much, but it was something. "Deke?"

"General?" He saluted me with his pencil.

"You're good at drawing."

"So kind of you to notice."

"And getting people to buy into your schemes."

He frowned for a moment, and then he nodded. "I suppose I am."

"So the enemy's weakness is money and our weapons are horses, French, drawing, persuasion, and the consummate Southern gentleman."

"Sounds about right. So what are you going to do with us, General?"

"Something. Just . . . give me a minute here to think."

As Otter and Dandy went back to playing cards and Deacon went back to his sketchbook, I let my gaze drift over them. Money.

Money was the key to victory. We needed to get Pennyworth to give us his money, *my* money, however much of it he still had left. But the only reason he'd want to do that is if he thought he had a chance to make more money. What we needed to do was swindle a swindler . . . with horses, a gentleman, and an artist.

"Dandy, you're from the South, aren't —"

"I'm from New Orleans."

"Right. So you know a thing or two about horses."

"Otter's the one who knows a thing or two about horses."

"Sure. That's right. But if I were a betting man, I'd say you know more about gambling than Otter does."

"Maybe."

I took that as a *yes.* "How about gambling on horses?"

Though he kept his gaze on his cards, he inclined his head in my direction. "I'm my father's son. Maybe even more than my mother's."

"Is that a *yes*?"

"It's a *yes.* And I'm blaming you for making me admit that." He made me feel as if I ought to apologize for the offense.

"And Otter? You can ride just about any horse in the academy's stable, can't you?"

"I suppose I have. At one time or another. Though I oughter say that York is no fun to ride — that's for certain."

"But you can, can't you?"

" 'Course I can."

"All right, then. And Deke . . . ?"

"General?"

"You remember that newspaperman from *Harper's Weekly* who came to draw one of our hops last year?"

"Sure. He was good, but not so good as me."

"Don't you think a magazine like that would want some drawings of our riding lessons too?"

"Maybe . . . What do you have in mind?"

In order for our plan to work, I needed to talk to Lucinda. After chapel, I snuck off the military reservation, hoofed it over to Buttermilk Falls, and waited outside the church. I had hoped to catch her there, but she wasn't among the congregants. As the churchgoers filed out, I caught Bobby Hammond's eye and gestured him over.

His eyes were wide as saucers, so I knew he'd heard about the parade. He was a decent lad, maybe more serious than a boy ought to be, so I didn't want to land him in trouble. I just kept him long enough to find out where Lucinda and her father were staying. Then I walked over to their boardinghouse, praying that I'd be able to find a way to talk to her.

I didn't have to wait long.

Just after the church bells rang noon, she stepped out of the boardinghouse. She joined me around the side of the building, out of view of the windows.

"I need your help."

Guilt darkened her eyes. "If I could give you my father's money I would, Seth. All of it. But the first person he'd suspect is me."

"I'm going to work all of it out. Don't worry. I'll get the money back and he'll never know you helped. No one will."

"You . . . you don't hate me?"

"I could never hate you. And I still stand by what I said — none of this is your fault. I have to admit that I didn't know what to think when you told me who your father was, but it's not as if you had anything to do with any of his schemes."

"But, Seth —"

"I will need your help with our plan though. We need to convince him to place some bets."

"What kind of bets?"

"There's a horse down at the riding hall named York. He's a holy terror. The only person who can ride him is Otter."

"Then you want to figure out a way to get my father to bet *against* Otter? Why would he do that?"

"If you bring him down to the riding hall on Wednesday afternoon, Deacon is going to help your father see that Otter — a true son of the South if ever there was one — can't ride a horse to save his life."

"But . . . ?"

"And the day after that, Dandy — a planter's son from New Orleans with nothing to do but amuse himself — is going to show up. You'll run into him at the hotel. Can you do that?"

She nodded. "Get my father to talk to Deacon on the first day and Dandy on the next? But I —"

"You can't give any sign that you know them."

"I won't."

"I know your father's the one who's been so cunning and deceitful, and I wish I didn't have to depend on you to be the same. I don't want you to think I assume that just because he does those things that you —"

"I understand. And I'll try my best."

"Do you think your father would try to convince Dandy to bet against Otter?"

"Perhaps. If he thought there was no way

he could lose the bet."

"If he heard Otter speaking, heard that Southern accent, and if he saw Otter ride truly terribly, do you think that would be enough?"

"It probably would. Everyone knows Southern men are good at riding. But you lost hundreds of dollars to my father. I don't think you'll be able to make it up in just one bet."

"At this point, I'll take what I can get."

"Then I'll do what I can to help."

"Just make sure your father's at the riding hall Wednesday afternoon."

45
LUCINDA

I watched Seth walk away wanting nothing so much as to go with him.

At least he didn't hate me. And at least he'd given me the chance to help him. Maybe that would assuage some of my guilt. I'd almost admitted to everything. But what would have been the point of that? As my father once told me, *"People don't want to know what they don't want to know so why tell them?"*

Why tell him?

He seemed to think of me in the same way he thought of his sister: hapless victim. What would be gained by telling him the truth? I might still carry my guilt, I might carry it for the rest of my life, but at least this way he would still have fond thoughts of me after he graduated.

The best thing to do, after he gambled back his money, was to put as much distance between us as possible. Maybe I could convince my father to move to the city for the winter. Maybe next time he went, I would go with him.

Or maybe I wouldn't. Maybe I would just take a steamboat up the river. Maybe I could do what I'd done here. I could start a finishing school. I could forge my references. And then . . . I would be the same deceitful person I'd always been. An honest life couldn't be built on a foundation of lies. My time in Buttermilk Falls had shown me that.

I'd just have to . . . what? My hands began to tremble as I felt my chin start to pucker. What was there left for me to do? I didn't deserve an honest life, and I had lost my taste for a dishonest one.

Maybe my father was right about me. I wasn't meant to live a respectable life.

I willed myself calm as I put a hand to my bonnet and retied the ribbons beneath my chin. I pulled my mantle closer about my shoulders and walked out toward the military academy to meet Mr. Conklin, as I had planned.

I pretended I was delighted to see him.

I let him pull me closer than was proper.

We strolled along Flirtation Walk together, and as we did, we came upon several other couples. Though we halted to let them pass,

Mr. Conklin didn't step off the path for them. They were obligated to go around us, even the girl who was wearing shoes ridiculously ill-suited to the terrain. But the cadets snapped salutes and quick-stepped away from us. I had the feeling Mr. Conklin usually got what he wanted.

As did my father.

It was odd that two men so unlike each other — one intent upon keeping the rules and the other on breaking every one — could be so similar. I'd spent my childhood following one man without question . . . if I kept to the path I was walking, I would spend the rest of my life following the other.

But what other choice did I have?

In spite of the frigid breeze coming off the river and autumn's vividly blue sky, the air suddenly seemed stifling. I tightened my grip on Mr. Conklin's arm. "What would you say if you discovered there were . . . ? What if there were disreputable people in your family?"

"*My* family?"

I nodded.

"There wouldn't be."

"But how do you know?"

"I promise you, my family is beyond reproach. The first Conklin on these shores signed the Mayflower Compact. There's nothing about us that we don't know."

"But what if there were." What if there were an outright criminal hiding in plain sight?

"Why would there be?"

"If there were, what would happen?"

"I assure you, they wouldn't be invited to Christmas dinner!"

"Not even if they had a good reason for what they'd done?"

"A good reason for being disreputable?" He said the words as if he didn't quite understand them.

"What if they didn't mean it?" But I had meant it. "What if . . . what if they didn't understand what they'd been doing?" But I had understood. "Or what if . . . what if . . . ?"

He took my hands in his. "Lucinda. My dear. All in good time. Anyone who joins the Conklin family would bring nothing but honor to their own family. Speaking of which, it's been so good to meet your own father. And your uncle. They're not Conklins, of course, but I know you must have your own sort of family pride."

46
SETH

I spent the rest of the evening planning our swindle.

The first thing we'd need were costumes. Deke had to look like a newspaperman, and Dandy had to look like the sire of one of those New Orleans planters. And none of us had a stitch of clothing between us that wasn't regulation issue.

"Got any ideas?" I asked Deke as we sat on the wall of Fort Put, looking out at the river and its valley.

"There's a girl works the laundry at the hotel who's been giving me the eye."

"I don't want you to have to do something you'd regret. Or that I'd regret you doing."

He heaved a sigh of relief. "Well, thank goodness for that! I knew you were a true friend."

A true friend who didn't have any better idea, unfortunately. "Do you know anyone in town? Someone who wouldn't ask why

403

you needed two whole sets of clothes?"

"No. You?"

"No. Or I would have asked before now."

"I don't know anyone in town . . ." He pushed himself to standing. "But I do know Benny Havens!"

"Benny? He wouldn't help us with something like this, would he?"

"If you told him you were planning to run a swindle beneath the commandant's nose? 'Course he would!"

"But he's a — No offense, because I know you like him . . . but he's not anyone's idea of a gentleman."

"Doesn't make any difference to me. I'm supposed to be a newspaperman, aren't I?"

I nodded. "It's Dandy I'm worried about. He needs to look just right."

"He will. I promise you. If anyone can do it, Benny can."

I left it to Deke to run to Benny's that night and beg for what we needed. That would take care of all my problems. At least I'd thought it would, until Otter and Dandy sat down next to me at supper that evening. One on each side of me.

Dandy glanced over at the fellows sitting next to us, and then he leaned in close. "I've been thinking about your plan, and I just don't know that I can go through with it."

If Dandy wouldn't do it, the whole thing fell apart. "All I need you to do is . . . Blast it, Dandy! You don't even have to pretend to be a Southern gentleman, because you are one. It's not as if you're lying. And even if you were, this might as well be a military operation: we've got an enemy that we're trying to defeat through subterfuge, misdirection, and deception." I clapped him on the back. "Your integrity won't be compromised. Besides, all *you* have to do is be yourself. It's everyone else who has to do the pretending."

"I'm fine with all of that. It's the part about betting on Otter."

"The part about . . . ?" Now I was mystified. Why wouldn't he bet on Otter? They were the best of friends, and Otter was the best horseman among us. "Why wouldn't you? Don't you trust him?"

"Of course I trust him. I'd trust him with my life."

"Then what's the problem?"

"It's the part you said about why. It's what I'd have to say to Lucinda's father."

"All you have to say is something about betting *with* your compatriots instead of against them. And everyone knows you Southern fellows are better with horses."

"First thing you have to realize is they're not my compatriots. Second, it's not —"

"They're not your compatriots? Last thing I knew New Orleans was south of Arkansas and east of Texas. That is the deepest South there is."

"But —"

He was starting to make me mad. "And don't even try to say it's not true about Southerners being the best at horsemanship." I rattled off half a dozen of the best horsemen at the academy, and all of them were from the South.

"I don't think you understand that —"

If I didn't stop him, he was liable to argue with me for the next ten minutes. Sometimes all a soldier needed was reassurance and a direct order. "I don't need you to ride the horse yourself. I just need you to put on that accent of yours and say what everyone else believes to be true. Is that going to be a problem?"

"If it were anyone but you, I wouldn't be doing this. Just so you know."

"And I appreciate it." I nodded and went back to contemplating the poor excuse for supper that we were being served.

"Uh . . . General?"

"Otter?"

"Yes sir, General."

"What is it? Are you not going to be able to do this either?"

"I want to say, yes, I will, but I oughter be honest with you. Just doesn't set right. Asking me to ride poorly is like asking a man to go back and crawl after he's been walking around on his own two feet for twenty years. I might as well be lying. And a gentleman's word is his bond. So how am I supposed to do that?"

I could think of lots of ways. And any one of them would work just fine for my purposes. But it wasn't me I was trying to reassure. "Didn't you hear me tell Dandy this was a military operation? Can't you just pretend?"

"I suppose, on reflection, I might could . . . but a horse don't forget a thing like not being ridden well. And I tell you, most of the time, the only thing I like about this place is the horses."

"So what you're saying is you don't feel right about pretending . . . to your *horse*?"

"No, sir. Mother always says, if nothing else, I've always been an honest man."

"So what you're saying is you want to be honest about this whole swindle? Is that what you're saying?"

"I just, I want to help you and everything, but . . . I sure would feel better about this if

I could feel like I was telling the truth. That's all."

"I really need you to do this for me, Otter." He was the only one who could ride York.

"I know you do. I realize that."

"But I wouldn't want you to do it if it doesn't seem right."

He broke out into a grin. "Thank you, General. Thank you so much." He dug into his puddle of boiled carrots with much more enthusiasm than I could muster.

Dandy had been listening to our conversation. Now, he set his fork down. "Does this mean we aren't going to do it?"

"We're going to do it."

Otter looked at me with drawn brows. "But you just said —"

"I just said I'd save your conscience."

"But —"

"I think I can figure out another way to do the whole thing. A way that will make you able to sleep at night, Otter. Would you agree to a plan like that?"

"Of course I would! Anything that gets you out of trouble and doesn't get me into it. That's a plan I can agree to."

With Dandy and Otter satisfied, I went back to eating. Otter's request might make things more difficult, but there were ways to work around it. What if he never made it onto the horse that first day at all? Or what if he made it into the saddle, but couldn't get any further? The only thing I had to do was make sure Lucinda's father heard his accent and make it look as if he couldn't sit a horse. What could be so difficult about that?

47

LUCINDA

Wednesday came too soon. And not without trepidation. Seth thought he could out-gamble my father? That was . . . Why, that was insanity!

When my father wasn't peddling his deeds to land in make-believe towns during the spring and summer, he was plying the Mississippi River as a professional gambler in the fall. If Seth thought he could just fancy talk my father out of his money, he was greatly mistaken. But I did want to help him get his money back. If there was any chance that he could succeed, shouldn't I help him?

At least my father wasn't planning to go into the city on Wednesday. That meant all I had to do was get him to the riding hall. I knew a dozen ways to make someone do what I wanted, but I'd never tried any of them out on my father. I went into the parlor after breakfast praying that I could convince him to do what I needed him to.

"The weather looks fine today."

He gave a glance toward the window. "For November."

"I was thinking of taking a walk to the academy."

"Suit yourself. I plan on trying to talk Mrs. Holt out of one of those pies she's baking." He propped an ankle on his opposite knee and took up a copy of some newspaper.

Why not get directly to the point? "I was thinking that maybe we should figure out how to make some money here as well as in the city."

He sent me a keen glance over the top of the newspaper. "What did you have in mind?"

"Was there a riding hall when you were here?"

He nodded as he turned a page of the newspaper. "We received training on horses every week."

"They built a new riding hall just this year. All the cadets have been rhapsodizing about it."

"Hmm." He was scanning the articles, no doubt assessing who or what might be good for a swindle.

"It's seems like the perfect place to lay down a wager or two."

"Hmph."

"Perhaps we should take a look."

He sighed and then his brows peaked. He rattled the newspaper. "They say the army is starting a camel corps."

Camels? "Whatever for?"

"Transportation in Texas. And New Mexico. Hard to figure out a way to profit from that, though. Wonder if they'll bring some out here for those cadets to practice on?"

"But don't you think we ought to?"

"Ought to what?" He glanced at me over the top of the newspaper.

"Have a try at gambling down at the riding hall."

"I don't think so."

What? "Why not?" He had to!

"Too risky."

"Risky?" Risk was the whole point. He'd lived his entire life — *my* entire life — on a knife's edge of risk.

"I don't think anyone will recognize me, but you were right in thinking it might not be smart to take chances."

He always took chances! If we didn't take anything else away from a scheme, we always took chances. "Maybe you're right." But I couldn't fail Seth. Not again. Even if his plan was doomed to failure, if I could do nothing else for him, I must get my father to the riding hall.

A long-ago phrase echoed through my thoughts. Sometimes when things were going poorly, my father would simply give in. "I suppose we could just go back to Buttermilk Falls."

He stopped reading, and for the first time that I could remember, he focused solely on me.

"But I was thinking that maybe —"

A chuckle rattled around his chest for a moment, and then it erupted into a roar. "Sorry." He pulled a handkerchief from his coat and patted at his eyes. As he tucked it away, his eyes were still dancing. "And what was it, my dear, that you were thinking?"

"Why not take advantage of any game we might propagate right here? It would be a shame to let good money go to waste."

He was silent for a long moment while he stared off into the distance. And he finally nodded. "Why indeed?"

I felt my shoulders sag in relief. I'd done my part, I would take my father to the riding hall. I could only hope that now Seth would do his.

We decided to stop by the hotel before walking across the Plain and down to the riding hall. That way we might be taken for tourists who wouldn't know anything about the horses or the cadets who rode them. Once we gained entrance to the hotel, I made a show of pretending I had forgotten my gloves. I apologized to my father and darted up the stairs. After walking the length of the second floor twice, I took my gloves from my reticule and pulled them on as I descended.

Father smiled at me and offered up his arm.

I threaded mine through it. As we departed, he asked the desk clerk for directions to the riding hall.

"The new one, sir?"

"Unless there's an old one." He winked.

"No, sir. Just cross the Plain in the direction of the academy building, and once you've crossed, follow the path to the left on down the hill."

We started toward it at a leisurely pace. I hoped my diffident manner belied the hammering of my heart. I didn't know what I was supposed to do beyond getting my father there. What was Seth expecting of me?

"We'll do it the way we usually do."

"Pardon me?"

"If I determine there's betting to be done, we'll do it the way we've bet on horses in the past."

That meant I was supposed to circulate through the crowd until I found a regular attender. When I feigned an interest, it generally didn't take long for the man to tell me everything he knew about the horses and their riders. I would relay that information to my father, who would check it against his own sources and his own instincts, and then he would attach himself to some man who looked fresh from the countryside. Father was particularly skilled at using big words that meant nothing at all to convince a man to bet against him. And sometimes he even used me to flatter the man into parting with his money.

Seth had no idea what he was up against.

Constructed of stone, the riding hall was long and imposing and topped by a curiously curved roof. Stepping inside it was like stepping into a deep cavern. The floor was dirt and was covered with tanbark. The walls were high. Rays of light streamed from parallel lines of tall, narrow windows, setting each particle of airborne dust to glimmering. I drew a handkerchief from my reticule and held it to my nose to try to stay the equally pungent odors of horse and haystraw.

My father elbowed me in the side.

I followed his gaze to a cluster of men who lounged about the edge of the riding ring.

Taking in a gulp of linen-strained air, I crumpled my handkerchief into my palm, widened my eyes into a gaze of innocence, and meandered toward the men. Behind me, I knew my father was scrutinizing both the cadets and their mounts.

I chose a stretch of railing close to the men and curled my gloved fingers around it. In front of us, the cadets were being put through their paces, jumping hurdles at the far end of the hall and slashing at leather balls with their sabers at our end. My gasps at the intensity of their exercises were entirely real. Fortunately they served to attract attention. As I watched, a cadet in the middle of the hall reached out toward a brass ring with his saber as he jumped his horse over a hurdle.

I held my breath.

He caught the ring.

I exhaled.

Then he tumbled from the horse.

"Oh!" I couldn't keep myself from exclaiming.

He picked himself up and stalked off, spurs marking his progress through the tanbark.

Beside me, a man pulled a coin purse from his pocket, grumbling. He lifted his gaze toward me. "Beg pardon. No offense."

I smiled. "None taken." I glanced beyond him to the other men. "This looks quite dangerous. Does the army know these cadets are doing things like this?"

One of the men hid a smile in his sleeve and turned back to watch the cadets. But another man, one who was sketching in a book, glanced up at me. "They surely do, miss. And just as surely, I expect they don't much care."

"You can't tell me the army *approves* of this sort of thing!"

The man grinned at me. "The army *encourages* this sort of thing. At least that's what they tell me."

"And you're drawing them?"

He held up the sketchbook for the rest of us to see. "I am. That's what I'm paid for. Mostly." He winked. "I'm not much good at anything else."

I had a difficult time trying not to smile back. The man was Seth's friend, Deacon.

"And how do you know which ones are good?"

"The horses or the men?"

"Either. Both."

He shrugged. "They all look good to me.

But if you want to know, ask this gentleman here. Mr . . . ?" He gestured toward the man who had just collected some coins from the others.

"Mr. Angersly. At your service."

I beamed a smile at him.

Deacon pushed his pencil into the hair above his ear. "Seems this lovely lady doesn't know much about horses. Come to think on it, neither do I. Except to always bet on the Southern boys."

Mr. Angersly frowned. "That's not any kind of tip. Everyone knows that."

Deacon sent me another surreptitious wink before he bent back over his drawing. Mr. Angersly cleared a place for me next to himself and began to tell me everything he knew about the cadets and their horses.

48
SETH

I leaned close to Otter as the soldiers brought in the horses. "We got some tourists today."

Otter looked over his shoulder toward the railing where a knot of men had gathered.

Lucinda was standing there in a wide, green skirt, her bonnet pushed toward the back of her head. One of the men was talking, and I could hear her reply every now and then. I hoped this worked. It had to work. My sister and I needed our money back. And Lucinda . . . she needed this too. Down at the other end of the hall, Lucinda's father was talking to one of the instructors. I hoped his attention stayed down at that end. I didn't want him to notice me or Dandy. But I sure as anything wanted him to remember Otter. "That's Lucinda's father, down there at the other end."

Otter was focused on his horse, but he took the time to glance down the hall. "The

419

one what looks like he stepped out of a bandbox?"

"That's him."

"He looks nice enough." He gave a tug on a stirrup. Checked the bridle. Otter might look like a slouch, but he was fastidious about the state of his horses.

"So do snakes. Until you step on one."

"That's true." He scowled in the man's direction.

I put a hand to his arm. "Wipe that look off your face. You don't want him to know that you know him."

"Anyone takes advantage of girls or orphans deserves a whole lot more than a dirty look in my opinion."

"Which is why we're doing what we're doing."

His lips clamped together in a thin, determined line.

I put an arm about his shoulders and turned him around so we could have a private conversation. "You do remember what it is that you're doing?"

"I remember. But you remember what you promised, right?"

Behind my back, I waved my hand at a classmate. I'd promised him an extra serving of our next hash in exchange for lengthening one of Otter's stirrups. "Of course I do. I promised I'd keep your conscience clear. All you have to do is . . . ?"

"Right down there, when we're waiting on riding, I'm to say 'They just don't do it like this in Kentucky.' "

"That's right."

"Which is strange because you know I'm not from there."

"I know it. But you've heard that said before, haven't you?"

"Depends on what you're referring to about horses. But sure I have. Everyone thinks those folks from Kentucky are the only ones who know horses. But the way they do things isn't the only way to train a horse, 'cause training all depends on the horse. I must've said that a thousand times."

"Just say that one line, Otter. Just the one sentence. Nothing else."

"I will. Of course I will. It's just that it don't mean anything. That's all."

"Eventually it will mean a whole lot to me and my sister."

He flashed me one of those grins of his. "And that's why I'm helping. That's why we all are."

We finished watching the others jump hurdles, and then I took the reins of Otter's horse as well as my own and pulled them back toward the end of the riding ring. Once we came abreast of Lucinda's father, I gave Otter the nod.

"They just don't do it like this in Kentucky!" Thank goodness he wasn't hoping to take to the stage any time soon. He was more than obvious, but at least his accent had come through loud and clear.

It was our turn for the hurdles. As Otter occupied himself with talking to his horse, out of view of Lucinda's father, I loosened his saddle. He'd wanted to be honest about this whole thing. I was just trying to abide by his wishes.

At the command to mount up, we all hopped on our horses.

A confused sort of look rippled across Otter's face, but there was no time to waste. We'd been ordered to jump the hurdles, and that's what we had to do. And if we didn't, or wouldn't, we faced being awarded demerits.

I jumped the first hurdle and then dismounted on command. I mounted again and jumped the second and third hurdles, then dismounted again on command. When I glanced back, Otter was off balance and spluttering, his saddle halfway down his horse's girth. The way his cheeks had flushed bright red made him look every bit

422

the country boy that I'd been hoping for.

Lucinda's father was looking on, a smile curving half his mouth.

Once Otter had cleared his last hurdle, he came to a stop beside me. Those clear blue eyes of his were troubled. "Could have sworn I checked the saddle on this horse. I always do!"

"What's that?"

"My saddle's loose!"

"That's not like you."

"No, it ain't. I make a fool of myself in every other class here. This is the one thing I'm supposed to do well."

"Don't say that so loud!"

He sent a glance down the ring toward Lucinda's father. "Sorry."

49

LUCINDA

Otter had done such a good job at losing his balance that it looked entirely natural. Maybe Seth's scheme would work. I tried to keep Mr. Angersly talking as my father approached. "Such a lovely location, here at the Point. Do you live here?"

"Me? No. I just came up for the day. Wanted to take a look around."

I cast my gaze wider. "Are you all just visiting?"

The rest of the men nodded.

"I've been here for most of the week." Deacon flipped through the pages of his sketchbook. They were filled with drawings of cadets and their horses.

My father extended his hand, and Deacon gave the sketchbook to him. He gestured me over and flipped through its pages. They chronicled what must have been at least a week's worth of exercises. There were sketches of cadets jumping hurdles, slashing at the leather balls, riding at full tilt with their sabers drawn. My father turned another page and burst out laughing, angling the sketchbook so that I could see it.

Seth's friend Otter was drawn midair, his horse racing out from beneath him. The expression of bewilderment and surprise on his face was supremely telling.

Deacon pushed away from the wall and came to stand beside us. Father showed him the sketch. "Oh! Him." Deacon smiled. "I couldn't help myself. Not fit for publication of course." He sighed and glanced back down the hall. "During my time here I've come to realize that some cadets are better at this sort of thing than others."

My father closed up the sketchbook and offered it back. "I've heard he's a Southern boy, though."

"Could be." Deacon accepted it with a grave nod. "I don't think any of them have actually killed themselves, but . . ." He shrugged and drew a cloth cap from a pocket. "If you'll excuse me. I think I've probably drawn all the pictures I need." He nodded and headed toward the door.

My father leaned close as we watched Deacon leave. "That cadet is a menace."

"Which one?"

"The one that nearly fell off his horse. The

one that newspaper fellow made the drawing of. But I overheard that cadet talking. He's from Kentucky."

"Everyone's from somewhere."

"Kentucky folks are supposed to be good at this sort of thing. I wonder . . ."

So did I. I wondered if my father would follow the trail of bait Seth had so carefully laid down.

"It's a rare thing."

"What is?"

"To find a Southern boy who isn't good at riding."

I willed myself not to smile, even though my soul was leaping in elation. It really might work.

The next morning, my father took me into the parlor directly after breakfast. "I've come up with a plan."

A plan? In my father's terms that meant he'd come up with an idea for a swindle.

"It's perfect. Just like out west, it takes advantage of the transitory nature of the area, only we won't have to do any transiting."

I tried not to get my hopes up. "Everyone I've met has lived here for years —"

"I'm not talking about these townspeople."

"— and the cadets hardly ever leave the Point."

"I'm not talking about them either. It's the tourists!"

"The tourists? But . . . there aren't that many. Not at this time of year."

"Which is perfect."

"For what?"

"For the plan. Here's what we're going to do."

Two hours later, we were sitting in the parlor of the West Point Hotel. My father was looking for just the right man. He had to be very obviously wealthy. It would also help our cause if he were from the South.

As we were sipping our tea, Dandy walked into the room. If I hadn't already known who he was, if I hadn't already given my heart to Seth Westcott, he might have swept my breath away. Dandy walked across the room, cigar in one hand, a cane in the other, measuring and then dismissing each of the hotel guests in turn.

In his frock suit and winged shirt collar, with his hair combed precisely back from his brow, he looked like the young scion of a wealthy Southern planter. One of those dangerous, deadly young men who live for amusement and pleasure. In short, he

looked every inch the dandy. The casual dif-
fidence in his manner, the disdain in his
eyes, and the way he slapped his gloves and
hat onto the table next to ours as if he
owned the place spoke of a life lived in
absolute mastery of everything — and
everyone — in it.

My father nodded at him.

Dandy returned the look but neither
smiled nor nodded. He simply paused in
his perusal of the room.

"You look like a man who knows a good
horse."

Dandy seemed to take his measure. "I
know several good horses."

"We're just visiting — came up the river
to see the military academy. Reason I mention horses is that I've heard there's a riding
hall down the hill."

Dandy glanced up at the woman who was
placing a cup of tea in front of him. For the
first time since I'd known him, I saw a
softening in his eyes. And if I could believe
my ears, I think he even thanked her.

My father was still trying to pique his
interest. "Not a lot to do here — after
you've seen the place, of course. We walked
around a bit yesterday."

Dandy raised the cup to his lips and took
a sip.

"My daughter and I were thinking of taking a walk down to that riding hall this afternoon."

Dandy nodded at me.

I returned the gesture.

"Would you care to join us?"

He sighed. Then the faintest smile lifted the corners of his mouth, as if he couldn't be bothered to fully extend it fully to his lips. "Why not?"

We walked together into the riding hall. While my eyes accustomed themselves to the dust-filtered light, the odors of the place assaulted me. I saw no need to hide it, and once more, I pulled out my handkerchief.

These cadets appeared to be from one of the more junior classes. Some of them were riding at full tilt toward the hurdles. Others were more intent upon putting their sabers to good use. As the soldiers called out instructions, the cadets wheeled their horses to respond. It did not take long to pick out the best of them. Father subtly placed us at a point along the rail where the cadets gathered before mounting. From there, we could overhear their conversations. Father and Dandy watched the cadets in silence for a long while.

After a particularly impressive feat, my

father whistled.

Dandy fingered his cigar as he turned to him. "Are you a betting man?"

"I am. And yourself?"

"I've been known to place a wager a time or two."

My father nodded. They directed their attention to a new group of cadets who were gathering along the rail in front of them. "Want to wager on who makes it through the hurdles the fastest?" My father withdrew a pocket watch from his coat.

Dandy shrugged. "Why not?"

They placed several bets, all of which my father won, though not by much.

After each one, Dandy challenged him to another. After a third loss, with an accumulated debt of one hundred dollars, Seth's friend was wiping sweat from his brow.

My father was smiling serenely. The group of cadets left and another came in. They were Seth's group.

Dandy pointed with his cigar. "Let's make another, on that young man over there. For double my losses. I'll wager he can do it fastest."

"Double? I hate to try to talk sense into you when you've been doing so well by me, but don't you think you ought to quit? No sense in digging your hole any deeper."

"Are you saying you don't think I can pay my debts?"

"I said no such thing."

"Double."

"All right, then."

Dandy lost that bet too. He was down for two hundred dollars now. "If you're any kind of gentleman at all, then give me another chance to recoup my losses." Dandy made his words sound almost plaintive.

Daddy's boy. I could almost hear my father saying the words. Daddy's boys were the best for a scheme like this. They didn't know what to do when they started to fail because they'd always been rescued. Their first instinct was to double down and try harder, make more bets, wager more money. It sometimes took a while for them to realize it would only make things worse. The trick of it was in judging properly. In stopping just before that realization dawned.

I saw Seth but could tell that he was trying to stay out of sight. Otter and Deacon were speaking, however. I hoped my father wouldn't recognize him as the newspaperman! As they talked, Deacon edged Otter toward us while keeping his face out of view. His voice, however, carried quite well. "What did Mrs. Ames decide to do about that land she was thinking of selling?"

Otter huffed a breath. "That land? Well . . . those Holifields said they'd pay even more for it than they offered at the first. Said they'd throw in one of those prize sow pigs of theirs and if she gave them access to the holler, they were going to let her have their rooster as well." Otter's accent was thicker than molasses. "But there was something about it just didn't set right, so she did some poking around and found they had them a still right close to the crick, and . . ." He shrugged. "Don't think they oughter been surprised when they came round one night and found it all destroyed to pieces. Mother sure can be a terror when she wants to."

"So she's not going to sell, then?"

"Well, now . . . I didn't say that exactly." Otter paused as the soldiers assigned them their horses. Deacon was given a bay I recognized from the day before. Otter was assigned the fearsome York, who came into the ring kicking.

Father and I exchanged a glance. Thinking that Otter was the worst of horsemen, he would consider this even better luck than he had hoped for. Knowing Seth was counting on Otter to win Dandy's bet, I considered it worse. Father pointed the pair out to Dandy. "I'll bet that even a Southern man isn't the equal of that horse."

Dandy looked at him coolly. "My belief, sir, is that blood will always win out."

The horse's ears went flat as its tail swished. It let out a strident whinny. "I don't think so, son. Not even a demon could ride that one."

"I would not wish to leave the honor of one of my compatriots undefended. What are you willing to wager?"

Father put up his hands. "I'm an honest man. I don't want to trick you. I don't think this would be a fair bet."

"You refuse?" Dandy seemed bloated with injured pride. "You've impugned my compatriot, you've taken my money, and now you wish to leave me without the means to redress it?"

"I just don't want to see you lose more of your money on a bad bet. Why don't we wager on one of the others? I'd feel much better about it."

"That one or no one."

"Well . . . I . . . uh . . . I suppose I can't back down now."

"Then I'll wager you double."

"Four hundred dollars? I don't think —"

"Are you no longer so certain of your opinion?" Dandy was playing my father exactly right. Exactly the way my father had played hundreds of victims in the past.

"No, no. It's just —"

Dandy extended his hand.

After hesitating for one long moment, my father extended his and they shook.

The bet was on.

50
SETH

As I stood watching, Dandy and Lucinda's father shook hands. It made me want to whoop. But celebration could be premature. My friends had taken their positions, they were armed and ready, but the battle still had to be won. And sometimes the best way to start was to make the enemy believe he had control over the battlefield.

I winked at Deke to signal the start of the next part of our plan. While he mentioned there was a fly on Otter's back, I pointed out a splotch of mud on the back of his opposite leg.

Otter tried to spot both at the same time, which had the effect of him turning first this way and that, like a puppy chasing after its own tail.

Out at the rails, Dandy scowled while Lucinda's father seemed barely able to contain his glee.

"Where?" Otter asked me.

Deacon answered. "Where what?"

"Where is it?"

"The fly?" Deke reached out to his shoulder and pretended to brush something off it. "Got it. Don't pay it any more mind."

A soldier led old York to Otter. "Think you can manage this one, private?"

Otter nodded with grim determination. "Can't say I'll enjoy it, but sometimes stone meal gets mixed in with the grits." He put a hand to the horse's muzzle and gave it a pat.

"You will mount at my command!"

Some of us sighed in relief. At least we wouldn't have to perform a running mount.

"You will ride with sabers, cutting at the leather balls!" The enlisted men moved to distribute the balls through the riding ring. "First on the ground, then on a post! You will jump the first hurdle and catch the ring! You will cut at the ball on the ground. At the second ball on a post you will jump the second hurdle and catch that last ring!"

My heart sank. Having to ride York on a bet was bad enough. But to have to do hurdles and sabers and rings as well . . . ?

Otter mumbled something beneath his breath.

I leaned close. "What's that?"

"Of course it'd be the full course today,

while I'm riding York."

"Can you do it?"

"I blessed well better try. Mother always says I'm not anyone's coward."

At the soldier's command, we all mounted and raced off to accomplish our orders.

But Otter's horse flat out stopped halfway down the arena, after he cleared the first hurdle.

My heart fell to my stomach. Dandy wasn't carrying any money. He didn't have any. None of us did. He couldn't lose this bet. Losing was not part of the plan.

For one long moment, Otter hovered in the air above the horse. And then he let out a blood-curdling yell, grabbed the horse by the ears, and jammed his knees into its neck.

Just as I started to breathe again, the horse began to kick.

Dandy, Deacon, and I stared, transfixed as it reared and then hunkered down and kicked his legs out at the back. But Otter clung to it like a burr.

And then it started spinning.

That's when the rest of us stopped riding and pulled up to watch.

I don't know if it bucked and heaved and spun for one minute or ten, but finally it suddenly stopped, flicked up its ears, and began trotting down to the end of the ring just as pretty as you please.

But Otter wasn't finished with it. He dug his heels into its flanks and wheeled it around. Then he galloped down to the far end of the ring and started all over again, cutting at the balls and sailing over that first hurdle.

When he cleared that second hurdle, the rest of us cheered.

All of us but the captain in charge of the drill. "Mr. Ames!"

Otter turned his horse around smartly. "Yes, sir."

"For dawdling on the course, three demerits."

Otter sighed. "Yes, sir."

"The rest of you — two demerits each for failure to obey a command."

We all spurred our horses into motion and joined Otter, whose horse was blowing heavily, down at the end of the hall. Once there, I was able to observe Lucinda and her father.

His face was frozen in disbelief as he watched Otter through narrowed eyes.

Had we been too obvious? Was he going to refuse to pay his debt?

51
LUCINDA

My father was livid. Rage vibrated from his features. "Yesterday, that boy couldn't sit a horse to save his life."

Dandy appeared as overcome with boredom as ever before, but deep in those dark eyes of his, I thought I detected a twinkle. "Blood wins out. That's what I always say . . . and sometimes a man can get lucky. Good idea, to come down here. Watch the cadets. Suppose I'd better go now." He extended a hand.

My father hesitated, looking out at the cadets as if he couldn't quite believe what had just happened. But he dug into his coat and brought out his wallet. He fisted the money into his hand and slapped it into Dandy's waiting palm.

Dandy transferred it to his own coat with what seemed like a smooth, practiced motion. "I'll be on my way now. Much obliged." He put his hat on his head, nodded at my father, nodded at me, and then he was gone.

Father stared at him as he walked away. Then he swung his attention back to the cadets. The horses were being led away. The cadets were bunched into groups, talking.

I reached out to touch my father's arm. "I don't suppose there's any reason to stay."

"Suppose not. I just wish I knew . . ."

I needed to get him away from the riding hall before he spent too much time thinking about what had happened. "Let's go, Father." I linked my arm with his and practically pulled him from the building.

But after about ten paces, my father suddenly stopped. "There's something . . . something I just . . ." He broke from me and strode back toward the riding hall.

"Father, wait!"

"In a minute." He disappeared into the building as my heart dropped to the bottom of my feet.

By the time I caught up with him, it was too late. At the end of the riding hall, Seth and Otter and Deacon were congratulating themselves. And as we stood there watching, Dandy, who was now dressed in his uniform, walked up and joined them.

"You there!" My father's outstretched finger was pointing toward Dandy.

Dandy's eyes widened.

"Captain!"

The captain in charge of the drill came toward us on the run. "Sir?"

"These cadets have stolen my money."

"They . . . they stole your — ?"

"They stole my money. Not ten minutes ago."

"But they've been riding horses this whole time." His gaze widened as it came to rest on Dandy. "Except, perhaps, for Mr. Delagarde. Did you steal this man's money?"

"No. He lost it honestly."

My father snorted, the very picture of righteous indignation. "I lost it in a dishonest gamble."

"A gamble? There's been gambling?"

"I insist upon speaking to your superior."

"That would be the commandant, Major Walker." He sighed. "You'll have to follow me." He held an arm out toward Seth and his friends. "And all of you might as well come too."

I struggled to keep up with the men without breaking into a run. One hand steadied my bonnet, the other clutched my skirt. When I was able, I grabbed my father's sleeve to slow him. "I don't know that this is the best idea, appealing to the authorities. What if someone recognizes you?"

"No one will recognize me. And if they do, then I'll deny it, just the same as I always do."

"But you have a history here."

"A history no one will connect with me."

I put a hand to his chest to stop him. "Don't go through with this. Don't accuse them."

"I accuse them of nothing. I'm simply stating the truth." He pushed my hand aside and strode toward the captain.

I called out after him. "The truth is you're just as bad as they are! And the only result will be their dismissal!"

He came back to me, took up my arm, and yanked me along with him.

"I just wish you'd —" I fell silent as we were escorted into a building.

We followed the captain, the cadets trailing us, as he rapped on a door and gained entrance. He directed us inside with a sweep of the hand and entered behind us. "Major Walker, sir. This gentleman has an accusation to place against these cadets."

The commandant rose and came from behind his desk as he considered each of the cadets standing before him. Then his curious gaze settled on my father. "All of them?"

My father nodded. "They enticed me into gambling."

The commandant seemed to take my father's measure from the tip of his toes to the top of his oiled head. *"They* enticed *you?"*

I knew the flush that swept my father's cheeks had nothing to do with shame and everything to do with anger. He was furious that he'd been taken at his own game. "These cadets — all of them — were involved in a scheme to cheat me out of my money."

"A scheme?"

"They tricked me into gambling against him" — he pointed to Otter — "in the riding hall."

"Against Mr. Ames? He's the best horseman we have!"

"Which simply goes to prove to what lengths they were willing to stoop in order to take my money."

"What exactly are you saying, sir?"

"They were gambling."

"Gambling?"

"They were. On academy property."

"You realize this is a serious accusation. These men would be summarily dismissed if that were the case."

"It was most definitely the case. That one"

443

— he nodded toward Dandy — "posed as a gentleman from the South and —"

"And *he* tried to talk *me* into betting on what he considered was a losing man." Dandy took a step toward my father.

My father swallowed.

"Is this true?"

Dandy nodded, defiance shining in his eyes. "You might say he enticed me into gambling. He was the one who tried to steal *my* money."

"You had money? On your person?"

Dandy's gaze dropped toward the floor. "No, sir. I did not."

"See?" My father's voice was strident. "It wasn't an honest gamble. It was designed to lure an unsuspecting visitor into parting with his money. I can't imagine the public would be happy to see their taxes spent on a military academy that harbors insolent youths like these."

The commandant frowned as he considered my father's words. "Who is currently in possession of this man's money?"

Seth stepped forward. "I am, sir."

"Give it back to him."

Seth's chin lifted. "No, sir."

"Excuse me?"

"It's mine, by right."

"By right, I should dismiss you this very

minute."

Seth's eyes glinted as he continued to speak. "You could ask him where he got that money, sir."

"How could that be relevant? It's whether you were gambling that I'm interested in."

Seth's face went as hard as a block of granite.

"Were you?"

Seth snapped out a reply. "This man went by the name of Pennyworth this summer out in Nebraska —"

My father puffed up with indignation. "I've never once —"

Seth ignored him, addressing himself to the commandant. "You'll remember, sir, that my mother died, and when I requested leave to settle her estate and establish my sister with relatives, it was denied."

"Cadets are not allowed —"

Seth kept speaking, overriding the commandant's words. Even my father raised a brow at that. "While she was preparing to travel, this man swindled her out of our money. He talked her into buying a hotel in a town that didn't even exist."

The commandant's frown deepened. He addressed my father. "Do you deny this?"

"Of course I do!"

He addressed Seth. "How do you know

this is the same man?"

"I . . ." Seth's gaze darted toward me. "I just do."

"If your sister hasn't come to town — ?"

"No, sir."

"Then I fail to see how you could identify him."

My father's brow had already begun to rise in triumph. I could see so clearly what would happen. Seth would be made to return the money, he and all his friends would be dismissed in disgrace, and my father would remain free to perpetuate his swindles. Not one of those results was just. I couldn't remain silent any longer. "I did."

The commandant's head turned sharply in my direction. "Pardon me, miss? Did you say — ?"

"I said that I identified him."

"Lucinda?" The mask of innocent victim had fallen from my father's face.

"I came to Buttermilk Falls in August to stay with my uncle, Professor Hammond. As I became acquainted with Mr. Westcott these months past, he told me what had happened to his sister. The things he told me led me to believe that the person who swindled his sister was my father. So when my father came to town, I thought it only right that Mr. Westcott should know."

"It's not true. What she says isn't true!"

"She's not your daughter?"

"She is my daughter. But she's been at finishing school these past few years. Even if I had done these things I'm being accused of, how could she have known it?"

The commandant turned his eyes to me. "Were you in Nebraska this past summer, miss?"

"No, I wasn't."

Clearly disturbed by the accusations and counteraccusations, the commandant retreated behind his desk. He sat in his chair as he glowered at all of us. "The only thing I'm certain of is that gambling took place at the riding hall and that you four men were a part of it. Am I mistaken in any of that?"

Seth spoke for all of them. "No, sir. You are not, but —"

The commandant raised a hand. "Just . . . let me think for a moment." His gaze probed us all. "Is there anything I'm missing?"

I had told Seth that I'd be willing to do anything to help him get his money back. I was. And I had. It wasn't right that his sister had been so ill-used. It wasn't honest, but more than that, it wasn't decent.

But I had helped my father take advantage of a dozen girls just like her.

I was as guilty as my father was. Maybe not in this particular instance, but I doubted Phoebe's God would care about finer details like that. When I'd admitted to knowing my father's business just now, Seth had looked at me as if I were some sort of savior. But I wasn't.

I didn't want to be the kind of girl who took advantage of others' gullibility or misfortunes. I didn't want to be the kind of person I used to be. What I wanted, more than anything, was to deserve the regard, the admiration, that shone from Seth's eyes.

There was only one way I could think of to do it. Only one way to ensure that Seth and his sister got their money back. "Yes, sir. There is something you're missing."

52
SETH

Lucinda had already told the commandant how terrible her father was. I didn't understand what she was trying to say. The best thing to do in these situations was to answer the questions that were asked. It never paid to volunteer information. Sometimes that made things more difficult than they had to be.

"I need to be completely honest." She looked straight at me for one long moment and then turned toward the commandant.

"Lucinda." Her father grabbed her around the forearm.

She extracted herself and took a step away from him.

"The reason I know my father took Seth's money is because he's done it many times before and —"

The commandant sighed. "But if you weren't there, nothing can be proved, miss."

"— *and* I know it because I've helped him."

Dandy's eyes widened, and Otter's mouth fell open.

"I've helped him swindle many people out of their money for many years. His best, most lucrative, swindle was the one he perpetuated on Miss Westcott. He sold deeds to a town called Greenfield that doesn't exist. I've helped him do it. I've helped choose his victims. I've helped talk them into it."

My father protested. "She's lying."

"I'm not lying."

"She's like her mother. She's always suffered from delusions. And you'll notice . . . she offers no proof."

"Perhaps I don't, not right this moment, but if you will allow me to return to our boardinghouse in Buttermilk Falls, I can give you the plates he used in printing the deeds for the town."

What was she saying? "Lucinda . . . ?" She wasn't telling the truth — she couldn't be. She didn't have to sacrifice herself to save me. If I could just talk to her, if I could just get her to look at me, then maybe she would understand.

She turned to me then. "I wanted to be different, Seth. I really did. I was trying.

Before my father came, I might even have said that I was succeeding. But don't you see? I'm not . . . I'm not a lady. I'm neither innocent nor naïve, and I never have been. If I'd been with my father in Nebraska, I would have helped him swindle your sister —"

"No, you wouldn't have. You wouldn't have done — !"

"Yes. I would have. It's what I do. It's what I've always done. I've been perpetuating an illusion ever since I've come here. The only thing I regret is that you believed it." She turned away from me and looked at the commandant. "If you would like to send someone to accompany me?"

The commandant assigned a sergeant to escort her. As they left, her father moved to fall in behind them, but the commandant gestured for Deacon to close the door. "I think we'll just all wait here until we see what Miss Hammond brings back."

Lucinda's father clapped his hat on top of his head. "I regret that I will be unable to wait with you. I've a steamboat to catch."

"And I regret that I am unable to let you leave. Perhaps you would like to take a seat." The commandant gestured to a chair, while Dandy and Deacon posted themselves as guards in front of the door.

After he realized he wasn't to be allowed to leave, he sat. "I find this highly unusual."

Otter stepped toward him. "Hadn't you oughter say that it's unusual to turn a daughter into a criminal? That's not a very nice thing to do."

Lucinda's father made no reply.

"I guess you oughter say it's not nice to take people's money neither."

"Exactly! In fact, I should like to ask for the return of it."

The commandant raised a brow. "Of . . . ?"

"My money."

"All in due time."

We waited, in silence, for at least another ten minutes before there came a rap on the commandant's door.

I sent Deacon a puzzled glance. Lucinda and the sergeant wouldn't have had time yet to return from Buttermilk Falls.

The commandant gestured toward the door.

Dandy opened it.

Campbell Conklin stepped into the room, snapping off a smart salute.

The commandant returned it. "I didn't expect you so quickly."

"When there's a problem with the corps of cadets, I try my best to help resolve it quickly."

452

"Mr. Westcott, Mr. Hollingsworth, Mr. Delagarde, and Mr. Ames have been accused of gambling at the riding hall. They say, however, that this gentleman" — he indicated Lucinda's father — "swindled Mr. Westcott's sister out of an inheritance."

"Miss Hammond's father? I find that difficult to believe. Is there any proof, sir?"

"I'm trying to obtain proof at the moment."

"But what of the charge of gambling?"

"They've admitted to it."

"All of them?"

"Indeed. In your opinion, what should happen to your classmates?"

"They should be dismissed. Without question!"

"And this man?" He indicated Lucinda's father with a nod of his chin.

"It must be a case of mistaken identity."

"What if the accusations turn out to be true?"

"What of it? They were still gambling, were they not?"

"So you would see four good men dismissed on account of one criminal?"

My hopes began to rise as Campbell Conklin's face flushed.

"How would that see justice served?"

Campbell's brow had furrowed as if he

were confused by the commandant's words. "But if rules are meant to be followed —"

"Then in some cases an injustice can be perpetuated. Enforcement is always left to the commanding officer's discretion."

Conklin's eyes darted between us and the commandant, as if he didn't know what to think anymore. "But —"

"Compliance ought never trump justice. An officer ready for command should know that."

"Sir? I don't think that —"

He was saved a reply by the commandant's dismissal. And before the hour was gone, the sergeant returned with Lucinda.

He saluted.

The commandant put him at ease.

The sergeant came forward and placed a blanket-wrapped bundle on the commandant's desk.

The commandant unwrapped it to find two engraved metal printing plates. "Where did you find these?"

"In the man's room."

The commandant began to inspect them.

Lucinda's father lunged for them, but Otter stopped him.

"This is outrageous! How dare you violate my privacy! I can assure you these are mere nothings. Simple mementoes of my time spent out west."

The commandant smiled. "There's an easy way to tell." He took up his ink well and dribbled ink across the top of one of them, crumpled a piece of loose leaf, and smeared the ink across the plate. Picking it up, he pressed it onto the blotter that lay atop his desk. He picked the blotter up and began to read it. Dandy, Otter, Deacon and I stepped forward.

The commandant's brow rose. He left off reading to address Lucinda's father. "Mr. Pennyworth, I presume?"

"I assure you, I have no idea how those got in my room."

"Your simple mementoes? You didn't place them there?"

"I swear that —"

Lucinda put a hand on the commandant's desk. "He did place them there. He's had them for years. I've been present when he's had deeds printed from those. I've even helped him sell them."

I couldn't believe what I was seeing. It looked exactly like the deed my sister had sent me. But if that was the case . . . ?

"Sir? I have one of those deeds. My sister sent it to me."

He glanced up at me. "I'll have you retrieve it in a moment. And Miss Hammond? Will you testify to what you just said?"

She came close, in that moment, to meeting my eyes. But then she closed them and took in a deep breath. When she opened them she was looking at the commandant. "Yes. Consider me a witness."

I didn't understand what was happening. "Lucinda? What . . . ?"

She did look at me then. "I'm not the person you thought I was, Seth. I wish I were, but I'm not. And I never was."

The commandant summoned the sergeant with a nod of his head. "Confine this man. He was selling these deeds in Nebraska Territory. Perhaps that makes it a federal offense. If not, at least we can hold him until we can remit him to the proper authorities."

My father shrugged the sergeant's hands from his arm. "You still have no evidence. She put those plates there without my knowledge."

The commandant stood. "Mr. Westcott?"

"Sir."

"You say your sister had dealings with this man."

"Yes, sir."

"Where is she?"

"Sir?"

"At this moment. Where is she?"

456

"Fort Laramie, sir."

"Then we'd best see about getting a corroborating statement. Mr. Hollingsworth?"

Deacon saluted. "Yes, sir."

"Can you draw this man?"

"Draw him? Sir?"

"With your pencil. Can you *draw* him?"

"Yes, sir!"

"Fine. Then I'll have that drawing sent to Miss Westcott just as soon as you finish it." He eyed Dandy. "About the bet . . . what exactly was it?"

"I bet that Otter would be able to ride York, sir. And that man bet that he wouldn't."

"A fool and his money are so easily parted, aren't they?" He took up the money and held it out to me. "I expect that you'll place this into the safekeeping of the Treasurer. I wouldn't want you to be caught with money on your person. At least not before you graduate. In that case, I would have to recommend you for dismissal."

"Yes, sir." I would have thought that getting that money back would have resolved all my problems, but all I could think was that I wanted Lucinda back too. The old Lucinda. The one I'd known before her father had come to town.

Lucinda had shrunk against the back wall,

457

hands clenched together, looking for all the world as if she wanted to disappear. And for the first time, as I looked at her, I didn't feel anything at all.

53
LUCINDA

I couldn't bear to look at Seth. Or the commandant. Or my father. In the past, a bright smile and a wide-eyed look had gotten me past some terrible accusations. No one wants to believe the worst of a pretty girl. But there was no point in pretending at respectability now. I'd told the truth. I had admitted to everything. Stepping back into a shadowed corner, gripping my own arms by the elbows, I let the talk swirl around me.

How long would it take for word of our deceptions to spread through Buttermilk Falls? Mrs. Holt had to have known that something was happening when that soldier escorted me to my father's room. The hope that she might have interpreted it as a liaison crept into my thoughts. The fact that I preferred that interpretation to the truth showed me just how far I had fallen.

Where would I go now?

With any sort of luck, my father would be jailed for a very long time. But even so, staying in Buttermilk Falls could no longer be an option. Not when the townspeople would soon learn the worst about me.

What would I do?

I would have fallen back on marriage in times past, the way I had meant to do when I'd first come here. But falling in love had changed my mind. Marriage wasn't a scheme. It was meant to be entered into with honesty. And love. But I'd ruined my chances with Seth. Ruined them long before I'd even met him. And now he knew it too.

I risked a look at him and flinched when it was clear he was steadfastly refusing to look at me. But he was in good company. My father was refusing to do the same.

At least when I was doing the wrong thing, I'd had my father to do it with. Now I had no one. I'd been in a similar situation when I'd come to Buttermilk Falls, or I thought I had been. But then I had been able to rely on the kindness of family. If they had shunned me when my father came to town, I could not imagine what they would think of me now.

As I stood there, it was decided that my father would be confined until it was determined who held jurisdiction over his crimes.

And over my own.

When the commandant addressed me, I thought I saw sympathy in his eyes. "I'm sure, since you're cooperating, some leniency will be shown you."

I wasn't, but I smiled just the same.

"A case can probably be made that he coerced you into helping him."

Perhaps. But it wouldn't be true. And when the time came, I would say so.

My father stood and glared at the cadets, and then he turned his wrath on me. It was a terrible sight. His rage had twisted his mouth, and it glittered in his eyes. It was a molten, liquid thing. "I hope you're happy. I never thought I'd see the day when I was betrayed by my own daughter. How could you do this to us?"

Scenes rose, like phantoms, from my memory. Me: stumbling on a boardwalk, crying because I'd skinned my knee. Him: berating me, shaking a fist at the departing stage we'd missed because of my tumble. Me: hesitating to approach the drunken paramour he'd selected for me. Him: scolding me for caring more about my feelings than I did for him. Me: trying to do everything he'd ever asked of me. Him: always unhappy, never satisfied, because I was forever holding him back.

That was when I finally understood.

That was the moment when everything about my life finally made sense. "It was never about us." I spoke with the authority of revelation. "It was never about me. It was always about you." There never had been an "us." And now, for better or worse, there never would be.

"You've given me up. Turned me in!"

"But I've done the right thing. I've done the right thing for the right reason. Isn't that what any father would want his daughter to do?"

As he scowled at me, the sergeant took him by the arm.

"Wait!"

The sergeant stopped at my command. The cadets, the commandant, my father all turned to look at me. "You might be interested to know his real name. You'll need it for the trial."

"Don't!" He barked the word at me.

"It's John Barns."

"I didn't want —"

Seth's eyes finally met my own. "Barns? It isn't Pennyworth?"

"No. It never was." Maybe someday he would understand.

All the turmoil and anger left the room with

my father. After he had gone it seemed there was no reason for the cadets to stay. They saluted the commandant, he dismissed them, and then . . . there was just me. I ought to have felt a sense of relief, maybe even of victory for justice having prevailed, but all I felt was terribly alone.

The commandant was standing behind his desk, looking as if he would very much like to sit once more in his chair. Was he . . . was he waiting for me to leave as well? "Do you need me to go with my father?"

"You? No. You're free to leave. As long as you let me know where you'll be staying." He said it with a lift of his brow, as if he expected that I had planned this out, that I had foreseen it all ending like this.

"I'll need to go back to the boarding-house."

He nodded and sat down. "Of course."

"I don't know where I'll go after that." I could use the money my father had left behind and take a room at the West Point Hotel, but surely news would soon find its way there too. And that money didn't really belong to me. It belonged to Seth — and to the others my father had swindled.

"Perhaps you should speak with your uncle."

"He had previous dealings with my father.

We aren't on very good terms at the moment."

"Moments have a way of becoming hours, and sometimes perspective is all it takes to change someone's mind about something."

"He was quite fixed in his opinion of me when I last spoke to him."

"I've never known a mathematician who wasn't enamored of proofs. If you present your evidence, he might just come to a different conclusion about everything."

"Perhaps." I nodded, though I didn't have much hope.

"Think about it. You have nothing to lose."

"Nothing to lose." He ought to have said nothing *more* to lose. I paused on the top step, my skirts swaying with indecision as I looked down the street toward the academy building. It was impossible for my uncle to think less of me than he already did. What if . . . what if I could convince him to welcome me back?

It could never be as it was before. I could never hope to earn back Phoebe's esteem. I could never again model for Milly all that was proper and right for a lady. Perhaps I could help my aunt in the kitchen, even if she wouldn't treat me as her long-lost niece. If I could bear to swallow my pride, what was left of father's money might just make up for the rest of what he'd taken from Seth's sister.

At the bottom of the steps, I turned toward the academy.

It didn't take me long to find my uncle. I could hear his voice from the hallway and followed it to his classroom. As I opened the door, his students turned to look at me. Perhaps sensing the change of mood, he glanced up from his notes at me. Then he lowered his head to look more directly, over his spectacles.

I didn't even try to smile. I couldn't. "If I might have a word?"

"I am instructing at the moment."

"The commandant suggested that I come."

The cadets were following our conversation as if it were a game of bandy.

He glanced at them and then at me. After placing his notes on his desk, he joined me, closing the door behind him with a click that echoed down the hallway. "Please do me the favor of making it brief."

Brief? How could I briefly sum up all the mistakes I had made in my life? All of the mistakes that had brought me here? A bubble of laughter rose in my chest, but it was choked by a sob once it reached my throat.

He crossed his arms as he looked down his nose at me. "I've no time for histrionics."

"My father was arrested today."

"Good."

"On the proof of my evidence."

"*Your* evidence?"

"The evidence he had in his room at the boardinghouse . . . as well as the evidence I've been collecting all my life as I've worked beside him to swindle innocent people."

He blinked. "You *helped* him?"

"Yes."

"Did you come to Buttermilk Falls to swindle us?"

"No. I came because I thought he was dead. I wanted to make a new life for myself."

"Then why?"

"Why . . . ? Why . . . what?" What else was there to say?

"What made you decide — I assume you've decided — to testify against him?"

"I have."

"Why?"

"How could I not?"

He blinked. "You implicated yourself in

466

his crimes. You didn't have to do that. At least, I presume that you didn't. I'm sure he's done more than enough in his life to implicate himself."

"Back in Nebraska, he swindled Seth Westcott's sister out of their money." The whole story tumbled out of my mouth before I could stop it. About Seth not being given leave. About his sister being stranded in Fort Laramie. His plan to be assigned to the cavalry and the way he and his friends had been caught trying to trick my father into giving them his money. "Don't you see? My father ruined all of their lives. And more than Seth's money, he stole his good reputation. If I had said nothing, he would have been free to do it to someone else."

"But now your reputation will be ruined."

"Don't you understand? Any good reputation I owned was false. What happens to me doesn't matter. Now Seth and his sister can have their inheritance."

He looked at me for a long moment. "I am sorry to hear you believe that." He glanced at the door to the classroom. "Wait here for a moment. I have something I want to give you."

As he opened the door I stood to the side, back pressed to the wall, so that the cadets wouldn't see me. I spent several agonizing minutes wringing my hands, trying to believe that everything might work out one day.

At last he appeared. As he closed the door once more behind him, he offered me a folded sheet of paper. "I'd like you to go to Buttermilk Falls and give this to your aunt." He extended it once more. "Go on. Take it. You can read it if you'd like."

I took it with trembling fingers and opened it.

This is my niece, Lucinda Barns. Please welcome her home.

I held it to my heart as I wept tears of gratitude and joy.

54
SETH

Deacon just couldn't seem to stop talking. He wasn't even trying to draw. He hadn't picked up a pencil since he'd done that sketch of Lucinda's father earlier in the day. I was tempted to leave our room so I could hear myself think. "And that was John Barns! Can you account for it?"

"For what?"

"The sheer coincidence. Here we were trying to get you to give John Barns a run for his money —" Deacon laughed — "and that's exactly what we did!"

I didn't find the coincidence so very funny. I found it rather frightening. I'd tried my best to be John Barns. To be worse than John Barns. It was his record for amassing demerits I'd been trying to break. Thank the Lord I hadn't succeeded. What kind of man might I have become?

"You don't think that's funny?"

"I think it's . . . it's wrong!"

"What's wrong?"

"A man like that, dragging a daughter around the West, getting her to do things no decent father would ever think of doing." With a father like that . . . with a father like that, she hadn't turned out half bad.

"She did you a favor to my way of thinking." He tipped his chair up on its two back legs and leaned against the wall.

I wished he wouldn't do that. It always made a mark on the paint. "What was that?" What was it Lucinda had said there at the end? *I wanted to be different, Seth. But don't you see? I'm not a lady.* What was it my mother had always told Elizabeth? *A lady is as a lady does.*

"Without her stepping in when she did and speaking up, we might have been dismissed by now. And you'd have been forced to give back all that money. And Pennyworth would have been free to turn around and swindle somebody else."

I wished Deke would quit talking. It made it difficult to think.

"Wouldn't you say?"

"Wouldn't I say what?"

"She did you a favor."

A favor? Of a sudden I could see it all so clearly. It was like having a view clear out across a battlefield. I could see where Lu-

470

cinda had feinted to draw in fire and how it
had all been a ruse. I pushed away from the
table and grabbed up my hat with shaking
hands. "I just . . . I just let her go. I walked
away!"

"Who? What are you talking about? Who
did you walk away from?"

"Lucinda!"

"That's what she wanted."

"What do you mean?"

He pushed away from the wall and let the
front two legs of his chair meet the floor.
"When people tell you the worst thing about
them, what they want is for you to let them
go."

"But what if she didn't? What if she was
hoping . . ." Had she? Had she really been
hoping?

"Hoping?"

"I'm a fool. She lied!"

"Yes. She did. Quite a lot for quite a long
time. That's what she said."

"No. Not about that. About telling the
truth."

"About . . . the lies?" Deke's brow had
wrinkled with puzzlement. "She told the
truth about lies?"

"Yes. But that's not what I'm talking
about. I'm talking about the other."

"What *other*? There is no *other*. She's a

swindler, just like her father. That's what she said."

"She was. That's what she lied about." Why hadn't I seen it before? I could only hope I wasn't too late. But . . . I didn't even know where she was staying. What if she'd already gone?

"How could you lie about being a swindler when you admit to — Seth?" His voice trailed after me down the hall. "I don't understand!"

I hadn't either. How could I have been so stupid? I left the barracks at a run, praying that Professor Hammond hadn't already left for home.

I didn't get very far.

Just as I rounded the corner of the barracks, I ran straight into Colonel Lee.

After recovering from a stagger, I straightened and saluted.

He returned the salute and then regarded me, hands behind his back. "Mr. Westcott. To what do I owe the pleasure of your company this evening?"

"I was just . . . just wanting to get a bit of air, sir."

"At a run?"

"Yes, sir."

He frowned.

472

"That is . . . no, sir."

"Which is it, Mr. Westcott? Yes or no? I expect all my first-year students to be decisive. Prevarication does not become an officer." Though his Virginian accent was mild, his words were sharp.

"No, sir. That is to say . . . I think I need some help."

"Some help? Considering the steep decline in your class standing, and the fact that you are hanging on to your appointment by a very thin thread, sir, I would have thought you might have asked for help much earlier."

"Yes, sir. I should have, sir."

He sighed and gestured toward the row of instructors' housing with one hand. "Then I suggest that you come along."

He took me to the office in his quarters and sat behind his desk while I remained standing.

When he put me at ease, I moved my left foot away from my right and joined my thumbs behind my back.

"Why must you men always insist upon hijinks? Why can't you simply obey the rules?"

I didn't even have the defense that I'd been trying to. "Sometimes the rules don't get you where you need to go, sir."

His eyes narrowed. "Explain yourself."

"It's, uh . . . It's rather complicated, sir."

"Then you'd best get started."

"Yes, sir." I desperately wanted to swipe at the sweat that was breaking out upon my forehead, but I restrained myself, locking my thumbs in place instead. "It started this past summer, sir, out in Nebraska. My mother died. And then my sister was swindled out of our inheritance."

"I am sorry to hear that."

"Sir. A man can't just stand by when his family is attacked. It was a trial, knowing that I wouldn't graduate until June, and after that, I wouldn't be at liberty to pursue the swindler until my eight years are up. It, uh . . . It seemed to me, considering that I was at the top of my class, that I might be assigned to the Corps of Engineers."

He raised a brow.

"Which would have been a very great honor. But the idea of that man, that swindler, being able to circulate freely just didn't seem fair." This next part was going to be tricky. "It . . . it seemed to me that, if I were assigned to the cavalry, to some fort out west, in the course of my duties I might be able to catch up with the man and bring him to justice."

"Which accounts for the steep decline in

your class standing."

"Yes, sir. I didn't think the army would assign someone like me to the cavalry just on my asking."

"No. I would not have allowed it. The army needs its best men in its most important positions. Lest you begin to congratulate yourself on being clever, however, I think that was a poorly thought-out plan. And you still haven't explained the reason for your unauthorized departure from the barracks."

"The man, that swindler, came here, sir. To Buttermilk Falls."

"Here?"

"Yes, sir."

"Which puts into question all of the trouble you went to in order to get yourself into the cavalry. Poorly thought-out plan, indeed."

"Yes, sir. I do realize that, sir. But I couldn't let him get away, so I came up with a swindle of my own."

"A *swindle*?"

"Yes, sir. To get my money back. And I did, sir. Just this afternoon."

"And how did you come by this money? If you were in class all day?"

Was there nothing that escaped the superintendent's attention?

475

"I would rather not say, sir."

"And I would rather not have to dismiss you from the military academy, Mr. Westcott. Though your attempts at justice and revenge were misguided, I find your sentiments admirable, and your concern for your sister could be called exemplary. Those are qualities of a gentleman, and it is my opinion that they ought not be overlooked in an officer either. So I'm going to give you another chance. Why don't you tell me what really happened?"

"Sir?"

"I already received a report from the commandant about your activities this afternoon. You have cheated the military academy out of the benefit of your hard work. You have lied about your true academic aptitude. You have played the fool in front of the corps of cadets, and you have made all of us who previously had good reason to believe in you as both an officer and a gentleman question our better judgment. The commandant felt that all could be forgiven, but I must tell you, Mr. Westcott, that after reviewing your accomplishments this semester, I have no choice but to recommend you to the secretary of war for dismissal."

My face grew hot as my ears buzzed.

Dismissal? "Yes, sir."

"What have you to say for yourself?"

I opened my mouth to offer a defense but realized I had none. I'd made my choices; now I had to pay the consequences. "I have nothing to say for myself, sir. I did exactly as you say."

"I am not an unfeeling man. I do understand the ties of family. And I do still believe in your capacity to become a useful officer. I'm going to reinstate you."

My knees wobbled with relief. "Yes, sir!"

"A smart man, Mr. Westcott, one who applies himself to his studies and to comportment, might be able to raise his class standing to a respectable level before graduation. I would expect no less of you. And quite a bit more, in fact. Is that understood?"

"Yes, sir."

"I haven't told many yet, but I've received a new assignment. I'll be second-in-command of the Second Cavalry, heading for Texas this summer."

"Congratulations, sir."

"I find myself looking forward to it. A combat assignment can be the making of a man."

It seemed to me that in his pause he was waiting for me to respond. "Yes, sir."

"I'll be made to take some of you men

with me, but it would mean quite a bit if I knew I could count on at least one of my junior officers."

"Sir?"

"I've no doubt you can pull yourself up through the files, though you'll never make it back to the top of your class this late in your senior year."

"No, sir."

"Some decisions you can't recover from once they've been made, but a smart man always finds a way to make the most of what's been done — to manage those things he can't change."

"Yes, sir."

"And sometimes, if God smiles upon him, it turns out better than he might have imagined."

Was he inviting me to join the cavalry? If an officer like Colonel Lee was looking forward to the cavalry, maybe it wouldn't be so terrible. I'd hoped to follow in his footsteps. I never thought I'd have a chance to walk right along beside him.

"There is one thing, however, you still have not told me."

"Sir?"

"Where is it, exactly, that you were headed this evening?"

55

LUCINDA

To my great surprise, my aunt and Phoebe welcomed me back with open arms. Milly nearly strangled me with her embrace, and Ella planted a dozen wet kisses on my cheek. Even Bobby, great lad of ten years that he was, did a poor job of feigning indifference. At the end of the night, Phoebe and I talked our way into sleep just the same as we always had, and by the next day, it felt as if I'd never been gone.

On Saturday afternoon, my aunt claimed me for the kitchen since we were having guests for an early supper. I helped her ready some vegetables for the cooking, took charge of the biscuits, and unmolded a pudding, but sooner than I expected, company was announced. She unpinned my apron and pushed me out the door toward the dining room.

I didn't quite know what to do when I saw Deacon, but he greeted me with a smile.

Dandy was otherwise occupied in trying his best to avoid Phoebe, although he didn't seem to have any problem sending her inscrutable glances. Otter shook my hand and thanked me for saving them all from dismissal.

"I didn't have anything to do with it. I really didn't."

Seth stepped into the sitting room. "You had everything to do with it." As he sent a smile in my direction, I felt my heart turn over. But then Mr. Conklin appeared at his side. He bowed. "Miss Hammond."

I nodded.

Seth saved me from replying by crooking his arm for me and escorting me toward the dining room.

Milly had been watching us, and she spoke up as Seth and I passed her. "Hadn't you ought to be escorting my mother? As the most senior gentleman?"

He winked at her. "It's Mr. Conklin's responsibility. He outranks me."

"I'm so glad." I whispered the words beneath my breath.

He leaned toward me. "Pardon me?"

"I said, 'That's too bad.' "

A quirk of his lips and a tightening of his arm let me know he'd heard me correctly the first time.

■ ■ ■ ■

The meal was delicious. The company was engaging. It seemed we'd just sat down when it was time for dessert. My uncle made a show of looking for it while Ella giggled and Bobby rolled his eyes. "Where's that pudding I've been smelling?"

My aunt smiled at me as she nodded toward the sideboard. "Lucinda made it, so it ought to be hers to present."

"I didn't actually —"

He nodded. "So it ought."

I excused myself to get it while my aunt brought the dishes. My uncle's smile was almost jolly as I placed it in front of him. "Tonight is a night of celebration. First, because Lucinda's come back to us."

I felt my cheeks warm as the children cheered.

"And second, because I have it from a very good source that Mr. Conklin's got himself engaged to be married."

Mr. Conklin blinked in apparent surprise and began to splutter.

"To one of the Boston Phillips if I'm not mistaken." My uncle's eyes were on me.

I smiled. "Congratulations, Mr. Conklin. I wish you every happiness."

481

My uncle was regarding him with a censorious look. "After such a splendid meal, I would much rather take dessert at leisure, but I expect, Mr. Conklin, that you'll be needing to get back to the Point to make certain everything's as it should be."

"Yes, sir."

"And I'm sure that you won't mind if Mr. Westcott enjoys the full benefit of his pass. After all, he doesn't have nearly the responsibilities that you do now."

"No, sir. Perhaps you'll excuse me if I leave now, sir."

"I most certainly will."

He rose from his chair and bowed before turning on his heel and stalking toward the hall.

As we heard the front door shut, my uncle let out a chuckle and leaned over Mr. Conklin's vacated chair to cover my hand with his. "I hope you'll forgive me for springing that on you, but he deserved it. And you deserved to see his true character."

"His father is a senator. His family is influential. You could just as well have pressed him to make some commitment to me."

"And have you bound to a liar and a cheat for the rest of your life? Family takes care of each other."

From across the table, Phoebe was beaming in my direction.

"I apologize that I invited him to court you. I haven't been a very good judge of character lately." My uncle's gaze locked on Seth's.

Seth raised a brow.

My uncle nodded.

At my side, Seth shifted to face me. "I told your uncle, Lucinda. I told him everything. Everything I should have told him from the beginning. About my mother and sister, and about your father. About why I was trying so hard to become an Immortal. All of it."

"I'm glad, Seth."

"I ought to have told him sooner. I ought to have told you. I wish I had. I don't deserve the least of your esteem. I am a man who has cheated his classmates out of good leadership, who has lied about his talents, but I find myself hoping that you might be . . ." His gaze drifted toward the head of the table, and a blush swept his face. "I, uh . . . I hope that you can overlook all that."

I nodded, afraid to speak.

My aunt grabbed up Ella and took Phoebe's arm, shooing Milly and Bobby into the sitting room ahead of her. Seth's friends quickly filed out behind them. And then my uncle excused himself for the purpose of finding his pipe. I would have told him it was on the desk in its normal place, but he abandoned us too quickly.

Seth placed his hands on the table, next to mine. They were so big. I felt so small. So much less.

He looked over at me through his clear blue eyes. "Thank you for getting my money back."

I reached down into my lap for my napkin, but he caught up my hand in his and wouldn't let me tug it away. "I'm so sorry, Seth, about my father. And about me. I don't care what you think of me, but I wanted to help you to get your —"

"I love you."

He . . . ? "What?"

"I love you."

"You love me?" I tried to laugh, but it died, unformed, in my mouth. "You can't love me."

"I do."

"You can't." There was such regard, such unspeakable kindness in his eyes. It was too much to bear, so I looked away.

"Why not?"

"Because I'm not worth it. I've schemed and cheated and lied my way across the country, Seth, and —"

He was shaking his head. "That's not the

kind of person you are. I know you're not like that. You once looked beyond the obvious and told me that you believed in me. Now I'm telling you the same."

"Don't say that."

"Why not?"

"Because it's not true. That's exactly the kind of person I am."

"It's the kind of person you *were*. But you're not like that anymore. You haven't been like that since I met you."

"But what if I am, Seth?" As I grasped at his hands, I couldn't keep the fear from my words. "What if . . . what if that person is still there, waiting to show herself again? What if I'm just a . . . just a big swindle?"

He cupped my face with his hand.

I gave in to his gentle pressure and looked up into his eyes.

"You were willing to give up everything to make amends. Your father. Your reputation. Your family."

"They weren't really mine to begin with. You're the one who gave up —"

He pressed the softest of kisses to my lips. "I gave up nothing. I purposely *ruined* everything. My grades, my standing. Dare I say . . . us?"

Us? Was *us* still possible? "Please do, dare." I laughed at that incongruous phrase.

I couldn't help it.

But he laughed too as he gripped my hand more tightly. "I won't be able to join the engineers now. I might never be able to take you to Europe."

"That was my father's dream, not mine."

"I've half a year left here, and all I can offer you afterward is the chance to head west with the cavalry." He was looking at me very carefully.

"I happen to like the West."

"You do? Truly?"

I nodded as a smile swept across his face.

I'd met so many men in so many towns that I'd lost count. Some were better looking than Seth was, many were better dancers, but there was no one I'd ever met who was a better man. No one — except Phoebe's God, perhaps — who knew me better or loved me more.

He lifted my hand to his lips.

One of my tears fell onto it.

He kissed my tear. Kissed my hand. Leaned forward to kiss my lips once more. And I knew then what I'd tell Phoebe later that night when she asked. I'd tell her that I'd finally found someone worthwhile to kiss. And the quality of the experience? My goodness! I'd have to say it was . . . Well, I wasn't really saying anything at all at that moment. There's just something about those West Point cadets. . . . They never do anything by halves.

A NOTE FROM THE AUTHOR

A con woman and a good boy going bad? *Really? This* is who character casting central sends me? As a character-driven writer, I have to go with whoever shows up when I'm planning my stories, but frankly, I wasn't sure how this one was going to turn out. I set a challenge for myself with each book I write, but I kept wondering if this challenge was just too big.

As I worked through the story, however, I realized that there's a bit of the con man (or woman) in all of us. How else to explain the front we sell to others even knowing, full well, that inside we're not as together as we appear to be? We too often convince ourselves that seeming is just as good as being, and we content ourselves with less when we could have much more.

This is the third time I've featured the military in my stories. The first two times were in contemporary settings. With this book, I was struck by just how little the life of a cadet has changed through the centuries.

A young version of the American Civil War's General Robert E. Lee, who so quickly forgave the faults of many of his officers, can be found in this story's longsuffering academy superintendent, Colonel Lee. In Stanley Horn's *The Robert E. Lee Reader,* he is quoted during that time as saying, "I wish boys would do what is right; it would be so much easier for all of us." He always hoped for the best from his cadets and gave them more chances at redemption than most superintendents. A West Point alumnus himself, he graduated second in his class in 1829, having never acquired a single demerit. He returned to the military academy as superintendent from 1852–1855.

Jefferson Davis, who would go on to serve as president of the Confederate States of America during the Civil War, served as secretary of war during that same time period. He graduated twenty-third in a class of thirty-three, having accumulated an average of one hundred demerits a year.

Historically, class ranking has had little to do with success in battle. Some of the most famous soldiers in the Civil War, men like George Custer, George Pickett, James

Longstreet, and Beauregard Ambrose Burnside, were Immortals during their time at the military academy. The writer Edgar Allan Poe and the artist James Whistler were also numbered among the Immortals before they were found deficient and dismissed.

Edgar Allan Poe came to the U.S. Military Academy in 1830 at the age of twenty-one after his foster mother had died. He'd previously served in the army as an enlisted soldier from 1827–1829. He may have been hoping for an eventual inheritance of some sort from his foster father, but after his foster mother's death, the man remarried. At that point, Poe simply stopped caring. He stopped attending classes, stopped going to formations; in short, he forced the academy to dismiss him.

The hijinks my Immortals engaged in were inspired by some of theirs. Deacon had Whistler's skills with a pencil. Otter had General (and later, president) Ulysses S. Grant's facility with horses. Grant's favorite mount was the famously bad-tempered York. To learn more about the Immortals, read *Last in Their Class,* by James S. Robbins.

As I was double-checking my facts on a final edit of this manuscript, I ran across the legend that West Point alumnus General J.E.B. Stuart, renowned cavalry commander of the Confederate States of America's Army of Northern Virginia, was rumored to have moderated his academic performance so that, instead of being assigned to the Corps of Engineers, he'd be free to go into the cavalry. Assignments from the U.S. Military Academy are still awarded based on the order of merit, but now those with the highest standing in their class get to choose first from among the open assignments.

There has always been tension between the top of the class and the bottom of the class at the military academy. The top accuses the bottom of not caring. The bottom accuses the top of caring overly much. In my research I came to understand there are two types of failing cadets. Those who become overwhelmed by their studies, due to the subject matter or deficiencies in time management, and those who simply feel there's more to life than studying. They would describe themselves as more well-balanced and more efficient at using their time. Why study harder than you have to?

Cadets at all the service academies are subject to regulations and restrictions that would send a civilian college student screaming in horror. The great care cadets take to interpret rules to the letter often leave them far from fulfilling their spirit. But when daily life is so restricted, when even the way you fold your underwear is inspected and regimented, the creative mind has to come up with some way to gain temporary freedom. Although these antics are never officially condoned, they are expected, and it's widely assumed that a successful career in the military requires swift obedience as well as boundless creativity. Which leads to that fine balance between obeying the rules and rubbing others' faces in them. We would all do well to remind ourselves what cadets, no matter the era, have always known: We're all in this together, and no one likes a snitch.

In writing this book, I appreciated more fully the tragedy of the American Civil War. Five short years after graduation, cadets like Seth, Deacon, Dandy, and Otter would face each other across battle lines. It's a testament to their military training that they were able to prosecute war against each other at all. But it's a testament to the close ties of friendships they formed as cadets that whenever they saw each other during those terrible years, in victory or defeat, they reached out to each other with kindness. And after the war, when the nation had such difficulty with reconciliation, they still viewed each other as friends.

It's quite difficult to erase a first impression, be it good or bad. Often, if you try hard and make an effort early at your job or in your course work, people are willing to give you the benefit of doubt as time wears on. Any soldier (or airman or seaman) knows that the needs of the army (or air force, or navy, or marines, or coast guard) trump the needs of the individual. No officer who recognized a talent such as Seth Westcott's would have thrown away that talent by assigning him to the lesser ranks of the infantry or cavalry during that period.

There really was a Benny Havens. He and his wife originally kept a tavern near the academy grounds, but they eventually earned the superintendent's disfavor when they were caught selling liquor to academy cadets as well as to the general public. Forbidden from setting foot on the military reservation, they relocated to the village of Buttermilk Falls. By all accounts Benny and his wife offered much more to cadets than liquor. They offered a warm room, hot meals, and unconditional love. Benny was also reported to be quite adept at mathematics. To be found at Benny Havens, however, meant automatic dismissal from the academy for having been guilty of consuming liquor. Jefferson Davis (future president of the Confederate States of America) was sentenced to be dismissed for being caught at Benny Havens but was saved by his prior record of good conduct. His runs to the tavern, however, almost got him killed when he fell over a sixty-foot cliff on his way back to the Point one night. The song "Benny Havens, Oh!" commemorates the old tavern and is still a part of the military academy tradition.

Being married to a graduate of the U.S. Air Force Academy and knowing several graduates of the U.S. Military Academy at West Point, I have tried my best to capture the unique atmosphere and humor that flourishes at service academies. The joke goes that one can be an officer or a gentleman, but not both at the same time. Perhaps they'd like to think that's true, but I suspect that you, like me, know better. Most graduates I know, be they men or women, manage to be both. That's probably due, in part, to the Cadet Honor Code, which influences every part of a cadet's life: *A cadet will not lie, cheat, steal or tolerate those who do.* Although its current wording dates to 1970, those principles have governed the conduct of cadets since the founding of the military academy.

In the prewar era, the purpose of West Point was to graduate engineers and gentlemen. Both were a particular fixation from the very founding of the academy. West Point developed as an engineering school modeled on France's legendary École Polytechnique. Many of its professors and department heads were acknowledged worldwide experts in their fields.

The most prestigious assignment coming out of the academy was to the Corps of Engineers. Americans like to say that the West was won by cowboys and pioneers, but in actuality, it was won by the army's engineers and topographers. They surveyed the land, they built dams and levees, they constructed forts and harbors, and they charted the railways.

America was also built by con men. They plied the rivers and byways of the developing West as they sought to take for themselves a part of others' American dreams. Land swindles abounded. Colonel Lee's father was impoverished by one. The sons of William Penn enacted another. Patrick Henry became ensnared in and lost his fortune through land speculation. George Washington, James Monroe, and James Madison all acquired land in what would

become Ohio for the purposes of investment. I imagine Mr. Pennyworth's land
swindle to have been in the vicinity of the
Farson-Eden Valley of Wyoming. The Oregon Trail forded Big Sandy River in that
location, but a town was never built until ir-
rigation came to the valley in 1907. The current census lists the population of Farson-
Eden as 660.

Lucinda's father would have been labeled
"morally insane" in the 1850s. Today he
might be diagnosed with Narcissistic Personality Disorder (NPD). Those with NPD
exhibit a lack of empathy, an inflated ego,
and are willing to go to incredible lengths
for self-promotion. Some of the symptoms
he manifested were pathological lying,
blaming, selective memory, denial, lack of
conscience, entitlement, intimidation, ne-
glect, and normalizing.

The village of Buttermilk Falls, located
about a mile south of the West Point military
reservation, was incorporated in 1906 under
the name of the Village of Highland Falls. It
is part of the Town of Highlands. In 1860,
it had a population of 307. In the years after
the Civil War, as New York City titans such
as John Pierpont Morgan built summer
homes there, its population boomed. Billy
Joel's *Turnstiles* album song, "Summer,

Highland Falls" was inspired by the town.

Flirtation Walk is just as popular now as it was in the nineteenth century. It's strictly off limits to visitors, however. In order to walk that lovely path, you have to be escorted by a cadet. Kissing Rock still juts out over the trail, and I'm sure every year at least one guest is convinced to come to the rescue of a hopeful cadet.

During the 1800s, most instructors at the military academy lived on the military reservation. I've been around enough military bases to know that the housing areas always seem to be in need of repair. It should not have been surprising then to read that several instructors at West Point had to leave their military housing during the 1850s and take lodging in the surrounding areas so that their quarters could undergo renovation.

In a world where streakers routinely show up at sports events, it can be difficult to understand just how shocking it would have been in the nineteenth century for a cadet to report for parade in his underwear. In the mid-Victorian period, however, modesty was most definitely a virtue, and at an academy that was meant to produce gentlemen, this would have been close to an unforgiveable sin.

I've toyed with the idea of turning this book into a series, intending Phoebe and Dandy to pair up after graduation and Deacon and Seth's sister, Elizabeth, to do the same a bit later on, out West on the frontier. Otter, God bless him, just seemed so close to his mother that I couldn't ever quite figure out what to do but let him go on home. As I worked through successive drafts, however, it became quite clear that Dandy and Deacon weren't the only characters with secrets. Otter had a secret too. Though I don't currently have any plans to develop the stories of Phoebe or Elizabeth, I did turn Otter's secret into a short story. If you visit my website and sign up for my newsletter, I'd be happy to send it to you. Beware: Once you read it, you'll probably find yourself flipping back through the pages of this book to see how you could possibly have missed it. Intrigued? Visit www.sirimitchell.com to find out!

ACKNOWLEDGMENTS

My agent, Natasha Kern, kept believing I could get through this one. Turned out, she was right! My editors, Dave Long and Karen Schurrer, did a terrific job, once more, of shepherding this book through the development and editing process. Mark Waclawski (USMA Class of 1979) graciously agreed to lend me his firsthand knowledge of the U.S. Military Academy and its traditions. Any errors regarding the USMA are mine, not his.

Once again, my street team — Jamie Lapeyrolerie, Denise Harmer, Jaquelyn Scroggie, Kathleen E. Belongia, Amy Putney, Brenda Veinotte, Kelsey Shade, Debora Wilder, Beth Bulow, Lindsey Zimpel, Melissa Tharp, Julianna Rowe, Lorraine Hauger, Martha Artyomenko, Nancy McLeroy, and Pattie Reitz — cheered me on enthusiastically from start to finish. Thank

501

you, ladies! And through it all my husband, Tony, kept a smile on his face even as I spent the better portion of many days this past year communing with my imaginary friends.

QUESTIONS FOR READERS

1. What's the worst piece of advice you've been given? The best?

2. Lucinda's father gave her many pieces of advice. Were any of them valid?

3. How do you know what advice to listen to?

4. Why was Seth attracted to Lucinda? Why was Lucinda attracted to Seth?

5. Campbell always played by the rules, and Lucinda's father never played by the rules, but in many ways they were similar. Why?

6. Campbell and Phoebe were both moral characters, but one was winsome and one was not. What accounts for the difference in the way you reacted to both of them?

7. In Chapter 13, Phoebe is talking to Lucinda of her accident. She says, "But how would you have wanted it to end? For me to wander home with no one the wiser? If nothing at all had happened, if there hadn't been any consequence for my disobedience, would that not have been unfair as well?" How does your perspective influence your concept of what's fair and what's not?

8. Seth, Deacon, Dandy, and Otter came from different parts of the country and had very different personalities. Why were they friends?

9. Seth and Campbell were both at the top of their class, both served as captain to their cadet company, yet one was loved and the other feared. Why? Which was a better captain?

10. If you're like me, you enjoyed Deacon, the consummate rule breaker, much more than Campbell, the consummate rule keeper. Why? Did it make you feel guilty?

11. What benefits and drawbacks do you find in obeying a law to the letter? In

obeying it in spirit?

12. What happens when a person of faith *requires* obedience to its laws? What happens when they *hope* for obedience? How do you reconcile the two?

ABOUT THE AUTHOR

Siri Mitchell is the author of over a dozen novels, three of which were named Christy Award finalists. A graduate of the University of Washington with a degree in business, she has worked in many different levels of government and lived on three continents. She and her family currently reside in the D.C. metro area. Visit her at www.sirimitchell.com.

The employees of Thorndike Press hope you have enjoyed this Large Print book. All our Thorndike, Wheeler, and Kennebec Large Print titles are designed for easy reading, and all our books are made to last. Other Thorndike Press Large Print books are available at your library, through selected bookstores, or directly from us.

For information about titles, please call:
  (800) 223-1244

or visit our Web site at:
  http://gale.cengage.com/thorndike

To share your comments, please write:
  Publisher
  Thorndike Press
  10 Water St., Suite 310
  Waterville, ME 04901